'Eirik'
A Time Travel P

By

Joanna Bell

ABOUT THE AUTHOR

Amazon Author Page: https://www.amazon.com/Joanna-Bell/e/B0768K811G

(click the orange 'Follow' button on the left)

For more information:

authorjoannabell@gmail.com

Website coming soon!

Contents

Chapter 1
9th Century

I know at once that something is off. The light is all wrong, for one thing. I didn't know what real darkness was until I became a regular visitor to Caistley – and now there is a strange orange glow coming from the direction of the village. A few seconds later, a sound my mind shies away from recognizing fills my ears.

Screaming.

Fire. It must be a fire. All I can think of as I start to stumble through the woods, down paths whose changing contours and curves have become unfamiliar to me in my absence, is Eadgar and his sister Willa. *They're both young and strong,* I tell myself. *It's the old people and the little ones who are in the most danger.*

When I come to the clearing and see that my fears are true – the entire village seems to be on fire, the flames leaping up into the black night sky as huts and storage buildings combust – I don't even think of turning back. But just before charging forward I suddenly note that the figures I see running back and forth don't all seem to be fleeing. No. A lot of them seem to be – are they *fighting?*

My blood, hot with adrenaline and fear, freezes instantly as my eyes pick out the larger figures carrying weapons – *using* weapons. I know who attacks villages like Caistley, burning and looting and murdering. I know it because I've heard Eadgar and Willa talk about them countless times, always in hushed tones and with eyes as big as saucers. Northmen. *Vikings.*

Snippets of conversation come back to me. "They kill the babies, Paige. They slaughter them like they were lambs." "They burn the fields so those they don't kill die of starvation not a few moons later." "Wulfric says they cave in your skull with a stone axe if you try to escape, and then they use your blood to decorate their faces like demons."

I'm rooted to the spot, absolutely torn between terror for my friends and, should I decline to run back to the tree and go home, terror for myself. I have no weapons. Even if I did, I'm no match for even a woman from Caistley, let alone a Viking. I can't leave them to their fate, though. I can't. I know the woods around the village better than anyone, certainly better than a party of raiders from the north. If I can just find Willa and Eadgar we can hide in the undergrowth until –

I am suddenly hanging in the air. Literally. I paddle my legs, seeking purchase on the ground, but my feet find none.

"What the –" I shriek, twisting my body until a grip of such finality that I might have guessed it belonged to a god falls upon the back of my neck.

"Stop struggling, girl, or I'll –"

But I don't stop struggling, because the voice is deep and male and heavily accented and I know at once that I am in more trouble than I have ever been in before. A moment later, in exchange for my continued desperate attempts to free myself, I get blackness.

* * *

I wake up confused, with a throbbing headache, and it comes back to me quickly that I'm in Caistley, not River Forks. I'm seated on the ground beside the village well, my hands are tied behind my back and I'm not alone. Other people with their hands tied behind their backs sit all around me, some of them bleeding and whimpering, others slumped forward as if they might be sleeping. I blink, trying to focus my vision on faces, but even if there were enough light to see properly almost everyone has their hair in the way, or is bloodied to the point of being unrecognizable.

"Willa!" I whisper, waiting to see if there is any reply, any movement or sound of recognition, before saying it again, louder the second time. No one replies, and in exchange for my trouble I feel a sudden sharp blow on my left side, right in the ribs, and turn my head to see a man standing there, aiming to kick me again. I use my feet to scramble away, toppling over in my haste, but the man catches me easily, yanking me up by the scruff of my neck and raising his hand.

"Leave it," a voice says behind him. "Not the women, Veigar."

I don't get a look at who's speaking but I do find myself back on the ground again, among the other captives. I stay quiet and keep my head down, listening to the sound of my own heartbeat thudding in my ears. I've never been struck before – not like that – and the casual violence is shocking. Part of me expects someone to speak up, to remonstrate with Veigar, but the other captives do as I do and keep their mouths shut.

At some point, it begins to rain gently – the kind of soft rain I remember from many an afternoon spent playing in the woods with Eadgar and Willa. Sometimes we would even designate one of us as a 'Northman' and play a variation of hide-and-seek that involved two of us hiding and the third person using a stick as an axe to 'chop' off the heads of the vanquished when he (or she) managed to find them. But nothing about sitting in the rain with my head – and now my sides – aching is playful. Nor do I have the luxury of it all seeming unreal, the way a normal person would if confronted by an actual Viking in, say, a parking lot outside the mall.

Soon, the light of dawn is visible to the east and two men, who I can see now are dressed in skirt-like leather garments and boots made of furs and leather bindings, approach the pitiful group of captives. I watch out of the corner of my eye, too afraid to raise my head, as one of them nudges a man with his foot and the man falls neatly to the side, clearly dead. Caistley and the part of my life that has been lived here have exposed me to many things that modern people are not exposed to. I've watched them slaughtering a pig in November – the 'blood month.' I've heard the sounds and breathed in the scents of death, and I know it's an everyday occurrence in Caistley, a part of life like eating or making love. But I haven't seen it up close like this yet. A dead body – an older man, someone's father. Nobody else is looking at it except me and I even I turn away when one of the two Vikings begins to drag it away by the ankle and the head thuds against the stones that stick up out of the dirt around the well.

I try to listen as they speak to each other but they're too far away, their accents too heavy. They seem to be making plans, gesturing at the captives. My wrists are still tightly bound, and I can feel there's no hope of escape until someone removes the bindings. Sooner or later, though, I know they're going to have to do just that.

Not that there is time to plan my escape because Veigar, the man who kicked me during the night, is suddenly among us, looking around, choosing people to drag to their feet and shove towards the smoking ruins of one of the nearby huts. When he reaches for me I force myself not to resist, desperate as I am not to give him an excuse to strike me again.

Soon, there is a group of about ten of us standing side by side, waiting to find out what we have been chosen for. I look around me and realize we are all women, all between the ages of about 16 and 35. Willa, although she's 24 and of the appropriate age, is nowhere to be seen. Maybe she escaped? She's always been smarter than her brother and I, and she probably has children to protect now. Yes, she must have escaped. I don't allow other, darker possibilities to enter my mind, because I can sense it's not the time to draw attention to myself with weeping or trembling or acting out. All the women standing with me are as still as statues, and as silent.

When Veigar is satisfied, after one more perusal of the captives, that he has everyone he wants, he leads us away from the wreckage of Caistley and down the path that to the sea. The wind picks up when we emerge onto the beach and my hair whips around my head, stinging my bare cheeks as I squint into the morning sun. Anchored in the bay, I see four wooden ships, of exactly the type I have seen before in history books. The Vikings are taking us away. I can't allow that to happen. I don't know where Caistley is, and in all my time there neither me, nor Eadgar or Willa have ever wandered beyond the natural boundaries of the village – the woods to south, the sea to the east and the marshes to the north and west. I stop walking. I can't get on one of those boats.

"MOVE!"

A shout from behind me and a push hard enough to send me flying into the sand, unable to break the fall with my hands. It's not Veigar this time but a different Viking, a short man with blond hair and a broad, ruddy face.

I cry out in shock and fear as I'm yanked immediately to my feet and the man grabs a generous handful of my hair at the nape of my neck, jerking my head back and getting right up in my face. His eyes are as cold and gray as the sea.

"Why are you fighting, girl? You're one of the lucky ones. The Jarl is going to have his pick of —"

But I'm not listening. I'm struggling, working my hands back and forth in their bindings, panicking.

"No," I gasp, desperate. "No, please. I can't leave! My father needs me. I can't — I don't know how to get back here. Please! I —"

The Viking's expression changes as I beg him to free me, from mild annoyance to amusement tinged with curiosity.

"You've got an accent - you not from here, girl? A foreigner! And a pretty one at that. Look at those teeth. I reckon the Jarl's going to give me ten barrels of ale when he lays eyes on you."

"No," I beg. "Please! Please, if you let me go I can give you more than ale. I can give you —" I stop, realizing I don't actually have anything to offer. But I can't give up so easily. If they take me from Caistley, and I can't get back, then I'll be stuck in the past for good.

Just as my captor is about to turn away I close my eyes and do something that makes my mouth go dry with fear. I step towards him and press my body against his, nestling my head into his chest, half-terrified he's going to respond positively and half-terrified he isn't.

He waits for a moment before pushing me away with a heavy sigh. "No, girl. Not until the Jarl's made his choices."

"But —"

"Stop talking. I won't ask again."

I stop talking. The Viking mentioned someone – a Jarl, was it? Someone important. Maybe I can talk to this Jarl? Maybe I can make a case?

No. If I'm taken away from here, if I get a chance to beg this Jarl to set me free, it might already be too late. The Viking's grip on me has slackened, he doesn't think I – or anyone – will dare to flee. He's wrong.

I make my move a few seconds later, because I know if I don't do it soon my nerve will desert me. I twist out of the Viking's hands and run across the sand, back towards the path that leads to the village and the woods and the tree that will take me home. My heart is in my throat, the fear so thick it's almost difficult to breathe.

Fifteen feet? Twenty? That's about how far I make it before being swept off my feet by the blond man, who expertly grasps my hair and pulls me away from his arm when I move to sink my teeth into his flesh. I am filled with hopelessness as the total futility of my escape attempt – and my situation – sets in. I am going to go where these men want me to go, not where I want to go. The law here is simple physical power and I am no match for a young warrior.

The Viking makes sure I'm held at a distance, to keep himself safe from my teeth. When he spots the fact that I'm emotional, he looks inexplicably surprised.

"They don't usually cry," he comments to Veigar before looking back at me, as if he's trying to figure me out. "Look at the others, girl. They know they're lucky to be chosen. They're going to eat better now than they ever have in their lives. And here you are weeping like a child."

"You might cry, too."

"I wouldn't cry, girl. As I said, look at your kin – are they crying? What high estate have you come from where anything less than death is a reason to spill tears?"

"They're not crying because they're too afraid to cry," I say quietly, feeling a kind of recklessness rising up inside me. If he takes me away from Caistley, it's over for me. I'll never see my dad again. I'll never see Emma again, or River Forks, or my mother's grave. I'll die is what I'll do, of a minor cut or a fever or any one of the countless minor things that become life-threatening the moment you step outside of the modern world. So what does it matter if my kidnapper is annoyed by me? Perhaps if I annoy him enough, he'll decide I'm not worth the trouble and leave me behind on the beach.

"They're right to be afraid," the Viking tells me. "And you – I can't decide if you're an idiot or if you just don't understand what's happening here. You belong to us now – to our Jarl. What do you think your King would do with us if he captured us? Would he feed us and gives us furs when we're cold? I'm only speaking to you as a courtesy and yet I see you standing there with fire in your eyes, as if I don't hold your very life in my hands."

Veigar approaches as his friend eyeballs me and shoves me forward, angry at my escape attempt. And when I'm on one of the ships, soaked to the waist by the cold saltwater I've just been dragged through and only barely able to see the shore over the row of shields tied along the side, I concentrate on details. I've never seen Caistley from this vantage point – in fact Caistley itself isn't even visible. All I see is trees and beach.

This probably looks like every other stretch of shoreline along the coast. There are no structures, no lighthouses. You won't be able to find your way back here!

I force the panicked thoughts aside and search, desperately, for something to remember the scene by. The bay. We are in a small, protected bay. The beach is sandy, crescent-shaped. A sandy beach and a bay, a backdrop of trees. It's not much but, should I find myself free at any point, at least I'll be able to narrow it down a little.

We sail north, hugging the coastline – which is a good thing for me. If we stay with the coast, then all I have to do is head south again when I'm free.

When I'm free. Although there is a feeling of heavy dread in my chest, I cannot allow it to take over. There will be a chance to escape. There will probably be many chances. I just need to be smart and patient, I need to wait for the right one.

The wind blows relentlessly as the ship cuts through the water and I turn my head to look at the woman sitting next to me.

"Where are they taking us?" I ask, realizing too late that she probably doesn't have any more of an idea what's happening than I do. "Do you know Willa and –"

The woman shakes her head at me quickly, eying one of the Vikings, and I understand she doesn't want to talk. I lean my head back against the sack of grain I'm propped up against and close my eyes.

Two irreconcilable facts:

1. This can't be happening.

2. This is happening.

I've missed Caistley before, when I've been away for long periods of time. I've even felt something akin to homesickness for it – I have been visiting since I was 5 years old, after all. But as a Viking ship takes me further and further away from my only route back home, I feel for perhaps the first time the profound foreignness of the place. I don't belong here. And I certainly cannot stay for long.

Chapter 2
21st Century

My mother died on February 15th, 2001, when I was 5 years old. Her illness was brief and I was told very little of it, although I later came to understand it was cancer, that it had been caught late, and that she hadn't wanted me to see her in the hospital. She didn't want me to be scared.

And I wasn't scared, not at first. At first I was just shocked, as silent and blinking as a person who has just been hit – but not killed – by the sound-wave of a bomb as it cracks over their head and leaves a ringing in their ears. Years later, and the ringing still hasn't stopped.

And, like a victim of a bomb blast, I've had to deal with the bodies. My father, for one. I suppose you could say he's still alive. He breathes, he eats – every now and again he speaks to me. But his life ended that day as surely as my mother's did. I was the sole real witness to my handsome, funny, playful dad's shrinking into himself over the course of the next few years, until the drapes were no longer opened and I learned how to prepare my own meals – and his.

Every therapist I've ever had has tried to get me to admit that I am angry at my father. But I don't think I am. It seems to me that my father is no different than one of those people you see in a video clip from a warzone – bloodied, broken, literally incapable of getting up and walking away from the wreckage. My father couldn't walk away from it, because he *was* it. Human wreckage.

I might have been human wreckage too, if not for the fact of being 5 years old and possessed of the inborn resilience of a person young enough to bend and twist with the fates, like a slender green branch in a high wind.

There was also Caistley. I had Caistley. My father did not.

Within a month of my mother's funeral, the visits from neighbors and friends lessened considerably in frequency. They had their own lives to get on with, and my dad had already begun to withdraw. The first thing I noticed was his face. He began to grow a beard, and I can remember sitting on his lap, running my fingers over the stubble, marveling at how sharp it felt as his eyes stared blankly ahead.

Our property was large and I was almost entirely unsupervised. The spring came early that year, taunting my father and I with its warm breezes and promises of life and renewal as our psychic landscapes remained bleak and dark. I began to wander further from the house than I ever had before. We had a farm, over five-hundred acres, but my mother had always cautioned me to stay in the yard. As well as cautioning me she had watched me, though, and now there was no longer anyone watching. I put my rubber boots on one day and headed out after finding my dad fast asleep in his darkened room at one o'clock in the afternoon.

The sound of water was everywhere that day, dripping from branches as ice melted and flowing in rivulets down to the little creek that ran dry every summer. There was warmth, too, of the kind only people who have known a cold winter can fully appreciate. I stood in the woods and turned my face up to the weak sunshine, drinking it in like a flower taken out of the shade.

And then I turned, suddenly, as someone whispered behind me – but there was no one there. It was mid-afternoon and the whisper had sounded friendly, almost like a stifled giggle. I wasn't afraid, but I *was* curious. I wandered over to the big tree that grew along the bank of the creek, where the voice seemed to come from. To my surprise, I heard it again – not a whisper this time but a distinct laugh. A person. I clambered up the hill – the tree's trunk was very large, and the roots spread over a large area – but there was no one on the other side, either. Was someone playing a trick on me? Was one of my classmates from school hiding in one of the hollows beneath the tree's massive roots?

I was getting overheated in my winter parka so I shucked it off and continued exploring, pausing every now and again to cock my head slightly and try to pick up the voice once more. And it was there, still – two voices, maybe. More giggling, more whispering. I looked briefly back through the woods towards the house, aware on some level that I shouldn't have wandered so far, but too curious to leave by then. And then I climbed over one of the thick, gnarled roots and in doing so put my palms flat against the tree.

In an instant the trees were gone, the light was gone, the warm spring air was gone. I clutched at my throat, gasping for air as it suddenly became difficult to breath and then, just as quickly as it had happened, I was once again in the woods. Not the same woods I had been playing in mere seconds before, though. No, these new woods were thicker and much darker and I couldn't understand how I'd gotten to where I was. Had there been a tornado? I knew what tornados were. I knew that sometimes they picked people up and carried them miles away. I knew that sometimes these people even lived. But there were no tornados in New York state – I knew that because my mother told me as much, when I had asked her what we were to do if one blew over our farm. So how had I got from the little stand of trees at the bottom of my yard to this other, darker and – now that I realized it – quite badly smelling place?

I sat up, trying to figure out whether or not it was time to be afraid, and two figures appeared out of the gloom.

They stood there, the two of them – a girl who looked to be about my age and a smaller boy – staring at me, while I sat and stared right back. They were both filthy, dressed in rags, and they made me think of Halloween. Did they think it was Halloween? Is that why they were dressed so strangely? Had their mothers marked their faces with stage make-up the way my own had last year, when I wanted to be a green-skinned witch?

"Why are you dressed like that?" I asked eventually, when it became clear that the two strangers weren't going to speak first.

The girl looked down at her clothes, confused, and the boy just kept staring at me. "Dressed like what?" She asked. "It's our clothing, isn't it?"

She sounded strange. The words came out of her mouth in an odd rhythm, almost like she was half singing them. And why was she asking me if her clothing was her clothing? Who was this weird girl?

"Was that you?" I asked, making a second attempt. "I heard someone laughing. Was that you?"

"Probably," she replied. "There's no one else in these woods but us. Maybe some pigs, but pigs don't laugh."

I laughed at that, at the idea of a pig laughing. And then the girl laughed and so did the little boy. I liked that.

"My names Eadgar," the boy announced, not making any move to shake my hand.

"I'm Paige," I responded before turning to the girl. "What's yours?"

"Willa. Are you from the big house?"

I didn't know what Willa was talking about, but I knew my house was close by and that it was quite big, so it seemed reasonable to assume that's the 'big house' she was speaking of.

"Yes," I told her. "I'm 5."

There was a pause while Willa stared at me suspiciously and then she threw her head back, giggling. "Half-ten? You? You're not half-ten! I reckon you're older than me!"

"How old are you?"

"Ten even."

Ten? There was no way. I laughed right back at her and told her it was a good joke. She was scarcely bigger than me, and much paler and skinnier. Her collarbones jutted out against her bone-white flesh and her wrists looked so thin and delicate that I imaged they would snap like twigs if she fell over and tried to catch herself.

"You're not ten," I told her, a little annoyed that she thought I was stupid enough to fall for such an obvious lie. If she'd said 6 or 7 then maybe, *maybe* I would have believed her. But not 10. "What grade are you in?"

Willa looked at me, confused. "What?"

"What grade are you in?" I repeated, grinning because I knew I'd caught her now. And sure enough, she pretended she didn't know what I was talking about. Not that it mattered too much, because I was happy to meet Willa and Eadgar and they seemed happy to meet me, too. There were no other kids who lived close to me, so if two had moved in nearby, I was pleased to have them.

"We're playing pig-and-acorns!" Eadgar announced and, when he saw that I didn't know what he meant, he explained. "I'm the pig and Willa is the acorn. She has to hide and then I try to find her. Or Willa is the pig and I'm the acorn – we take turns."

Hide-and-seek. That's what they were talking about. I was definitely up for a game of hide-and-seek.

"I'll be the pig!" I told them, excited, before Willa shut me down in her kind but firm way.

"No I'm the pig. You two go hide, you can be the pig later."

So we played in the woods for who knows how long – hours, I think. Eventually the two of them seemed to trust me enough to allow me to take on the status-heavy role of 'pig' in the game of pig-and-acorns and I did as I always did during hide-and-seek and crouched down to cover my eyes while they hid. But in doing this I toppled over sideways and had to catch myself by putting my hands against the tree I had first emerged into this place next to.

At once the airless darkness sucked me back in and I opened my eyes in the waning sunshine of afternoon in the woods at the bottom of my yard. Willa and Eadgar were nowhere to be found. I blinked, looking around, half-wondering if I'd been dreaming. But I hadn't been, I knew that. I looked down at my hands, smeared with the dirt of that other, darker forest, and couldn't figure out what had happened.

But I was 5 years old then, and I was also hungry from the adventures of the afternoon, so I headed back to the house with my parka under one arm and a thought to making myself a honey and peanut butter sandwich if my dad wasn't up yet.

Chapter 3
21st Century

I went back to the 'other place' – as I was still calling it then, before I heard Willa and Eadgar referring to it as 'Caistley' – a few days later, after school on one of the afternoons my father could not be roused from bed. Willa and Eadgar were not there the second time so I didn't stay for long, not daring to explore very far from the tree (which I had now figured out, in both places, was the key to getting from one to the other) and then frightened by the sudden appearance of big, red, hairy animal that made a grunting sound at me before disappearing into the undergrowth.

The third time, though, my new friends were there, and they both fell over laughing when I asked them about the hairy creature.

"A pig!" Willa giggled. "You don't even know what a pig is, Paige?"

I laughed too, because I was starting to understand that there were some big differences not just between the woods at the bottom of my garden and the forest where Willa and Eadgar played, but in our lives as well – differences that ran a lot deeper than clothing. If they said the animal was a pig, I believed them. Maybe it was a pig? It sounded like a pig, that's for sure. Maybe it was a different kind of pig?

"What's that?" Eadgar asked that time, running his hands over the glittery unicorn appliqué on my t-shirt.

"What?" I asked, not realizing he was probably asking about the glitter effect itself. "It's a t-shirt."

Willa and Eadgar didn't wear t-shirts, that was one of the differences between us. They didn't wear pants, either. Both of them wore thin, cream-colored tunics that stopped at the knees. When I told Eadgar it was a t-shirt he repeated the word back to me, obviously hearing it for the first time.

And it's not like I didn't wonder why they didn't know what a t-shirt was, or why what I thought was a pig was different to what they thought was a pig, or why they both kept insisting they were 10 and 6, despite their small sizes – I did. But I was also 5. At 5, most of us still believe in Santa Claus and the Easter Bunny and that the grown-ups know everything and will always do right by us. If a fat man on a magic flying sleigh delivered presents all over the earth every Christmas night, then it didn't seem outside the realm of possibility that a tree in the woods at the bottom of my garden somehow took me to another place, and that in that other place I had two friends who always looked like they needed a good bath.

I even talked about Caistley openly back then, regaling my sleepy, grunting father or my teachers with tales of what I'd gotten up to with Willa and Eadgar. All of them listened – well, maybe my dad didn't listen all the time, but I understood in my childlike way that he wasn't trying to be rude, he was just very sad. I kept talking about Caistley, too, as kindergarten turned into the first grade, and then the second, and I began to spend more time there as my father retreated further and further into himself.

It was just before my eighth birthday that I was pulled out of class one day by the school nurse, who took me into her small, antiseptic-scented office and introduced me to an older man with short, curly gray hair and a sweater with patches on the elbows.

Dr. Hansen wanted to talk to me, the nurse said, and I was pleased because other than Willa and Eadgar, no one seemed to want to talk to me very much. I thought it was because my mother was dead, because her death had marked me somehow, made people afraid of me. And it was about that – but not only that.

I began to see Dr. Hansen twice a week, and I enjoyed it very much at first because he seemed quite interested in me and what I thought about everything – and Caistley. He was very interested in Caistley. Sometimes he would take notes and peer at me as I detailed a trip to the beach with Willa and Eadgar, detailing to him how they taught me to distinguish between the edible seaweed and the stuff that would give you a sore belly.

"Extraordinary," he would whisper sometimes, as he scribbled on his note pad. "Amazing."

I thought he was talking about me. I thought *I* was extraordinary and amazing. My mother was dead, I was 7 years old, I was starved for attention – can you blame me? But it soon became clear that Dr. Hansen's interest wasn't in me, specifically. It was related to me, I knew that, but it wasn't entirely *about* me. One time, he went to the bathroom during our session and I grabbed his notepad, skimming the first few scribbled lines before I got too afraid he would catch me and put it back. I don't remember precisely what it said, but I do remember the word 'fantasist.' I went home that night and searched the internet, on our dust-caked family computer, for its meaning.

fantasist

noun

someone who often has fantasies, or confuses fantasy for what is real

I sat back in my chair, wounded. I knew what fantasy meant. Dr. Hansen, who I had thought my friend, thought I was making it all up? About Caistley and Willa and Eadgar? Is that why he was always asking me for details?

The betrayal cut deep, and I stopped talking about Caistley so much. Eventually I stopped talking about it altogether and Dr. Hansen informed me one day, with a big smile on his face, that he thought I was going to do "just fine."

Just fine? What did that mean? How was I not 'fine' before? I wanted to protest. I wanted to inform him that Caistley and my friends there were as real as the desk between us, and the notepad full of scribbles and the clock ticking on the wall. I didn't, though. Dr. Hansen seemed pleased with me, approving. I had stopped talking about Caistley and somehow that had made him happy.

To my great disappointment, I didn't see him anymore after that – although sometimes I would pass him in the halls and he would nod, the way my dad used to do when we drove past someone he knew on the road.

Once, when I had been sent to the staff room on some errand or another, I almost ran into Dr. Hansen as he talked to a woman I didn't recognize, but managed to stop myself just in time when I heard my own name spoken aloud.

"...the detail was amazing. She even talked about the seaweeds, which ones were edible and so on. I've never met a child with such a richly detailed fantasy life."

"Did you look it up?" The woman asked, chuckling softly. "Who knows, maybe she really does have a magic tree in her backyard?"

***

I can't say when it became clear to me that Caistley was more than a different *place*, the way Chicago or Australia or Germany were different places. It didn't happen in a single moment of revelation, either – I didn't suddenly realize what was going on. No, it was more gradual. You have to understand how normal it all seemed to me. As far as I was concerned and for all practical purposes, it *was* the same as Chicago. It wasn't River Forks, it wasn't the place where I lived, but it was somewhere real, somewhere that existed at the same time as River Forks, somewhere that could be reached with a car or a train – or a tree.

And even as I say it was normal to me – and it was – I must admit there was something that all three of us understood, some strangeness that we acknowledged silently, seeing no need to discuss it. Willa and Eadgar never actually brought me into their village, for one thing. We stayed in the woods outside and sometimes the shoreline a short walk away, playing games and making up silly little songs that we would sing to each other as we tramped through the forest. And I knew, partly from Eadgar's reaction to my glittery t-shirt and partly just through a kind of intuition, that there were certain things I couldn't do, certain things I couldn't talk about or items I couldn't bring with me when I visited.

I screwed up once, forgetting to leave my cell phone behind and watching as Eadgar picked it up, fascinated, after it slipped out of my pocket. His fingers crept over the smooth surface until one caused the screen to light up and he dropped it, screaming with fear, and scrambling away from it – and me – so fast he fell over. Willa wasn't there that day, and I don't know if Eadgar ever told her about my terrifying gadget, but he was skittish around me for days afterwards, glancing at me out of the corner of his eye and shying away when I went to put my arm around him or give him a playful shove. I was more careful after that, even going so far as to take a little plastic storage container from the house and keep it near the base of the tree so I could put whatever items I thought Willa and Eadgar would not understand into it before I visited them.

It wasn't just technology, either – it was almost everything. Even the buttons on my blue-jeans caused wide-eyed stares and whispered comments. Eventually I took to wearing a plain white cotton nightgown and nothing else – not even any shoes – so as to avoid the suspicions and curiosities of my two friends and to look as much like they did as possible.

Sometimes, Eadgar and Willa weren't in the forest. They had work to do, I understood that, the kind of work that in my life only adults did. Willa had to help with her younger siblings and both of them seemed to be involved in a lot of farm work. So when I came through the tree and found myself alone, I eventually built up the courage to explore farther, creeping down the narrow paths that ran through the undergrowth until I could see – and smell – the village itself. It smelled like wood smoke and, well – poop, if I'm to be perfectly honest. Even from a distance I would often catch myself pulling my dress up over my nose and gagging a little.

I suppose it was the village itself that first got me to thinking about whether or not Caistley might be something more than a different place – like Chicago or Australia or Germany. The buildings were not like any buildings I had ever seen before. Where River Falls had structures made out of concrete and brick Caistley seemed to be constructed almost entirely of mud and straw. I'd never seen anything like it – not until I saw something similar in an educational documentary about the Middle Ages in the fourth grade. There were no cars in Caistley, no trucks, nothing at all that seemed mechanical. The people moved their goods around in wooden carts on paths that turned into muddy quagmires when it rained (which seemed to be often).

By the time I was 9 or 10 I knew Caistley wasn't just a different place, but a different time. And once again, because the realization came so slowly and naturally, there was no single moment of shock. I'd been going there since I was 5, I always knew it was different, and now I knew why. It made sense. I didn't understand quite how I was getting there, that's true, but I didn't understand how airplanes stayed in the air, either, and they didn't strike me as particularly mysterious.

And with the realization that Caistley existed in another time came the dawning acceptance that my experience was – or appeared to be, anyway – unique. Other people weren't just traveling to different times the way they traveled to the next town over, the way I had once assumed they were. I stopped talking about it so much then, especially to grown-ups, and began to understand just how strange I must have made myself to my peers, with all my talk of traveling through trees and villages where no one owned cars and everyone was dirty all the time.

It was too late for my social life, though. I was already the designated 'weird kid.' Even when I stopped mentioning Willa and Eadgar or Caistley itself, some of my crueler classmates would ask me about them, faking an interest they didn't feel. And I, naive and outcast as I was, would answer in good faith, excitedly telling them about the bonfire Eadgar and I had built in a clearing, or the rabbit we roasted over the coals, or the fact that Willa was starting to talk about one of the boys in Caistley a lot more than she talked about anyone else. It all came to a head one spring day in fourth grade, when the most popular girl in class cornered me outside the gym.

"Hi," I said, not realizing what was happening at first, but noticing she had her three little handmaidens with her, all of them eying me with an air of malevolent anticipation.

"Hi," Kayla replied, mimicking my tone of voice.

I felt my cheeks begin to heat up. "What's up?"

"What's up?" She sing-songed back to me and I gave up trying to make conversation.

We were 9 years old. Kayla was wearing a pink velour Juicy Couture hoodie, of the kind I could only dream of being able to own, and she flicked her blonde hair over her shoulder as she looked at me, radiating impatience even as she was the one forcing me to continue with the interaction.

"So," she started, when she realized I wasn't playing anymore. "Have you been to *Caistley* lately, Paige? Have you seen *Willa*? Or *Edgar*?"

She emphasized the words 'Caistley' and 'Willa' and 'Edgar' the way you might if you were talking to a toddler. It made me want to punch her in the face, even as I knew that doing so would be the end of any slim chance I had of ever fitting in.

"It's Eadgar," I replied. "Not Edgar."

"Whatever. Edgar is a stupid name anyway. So have you seen them or what?"

I nodded. "Yes."

"And you went through the tree to get to them? Is that the story you're sticking with, Paige?"

Wow. I really did not like Kayla Foster. I didn't quite know how to respond, either. She knew as well as I did that I'd been talking about Caistley – and how I got there – for years at that point, the way the other kids talked about their ski trips to Colorado or their summer vacations to Disneyworld with their grandparents. Lying and telling her it was a normal place wasn't an option, and neither was pretending to admit I'd made it all up, which I sensed was what she wanted to happen.

"It's not a story," I said quietly.

Kayla snapped her gum. "Yes it is, Paige. *Everyone* knows it. We're not in kindergarten anymore, you know. We're old enough to know you're lying. You probably still believe in Santa, too!"

"I don't!" I snapped. "I don't believe in Santa."

Kayla and her friends looked down their noses at me. "Whatever you say," she replied haughtily. "But if you think you're ever going to get a boyfriend while you still believe in dumb kid stuff like magical trees, I'm sorry to say but you're wrong."

I said something, then, that I shouldn't have said. Kayla Foster's 'boyfriend' (the word is in quotes because in fourth grade having a boyfriend mostly meant eating lunch with him and sometimes, at the bus top, ostentatiously holding hands with him so all your friends could see he was your boyfriend) had dumped her the previous week, a juicy scandal for all. I'd even heard rumors that someone had seen Kayla crying in the girl's bathroom in the C hallway.

"Maybe I won't," I said calmly, before sticking the knife in. "But I bet if I do he won't tell all my friends that kissing me is like making out with a vacuum cleaner."

I didn't even understand the vacuum cleaner comment, nor did I know if Chris Ward – the erstwhile boyfriend – had even said it, but I did know Kayla was well aware that it was being passed around as truth. I enjoyed the way the smugness drained out of her expression when I said it though, even as I knew I was going to be made to pay.

"Bitch," she sneered, glancing around first to make sure there were no teachers nearby to hear. "You're such a stupid bitch, Paige. Nobody likes you. Everybody knows you're just making it all up about Caistley to make it seem like you actually have friends."

My hand itched to punch Kayla Foster as she got right up in my face, breathing her lip gloss-scented breath all over me and pushing me back against the wall. And as I considered it, weighing the look of hurt and surprise on her face if I allowed myself to do it against the years of even worse social torment than I was currently suffering, an idea popped into my head. A mean, irresistible idea.

When Kayla backed off I looked her in the eye. "It is real. I could take you."

She scoffed. "Yeah right."

"No," I insisted. "I mean it. Right now. I could take you right now. What – are you scared?"

"No!" She replied hurriedly. "Of course I'm not scared, you dumbass. I mean, fine, sure, let's go."

The best part was that she thought she was calling *my* bluff when, in reality, it was just the opposite.

Chapter 4
21st Century

Some instinct inside me told me to blindfold Kayla Foster before leading her down to the woods. Maybe it wasn't an instinct, maybe it was just latent control freakery, I don't know. What I did know is that I definitely did not want her to know how to get to Caistley herself, even if I wasn't sure it would even work if she was alone.

When we got to the tree and I pulled the blindfold off over Kayla's head, she scowled at me.

"Well?"

"I just wanted to make sure you really want to do this," I said, shrugging.

"Do what?" She asked. "Stand in the woods with you while literally nothing happens?"

She was so sure of herself, so perfectly certain that I was lying, and that she was going to be the one to finally inform everyone of that fact, to great social acclaim. I, on the other hand, was doing everything I could to hide the fact that I was dying to get Kayla through the tree to Caistley, because some part of me knew that she was going to lose it and I wanted to see the look on her face when she did.

"Here," I instructed. "You have to put your hands on the tree."

Kayla rolled her eyes and leaned forward and just as she did, the sound of a pig or some other animal rustling through the undergrowth came to us. Kayla jerked up, looking around, and I saw the confusion in her eyes when she realized there was no animal. Of course, I knew we were hearing something in Caistley, but as far as Kayla was concerned she was experiencing auditory hallucinations.

"What was that?" She barked at me, irritated. "What are you doing, Paige? What was that sound?"

Behind the usual blustery bravado of her tone I sensed it —
fear. Kayla was frightened, a little, and she was trying to cover it.

"It's just the wind." I told her. "We can go back to the house
if you want. If you're too scared, I mean."

That did the trick. Kayla stuck her hands out again so they
were touching the tree, scoffing the whole time, and I laid my own
next to hers.

Even in the brief, airless blackness before Caistley, I could
hear Kayla panting with terror and I realized, at the moment it was
too late to turn back, that I had probably just screwed up very badly.

When we arrived she sat there, unmoving and unblinking, at
the base of the tree.

"See?" I said, pleased with myself. "I told you Caistley
existed. I told you —"

"Take me back! Oh my God, Paige, you — you crazy witch!
WHERE ARE WE?! TAKE ME BACK!"

I watched, horrified, as Kayla's words dissolved into
hysterical tears and she began to hyperventilate.

"Wait," I said a few seconds later, reaching out to touch her.
She shrank away. "Wait. You said you wanted to come here, Kayla.
You said —"

"TAKE ME BAAAACK!"

"But," I stammered, totally thrown off by her response.
"Don't you want to see anything? Don't you want to meet Eadgar or
—"

"AHHHHH!"

She was just screaming by then, and doing it loud enough
that I began to worry someone from the village might hear it. To
hear Willa and Eadgar talk, the woods we played in regularly were
infested with outlaws — not to mention demons and evil spirits — and

the sound of a child screaming her head off would certainly bring the men of Caistley to investigate.

"Shut up!" I hissed. "Kayla *shut up*. Someone will hear us!"

But Kayla did not shut up. She kept up her wailing and eventually closed her eyes, refusing to open them again. It soon became clear that there was not going to be any exploring on that day and I stepped forward to guide her hands back to the tree and take us both back to River Forks.

***

That little stunt with Kayla Foster nearly cost me my place at River Forks Elementary. Of course none of the grown-ups believed her when she started babbling nonsense about traveling through trees and floating in blackness but they knew one thing, and that was that Kayla was neither faking nor exaggerating her terror when she got back to her parent's house that day. Something bad had happened in the woods at the bottom of my backyard, everyone accepted that. Something I was at fault for. I told everyone I could that Kayla wanted it to happen, that she practically dared me to do it, but nobody wanted to hear it. Her parents, both lawyers, lobbied hard to have me permanently expelled from school and the only reason I wasn't is because a) there was nowhere else for me to go and b) no one could actually establish what it was, exactly, that I had 'done' to Kayla in the woods, and they therefore couldn't expel me for it.

They did manage to get my father on the hook for Kayla's therapy, though. And the way I was treated at school after the incident began to make my previous outcast status look like a walk in the park. As I said, the grown-ups didn't believe anything out of the ordinary had happened in the woods. I'd just played a trick on Kayla to scare her. But the other kids, they weren't so sure. Within days I was finding the word 'witch' scrawled across my locker and hearing loud whispers wherever I went. Even the other outcasts wanted nothing to do with me then, and I was truly alone.

It was during dinner one night soon after the incident with Kayla Foster that my dad made his way downstairs to the kitchen while I sat silently, eating a tuna sandwich. I looked up when I heard the floor creek, shocked. He hadn't been downstairs for months.

"Dad," I said, standing up. "Do you – I brought you a sandwich but I can microwave some soup for you if you want. Or – I bought some ice-cream, I can –"

My dad put his hand up. "No need, Paige, I'm not hungry."

If I showed you a photo of my father before my mother died, and another one taken that night, you would not believe they were the same person. The handsome, smiling twenty-something in all the photos was gone, replaced with a grizzled wraith who looked to be at least 50, his hair shot through with grey and his youthful strength wasted away. And he wouldn't eat. I was always trying to get him to eat, but no one had ever taught me how to cook or shop and so we lived on sandwiches, canned soup, apples, bananas, anything I could think of that was healthy-ish and easy to prepare.

I sat back down. "Are you sure? There's some apples in the – "

"No, Paige, I'm really not hungry. I just came down here to talk to you."

"Oh," I said, very quietly. "I'm sorry, Dad. I'm sorry about what happened with Kayla Foster and –"

My dad waved his hand in front of his face, a gesture of dismissal I was very familiar with by that time. It was as if someone had drained all the energy right out of him, as if even speaking left him as exhausted as a person who has just run a marathon. I know now that it was depression, of the deepest and blackest kind, but at 9 – how could I have understood?

"I want you to go and talk to someone," he said, and I leaned forward because his voice was so low I could barely hear it. "Like you did before, after your mother died. You can't talk to me, we both know that – I'm useless. So you need to talk to someone else. A professional."

I didn't want to talk to a professional. I most certainly did not want to waste any effort trying to come up with a way to talk about Caistley and Eadgar and Willa in such a way as to honestly portray my experiences without getting myself locked into some kind of institution for delusional little girls. But I did want my dad to be happy, and so far I seemed to be doing very badly at that. Maybe talking to someone would help him? Maybe if I did as he asked he would see that I cared, that I wanted him to approve of me and be proud of me?

"Ok," I said, taking another bite of tuna sandwich. "I'll go talk to someone."

So that's what I did, to try to make my dad happy. River Forks was a half hour drive from a larger town, and the school nurse found a doctor who worked with children in that town. Once a week I would take a taxi to talk to this person – Dr. Whittington – and to try to leave out anything to do with Caistley.

***

Dr. Whittington was younger than Dr. Hansen and I liked him better, although I was obviously very suspicious. He didn't make me talk about anything in particular, though. Sometimes we talked about how I was doing at school and other times about how I felt about my dad, or how I missed my mom, what I might say to her if she was there with me. Mostly, Dr. Whittington asked me questions. And one day, after I'd been seeing him for a couple of months, he asked me if I was holding anything back.

I shook my head and looked out the window, eager to avoid eye contact lest it give away the fact that I was lying through my teeth.

So once again, therapy became more of a social hour than anything psychologically constructive. I kept going, because Dr. Whittington was one of the few people on earth who seemed interested in me or how my life was going – and also to stop my father from worrying. Which didn't work, because he knew even better than I did that he wasn't up to the task of raising me.

It was around that time that my friendship with Eadgar and Willa deepened, the way friendships do at that age, ripening from shared activities and play into deeper connections, real knowledge of another person, real concern for their wellbeing. Their father died that summer, kicked in the gut by an ox. Eadgar relayed the story to me, and neither of them shed a single tear as they described the way their dad's belly had swollen up and turned a deep purple and how he had spent days in agony, unable to sleep or find any relief from the pain.

"Are you sad?" I asked tentatively when the story had been told and Willa had matter-of-factly informed me that they had buried him in the field just north of the village. It was, admittedly, a stupid question. And when Willa turned on me, her eyes aflame, I knew it.

"What?" She shouted. "Our father is dead and you ask if we're sad!?"

"I didn't mean that you didn't seem sad," I replied awkwardly, and in spite of the fact that that was exactly what I'd meant. "You just, um, you don't – you two don't really seem as, uh, you don't seem –"

I was trying to express that although I knew they experienced emotions as strongly as I did, they seemed less willing to show them. I'd never seen Willa cry, for instance, and she had seen me cry countless times by then, usually as I told them some story or another of being bullied at school, or fearing that what my dad was actually doing up there in his dark, airless bedroom, apart from being very sad, was dying.

"Because we're not spilling tears, you mean? What use are tears, Paige? Will they bring my father back? Will they plough the land and plant the seeds and harvest the grain?"

Willa's tone was harsh and unfamiliar. I sat back, chastised and guilty. "I didn't mean it like that," I whispered, looking down. "I meant to insult myself, not you or Eadgar. I cry all the time, but the two of you seem so strong. Nothing ever seems to leave you in your beds, unable to get up."

"She doesn't mean to be cruel," Eadgar said, putting one arm around my shoulder. "But you're different to us. You live in a big estate with servants and a big garden to grow all your food in. We don't stay in our beds because we can't – we'll starve if we do. My mother is outside this afternoon, cutting the wheat with the others, because if she doesn't do that we won't have any bread this winter."

I never really told Willa and Eadgar I lived on a big estate with servants and a garden, apart from that initial meeting when I had confirmed that yes, I lived in a 'big house.' They came to the natural conclusion that I did, based rationally on the fact that I always appeared healthy, never underweight, that my fingernails were always clean, my hands un-roughened by manual labor. I didn't see any point in telling them otherwise, either, because it helped all three of us put the larger mystery – of what exactly it was that a girl from a big estate was doing showing up in the woods outside Caistley day after day, and then year after year – aside.

As I sat on the old fallen tree in the woods, with the dappled sunlight falling on my head, Willa suddenly collapsed in on herself and began to weep. Shocked, and terrified that I was probably responsible, I wrapped my arms around her as her brother did the same, from the other side.

"It's OK," I whispered. "I'm sorry, Willa. I didn't mean to upset –"

"Oh Paige!" She cried, turning to me. "The reason I don't cry is because if I started, I would never stop! You never talk about any of the things that happen to us. You never say oh, my aunt's baby died for lack of food, your belly never growls, and I never ask about any of it because in truth I don't understand but life is hard for us, Paige. It's hard for us in a way I'm not sure you know. We haven't eaten a proper meal since my father left this world, we're hungry and scared but most of all we miss him and we don't know what to do without him. My mother has a look in her eye like she's half gone to the next world, too. I fear we will all be dead by this time next year."

Willa wasn't joking. About being dead by the same time next year. I could see in her expression that she was entirely serious. I opened my mouth to speak, to try to provide some comfort, but my throat was tight and no words came out.

Were my friends going to die?

The death of Willa and Eadgar's father was a turning point for them – and for me, for us. I'd always known their lives were hard, but it didn't quite make sense to me until I saw the real fear of death, of starvation, on their pale faces. I started to bring food after that, and there was no pretense at turning it down on their part, no protestations, no reassurances that they would be fine.

I tried to bring food that made sense, too, searching the kitchen at my house fruitlessly the first time. What would they have made of sugary, colorful breakfast cereal? I didn't know, and I didn't want to find out. Cheese slices? No, they wouldn't recognize those as food, either. Cheese was a good idea, though. They ate cheese. They ate cheese and bread. So before my next visit to Caistley I went to the store and bought an unsliced loaf of bread and a package of cheddar cheese, both of which I carefully took out of their plastic packaging and wrapped in a plain white kitchen towel before giving it to them.

Watching them devour the food made me feel terrible. I began to cry when they both set aside some of their bread and cheese, which I could see from their sunken cheeks they clearly needed to eat, for their mother.

"I should have brought you food before," I said, sniffling. "I'm sorry – I'm so sorry. I didn't realize it was so bad! I thought you had enough and you were just so skinny from working all the time. I didn't think –"

"No matter," said Eadgar, panting from the effort and speed with which he had consumed what I brought him. Willa joined in, patting my head. "No matter, Paige. No matter. It's not your job to keep us fed."

'No matter.' They always said that, usually at the same point I would have said 'it's OK.' Sometimes, in River Forks, I would use some of the phrases or words I learned in Caistley, and people would look at me oddly.

As to it not being my job to keep Eadgar, Willa and their mother fed, they were technically right – it wasn't. But I took it on anyway, using my dad's credit card to shop (I had long since set up an automatic payment process for all our bills every month, a system my father approved of, and I knew he wouldn't even notice the extra outlay) and then arriving in Caistley with my arms full of apples, bread, cheese, cream (which I had to transfer into a wooden bucket I found in the garage) and everything I could think of that would keep them fed. At one point, Willa brought me a little sample of something she called 'porridge' and, tasting it, I thought it mostly tasted like pea soup. It was what they mostly ate, she said, sometimes with pig bones from the landowner mixed in if he or his wife had seen fit to part with any. After that I brought sacks of dried peas and pork knuckles I bought at the butcher in River Forks.

It's no self-congratulation to say that nothing had ever made me happier than seeing Willa and Eadgar – my truest, best and only friends in the world(s), go from almost too weak to play in the woods with me after the loss of their father to, if not exactly glowing with health, at least substantially more robust than they had been. I actually had to scale back on my food deliveries at one point, because some of the other people in the village had grown suspicious, started to suspect them and their mother of somehow stealing or procuring food that wasn't theirs.

The three of us were as close as triplets, chattering and laughing and playing almost every day. Even Willa, always the more aloof of the two, seemed to warm to me greatly. It was unspoken, the way these things often are between children, but they understood what was driving my food deliveries – my care for them, my concern. And I in turn felt theirs for me, as they listened with serious expressions on their faces to my tales of loneliness and torment at school, and to my detailing of my father's inability to leave his bed, or even to shave off the beard that now made him look like some kind of crazed mountain man.

"I'll kill her," Willa said one day, when I told them that the bruise on my arm was from Jessica McAllen – Kayla Foster's second in command – punching me out of the blue as I walked past her in the hallway. "Why did no one punish her? Are her parents dead?"

I shook my head and explained that it just didn't work that way where I was from. And Willa and Eadgar's fury on my behalf did more for me than countless hours of talking to Dr. Whittington did, I have to say. I could have talked and talked and talked until the mountains turned to dust and nothing would have put the feeling in my heart that my friends and the fierceness of their affection – their love – did.

"Thank you," I said, after both had sworn they would help me take revenge on Jessica McAllen, and just before I left to go back home. It was dusk, and even Willa and Eadgar – the only kids in the village who were brave enough to spend time in the woods during the daytime – had never stayed there past nightfall, not for as long as I'd known them. Evil spirits, they said. Demons. Witches. Outlaws.

"You're one of us, Paige," Eadgar said simply, as if it was obvious. "So anyone who hurts you hurts us, too. What happens to you happens to us."

Chapter 5
9th Century

Our childhood idyll didn't last. Not because of any one act or event, but because that's the point of childhood idylls – they don't last. They slip away so slowly, so almost imperceptibly that sometimes it's years later before you even realize that they've ended and that your memories are tinged with a kind of golden light, making you wonder if they ever happened at all, if you were ever truly that content, that at ease in the world.

Not that childhood is a time of pure contentment or ease – only the luckiest can say that and neither myself nor Willa or Eadgar would describe the early parts of our lives as 'easy.' But we had each other – and that's no small thing – and we had the forest and the beach and the sunshine and the games we invented and then forgot about as the days and years passed.

I was twelve when Willa had her first baby. There was pressure, after her father's death, to marry and have a child as soon as possible. Children were mouths to feed in Caistley, just like they were in River Forks, but not for as long. By 3 or 4 the little ones in Caistley were helping out and by 6 or 7 a lot of them were doing as much work as the adults. If anything, Willa and Eadgar turned out to have been a bit of an exception to the rule, born to parents who didn't believe in working them to the bone as early as possible.

Even before Willa's marriage, I was seeing a lot less of both her and Eadgar. They were busy doing the things their father had done before them. It didn't stop me going to Caistley, but it did mean I spent a lot more time there on my own. I started to take books with me, reading them in a little clearing close to the beach where none of the villagers ever came. The villagers – some of them – seemed to know about me. Or, to know that Willa and Eadgar had a little friend who wasn't from the village itself and that we used to play together in the woods, anyway. I was wary of them – and they, I think, of me.

It was Willa herself who announced her marriage to me, after it had happened. I was hurt at first, and asked her why she hadn't mentioned it.

She shrugged. "I didn't think you approved, Paige. I thought you'd try to convince me otherwise, when the truth is I had little choice."

"Did they force you?" I asked. "Your mother, I mean – did she force you to get married?"

Willa laughed. "No one forced me, girl. Unless you can call life itself a force. My father's gone, my mother's getting old (Willa's mother was in her mid-30's when she told me this), we need people to help with the garden and the crops and the animals. This is just how it is here. I don't know how it is in River Forks or on a grand estate, but that's how it is here."

"Well who is he, then?" I asked, curious and not entirely happy.

"Aldred," Willa replied. "He's ten and seven, just like me, and he's as tall and strong as an ox. I hope our babies will be tall and strong like him."

Seventeen. Willa was married at 17, to another 17 year old. It was no scandal, either, nothing out of the ordinary. Neither was it a surprise to anyone when her belly started to grow and I saw even less of her than I already was at that point – which wasn't very much.

The day she crept into the woods with a tiny, snuffling bundle in her arms, with all of her attention focused on him, I knew it was the end of something for all of us. Her baby was tiny and beautiful and Willa was in love. I was slightly unmoored, fiercely jealous of the new person who had taken my stand-in big sister and her stern, maternal attentions away from me.

I was old enough to realize it would not be right to express any of these things, but I felt them all the same.

Dr. Whittington noticed something was wrong, too. I'd been seeing him for awhile then, talking around and around the central relationships of my life, searching the chambers of my heart where River Falls and my father and my long-lost mother lived for new material. When he asked me one afternoon after class why I was so quiet, for some reason I decided to tell him some of the truth, for once.

"I think I lost a friend," I told him, looking out that same window I always looked out of. "A good friend – my best friend."

Dr. Whittington tried, somewhat unsuccessfully, to keep the surprised tone out of his voice. "Your best friend?" He asked, knitting his brows. "Who is that? I don't recall you mentioning a best friend before, Paige."

"Her name is Willa," I told him. "She doesn't live here in River Falls. Anyway, she's been looking after me for a long time. Not like a mother, really, maybe more like an older sister. It's not just her, either. There's Eadgar, he's her younger brother. They're both my best friends."

"She's been looking after you for a long time?"

I nodded and swallowed as a sudden lump formed in my throat. I couldn't speak without crying so I just nodded quickly in response.

"You're emotional," Dr. Whittington said calmly. "Willa and Edgar must be very good friends to you."

"Eadgar," I whispered.

"Why haven't you mentioned these friends to me before?"

I shrugged and wiped my nose on my sleeve. "It's complicated. I guess I haven't mentioned them because no one really believes they exist."

I didn't tell Dr. Whittington everything. I didn't tell him about Caistley itself or the tree or any of that. But I did tell him more than I ever meant to, and he was good enough at his job not to push me when I didn't want to give specifics on this or that little detail. After that, and ironically at the point that they both began to play smaller and smaller roles in my own life, I began to talk to the doctor more and more about my friends.

That's not to say that I knew whether he thought they were real or not – even as I tried to make it sound like they were friends from a few miles away, perhaps ones who attended a different school, I slipped up fairly frequently, dropping mentions of the 'demons' in the woods (demons I definitely did not believe in, but demons that were real enough to me in that my friends did) or the fact that Willa and Eadgar's father had died after a kick from an ox. No one in River Forks in the 2000s died from being kicked by an ox. But the doctor *listened*. When I told him how much it meant to me to have friends, as an outcast at school and someone who might as well have been an orphan at home, he nodded and I could see some human empathy in his brown eyes, some acknowledgement that even if I was making it all up, he understood what it was to need company, to need people on your side.

Dr. Whittington nodded quietly when I told him how sad I was not to be seeing Willa and Eadgar so much anymore and, as the weeks passed, almost at all. I barely ever saw Willa at that time, and Eadgar maybe once or twice a month.

"They're growing up," he said to me one day. "They have responsibilities. It sounds like they come from a different kind of family, and with their father gone Eadgar will be stepping into the role of man of the house – and Willa has her child to attend to. I wouldn't take it personally, Paige, as painful as I can see this is for you. People grow, relationships change, but love remains."

It applied to so much of my life, and not just the one that took place in Caistley. I still loved my mother, a woman whose face I could hardly remember without a photograph to remind me, and I still loved my father, too, even as he became a kind of living ghost. I went home from therapy that night and sat in my room, looking at myself in the dusty mirror and wondering what was going to become of me. My mother was gone, my father might as well have been gone, and my friends were far away, busy with their increasingly adult lives.

Love remains. I whispered the words out loud as my eyes brimmed, desperate for it to be true.

Chapter 6
9th Century

I wake up in the midst of vomiting, my head woozy with nausea, and only remember I'm on a ship when I finish and the sound of the water slapping against the wooden sides reminds me. In a panic, I crane my neck up, looking to the left and going limp with relief when I see it there, a strip of blackness even darker than the star-studded night sky. Land. We're still sailing north, still hugging the coast. I can still get back to Caistley.

The other women are with me, all seated, all with their hands still bound behind their backs. Most of them look to be asleep, their heads lolling forwards, only waking up to be sick – and sometimes not even waking up for it at all. I'm thankful for the brisk, briny maritime air and the way it carries away the stench of seasick human beings who do not have access to bathrooms or water.

I doze off again, waking to the light of dawn when it creeps into the sky to the east and the sound of the Vikings speaking to each other. We appear to be anchored in a bay, and spoils from Caistley are being unloaded – casks of ale, sacks of grain and peas, wooden crates filled with apples. Live pigs, too, squealing with indignation, are lowered down over the sides.

That's what you are, I think as somebody whose face it's still too dark to see lowers me into the thigh-deep water and prods me towards the beach. *A sack of peas. A resource. Keep your eyes open, Paige, you have to get out of here.*

I look to my left when I emerge out of the water and onto a sandy beach, but it isn't going to be possible to make a run for it, not before I've at least been able to get a look at the terrain. Just north of Caistley it's all marsh, and I certainly don't want to get caught in anything like that with a pack of Vikings on my heels and no food in my belly.

At the top of the beach, and in the growing light, I spot a woman waiting, looking right back at me. She's short, but solidly built, and her straw-colored hair has been braided and wound around her head like a crown.

"Did you treat them gently?" She asks the Viking bringing up the rear, making sure none of us are dumb enough to try to make a run for it. "You know Jarl Eirik doesn't – "

"They're fine, woman," the Viking grumbles. "Not a scratch on any of 'em."

The woman steps forward as he approaches, looking up (for she is at least a foot shorter than him) and smacks him square across the face. I cringe away, anticipating the return blow, but the warrior does nothing but hang his head and rub his tender cheek.

"You want a seeing to, Hildy, is that it?" He asks a few seconds later, grinning. "I can come to your bed and put an end to this foul mood, but I need to get these girls up to the –"

Crack. She slaps him again, and then turns her attentions to us. "Come with me, girls. We need to scrub that filth off you before you're presented to the Jarl."

The Jarl. There's that title again. The woman's tone of voice is slightly reverent when she says it. As we follow her up the beach and over a series of grassy sand dunes, I steal another glance to the south. It's lighter now, and I can see that the land here isn't treed. Even if it gets marshy, I could just follow the coast, couldn't I? Walk along the beach?

It took us hours to get where we are, though. All night, and I have no idea how fast the ships were sailing, how much ground we've covered. If this was my first visit to the past, I might consider an escape attempt right now, with only the stout Hildy to chase me down. But it's not my first visit and now I've seen what hunger can do to a person. I can't cover miles of terrain on no food and possibly no water. My escape – and make no mistake, there *will* be an escape – will have to be better planned than this. It will have to wait.

Hildy leads us to a deep stream, about five feet in breadth, and slices the bindings from our wrists with a small knife. Then she commands us to take our clothes off. The other women do so at once, and they do it easily. It is not so easy for me. I am not comfortable being naked, especially around strangers.

"What is it?" Hildy barks at me, slapping me upside the back of my head. "You deaf? Take off your tunic so the Jarl doesn't take off my head for presenting him with a pack of dirty rats."

When I move too slowly in pulling my dress off over my head, Hildy slaps me again. She's stronger than she looks – and she doesn't look weak. I shrink away from her and draw my legs tightly together when the thin layer of fabric between my nakedness and the world is finally removed. Hildy leans her head back and laughs out loud.

"Preciousness won't get you anywhere with us, child. Now get in the water and wash yourself."

She shoves me into the stream and then raises her eyebrows, surprised, as I come back up and tread water in place. The rest of the women are hesitating and I know why – none of them can swim. Willa and Eadgar couldn't swim, either – it just wasn't something the people of Caistley learned how to do – and they displayed a healthy amount of fear about any kind of water, often hinting at strange creatures or sickness lurking in the depths. Fortunately I'm a strong swimmer, and Hildy's attempt at scaring me hasn't worked. She turns her attention to the other women, screaming at them to get in deeper, smiling as they whimper and cling to each other.

Ten minutes later we're led naked and shivering to a round wooden building that doesn't look like anything I ever saw in Caistley. Inside, a small fire is burning. It doesn't offer much heat but something is better than nothing and we crowd around it, our teeth chattering audibly.

"I'll be back to get you soon," Hildy says, dropping two more logs onto the fire. Dry yourselves and pinch your cheeks – the Jarl will choose his favorites before the feast."

And then she's gone and we're all standing there looking at each other with wide, scared eyes.

"What about those of us he doesn't choose?" Asks one girl who looks to be about my age.

"They'll chop off our heads," comes the reply and then, followed by that, a rising collective wail.

"They don't seem like the type," I respond, an attempt to convince myself as much as it is any of them. "Why would they kill —"

"They killed my brother," a woman with long, wet hair hanging down over her shoulders tells me. "Back in the village, the big one bashed in his head with a rock."

I almost laugh when she says this, because it sounds like a joke. Willa and Eadgar have told stories of savage 'Northmen' before, but I always assumed their tales of brutality were more exaggeration than faithful description. But the woman isn't exaggerating and soon I'm hearing more of what the Vikings have left behind in Caistley – of destruction, of brothers and uncles, fathers and sons murdered. A pit opens in my stomach.

"What? You don't believe us?" Someone asks me. "You're that girl from the woods, aren't you? The little witch from the ealdorman's estate? This your first time with the Northmen? You're lucky. Mark my words, their Jarl is more likely to slice you open than he is to set you free tonight, if he doesn't like what he sees. Not that I reckon you're in any danger, not with that body."

I look down at my body, still naked, as the light from the flames dances across my skin. The woman speaking is right, I don't look like the rest of them. Even the youngest of our group are bent and pock-marked. A couple of them have limps and at least one has a withered, useless arm that dangles from her shoulder. Breasts appear deflated, nipples rough and cracked from breastfeeding infants and bellies sag low, marked with silvery webs of stretch-marks. My own skin, in comparison, seems unrealistically flawless, almost photo-shopped, like a model in a men's magazine. It's literally the first time in my life that I have ever been in a roomful of other girls and found myself to be the most attractive one. It's a strange feeling, heavy with importance. Will I, Paige Renner, be saved by my *beauty*? Once again the urge to laugh out loud seizes me. Talk about a fantasy story – none of the girls back at River Forks elementary school would ever have believed it, not in a million years.

Too soon, Hildy returns. She's quieter this time, her expression more serious.

"Come," she says, gesturing for us to follow her and we do, emerging into the sunlight blinking and cringing.

I can't get over the feeling of being naked out in the open, of the breeze skimming over parts of me that weren't meant to see the sunlight. There's a tension inside me, too, a submerged shot of adrenaline waiting in the wings and ready to surge into my bloodstream should a chance present itself. I look around, to try and get some idea of where I am, and see more wooden buildings and, to my grim disappointment, a palisade of upright wooden posts that appears to encircle all but the eastern edge of the makeshift village. I try to get my bearings, shading my eyes with one hand and looking up to find the position of the sun in the sky, but the sound of – is that a party? – interrupts me.

In front of us is another wooden structure, long and narrow, and filled with what sounds like a great number of shouting, singing men. As Hildy moves to push me inside I balk, digging my heels into the sandy earth without even meaning to and she grabs my ear, yanking me towards her.

"Keep going girl, I promise you you'll begging to spend more time with me if the Jarl sees you hesitating."

So I keep going, putting one foot robotically in front of the other as my eyes adjust to the candlelit darkness in the windowless longhouse. A series of ornately carved wooden tables set end-to-end run the length of the room, and every single inch of them is covered with either candles or food. And the smell! Roasted meat, bread, vegetables, bowls heaped with bright yellow butter, ale, plates of fruit. It's been hours since I last ate, and the urge to step forward and snatch an apple or a scrap of meat is almost impossible to resist.

Resist I do, though, because as my eyes travel the length of the table I see many pairs of eyes looking back at me, and none of them appear particularly friendly. I'm starting to recognize that look, actually. It's the look you give a thing – a piglet, a slice of buttered toast – not the look you give another human being. Slowly, the attention in the room comes to settle on the group of frightened women I am part of, and a chant I can't quite make out begins to rise from the seated Vikings as they beat their curved drinking cups on the table in time to it.

I don't have any idea what's happening, but it would take an idiot not to feel the tension rising, the anticipation of the room reaching a raucous, shouted peak.

And then *he* appears. The Jarl. It must be him.

I don't even see him at first. No, what I see is the way everyone's eyes move to the other end of the longhouse and then the way they fall respectfully silent as a large figure emerges from the gloom. He begins to walk towards me – towards us – and he does it slowly, accepting congratulations, big manly bear-hugs and slaps on the back that would send a lesser man sprawling across the ground. He's being congratulated for the raid on Caistley, I assume. The longhouse has been packed with the fruits of that raid, too, the sacks of grain piled against the walls and the crates of dried fish and apples stacked one on top of the other in a proud, victorious display.

As he gets closer, I see that, if anything, the Jarl outdoes his own reputation. He is – for one thing – huge. Huge enough that he towers over men like Veigar as they follow behind him. He wears a thick, silver-tipped fur around his shoulders, bound with leather ties, but his chest – broad and muscled and marked with a single curved scar – is bare. His eyes are a piercing, icy blue, the kind of eyes that can cut like a blade, and his hair is black.

At once I understand that the singing and back-slapping, the display of spoils, all of it, are tradition, not necessity. The Jarl –

although I don't quite understand how I know this, but I do – is the kind of man who draws attention to himself the way iron draws a magnet. He doesn't strut or preen, because he doesn't need to. His authority is self-contained, naturally manifested, in need of no outside praise or acknowledgement. I, like everybody else in the room, cannot take my eyes off him.

Hildy kneels as the Jarl approaches. Beside her Veigar and three other men I recognize from the journey north take their places. The men don't kneel but they do cast their eyes down reverently.

"The girls," says Veigar, his voice soft. "We chose the prettiest and the strongest for you, Jarl."

We are lined up, us women, one next to the other, and I feel the Jarl making his way towards me rather than seeing him, because my eyes are cast down then, too. There are sounds – a male grunt – the Jarl? Is he pleased? Displeased? A woman's gasp. I want to look up but I don't dare. The longhouse is warm, much warmer than outside, but I feel my nakedness acutely as the Jarl closes in on me. I force my arms to stay at my sides rather than crossing over my breasts, which is what they desperately want to do.

A pool of light follows the Jarl, cast by a torch he holds in his hand. It is this light on the bare dirt floor that I watch approach the woman next to me. I make a mistake, then, flicking my eyes up and to the side before I've even had time to think about it. And there he is, not just right beside me but *looking right at me*. His eyes are a bright, piercing blue, his gaze unwavering.

"I'm sorry," I mumble, looking away, balling my hands into fists as they begin to tremble. *Please go back to looking at the other woman. Please. Please.*

But the Jarl does not go back to looking at the other woman. He turns to me and reaches out, brushing the fingers of one massive hand down over my waist in a gesture that tightens every single muscle in my body.

"Look at me."

His voice is a deep rumble, devoid of all uncertainty. He knows my disobedience is as likely as the sun rising in the west the next morning. I swallow and my mouth is so dry my tongue gets stuck so I swallow again. And then, I look at him.

It's difficult to look at the Jarl. I fight the urge to blanche, to turn away the way one turns away from looking at the sun.

He's gorgeous. You might think it a stupid thing to notice, given the circumstances but the thing is, it's impossible not to notice. It's difficult to breathe standing there in front of a man like that, with his attention like that of a tiger's taking in a gazelle. His cold eyes flicker down over my mouth, and then further still. I feel goose-bumps rising on my skin, shame and embarrassment boiling pink and hot into my cheeks as he keeps going.

"Bashful," he pronounces, running a finger down the left side of my face. "Where did you find this one, Veigar?"

"Just outside the village, Jarl. She was watching."

The Jarl, who hasn't looked away from me for one second, peers at me with interest. "You're not from the village are you, girl? Look at you, look at –" he pauses, then, and opens my mouth with one finger – "these *teeth*. Where did you grow up to have teeth like this? Not a single one missing – not even the King can say as much."

"I –" I stammer, my brain whirring with multiple possible responses but refusing, in its panic, to settle on a single one. "I – I'm not –"

The Jarl laughs then, and the entire row of women, myself included, jump slightly at the sound. "It doesn't matter if you're the King's daughter herself, girl – all the better if you are. But tell the truth, now."

"I'm not the King's daughter," I rasp, my mouth still dry with fear.

"You're someone, though, aren't you? You're someone who knows how to be evasive with a Jarl."

"No!" I cry, desperate not to anger the man mere inches in front of me. "No, sir. Uh, Jarl. No, Jarl. I'm telling the truth. I'm not the King's daughter."

Seeming to forget his interest in my origins, he reaches out again, pressing the tips of his strong, agile fingers into the flesh of my hip. When he takes his hand away my skins burns warm where the contact had been made. "How old are you? Ten and three? Have you had your blood yet? You're tall, but there's less wear on you than I see on babes in arms."

"Ten and ten," I whisper, causing the Jarl to chuckle aloud again.

"Ten and ten – who do you take me for? An idiot like Veigar? Do you think they catch me out in the fields at night, trying to grasp the reflection of the moon in a puddle of water?"

There is general laughter in the room at this comment on Veigar's stupidity, but I'm being asked questions and I'm going to have to answer them. I lower my eyes to the ground in a manner I hope the Jarl sees as respectful and repeat myself very quietly.

"Ten and ten."

He's staring at me, I can feel it. "You're lucky it's a feasting day," he tells me calmly. "You're lucky the men came back with spoils and not empty hands. I've killed men for less than lying to –"

"I'm not lying! I'm ten and –"

I stop talking when I hear a collective audible gasp and realize I've just done something very bad. Hildy marches forward and slaps me across the face so hard it stings.

"Who are you talking to the Jarl like that?!" She demands, slapping me again for good measure.

Suddenly Veigar is at my side, his body tense, ready for action. "Shall I take her outside and kill her, Jarl? Nothing would please me so –"

The Jarl raises his hand, silencing everyone, and then he smiles at me. A man has just casually offered to kill me, and the Jarl smiles.

"Veigar's bloodthirsty," he tells me, in a voice that suggests we're participants in a private conversation and not surrounded by people. "Here, Veigar, look at her eyes – she's not afraid of you. Are you, girl? No, there's been enough flesh for your blade today, go and bring us another cask of ale."

Veigar looks at the Jarl briefly, as if he's about to say something, but the Jarl just looks back at him and that shuts him up. He storms out of the longhouse and the attentions refocuses on the Jarl – and myself.

"Are you hungry?" He asks.

Is it a trick question? I look into his eyes and see no trickery. I nod.

"Her alone?" Hildy cuts in. "None of the others?"

The Jarl glances down the line of other women, distracted and then shakes his head after a few seconds. "No, Hildy, this one will do. And I'll have her sit with me during the feast, you can bathe her later."

With a nod, Hildy leads the other women out of the longhouse and the Jarl walks to the other end of the longhouse to take his seat at the head of the room. I follow behind him, because it seems to be the most obvious choice, and stand to the side after he sits, waiting for instruction, praying I haven't transgressed. The smell of the food is torment now, my stomach aching with hunger and my mouth watering. The feast begins again when the Jarl reaches for his cup and drains it, to the cheers of his men, and I stay where I am, still naked, still terrified.

It's minutes later when the Jarl turns and gestures to me to come to him, pulling me onto his lap as I get close. He's wearing a skirt-like leather garment, like his men, but his is tied at the waist with straps from which hang various beads, shells and tools. Leaned against the table is a sword, it's pommel inlaid with what look to be colored gemstones and its blade gleaming in the firelight. It's still difficult to believe that what's happening is – well, what's actually happening. I am naked on the lap of a Viking warrior, his arm slung casually around my waist, and surrounded by roaring, feasting men. Mostly, they keep their eyes to themselves but every now and again, when the Jarl's attention is elsewhere, I feel eyes on me, drinking me in.

"Here," the Jarl says, passing me a roughly carved wooden bowl full of what looks and smells like meat stew of some kind. "Eat this, girl. Your eyes are just about bursting out of your skull looking at all this food. Are you thirsty? Bring her some ale!"

A few seconds later there is a cup of ale in front of me, but it's going to have to wait. Someone hands me a wooden spoon and I dip it into the stew.

"Oh my God," I breathe, the only words that have time to slip out of my throat between mouthfuls of stew. It's the best thing I've ever tasted, meaty and thick and steaming hot. I keep going for quite a long time, too, cramming spoonful after spoonful into my mouth until it's dripping off my chin and onto my bare thighs and I'm breathless with the sheer effort of eating. It's only then that I realize the Jarl himself has stopped eating and has instead chosen to watch me, leaning back with a deeply amused expression on his face.

"Ale?" He asks, causing the men seated nearest to us to break out laughing as he passes me the cup of ale. I gulp it, pausing after the first taste because it's sweet – not what I was expecting – and then drinking the rest.

"More ale!" The Jarl bellows. "And more stew!"

Halfway through the second enormous bowl of stew, I begin to slow down. And as my hunger and thirst are satisfied, I become more conscious of the hand resting heavily on my thigh.

Well what did you think he was choosing women for? The words flit through my mind as I look at the Jarl out of the corner of my eye. The man is a colossus. Surely he has a wife? Many wives? But there is the fact of that hand.

There is something else, too, besides the hand. Something I don't understand. I'm afraid, that's true. I need to get home, that's also true. The man whose muscular thigh I'm perched upon is as clear a danger to me as there has ever been – and not just to my honor (my virginity has, if anything, been more of a millstone around my neck than anything I've sought to preserve). One of his men was threatening to kill me not an hour ago!

I should feel fear, and I do. But I'm not as afraid of the Jarl as I would have expected, and it doesn't make much sense.

As the feast goes on, and my belly fills further, the lack of sleep over the past 24 hours begins to catch up with me and I catch my head nodding. The Jarl notices it too, catching my chin at one point before it hits the table.

"You're tired," he says, speaking only to me. It hasn't been long but I've already noticed that when the Jarl speaks, it is often to a whole group of people at once. And when it is directed at one person, they glow from head to foot.

The food has hit me hard – my eyelids are so heavy I can barely keep them open. I'm aware that the Jarl is looking at me, though, perhaps trying to assess whether I'm trying to fake him out so I can make and escape attempt. A few seconds later he gestures for someone to come to us. Hildy.

"Take her," he instructs the woman. "Put her in my bed but let her sleep."

The words 'my bed' barely register and Hildy helps me up, throws a rough woolen blanket around my shoulders and guides me out of the longhouse. Outside it is still daylight and if I were any more awake I would enquire as to how long the feast is expected to continue. But I'm hardly awake at all so I just allow Hildy to lead me to a round wooden building like the one we were first made to wait in, and set me down on a bed of furs. She begins to place wood in a central fire-pit to start a fire but I've drifted off to sleep before I can begin to feel its warmth.

Chapter 7
9th Century

When I wake up, I am disoriented and alone, but nestled into soft furs. Where am I? Oh, yes. Embers glow orange in the fire-pit and I'm thankful for the warmth. I push myself up on my arms and look around – is Hildy lurking? No. I lie back down and listen attentively for any sounds. A dog barking in the distance, nothing else. The feast must still be happening? I have no idea if I've slept for two hours or twelve.

Beside the bed the blanket Hildy wrapped around me has been thrown over a wooden stool. I pick it up and wrap it around my body twice, pulling the corner over my shoulder the last time before tucking it underneath itself near my armpit. Then I walk to the door, which is less a door than a sheet of leather hung over a tall opening, and pull it aside, leaning out into a cool, dark night. It's only late September but there is already a thin layer of frost covering the ground. In front of me, my breath is visible in the dim light from a crescent moon. I look to the left, then to the right, and see no one. In the distance, now, I can hear what must be the feast still going on, the shouts of high-spirited men carried to me on the breeze.

Where is Hildy? I don't know. Does this Viking camp have guards? Has someone been tasked with looking out for me? I don't know any of these things. I slip out of the roundhouse, pulling the blanket tightly around me and trying not to acknowledge the fact that it is far, far too cold to try and slip out of the camp without more to cover myself with. Just reconnaissance, then.

Within minutes my feet are wet and numb, but I seem to have found one side of the camp, because I'm running my hands along the thick posts of the palisade and standing on my tiptoes trying to get a look over the top so I can figure out which direction I'm facing.

"HEY!"

I turn quickly and make an instinctive attempt to flee, but am stopped by a hand wrapped around my upper arm. So the Vikings do have guards. This one is young, but he's tall and wiry and he's lifting his hand above his head. I squeeze my eyes shut tight, presuming it better to take the blow rather than to try to duck away and risk angering the guard further. But just as it should be about to land a female voice – Hildy – interrupts.

"No! No! The Jarl chose her, and he won't be happy if you mark up her pretty face."

Once again the word strikes me, even in a situation like that – which might not say too much about me. Pretty. These people seem united in the belief that I am pretty. Perhaps I can have them sign something before I go home, so I can take it back to River Forks and show it to Kayla and all the rest of those mean girls from high school. *See? I'm not an ugly witch. These Vikings said so.*

Hildy instructs the guard to take me back to the Jarl's roundhouse, and laughs at my attempts to claim I was looking for her.

"Save it, girl, for Veigar. He's the only one who might believe you. But hear this – it's cold and you've no furs, no leather boots for your feet. Even if you did manage to get out, you'd be dead of freezing by dawn. And if somehow you weren't, the Jarl's men would find you and drown you in the marsh."

Back in the roundhouse, the guard declines to leave me alone. He throws more logs onto the fire and comes inside with me, standing by the door and staring at me shamelessly.

"I'm not taking the blanket off," I inform him prissily, trying to salvage some of dignity after being unceremoniously dragged back here. "So I don't know what you think you're looking at."

Stupid. So stupid. I probably will learn to keep my mouth shut at some point, but apparently not yet. The guard simply crosses the distance between us in a couple of easy strides and tears the blanket off me, yanking it out of reach when I move to grab it. He gets an eyeful then, and I turn away from his gaze, humiliated.

A couple of moments later and I feel him there behind me, his hot breath on my shoulder. And virgin or not, I know what he's interested in.

"Hildy told you," I tell him, in a voice that shakes too much. "She told you the Jarl chose me. You should keep your hands off –"

The guard grabs at my breast and I try to twist away but it doesn't work. He pinches my nipple, hard, and I yelp with pain and surprise.

"Hey! Stop! What are you doing?! Please – I told you the Jarl –"

A smelly hand closes over my mouth and I reach up, clawing at it, screaming now although the hand prevents anyone from hearing it. The guard is too strong for me – even as I writhe and kick he's pushing me down – not onto the furs but onto the bare earthen floor. His hand slips briefly off my mouth, allowing a shriek to pierce the smoky air, but it's soon back in place.

I'm panicking now, because I know I can't get away. I know, even as he forces my legs open with his body, that I'm not strong enough to fight him off.

He's fumbling, trying to untie the leather straps around his waist and his breath is coming fast against my neck. So this is it. I stop fighting, knowing it's useless, wanting only to lessen the pain that I'm about to experience. I squeeze my eyes shut and then suddenly a great roar fills the roundhouse and the guard is no longer on top of me. My eyes fly open and I look up. The Jarl. He's standing over the cowering guard and I am flooded with relief.

The guard is whimpering, apologizing and begging. "I'm sorry, Jarl. I'm so sorry. She took off her blanket and I couldn't resist. She spread her legs and showed herself to me! I couldn't –"

"No I didn't!" I shout, desperate for the Jarl not to think I did anything to bring the guard's behavior on. "No I *did not* open my legs for you, you lying pig!"

The Jarl cuts in, speaking to the guard. "It doesn't matter. Hildy told you she was mine. Boy, you know the punishment for this!"

At that, the guard begins to physically grovel and I wonder what horrifically painful ordeal is now to be meted out by one of the Jarl's men – or the Jarl himself. I don't have to wonder for long, though, because the Jarl picks up a heavy stone axe laying by the door and brings it suddenly – and with a sickening thud – down onto the guard's head.

I look away swiftly, the vomit already rising in my throat, and the absolute silence tells me the blow has been final. I've never even seen an animal die.

The Jarl busies himself, doing something with his axe that I do not want to see – cleaning it, probably – and my heartbeat sings high in my ears as a terrible smell rises around me. It is the smell of blood, of flesh and bone and sweat and fear and all the things us humans are made of. I breathe through my mouth, desperate to get that smell out of my nose, but it's too strong to escape.

"What is it?" The Jarl asks, after instructing another guard to bury the one he has just killed, and to send the dead guard's father to see him the next day. I make the mistake of looking up, then, and subsequently seeing some lumps of something pink on the dirt floor next to the door. A girl appears, gathering them in her hands, but not before my brain has taken in the fact that it's looking at pieces of a person. I look up at the Jarl, filled with a terrible kind of awe – how is it possible to end a human life like that, with less guilt than I would feel over killing a spider? – and barely manage to lean away from the pile of furs before vomiting copiously onto the ground.

"Girl!" The Jarl barks at the servant. "Clean this first, I can't stand the smell of it."

But you can stand the smell of brains? I want to ask. *You can stand the fact that there are flecks of another person's blood on your cheek right now?* It's not even terror I'm feeling, it's a plain lack of comprehension, an inability to understand what has just happened.

The Jarl must see the look on my face as I retch and wipe the back of my hand against my sweaty brow. "What's the matter?" He asks, sitting down on the furs beside me and wiping one bloodied hand across one of them. I look at him, searching his face for some sign he's showing off, or pretending a nonchalance he does not feel. There is none. "What?" He repeats."Have you never seen death before, girl? It's not possible. But your face –" he takes my chin in one hand, a gentler touch than I'm expecting, and looks into my eyes – "you're as pale as winter milk. Come now, speak."

"No," I try to say, but all that comes out is a cracked whisper. "No," I repeat, my voice louder but still a whisper. "No I haven't. I – I haven't."

"It's not possible," the Jarl repeats, looking at me the way you look at someone you think might be pulling the wool over your eyes. "Even if you are the King's daughter, as I'm beginning to think you are, you cannot be ten and ten – or even just ten alone – and not have seen death before, not have smelled the blood I see you drawing away from now, as if a single drop of it will soil you. Are you surprised, girl?"

I shake my head because I do not want to displease the Jarl. I do not want to anger him. I do not want to give him any more reasons to question me, when I know most of my answers to his questions will not be adequate. "I'm not surprised," I lie. "I'm just sensitive. I don't like to see it. I don't know why you had to –"

The Jarl pulls back, an openly baffled expression painted onto the broad, sharp angles of his face. "He would have raped you – you know that, do you not? Are you slow, is that it? Have I chosen badly, a pretty face and a dull mind?"

Again I shake my head. "No! No, I'm not slow, I –"

"You don't have to explain it to me, I can see it in your eyes. You're sorry for him. Sorry that a man who intended to rape you has had his injustice turned back on him."

The Jarl is not the only one with questions. But he is the only one who dares to ask them.

When the roundhouse has been cleaned and the servant girl has left, Hildy enters and I notice that she is not meeting the Jarl's eyes. "Is there anything else you need, Jarl?" She asks.

A man has just died for putting his hands on me, but even I know it has nothing to do with the fact that it was I who didn't want them there. No. It was the Jarl who didn't want them there. And now I suspect the Jarl will put his hands on me, and it won't matter what my feelings on it are. I won't fight him. Not because I don't want to, but because I can't. I've just seen it spelled out for me in the most graphic terms possible what happens to people who don't do what the Jarl wants them to do. So I will not fight.

Maybe it will be over quickly. Emma and the girls at college joke about that, about it being over quickly. Maybe it will be the same now?

I try to turn away before anyone can see the fat tear that drops from one of my eyes onto the furs, but I'm not quick enough. Again, the Jarl is lifting my face up to his, gazing at me the way one might gaze at a creature one has never encountered before.

"I think this one might be dull," he says to Hildy, who immediately begins to apologize. The Jarl ignores her and continues. "Look at her, she's weeping over the guard. Whoever saw a woman weep over the death of a man who meant to rape her?"

He looks at me for a few more seconds, still with that same curiosity in his eyes, before turning away. "No matter, I'm not in the mood for weeping girls tonight. Take her and put her with the others, I'll decide what to do with her in the morning. Bring me Alva – and Hildy? Make sure she's clean."

I stumble ahead of Hildy as she prods me in the back, pushing me out of the roundhouse. And as soon as we're out of the Jarl's earshot she leans in close. I pull away, expecting a slap. Instead, she yanks my head back and hisses in my ear:

"What are you doing?! The Jarl chose you, girl, and now you sit in front of him like an unhappy child – have you any idea what will happen if he gives you up? You'll be a slave like the rest of them he rejected. Is he right, are you dull? Would you rather eat bones that the freemen and women have already picked clean, is that it? Would you rather there was no one to care if the guards take you ten times in a night?"

I don't respond right away – not because I don't want to but because by then I have no idea where to start – and Hildy spins me around to face her. "Well?! Would you?"

"No!" I reply. "No! I just – I don't understand how things work here. I don't –"

Hildy grabs me by the shoulders and gives me a shake. "Well you'd best learn soon, do you hear me? Do what he wants, girl. If what you say is true and you're truly ten-and-ten, then you already know what it is a man wants, be he a freeman of the North or be he one of the high men here, in your own country."

Hildy is right, I do know – theoretically – what a man wants. I wonder if this is how it was for Willa. Did she choose her husband, as I had always assumed? Or did he just take her, like she was livestock? And has Eadgar done the same thing – chosen a woman from a group and made her his companion without anyone ever wondering if she had any interest in the role? Hildy is probably also right about me needing to wake up. Will I be a slave if the Jarl rejects me? Will it be me cleaning still-warm brains from the dirt floor of his roundhouse?

"Think," Hildy instructs me when we get to a small, squat building near the fence. "Think about what's best. I already told you that you won't be escaping from here, and you won't, not unless death is preferable to life with us. I don't understand you, girl – you'll be better off as one of the Jarl's girls than you would ever have been as the wife of one of those peasants back in whatever village it is you come from. Do you want your children to eat or do you want them to starve?"

With that, she pushes me into the building and leaves me there in the pitch black, where I soon become aware of the sounds of other people sleeping. Everywhere I try to step I run into a warm body, so in the end I just sink to the ground where I stand and curl into a ball.

I don't sleep, though. I think about the things Hildy has just said to me, specifically the part about escape being impossible. Of course she would say that, wouldn't she? She's one of them and she seems to be nominally in charge of the women taken from Caistley – she would probably be in trouble if any of us went astray. She's not wrong about the weather, but the Vikings have furs and garments made of wool and leather. If I can manage to get my hands on some of them and if I can find my way out of the camp – another task which does not seem impossible – I can do as planned and follow the coast south again, back to Caistley.

The question of what to do in the meantime – because as naive and plain old stupid as I may be in this world, even I know I can't just blunder into an escape attempt and give the Vikings any more reason to supervise me – presses down on me. Hildy said to make him happy and I know what she means. I don't want to make the Jarl 'happy.' I don't even know the Jarl. And by the looks of him, whatever he wanted me to do would probably not be too pleasant, or gentle.

A conversation pops into my mind suddenly, one I had with Emma and a few of our friends from class one Friday night as we shared a bottle of wine before heading out to a party. We had been discussing prostitution, how desperate we would have to be to do it. And the consensus, apart from a single woman who had spoken up to admit she did have a price, had been that there was literally nothing on earth that would make us choose to use our bodies in that manner, to gain favor or money or gifts.

Lying on the cold dirt floor of a Viking roundhouse, surrounded by women who are now slaves, it's safe to say I begin to feel a new flexibility creeping into my perspective. I need food, for one thing. I've seen what a lack of food does to people – to Willa and Eadgar after their father died. How do I mean to escape, to walk for hours, probably days, along the coast, to evade anyone sent after me if I am weak from hunger?

The truth stares me in the face. I have to do as I'm told. I have to acquiesce. There's really only one question that matters, and it isn't what will I do to get home – it's what *won't* I do. The air in the roundhouse is stale and, in spite of the bodies packed in with me, cold. What is there I won't do to get home, to get back to my actual life? Here, right now, there isn't a single thing I can think of.

Chapter 8
21st Century

School never did get better. The bullying became less overt as we all got older, but I was never accepted, never anything other than the weird girl. The incident with Kayla Foster got spun, through the combination of rumor and passing time, into something horrific and extravagant. The last version of it I ever heard was that I had lured her into the woods against her will to participate in a Satanic ceremony – one that involved animal sacrifice. Of course, if all the rumors about me were true, and I really was some kind of powerful, dark figure, my fellow students showed remarkably little real fear of me.

All except Kayla herself, anyway. When she was with her friends she was as dismissive and haughty as any of them. When she was alone, though, she would refuse to meet my eye and turn away down another hallway rather than pass me by. I wondered if she ever told anyone the truth of what happened that day but I suppose she didn't understand it herself. To her it probably felt like a hallucination or a dream.

What I'm trying to say is that I was friendless and isolated. Not just at school, either. My father never recovered from the loss of his wife and by the time I was 15 or 16 I was basically his caretaker. He refused to see any doctors, but as far as I could tell whatever his affliction was it wasn't physical. He could still walk, he just chose not to. His world shrank down to the size of his room, which he rarely emerged from, and I was left to find my way into adulthood – into womanhood – entirely alone. I learned to cook a few basic dishes by watching Youtube videos and when I got my first period it was the internet that held my hand, advising me to stock up on Advil and tampons and to forgo the wearing of white pants when my 'aunt flo' was in town.

It was a difficult time. I say that as if it was brief. As if I could pinpoint some specific period in my teens when life was hard. But it wasn't part of it, it was all of it after losing my mother. For a few short years I was happy in another place – in Caistley – but as with all childhood contentment it was fleeting, ungraspable.

Watching my father taught me one thing, and that is that you would be surprised what a human being can endure. You would be surprised how much a person – how much a *life* – can shrink without ending. It wasn't just my father, either. He got used to existing instead of living, and so did I. Each day became a series of minor tasks to be crossed off an ever-renewing list. Wake up. Make breakfast. Go to school. Eat lunch in the library, alone. Go home. On Tuesdays and Thursdays, meet with Dr. Whittington. Make dinner – for my father and for myself. Do homework. Go to bed. Repeat. Repeat. Repeat.

Dr. Whittington suggested anti-depressants but he didn't push them on me because I think even he realized that I was depressed because my life itself was depressing.

At 15, a few years after definitively realizing that Caistley existed in a different time, I got more serious about trying to find out where exactly it was – and when. My total lack of a social life aided my new hobby, and I began to spend almost every lunch hour in the library, reading.

I was pretty sure Caistley was in what was now known as Britain, or the United Kingdom. The weather seemed to support this theory, as did Willa and Eadgar's talk of "Northmen" and "invaders." I was pretty sure they were talking about Vikings.

As I researched and read, a very rough picture began to emerge. Whenever Caistley was, it was a very long time ago. The Vikings were mostly active in Britain pre-1000 A.D. There were other clues, too. No one in Caistley had ever owned a book. When I described them to Willa and Eadgar both of them looked at me like I was mad. They hadn't just never seen a book – they didn't even know what a book was. When they spoke of the King it was the 'King of the East Angles' – and they referred to themselves as Angles. For a long time I thought the 'martians' they talked about were evil spirits but after paying closer attention to our conversations and reading a little further I came to the conclusion that they weren't 'martians' –

they were Mercians, and they were simply the citizens of a rival kingdom.

As far as I could tell, the Caistley I had spent my childhood visiting existed sometime in the mid to late 9th century in the Kingdom of the East Angles – known today as East Anglia. If I was right about that, and based on my reading, Willa and Eadgar had good reason to fear the Northmen who they spoke of in hushed tones. I wanted to warn them that the Viking raids they talked about were going to become more frequent and, eventually, more permanent. The invaders were going to move from brief forays into Anglian territory to secure resources to a pattern of settlement which was going to lead to two centuries of rule by the foreigners.

But Caistley itself had never been hit – not at that point – and when Willa and Eadgar spoke of the Vikings it was the same way they spoke of the demons they believed lurked in the woods at night – scary, but avoidable. Not an immediate threat. And perhaps they were right about that, given that I could not pinpoint exactly what year – or even what decade – it was.

I tried, though, one afternoon when I was 17 and visiting Caistley as infrequently as once a month. I hadn't seen Willa for ages, but Eadgar was there that day and, based on my readings, I tried to impress Caistley's vulnerability upon him. I tried to make him understand how welcoming the little bay would be to Viking ships, how short the path to the village, how completely undefended it all was.

Eadgar didn't disagree with anything I was saying but he did display the streak of what I took to be fatalism that I had come to believe was one of the deepest differences between myself, and the people in my time, and Eadgar and Willa and the people in their time. He even shrugged at one point when I reminded him of what he himself had told me about what the Vikings did to the inhabitants of the villages they invaded. I became annoyed.

"Don't you care?" I asked, wanting to see some sign that my friend was taking my words seriously. "What about Willa and your mother? What about Willa's son? Do you want to see them killed by Northmen?"

Eadgar had looked at me sharply then, something he rarely did, and thrown my questions right back at me. "Do you take me for a soldier?" He asked angrily. "Have you ever seen a sword in my hand? It is always this way with you, Paige, there is always this bridge between us, as if you assume me a King, with the powers of a King. You've never seemed to quite understand that however it is on the estate, or with your kin, it is not that way here in Caistley. Here in Caistley we are farmers. We grow food, we tend animals. We don't fight. If someone attacks us who will go hungry? Yes, we will go hungry. But so will the ealdorman – the King's man – and his family and it is their task to protect those who work for his estate. They protect their own interests in protecting ours. Everyone plays their part, and this is what you always fail to understand."

"So you're fine with that?" I asked, exasperated. "You tell me of invaders, of murder and plunder, and your response is to just act like there's nothing you can –"

"But there IS nothing I can do!" Eadgar shouted, losing his patience with me – for the first time ever, as far as I could recall. "Everyone has a role, Paige. I fulfill my role, Willa fulfills hers, all the others in Caistley do the same. The ealdorman has a role, too. And the reeve and the slave. And none shall go outside their role, lest it all fall entirely apart. Why don't you understand that? None of it would work if we all tried to do all the roles at once. Sometimes I question if you are even from the estate. Seems as if you might be from somewhere else, somewhere across the sea."

Somewhere across the sea. 'Across the sea' was the phrase used by Willa and Eadgar to mean 'incomprehensibly foreign.' And I can't say as I blamed him for using it during that conversation. I was being stupid and impatient because I was fearful for my friends, because I wanted them to be safe. And it was as difficult for Eadgar to fathom a different way of life as it was for me. Just as he couldn't wrap his head around people stepping outside their roles, I couldn't wrap my head around *having* an assigned role at birth, with no chance to improve my lot or follow a different path than the one laid out in front of me by biology and social class.

When I asked him a short while later if anyone in Caistley had thought of building defenses – even a fence of a kind to keep invaders out, rather than livestock in, he shook his head, annoyed again.

"If the ealdorman or the king want to put up fences, Paige, then they will put up fences."

"But surely you and some of the other men of the village could –"

"Could what? Put up fences ourselves? We are forbidden to cut down the trees, Paige! None of this land is our own. It belongs to the King or the King's men. We're not to take trees or animals from the woods or fish from the rivers without permission – to do so would mean losing a hand or even death."

***

A couple of evenings later, Dr. Whittington noticed the edge in my usually flat voice and commented on its presence.

"I'm just frustrated," I told him. It was true – I was frustrated. About the fact that even with a foreknowledge of what was coming there appeared to be very little I could do to help my friends in Caistley. But I was frustrated with Dr. Whittington, too, and the situation between us. I wanted to tell him the whole story but I couldn't. If imaginary friends are frowned upon at 9, there's no telling what could happen if you still have them at 17. And kind and tolerant as Dr. Whittington was, even I knew he wasn't just going to believe me if I told him what was really going on with my friends who lived 'out of town.'

When he asked me what I was frustrated about I frowned. "I don't think they're taking care of themselves," I replied. "I think something bad is going to happen to them but when I tried to warn Eadgar he just shrugged it off. It's not even because he doesn't believe me, either! He just has this whole fatalism thing going on, like there's nothing he can do about any of it!"

"Eadgar is your age, isn't he?"

I nodded. "About a year older."

"Perhaps your annoyance with him and what you perceive as his weakness, or his inability to help himself, has some parallels to your own life?"

I closed my eyes and took a deep breath – but only to keep myself from rolling my eyes and yelling "WELL, DUH!" at my doctor. Yes, my own situation was a seemingly endless grind of days, one the same as any other, but that didn't mean my worries with regards to Eadgar and Willa were wrong, somehow, or that they didn't exist.

Not that any of that mattered in my conversation with Dr. Whittington, because I couldn't really explain any of it.

Over the next year or so, Eadgar's irritation with me grew. The more I read about the Viking invasions the more I worried, the more I was unable to hold back from encouraging him to take his sister and her children (she had two by then) and move further inland. I totally understood his irritation, too. He couldn't move inland, as he repeatedly told me. It wasn't up to him where he lived. His parents were born in Caistley to work the land for an ealdorman, a person much higher on the social scale – and so Eadgar and Willa and their children and grandchildren would also work the same land for the ealdorman and his children and grandchildren.

It got so bad that I cried one day, when Eadgar threw down the branches he'd been weaving together as we talked and started back towards Caistley, so angry at me he didn't even bother to say goodbye.

"Maybe I should just take you to the – to the estate!" I shouted after him, immediately shutting up as I realized I'd just crossed an unspoken-of and generally unacknowledged line. Eadgar stopped walking away, too, and came to a dead stop with his back to me. He waited a few seconds before turning around slowly and peering at me.

"You never talk about the estate, Paige."

"I know," I replied, wiping my eyes and wondering what kind of enormous can of worms I'd just opened.

"So why are you talking about it now?"

I have a very clear memory of Eadgar that day, of the way it was just at the moment, over a period of less than a year, when he turned from boy into man. His face was still rounded near the chin, like a child's, but his voice had deepened and his shoulders broadened. He still would have been considered scrawny in River Forks, and none of the football coaches would have taken a second look at him, but I could see the difference. I remember he was half-obscured by shadows from the woods that crept right up to the edge of the beach where we'd been sitting and just for a second or two it looked like someone else – a grown man – walking towards me.

"Why are you staring at me in the way?" He asked as got back to me and maybe if the conversation hadn't already been about something else, I might have told him.

I didn't, though. I didn't tell my friend he was beginning to look like a man because I didn't want to embarrass him or make him think I was interested in him in a way that I wasn't. Instead I made a scoffing noise and he seemed to forget about it.

"So why now then, Paige?" He asked. "Why do you speak of the estate now, after all these years?"

"It's what I've already told you a thousand times, Eadgar. I'm worried about you – and Willa. I'm worried if the Northmen come to Caistley, you'll be taken or worse. I'm worried that you don't seem to –"

Eadgar stepped forward. He didn't put his hand on me but he drew himself up in a way he had never done before. I'd always been bigger than him, despite our being almost the same age, but he was as tall as me by then, perhaps even an inch or so taller. He leaned in close to me and shook his head."Don't say it again, Paige. I can't hear it again. I can't hear you telling me I don't care about my own kin, my own life."

He was right. I knew it, and he knew I knew it. "Alright," I replied, "I won't say it. But don't expect that to stop me from worrying. I worry about you all the time, you and Willa out here, with no one to call if the Northmen come, no one on hand to defend you."

"Is that why you mention the estate? Is that why you mention bringing us to the estate? You must know it's impossible, Paige. As impossible as me building a fence around the village."

But it wasn't impossible, because there was no estate and what there was – a literal different world – was not subject to the social customs of the 9th century. I'd already successfully brought one person through the tree – admittedly in the opposite direction – but there was no reason to think it couldn't work.

Even as I thought of it, though – and it was not the first time it had entered my mind – I remembered Kayla Foster's reaction. Kayla Foster from the 21st century, who had barely seen more than a few trees when I brought her to the past. I knew, even without having to imagine it explicitly, that neither Willa nor Eadgar could be prepared for the distant future. Not because they were too stupid, but simply because the future was too alien, too much. No one could have been prepared for it. No, bringing people from the past to the future was an impossibility.

Chapter 9
21st Century

"Are you going to your prom?"

Dr. Whittington was asking out of politeness, because the topic had come up. I could not imagine he was asking because he actually thought there was some chance I *was* going to my prom.

I shook my head no and we moved seamlessly on to another topic.

Prom night came, though, in the spring of my final year of high school, and I spent it at home, alone, the way I spent every evening. I ended up being more disturbed than I had anticipated, too. Why was missing out on prom such a big deal to me when I'd already missed out on so many other adolescent rites of passage? No boyfriends for Paige Renner. No parties, no driver's education classes, no first kisses or photographs of me next to a gangly boy in a tux.

I brought my dad's dinner upstairs to him at five o'clock – he ate early and went to sleep early – and then I tiptoed back downstairs and stood at the entrance to the kitchen, seized suddenly by a memory of my mother shooing me out after she'd washed the floor, telling me to wait for it to dry. I looked down at the tiles, clean enough because I kept them clean, but broken in multiple places, and uneven. I could clean floors, but I didn't know how to fix them.

It was the next thought that really got to me, that sent me scurrying down to the woods and the tree at a later time than usual. And that thought was what my mother would say, what she would *feel*, if she could see me at that moment, on my prom night. I have photographs of my mother from her childhood and adolescence. I was starting to look very much like her by then, the only thing difference between me and the grinning woman in the photographs was our clothing and hairstyles. My unruly, chestnut-brown hair was like hers, as were my round hazel eyes and my heart-shaped face. My mom was thinner than me – I seemed to have inherited a certain thickness of limb from my father's side of the family. I wasn't fat, but

I wasn't skinny either, and my body was generous and womanly way before I was ready for it.

Unlike me, though, my mother was popular. In so many of the photos she's wearing cut-off denim shorts and halter tops and standing with a crowd of other girls dressed the same way, all of them with their bangs teased way up into the sky and huge, wholesome smiles on their faces. The young, happy girl in those photos wouldn't have wanted her only child to spend prom night alone, in a dingy old house that was falling apart at the seams.

But I was alone and that night, it was too much. I checked that my father was asleep and then ran down through the yard to the woods to lay my hands on the tree and close my eyes with relief as the darkness pulled me away from my own loneliness.

The woods on the other side were empty. Willa and Eadgar avoided leaving the village after dark, suspicious as they were of whatever it was they seemed to believe lurked there after night fell. I wandered the trails for a little while and came out on the rocky point at one end of the beach. There was a wind blowing but it was a warm wind, carrying the promise of summer on its gentle gusts. I turned my face into it.

What are you doing?

The question just popped into my head unbidden, as if spoken aloud by someone standing a few feet away from me.

I'm sitting on the rocks, enjoying the wind on my face.

But the question wasn't really about what I was doing at that very moment, and I knew it. It was larger than that and it was the right time for it to be asked. High school was almost over. What was I going to do? Dr. Whittington and the librarian at school, who had taken pity on me after seeing me spend every lunch hour alone in the library, were both encouraging me – gently – to go to college. Kayla Foster and her crowd spoke of little else but college in those waning school days. College boys, college parties, prestigious colleges, state colleges, colleges in California, colleges hundreds of miles away from all parental supervision.

I felt what I felt often at that time – envy, exclusion. And sitting on the rocks outside Caistley I realized that there wasn't actually anything stopping me from going to college. If anything, it might be one of the last opportunities of my youth to start over in a different place, somewhere where nobody knew I was the weird girl or the 'witch' or that I had never kissed a boy.

It wasn't yet summer when I walked back through the dark, dew-sparkled woods to get home. It didn't cross my mind that it might be my last trip to Caistley – for a very long time, anyway. I reassured myself with the thought that it was months before September, that there would be ample time to come back, to say a proper goodbye to Eadgar and Willa.

But in the end, I didn't go back. I applied to a few different colleges, all within a day's drive of River Forks, so I could check in on my dad on weekends and holidays, and got into every single one. The final decision on what college I would actually attend was made for me one day at the grocery store where I overheard Kayla Foster's mother talking about the college – one of my own picks – that Kayla herself had chosen. It was one of the last two I was hemming and hawing over and discovering that Kayla would be at one of them made my decision for me.

"Grand Northeastern," I muttered the name of the institution that would not be favored with Kayla's presence as I exited the store, "here I come."

My father didn't want me to go away. Not at first, anyway. He didn't want it so much he actually got himself up and dressed one night and came downstairs to eat a dinner of boxed macaroni and cheese and steamed broccoli with me. Just before the meal was finished, he put down his fork and stated that it would be a bad idea for me to go to college.

"Why is that?" I asked, prepared to defend myself even as I was mortified at having to – what kind of parent tries to *stop* their child from going to college? I had a scholarship and everything!

"Why do you think?" My father replied immediately, without looking up from his plate. "Look at this place, Paige. Look at *me*. What am I going to do without you here to take care of everything the way you do?"

I was prepared for that conversation. I had known it was coming. I knew what I was going to say. But the sorrow in my dad's voice got to me and instead of calmly reciting all of the solid, rational reasons why I should go to college, I found myself tongue-tied and awkward.

"Dad," I whispered. "Dad!"

"What?" He mumbled, still studying the last few remnants of dinner.

"LOOK AT ME!" I shouted, shocking myself almost as much as I think I shocked him. It worked, though. He looked up.

"Jesus, Paige! Are you trying to give me a heart –"

"Dad why are you doing this?" I asked, the words all tumbling out in a rush because I didn't want to lose my nerve before I could finish saying what I suddenly needed to say. "Why are you trying to stop me going to college? You spend all day reading the news, reading how bad it is for my generation, how there are no jobs here and you want me to *stay?* I'm 17 years old, Dad! What would mom say? I don't even have to ask, do I, because we both know what she would say. Why do you want me to waste my life the way you –"

"Don't talk about your mother."

That was it, the entirety of his response. He stood up and stormed out, heading back upstairs to his room.

Five days later he emerged into the sunlight of a Sunday afternoon as I weeded the small patch of earth in the backyard where my mother used to grow tomatoes and told me I had to go to college. That's what he said, exactly those words: "Paige, you have to go to college."

I looked up, shading my eyes from the sunshine. "I know."

"I never would have let you stay," he told me, his voice shaking with emotion. "I never would have let you stay, Paige. I know it's time for you to make your own way in the world. I'm just an old man, and I'm afraid of losing the only person –"

I had never actually seen my dad cry before that day. He went dark and silent and mournful when my mother died, but I never saw him cry. He must have, of course, but he didn't let me see it happening. So when I saw it that afternoon it was like a dam had just burst in my chest and all the daughterly love and pain at what had become of my dad poured out at once and didn't stop.

"Dad," I gasped, choking back a sob as I stood up and wrapped my arms around him. "I know. I know you wouldn't have let me stay. I know it. I know."

"I'm just going to miss you, Paige. I'm going to miss you so much. And I'm so sorry. I'm so sorry, my beautiful girl. I've let you down. I haven't been a father to –"

"Stop!" I instructed, pulling away and holding my father by his once-solid but now frail shoulders. "Stop it. I may only be 17 but I'm not stupid. I know that life isn't a series of tests we all pass with flying colors and no lasting damage. Mom died. She died, Dad. In a weird way I've always thought what happened afterwards was kind of a testament to how much you loved her. To how much *we* loved her."

"You're a good girl, Paige," my father replied, stroking my hair and looking into my eyes for more than a second for the first time in years. "But you don't have to make excuses for –"

"I'm not, though," I told him firmly. "I'm not making excuses for anyone. She died and we fell apart. What point is there to lying about it now? To pretending it didn't happen? If I could go back would I change everything so she lived? Of course I would, but that's not how it was for us, was it?"

"OK," my dad breathed, nodding. "OK. I won't argue with you. I don't think I even know how to argue anymore. But what I'm trying to say, what I want you to know more than I want anyone else to know anything in this world, is that I'm sorry. I'm sorry I haven't been here for you. I'm sorry you've had to go through your childhood without your mother – and without me."

He meant it. I could see it in his expression, hear it in his voice, feel it in the space between us – my father was sorry. And even though at 17 I was still too young to truly understand what I'd missed out on – what we'd both missed out on – due to his self-imposed seclusion, part of me knew on some instinctive level that what my father had just done was to salvage something out of the wreckage of his – of our – current lives. Nothing was built yet, no blueprints had been drawn up, but my father had just taken a brick and held it up to me before placing it down into the soft clay between us. A gesture, a promise – hope for a future that might look different to our past.

"Thank-you, Dad," I whispered, suddenly absolutely seized with the need to let him know that I loved him, that I forgave him. "I won't be far, you know. I can come home every weekend. And holidays, too! I can do the shopping on Saturdays, I can –"

"You can come home when you need to come home," he responded. "And not before then. Your old dad is going to have to learn some new tricks. Or relearn old ones, I suppose. Either way, Paige, I don't want you going off to college with a millstone around your neck. You go and take care of yourself. You go and live your life, my beautiful girl. I'll be here when you need me, but you aren't responsible for me anymore. OK?"

"OK, Dad."

Chapter 10
9th Century

"Come on, girl!"

Hildy snaps a length of cloth at the bare backs of my legs and I jump, shrieking with pain, as it connects. She's herding us like cattle again, down to the stream to wash. And the whole way there she's complaining about how filthy we are, about how filthy the Angles are in general, how if she was blind she wouldn't be able to tell the difference between an Angle and a pig. *OK,* I want to yell. *WE GET IT, WE SMELL!*

It's been a day and a night since the incident in the Jarl's roundhouse with the guard. I haven't seen the Jarl once since then, and it would appear that I am now to be included in the rest of the group of women from Caistley. Hildy – and a couple of the women from Caistley – have chastised me a few times, told me I'm stupid for not sucking up to the Jarl or not doing whatever it is they seem to be implying I should have done. Honestly, though, it's a lot more relaxing not having to worry about whether or not I'm going to be killed or raped at any given moment. Not, I suppose, that that couldn't happen now, but I do feel a certain level of safety being in a group.

The water is cold and our skin is gray and mottled with goose-bumps when we emerge, teeth clattering, from the stream. Hildy tosses us tunics like the ones worn by the villagers in Caistley and we pull them on over our soaking wet heads. She eyes us sharply and lets a great sigh escape her lips.

"Winter's in the air and no doubt," she quips, to no one in particular. "I suppose it's time to get you some woolens, or we'll have you all freezing to death before sundown."

Twenty minutes later I'm still damp, but much warmer under a layer of thick felted wool in the form of another tunic layered over the thin linen one underneath. Hildy stands back appraising us.

"There you go," she smiles. "Those of you who don't make it through winter now are no fault of mine."

The phrase 'make it through winter' hits me like a ton of bricks, even though I'm immediately aware that it shouldn't. The only person keen to leave is me. I'm keeping my wits about me on that count, too – spotting guards, trying to pick up on the patterns and rhythms of life in the Viking camp, taking note of how far the temperature drops at night. My new woolen tunic causes a burst of optimism in my chest – it's heavy and warm and just the thing to keep me from freezing to death on the return journey to Caistley.

Now all I have to do is get out. It doesn't seem like it will be too difficult. In fact it appears to be very easy – people come and go all day, including slaves as they carry goods to and from the beach or herd animals – pigs or sheep – into or out of the camp. It's the ease itself that worries me. Surely if escaping is that possible, it indicates some confidence on the part of the Vikings that their captives won't even try to flee? Maybe it's just the natural obstacles that have been mentioned before – the cold, the distance, the fact that much of the land may be marshy and treacherous or impossible to cross? It's definitely something, though. Something is keeping the people who have been taken from other villages here with the Vikings, even as they get beaten and threatened with death for stepping out of line.

***

That night, just as I am about to settle down on the dirt floor of the roundhouse with the other Caistley women, the leather door-covering is snatched to the side and Hildy is there once again, her fists balled at her ample hips.

"You!" She shouts, pointing directly at me. "Come with me."

I stand reluctantly and follow her out into the night. She says nothing, marching down the paths worn into the earth by the camp-dwellers and expecting me to follow – which I do. Hildy is free with her slapping hand – and her kicking foot – and I don't want to get hurt again. Nor do I want to risk asking her where we're going, because she has a hair-trigger temper and as I said, I don't want to get hit or kicked.

A few minutes later we arrive at another building, circular but a bit larger than the usual roundhouses. Hildy pushes me roughly inside and I blink in the firelight, looking around. Two women who look to be a little older than me are tending a fire, and a wooden tub of some sort has been set up close to it. One of the women gestures to me to come forward and I turn to Hildy, unsure what's happening. She shrugs angrily.

"Don't look at me, girl, the Jarl ordered it. Do as the women tell you, now."

With that, she flounces out and I realize that the annoyance in her voice is – is it jealousy? Yes, it must be. Hildy has made a number of cracks about my stupidity already, rubbing it in my face that I had a chance with the Jarl and then I blew it – and now he's paid attention to me again, singling me out? No wonder Hildy is mad. I can't help smiling a little as the women lead me gently to the tub, which I can now see is filled with steaming water. As they undress me I ask questions.

"How did you get the water so hot?"

The shorter woman, who has a pronounced overbite and who tells me her name is Gudry, demonstrates how the water got so hot, pulling a heavy stone from the fire with a pair of tongs and dropping it into the tub, where the water briefly boils and sizzles around it before falling still again.

"Is that going to burn me?" I ask, pulling back slightly as they try to get me to step into the water. "Isn't that rock hot?"

Using the tongs, Gudry reaches in and removes it with a shrug. "The others are cool enough now, you don't need to worry. We wouldn't be the Jarl's maids if we left his women all covered in burn marks, would we?"

Good point, I want to say. But instead of speaking I take Gudry's hand and step into the tub, closing my eyes and almost moaning with the simple ecstasy of being warm, just warm, after so many days of shivering. I add it – warmth – to the ever-growing list in my head of things about the modern world no one even close to appreciates.

"It's nice, isn't it?" Gudry asks, grinning at me and then grimacing as a slap lands on her cheek. "Anja!" She squeaks, looking up. "What did you do that for?"

"You're too familiar," Anja, the clear senior of the two – in rank if not in age – replies. "And I see you leaving your arms in the water for too long, silly girl. You'll drain the heat too quickly and she won't be clean. Hildy will switch us with a branch."

I open my mouth, about to reassure the both of them that I won't say anything to Hildy but something keeps the words in my throat. It's only been a short time but already I'm learning – and learning in a way I never did in Caistley, where despite my friendship with Willa and Eadgar, I was never part of the village itself, never a participant in life there – that the ways of life here are so different as to be incomprehensible to me. I have no idea if promising to keep Gudry's apparent transgression to myself will actually help Gudry or just make whatever punishment she has coming to her even worse. It already backfired a day ago when I snatched a piece of bread back from one of the younger, stronger women from the Caistley group, and returned it to the old woman she'd stolen it from. Hildy saw it happen and took the rest of the old woman's food away, throwing it on the ground and mashing it into the dirt with her feet.

"There!" She'd bellowed, looking right at me. "Keep yourself to yourself, girl, or you just make it worse for everyone."

I still don't understand why Hildy was even angry – she was the one who handed out the food, including to the old woman – why would she be upset that I was trying to make sure we each got our share?

I lie back in the tub, exhaling a long, slow breath and letting Gudry and Anja dip their little linen scraps in the water and run them over my body. Sleep is lurking, dragging my eyelids down, making my limbs heavy. But I don't give in to it – not because I don't want to but because, aside from the pure sensual pleasure of the hot, clean water – I am aware that I am being prepared for something. For some*one*. The Jarl.

When Gudry's hand pushes the cloth a little lower on my belly than I'm expecting, I jump slightly.

Both women eye me. "What's wrong, lady?"

"My name is Paige," I reply, shaken out of my torpor.

A pause and then Anja repeats Gudry's question, wondering what's wrong. I have no answer. It's obvious they don't understand.

"Are you having your blood?" Gudry asks, ducking out of reach when Anja moves to slap her again.

"She's not having her blood, stupid! Why would we be bathing her if she was?! Unless..."Anja looks at me enquiringly. "Did it just start?"

Briefly, I consider lying and saying it did. But I'll surely be caught in that lie, probably by Hildy and the very last thing I want to do is give Hildy one more reason to be upset with me. I shake my head.

"What then, lady?"

Why are they calling me lady? Everyone else calls me girl. No one calls me Paige.

"N-nothing," I stammer, and then don't manage to keep myself from pushing Gudry's hand away when she moves again to wash me between my legs. "I just – I don't want you to, um – can I do it? Here, give me the cloth, I'll do it. I know how to do it better than you do."

Gudry is about to hand over the cloth when Anja stops her, grabbing it for herself and moving to do the job herself. I grab her wrist, hard, before she gets anywhere near my most intimate area, and look into her eyes.

"I said I would do it myself." The coldness in my voice surprises even me, but it works because Anja lets her arm fall limp and tosses me the rag. "Fine, lady. But if the Jarl complains I'll tell Hildy you –"

"You can do whatever you want," I snap. "Me, I don't want anyone to go running to Hildy. I'd rather we just got this done ourselves and no one got switched with a branch, alright? The Jarl won't complain."

Anja and Gudry both look doubtful as I speak that last sentence, and I suppose with how defiant I'm being I don't blame them.

"The Jarl won't complain," I repeat myself, because somehow it feels like maybe if I say it enough times it might come true.

I use the cloth to clean myself between my legs while Anja works on my neck and shoulders and Gudry uses a carved bone comb to run through my hair.

"At least I don't think he will complain," I say, trying to keep the fear I'm feeling out of my voice as I say it, and hoping one of the women will have some comfort to offer, some advice. Anja picks up on it right away.

"You're a maiden, lady? It's your first time?"

I squeeze my eyes tightly shut in response as what I've been dreading is confirmed. So far I've been able to tell myself the Jarl might just want to talk to me. To court me somehow, to get to know me. But now that Anja has said it out loud I suppose I already knew it. I nod quickly.

"Yes. It is."

Gudry smiles again, before a scowl from Anja wipes it off her face, but she can't help a little excited bounce as she scoots in closer to me. "Your first time, lady! And with a Jarl! Where I grew up the girls would have torn all each other's hair out to be with a Jarl. And this one is so handsome – the most handsome I've ever seen! I was just saying the other day that his eyes are as blue as –"

Anja rolls her eyes. "Enough, Gudry. She didn't ask for you to spill your own desires, did she? She's scared – look at her. Are you scared, lady?"

Of course I'm scared, I want to spit. Instead I just nod.

"It's not so bad," Anja says, lifting one of my feet out of the tub and running the cloth between each of my toes. "It only hurts at first – and when it stops hurting..."

Hildy barges in at the moment, raising her eyebrows impatiently at Anja and Gudry.

"Is she ready? The Jarl wants her now."

It's almost an out-of-body experience as Gudry helps me to my feet and Anja wraps a linen robe around my dripping-wet body. *Is this really happening?* Alarm bells are clanging in my head, every instinct I have is screaming at me to run, to just push my way past Hildy and keeping going, running out of the Viking camp and all the way back down the coast to Caistley. But I can't run and I know it – Hildy and Gudry and Anja know it, too. It's a chilly evening and I'm soaking wet. I'd barely make it down to the beach before the cold made my limbs stiff and clumsy and eventually prevented me from going any further.

"Wait!" Anja calls just as Hildy is about to lead me away. She pulls a small wooden box, like a jewelry box, out of the leather pouch she wears dangling from the belt around her waist, as all the Viking women seem to. Inside it is a waxy substance that smells strongly of – is that roses? It's floral, whatever it is. Strongly floral. Anja dips her finger into the substance and then applies it to the back of my neck and the little spot between my collarbones. "There," she says, nodding at Hildy. "She's ready."

Chapter 11
9th Century

I follow Hildy when she gestures at me to do so and don't duck away when we reach the Jarl's dwelling.

"Here she is," she announces to the Jarl, pushing me forward.

The Jarl is seated on a wooden chair, dressed in the extravagant furs and leather I first saw him in and he appears to be sharpening the blade of a sword. He looks up when Hildy speaks and although I don't dare look directly at him I feel it as his gaze lands on me.

"She's bathed and clean, Jarl," Hildy says.

And then, for a few excruciating moments, no one says anything. Am I being inspected? I still don't dare to look up.

"Come here, girl."

Is he speaking to me? He must be speaking to me. I step forward slowly, towards the fire, thankful for the warmth but so nervous I'm shaking. The Jarl reaches out and takes my trembling hand, bringing it close to his face and then looking up at me. He's got that expression on his face again, the one that says he doesn't understand. I hear the leather door flap shut as Hildy leaves.

"You cold, girl?" The Jarl asks. "Come sit by the fire, have some oxshot."

There is another wooden seat, this one with a dark fur laid over it, next to the fire. Gingerly, because I'm not sure whether he means me to sit on the chair or the floor, I lower myself onto it. The Jarl hands me a cup of carved horn with a dark, warm liquid inside. I bring it up to my nose and sniff, immediately coughing and pulling away. It's sharp and alcoholic, but salty as well. I'm going to have to drink it, too, because even though nobody in the Viking camp has explicitly told me it isn't done to turn down offers of food or drink from the Jarl, I'm beginning to understand it anyway. I take a very small sip of the drink and fail to suppress a cough afterwards. It *is* alcohol. And it *is* salty. Oddly savory.

The Jarl is watching me intently. He breaks into a wide smile at my reaction to the drink. "At least you didn't spit it out all over me. The Angles can't handle good, strong drinks like oxshot. You did well, though – better than most of the men of your kind."

Suddenly, a memory of a party enters my mind. Emma standing in front of a folding table on a lawn, doing five or maybe even six or seven shots of vodka in a row as she's cheered on by the crowd, slamming the last one down on the table before lifting her arms in drunken triumph. I chuckle at the thought of the Jarl witnessing such a scene. Something tells me Emma could drink most of his men right under the table, if it came to that.

"Have I said something funny?"

"What?" I look up, worried I've caused offense. "No. No, Jarl. I was just, um. No, no you haven't."

"You're more nervous than a pig in November," he comments, taking another gulp of the oxshot. "Have another drink."

I politely ignore the fact that I've just been compared to a pig and take another sip.

"It's broth," the Jarl tells me. "The cooks boil down the ox bones until the broth is dark and rich and then we add svass, the Viking drink, and serve it hot to warm our bellies and give us strength over winter. Women aren't usually allowed to drink oxshot."

"Oh," I say, realizing that he has allowed me a privilege. "Thank you. It's delicious."

It actually isn't half bad, once you get used to the idea of beefy alcohol – perfect for a night like tonight, anyway. I hold the horn cup in my hands and a warmth begins to spread through my belly. Whatever svass is, it's strong enough to have an almost immediate effect.

And then there's the Jarl. He's right there, his presence and sheer physical bulk impossible to ignore. He seems at ease, amused by me. I'm still having difficulty looking at him, though, which he notices.

"Look at me, girl."

I gulp and steel myself before turning my head up.

Even in the firelight, the Jarl's eyes shine as blue as jewels. His jaw is wide and strong, the angles and planes of his face sharp here and solid there. He isn't nervous, he's self-contained. The anxiety, the not knowing what to do or say or what expression to wear on my face is mine and mine alone. And he sees it. I *feel* him seeing it, seeing right through me. It's an odd sensation, being seen like that. There's nowhere to hide and that's not helping my nerves. On the other hand, it means I don't even have to bother pretending a strength I don't truly feel.

I wonder, briefly, how Viking society works. Was the Jarl raised from birth to be the man I see sitting in front of me? Was he born into his role? Or did he take it as his own, his inherent qualities arguing for themselves?

"What do you think of?"

It's taken me a few minutes, but I'm starting to see what's happening. The Jarl is talking to me. He's not going to throw me down, rip off my clothes and have his way. Not right at this moment, anyway. He's not an idiot like his man Veigar, or a dumb, lust-driven animal like the guard he killed.

"I think of you," I reply, emboldened by the oxshot or the realization that I am not in any immediate danger, or both.

"Of me? You're afraid of me, I see it in your eyes, girl. What is it - do you think I'm going to eat you?"

"No," I tell him, shaking my head. "I wonder how you came to be Jarl of these people. I wonder if your father was Jarl and you inherited the role or if —"

"*The* Jarl."

"Yes," I say, hoping I haven't caused offense. "The Jarl."

"It's a title, girl. It means King. Leader. My name is Eirik."

"Yes I know," I start, before stopping again. Wait. Did he just tell me his name? He did.

"Eric?"

"Eirik. But don't let Hildy catch you calling me by that name, or she'll whip you pink."

Eirik. When I repeat his own name back to him the Jarl smiles and comments that none of the Angles can ever pronounce it quite the right way.

"I am Paige," I say then, eager to return what I have perceived as a favor.

"Paige."

And just as he has chuckled at me, I can't help doing the same back to Eirik, the Jarl, when he tries to say my own name. I say it again and he tries again, more slowly. It still isn't right but I like it. I like the sound of it, of his voice saying it. And I don't even realize this until a few seconds later, when the fact that I'm smiling hits me.

Why am I smiling? In the roundhouse of this man who means to relieve me of my virginity whether I want him to or not – why am I no longer trembling? I can't say, not specifically. It's him, though. Eirik. Eirik with his blue eyes, his easy smile and his impossible-to-ignore presence.

"You aren't from the village."

I snap back to attention. "Well, I –"

"And you're not from the estate near the village, either. We captured the estate and no one had ever heard of you, none of the ealdorman's daughters were missing. So where are you from, Paige?

I'm tempted to say somewhere very far away, and if that's true the question is how did you get to where we found you? What were you doing standing in a field outside a village on fire, and thick with Viking raiders? Why didn't you run?"

Eirik has been asking his men about the night I was captured. Part of me – a small part – is flattered by his interest. Another part of me recognizes it as possibly useful. And yet another part, larger than the first two combined, knows that I don't have any answers to his questions. Not ones that would make sense.

"I have friends in the village," I respond slowly, worried about slipping up and triggering yet more questions. "I was afraid for them. I wanted to help them."

The Jarl leans forward and runs his fingers over his chin, looking at me still. "The way you speak confirms it – you are not from the village. And no one from the estate knew of you. They knew they'd be killed if we caught them lying. So where is it you from, Paige?"

My mind spins with possible stories as the Jarl repeats his questions. An outlaw's daughter? Willa and Eadgar spoke of outlaws often, people – men – who lived outside society, banished, always in danger of being caught and punished for whatever crime they had committed. They lurked in the woods, it was said, poaching what they could, stealing from the farm workers. But I'd never heard of them having any small children with them.

The Jarl is waiting for an answer. His eyes bore into me, but no words offer themselves up to be spoken. The heat from the fire has nearly dried my linen robe and I look down at my body, at the swells of my breasts under the clinging fabric. Then I reach up, tuck my fingers underneath and pull it down off one of my shoulders. The light from the fire dances on my bare skin. I'm not breathing. The air in the roundhouse is still. I keep going until one of my breasts comes free and then I stop, too timid to look up for a few moments. When I do, the Jarl's eyes are where I want them – on my body. He reaches out and I tense up just before his fingertips slide under the bottom curve of that one bare breast, his thumb brushing lightly over my nipple.

I don't know what I expected. Not the strangeness in my belly, which is not so different from the sensation of traveling through the tree, the feeling of falling away from something, of my breath being sucked out of my lungs. When I look up, wide-eyed and helpless, the Jarl is staring right back at me.

"Look at you," he whispers, and his voice seems to sound different now, slower – or am I imagining it? "You're a maid, aren't you?"

He knows. Of course he knows. It seems, sitting here in this roundhouse, in this place where Eirik's word is the last word on everything there is, that he might just know everything.

I nod quickly and he takes my chin in one hand before I can turn away.

"Do you think I mean to rape you, girl? Do you understand – do you know – who I am?"

I'm confused. He's the Jarl. I know it and he knows I know it. "You're the Jarl," I say quietly. "Eirik. The Jarl."

"Yes you know the words." He replies. "You know them, but I don't know if you understand what they mean. That guard the other night, he would have raped you – had I not been there to stop him. But I am the Jarl, girl. There's not a woman in this camp, or anywhere close to it, or in the whole of the my country – or yours – that would turn away from giving me the thing that women give to men." He pauses. "None except you, that is, and even you I doubt. No, Paige, you're not to fear that sort of thing from me. I don't take what isn't given. All is given to me."

The Jarl is speaking the truth. I've seen the way the women react – *all* of the women. Hildy, the other Vikings, the other women from Caistley and the raided villages. Their bodies go soft when his name is mentioned, an air of willingness surrounds them. I don't understand it.

Or maybe I do, because sitting there with the Jarl himself, I find to my surprised chagrin that the nipple on my exposed breast, the one he touched, is small and hard and sensitive to the wisps of cool night air that find their way past the fire's warmth.

All is given to me. That's what he said. And it wasn't an empty boast, either, like the ones I'm used to from young men. He didn't say it to impress me. He said it because it's true.

I shift on the fur, suddenly acutely aware of my own body, of the earth under my toes and the fact that the gown I'm wearing has only dried where it faces the fire. I'm nervous still, wired, but it's changed. I turn my face up to the Jarl as it dawns on me – I'm not fearing his attention any longer. I'm craving it. I open my mouth, wanting to speak, but I don't know how to put words to the chaos inside me.

"Where are you from?" He asks me again.

"Not here," I reply haltingly, because my mind has retreated somehow, stepped back. "Not – not Caistley, I mean. I'm not from Caistley."

I'm breathless, I can hear it as I stumble over my words. And if I can hear it, he can hear it. My cheeks burn.

"I already know where you're *not* from, girl. I'm asking you where you *are* from."

As he speaks he reaches out again and caresses my breast briefly, too briefly. It's impossible to think when his hand is touching me, that's something I didn't expect.

"Far away," I babble. "You don't know it – you don't know –" *Please put your hand on me again. Please. Please.* "You haven't heard of it, Jarl. Uh, Eirik. Jarl."

He stares at me and the seconds stretch out and distort around me. When he stands, suddenly, there is a quick glimpse of something – something insistent, something that glistens in the light – under the leather that is wrapped around his waist, but I look away before I can truly see. The Jarl chuckles and claps his hands. At once, a woman I don't recognize appears at the door.

"Take her back to her dwelling" he says to her, nodding at me.

No! I want to shout, looking back at him as the woman takes me by the arms and practically drags me out. No, no, no!

He sees my distress – and he knows what it is, far better than I do. "We're raiding tomorrow, Paige. I like to have my blood up when we raid. If I'm not killed by an Angle with a dull axe, I'll send for you when I return."

The walk through the darkness back to the roundhouse where the other women from Caistley are asleep is one of the most unsettled of my life. I don't know what I'm feeling. Or I do know what I'm feeling and I'm not sure how I should feel about *that.* One thing is undeniable, and that's the physical response in my body. I feel alert and alive, my veins surging with something that's half frustration and half awakening.

I'm wet, too. My thighs are slick with it, a response that no one has ever brought forth before – one I didn't even think was possible for me.

I lie down on the dirt floor when I'm back with the women, pulling my woolen tunic on over my head before I do so. So far, my thoughts each night have been organized, ordered. I observe during the daylight hours and at night, before sleep, I go over what I've observed, I allow my mind the space to come up with alternative plans and possibilities of escape. Mostly I give myself pep talks, reassurances that the woods outside Caistley, and the tree that will take me home, aren't going anywhere.

Not this night. Tonight my teeth are on edge, and it has nothing to do with my captivity. Tonight it's like I'm drunk, like I can't get away from the way he looked at me or the combined smells of animal fur and man when he leaned in close to me or the sharp, meaty taste of the oxshot. I've been invaded mentally as thoroughly as I had supposed the physical invasion was to be.

When I finally doze off, my dreams are not of home but of him.

Chapter 12
9th Century

It's warmer the next day, and Hildy speaks with some of the other Viking women of a 'second summer,' which I presume is their term for an Indian summer. I find myself at the stream during the afternoon, filling wooden buckets with water to be carried back to the enormous series of fire-pits where the cooking takes place. Most of the men are gone, only the male children, old men and servants remain.

"He's raiding," Hildy says, nudging me hard in the ribs when she catches me staring off into the distance. "He'll be back tonight or tomorrow, and if we don't have meat and ale and stew and fruit ready for the feast, it'll be our heads he takes."

I'm still not quite sure how to take all the talk of heads being chopped off, of beatings and whippings. Those things happen here, I have been unlucky enough to either witness or experience, but the Jarl is an intelligent man, he knows who he can do without and who he can't. And he can't do without Hildy, as painful as it is for me to admit that. She seems to run the camp – and most of the fighting men – with an iron fist, rushing from roundhouse to longhouse to stream to beach to shout instructions at people and clip them on the ears if she thinks they haven't understood. Only an idiot can't see that without Hildy, the place would descend into chaos in a couple of days.

I'm not alone at the stream filling buckets. Other women are with me, including some I recognize from the Caistley group. A familiar feeling takes over as I hear whispers behind me and I almost burst out laughing at the realization that I can't seem to get away from gossiping girls, whether I'm in the 21st or the 9th.

"What?" I ask, spinning around and facing them, because one difference between home and the Viking camp is that in the latter, I'm stronger than almost all the other servant women and girls. I'm also vaguely aware that the whispering is of a different quality than that to which I became accustomed in my younger years. It's envious rather than scornful, and the two girls I've caught stare up at me with something like awe in their eyes.

"We were just talking about the Jarl, lady. The Northwomen say he's taken a liking to you. We were just saying we wish it were us. You're so lucky."

And there's that word again – lady. It's an honorific of some kind, I'm coming to see that, a signal of respect.

"Oh," I respond. "Oh, uh – really?"

One of the girls giggles, the way I saw girls giggling together in high school, sharing their secret crushes. "Yes! You feel it too, don't you? He's so handsome! And so young still."

My ears prick up. "Young?" I ask, curious about the Jarl's age but previously too shy to ask anyone – even him. "Do you know how old he is?"

"Ten and ten and five." The girl responds, and her companion nods.

"Yes, ten and ten and five."

The two skinny girls both jump away a little as I shift my body and I realize that they're afraid of me. I want to ask why but I don't get the feeling I'll get a straight answer. At least I know the Jarl's age now – 25. It's younger than I had assumed, but it's more about the authority he has and the respect he commands than it is about whether or not he looks a certain age. I smile at the girls, and at the funny way the Angles have of communicating numbers, and move to take my leave.

"NO!"

A blow lands on my right ear as I trudge back to the cooking pits with two heavy buckets of water balanced on either end of a stick that lays across the back of my shoulders. I bend my knees and set them down before turning to see who's hitting me this time and of course it's Hildy.

"What?" I demand rudely, emboldened by the deference shown by the girls. "You said you needed us to bring water so I'm –"

A sudden sharp, stinging pain rings out across my bare shin and I shriek, not even realizing what's caused it at first. And then I see it in Hildy's hand – a length of thin, flexible branch that she's just brought down on me. I fight a sudden, crazy urge to shove her as hard as I can – but strong though I may be I don't favor myself in a fight with Hildy – and bite my tongue, waiting to be told what I've done wrong.

"Not you!" Hildy barks. "I need you to *fill* the buckets, not to *carry* them. You think the Jarl wants to see you all bedraggled and worn out when he returns? Stupid girl."

I stay exactly where I am, not moving, because I don't want to give Hildy a reason to hit me again. A few seconds later she yells at me to get moving.

"Where to?" I ask, trying to keep my voice as flat and free of all emotion as possible.

"Back to the stream!" She bellows. "You know some of the other slaves think you're dull, don't you girl? I don't think you are, as far as I can tell it you just seem like you're from another place, somewhere that does things differently. But I have to say, I'm starting to wonder if they aren't right."

Hildy is talking to me. Not screaming or yelling, and not threatening to rain blows down on my head. She's a tyrant, but she's not stupid. Her assessment of why I am the way I am is completely correct. I am from another place, one that definitely does things differently. Unlike the Jarl, Hildy doesn't seem especially interested in hearing about that place, to my great relief.

"You didn't get hit much before, did you?" She asks in the kind of conversational tone I don't usually associate with perpetrators of ongoing physical assault. "Your parents didn't hit you, girl? Were you their only one?"

I nod tentatively, not sure how long I can trust this mood of hers to last before she decides I need a switch to the leg again. "Yes, I was their only child. And you're right, they didn't hit me."

I leave out the part about my parents not beating me or whipping me with tree branches because where I come from, that isn't a normal thing to do.

"I can tell!" Hildy chuckles. "You walk around here with that constantly surprised look on your face, girl, like you're seeing everything for the first time. That's why some of the others think you're dull. If you're not dull, you'll see what an opportunity you've got with the Jarl. He likes you, you know. He likes you quite a bit. I've never seen him take to one of the captives this quickly – he had you bathed the other night! And I hear he killed a man who meant to rape you. Is it true?"

Ah, gossip. Hildy is pumping me for info. I didn't mind, anything is better than being beaten and screamed at. "Yes," I tell her as we go back to the stream and get to work filling the pile of empty buckets, handing them off to various other servants who come to carry them back to the cooking pits. "He did."

"Be smart then, girl. Make him happy, give him what he wants. The Jarl's bed slaves have easy lives compared to the rest of – "

"His bed slaves?" I ask, figuring I might as well do some digging of my own, and in spite of the fact that the term itself gives me a fairly good idea as to what Hildy is talking about.

"This is what I speak of," Hildy says, eying me for a second before getting back to the bucket-filling. "The way you act like you've never heard of a thing like a bed slave before! Now I know the Angles do things differently but you never heard of a powerful man taking a woman into his bed? A woman who is not his wife? Your King doesn't do that? His men don't do that?"

I have no idea what the King's sexual habits are, nor those of his men, so I shake my head.

"So a Jarl keeps his bed slaves?" I ask. "After he gets married? Is Eir – the Jarl – married?"

I don't manage to stop myself from uttering his name in time and Hildy's head jerks up, her eyes wide and staring right at me. "Girl!" She hisses. "Don't you ever, ever –"

"He told me!" I whisper back, desperate not to be smacked again. "He told me his name!"

At that, Hildy puts down the bucket she's about to fill and sits back on her haunches, studying me the way you study someone you're pretty sure is lying. "He told you?" She asks. "The Jarl told you his name? Did he ask you to use it?"

I pretend that I'm struggling to remember. "I don't know," I say vaguely, "I'm not sure if –"

"Because," Hildy cuts me off, "if he did tell you his name then you are in a better position than I thought."

"What do you mean?" I ask and she scowls at me.

"What do I mean? What do I mean? Girl, is there a problem with your hearing? Is that it? Because no matter how far away it is you come from, I presume that the men there are men and the women are women?"

I nod. "Yes."

"And the men where you come from want the same things that men everywhere want from women? And the women from the men?"

I nod again and Hildy throws up her arms. "There's not enough time to lead you by the hand, girl. I already told you he likes you. And no, he's a young man yet so he's not seen fit to take himself a wife. When he does, rest assured she'll be one of his own – so don't go getting any ideas about that. But to be a bed slave, especially a favored bed slave, now that is a nice development for any young lady from one of the villages we've taken. I advise you to be smart about it. None of this arguing, no more silly questions, do what he wants you to do. A Jarl has a great responsibility on his shoulders, and he values any that can lighten his burden. A pretty girl like yourself can surely figure out what I speak of when I say that."

Hildy stops speaking and it takes me a few seconds to realize she's waiting for confirmation. "Oh!" I say. "Yes! I know what you speak of."

I do know what Hildy speaks of, theoretically. I even know, now, what it is to want that theoretical thing, in a way I did not know before the Jarl brought me into his roundhouse and looked at me the way he looked at me last night, and spoke to me the way he spoke to me. But her pep talk hasn't worked – if anything it's made me even more nervous, more anxious not to screw up.

I don't want to ruin my chance, and not just because an exotic, alien flower bloomed warm and deep in my belly when I was with the Jarl. I don't want to ruin my chance because the way Hildy is talking it sounds like the 'bed slaves' have a better life than the others. It sounds like they might have better food, and more of it. Better clothes, maybe? Warm blankets at night? And I need to keep my strength up. Above all else, I need to prevent myself from weakening, the way I had always seen Willa and Eadgar as weakened. If I'm to make it down the coast to Caistley again, it won't be with my ribs showing through my skin, or my limbs stiff and creaky from sleeping curled up tight in a ball during the cold winter nights.

"So it's true."

I look up, taken out of my thoughts by Hildy's voice.

"What?"

"So it's true," she repeats. "You're a maid. One of the women mentioned it this morning, but I didn't believe her. Now I see from the way you are that it's true."

What does that mean? She can tell from the 'way I am?' But it's Hildy so I don't ask, because that risks annoying her.

She's being kinder to me now than she's ever been, though. And she seems interested in advising me.

"Yes," I reply. "I've never been with a man. I'm scared."

It's true that I'm scared, but I tack that phrase onto the end of my response not to be truthful but hopefully to encourage Hildy to keep talking to me. It hasn't been long but I think I can see that she is one of those people who is much better at being kind to those she perceives as lesser than herself somehow, more pitiable. I've already noticed that she tends to hit the other servants not necessarily for screwing up, but for talking back, for defiance.

It works. Hildy's expression softens instantly. "Oh, girl," she says, actually reaching out and patting my knee – a touch that it takes all of my self-control not to flinch away from. "You'll know what to do. Our bodies know, even if our minds don't. A woman is born knowing how to please a man, but she doesn't always realize it."

"Oh," I nod seriously, giving no sign that the lack of detail is unhelpful and wholly annoying. *I'll just know what to do? Great, thanks for that.*

Chapter 13
9th Century

The Jarl and his men haven't returned by late afternoon and then by nighttime. There is a feeling in the air of the camp, an anxious waiting. Everyone from the lowliest servants to the guards and the older, married Viking women is lifting their heads often and looking east, towards the sea, from where the warriors will return.

Dawn comes, after a night that has stayed mercifully above freezing, and then afternoon and still the Viking men are nowhere to be seen. I'm in one of the smaller wooden buildings close to the cooking pits, grinding whole dried grains between two rocks – by hand – with a few other women when a sound of shouting comes from outside. It's one person at first, and too far away to make out words. Then it's a few more people, and the sound of footsteps as people run past outside. The women and girls I'm working with put the stones in their hands down and stand up, looking around at each other questioningly? Are the men back? Are they victorious?

The men are back. I slip out of the grain-house and find a spot where I have a good view to the east of camp, holding back to watch as everyone else surges forward. It's only momentarily confusing to watch the servants, too, rushing forward with their hands raised above their heads. The triumph of their captors is their – our, I suppose – triumph, too. When they eat, we eat. When they prosper, we prosper. Still, I can't bring myself to join in. These people took me, and now they're keeping me, all against my will. How can I cheer for them?

The shouting and cheering gets louder and more frenzied when the Vikings appear, their limbs and faces bloodied, a few of them being carried by their fellow warriors. Behind them trail their captives, wrists bound behind them like mine were, and more Vikings carrying resources they have stolen from their vanquished foes. Crates of grain, pigs, tools, huge clay pots of animal tallow.

At the head of this entire crowd of goods and human beings – and human beings who *are* goods – is Eirik. He's smiling broadly, accepting kisses and little handpicked bouquets of wildflowers from the women. When he enters the camp itself he turns to one of his men and is handed something. A sword, which he raises above his head as the crowd noise reaches a crescendo. I shield my eyes as the sun glints off the sword's blade. I am happy to see the Jarl. I am relieved that the blood smeared across his chest and face appears to be someone else's. And even as I feel relief, even as the joy of the crowd infects me, part of me is still withheld, still troubled by what I'm happy about.

As the triumphant arrival turns to work, and the people – Vikings and slaves – busy themselves bringing the goods up from the beach and storing them in their appropriate places, Eirik and his men mingle with the crowd, accepting more kisses, speaking of their adventures. I stay where I am, watching.

The Jarl looks up as a woman hangs off his neck, squealing her delight at his return into his ear, and looks right at me. I'm surprised, I thought I was far enough away to avoid notice.

"Paige!" He shouts my name, holding one arm – still clutching his sword – aloft and then pointing its tip at me.

I give a nervous little wave as some of the people around the Jarl also look up to see what he's pointing at. Does he want me to come to him? Am I supposed to say something?

"Come here, girl!"

I walk down the path to where Eirik stands amongst his men and his people, and he looks down at me for a second, seeming to want something.

"You're back!" I say, stating the obvious, and he leans his head back and roars with laughter. People around us join in. I join in, even though I don't understand the joke – or if there even is one.

Up close, the warriors smell. Not bad, not of rot or filth. It takes a few moments for it to occur to me but it soon does – they smell of victory. Of blood, metallic and dark, and earth and the ocean winds that carried them home. Eirik reaches down with one arm and scoops me up as I were a feather, twirling me through the air before leaning his head in to kiss me.

It happens suddenly, and as it was before in the roundhouse, the Jarl's presence leaves me no mental room for anything except him. His mouth is firm on mine, his chin and face rough with stubble, which surprises me with its sharpness. My hand, clutching his shoulder, comes away slippery with another man's blood. My senses are gorged on raw masculinity, the animal smell of Eirik's neck, the insistent hunger I taste in his kiss, the feeling of his strong arm around my waist, holding me tight against his body, so different from my own. I can't speak. All I can do is react, bury my face in his shoulder so no one can see the startled look in my eyes.

"Look at you," Eirik says, whispering in my ear so only I can hear. "I could take you right here, Paige. Right here on the grass, before the feast, with everyone watching and the pigs nibbling our toes."

He pulls away, laughing, to see my reaction. It's a joke, I can glean that much, but there's something dark in his eyes, the same thing I saw when I was with him a few nights ago. When he puts me down he grabs my wrist suddenly and presses my hand against – well, against his erection. "See?" He says. "Look what you've done."

He's not hiding it, nor is he speaking quietly anymore. The people around us see the bulge in his leather wrap as well as I do, and they hear him telling me I caused it. My cheeks are instantly hot, prickling with embarrassment. But then I look around, and I see that the warriors are all over the women – the Viking women, the slaves, their wives – who can tell? All around me the sound of sloppy kisses fills the air, male grunts, more cheering. What is happening?

The Jarl looks down at me, still making no effort to hide his obvious desire. "Don't look so frightened girl, it's part of the raid. We'll feast, first, and then after my men have filled themselves, they'll fill the women. It is always this way."

I don't know where to look so I look at the ground. There's no sense of shame in the air, the only red cheeks in the crowd are my own. These people are not embarrassed about their lust.

The crowd begins to move further into the village and I move with it, losing sight of the Jarl as his people demand a piece of him. A hand on my wrist is recognizable before I even see the face. Hildy.

"Come with me, girl, quickly now!"

I assume we're going to the cooking pits to knead dough or chop up pork ribs, but Hildy is leading me in another direction.

"Where are we –"

Hildy doesn't respond and soon she doesn't need to because I recognize the bathing room. Gudry and Anja are waiting for me, arranging little wooden vials and bottles on a table and talking quietly over a selection of what look like tunics, although fancier than I'm used to, with beads and colored threads woven into them.

"You'll be seated with the Jarl tonight," Hildy tells me, in the midst of pulling my clothes off over my head. He won't want you smelling of grain and pigshit, so Anja and Gudry here will bathe you again, and dress you in something appropriate.

"But I sat with the Jarl last time," I begin, before Hildy breaks in.

"No you didn't, girl. You sat on his lap last time, you didn't have your own place at the table. This is a rare thing, a privilege, and I pray to Freja that you don't do something stupid and embarrass yourself." She turns to Gudry and Anja and addresses them directly. "You heard me, she has a seat – a seat next to the Jarl himself! Braid her hair with flowers, anoint her with your oils, choose the finest dress you have – if the Jarl is unhappy I promise it won't be me who pays!"

With that, Hildy sweeps out into the evening, off to bully the cooks and the serving girls and boys. My stomach rumbles as Gudry helps me into the bathing tub again, apologizing when I flinch at the coolness of the water.

"We didn't have time to heat the water, lady – Hildy said it needs to be done right away."

* * *

An hour or so later I am standing just outside the feasting longhouse, in a room built just off of one end. A fire crackles in a fire-pit, keeping me and Gudry and Anja warm. My hair has been braided and the braids have been woven into each other and decorated with the small white and yellow flowers that are still growing in the field outside the camp. Some kind of thick unguent, scented with the floral oil, has been rubbed into every inch of my skin. Even my feet, which are already growing hard and thick on the soles after only a short while without shoes, are soft and tender tonight.

There are no mirrors in the Viking camp but I *feel* beautiful. I feel clean and soft and, perhaps most of all, attended to. It's not something I'm used to, being fussed over. But Gudry and Anja take their tasks seriously and not a single inch of my body has been left untended to. My tunic is made of different fabric to what I'm used to – it might even be silk. It's light and smooth against my skin, slipping coolly over my curves whenever I move.

"I'm so hungry," Gudry whispers as we wait and Anja smacks her – gently – on the arm and tells her to shut up. They will not be attending the feast, of course, and I make a plan to steal some bread, maybe some apples, to give to them tomorrow.

People – men – stare when I am led into the feast. Not all the men, and their gazes are not lascivious this time, as they were before. Now, they feel almost respectful. Curious, too – and I know why. They want to get a better look at the girl who has captured their Jarl's attention. They want to know more about me, to determine if I am worth it or not.

I avoid their glances and take my seat next to Eirik who leans in close and breathes in the scent of my neck.

"How will I get through the feast?" He shouts, addressing his men more than me. "With this temptress next to me?"

The Vikings bang their horn flagons on the tables, spilling ale everywhere and roaring with approval. I have never been in a situation that reeked so much of battle and testosterone. I'm not afraid, there is just a very strong sense that I am in a foreign space, somewhere that, without the Jarl's explicit invitation, I would be neither welcome nor necessary. Next to me, he stands and a hush falls over the room.

"Brothers!" He starts. "A second feast during the same moon – the Gods surely watch over us."

Around me, the men repeat the last phrase, leaving out one word. "The Gods watch over us."

"Three of our lot have been chosen for Valhalla today," Eirik continues. His voice is steady, somber. Davyn, Asrod and Gilby. Neither their wives nor their children will ever go hungry or unprotected. And tomorrow we will send them on their way."

The Vikings nod and touch their foreheads with the tips of their fingers, an unfamiliar gesture but clearly one of respect. The Jarl goes on to recall the raid in great detail, right down to the number of pigs and how many slaves were captured. His men whoop and cheer at each pronouncement but all I can do is smell the food that is waiting to be brought in.

"And finally," Eirik announces as his speech draws to a close. "As you can see, I do not want for company this evening. The taken women will be brought in, but tonight I give them to my bravest warriors. Victory always makes a man run hot, but I have a feeling this one –" he looks down at me as he says this, grinning, and God help me I cannot help the way my blood rushes quick in my veins – "will be enough to settle the flames."

Chapter 14
21st Century

After a lifetime of social exclusion I was used to the solitary nature of my existence. It didn't bother me, because it was just how things were. Maybe it bothered me a little. I tried not to get my hopes up about college, constantly repeating to myself that I was there to get my degree and nothing else.

And then one day I packed a small suitcase, bid my father – and our house – farewell and took a three hour bus trip to Grand Northeastern University with a stomach that was sour with nerves and a fervent hope that I was doing the right thing for myself.

Within days, I had a friend. Her name was Emma, she was British and loud and she was my roommate in the shabby little apartment we were sharing with two other students just off campus. She was the only person there when I arrived, yanking open the door after she heard me dragging my suitcase up the three flights of stairs and grinning widely at me.

"You must be Paige!"

"Yes," I smiled, terrified that I was going to emit some kind of 'loser' scent and put her off me immediately.

"I'm Emma! Here, let me take your bag. Wow, I love your hair. OK, so, yeah," she led me into the apartment, "it's not One Hyde Park, but it'll do."

I laughed again, even though I didn't know what or where One Hyde Park was. Emma was an exuberant whirlwind of emotion and color, everything I was not. She showed me around the place, showing me how to work the tap in the shower – "stand to the side when you turn it on or you're going to freeze your arse off" – and pointing out the fact that one of our other roommates had used stickers to label their yoghurt and sliced deli meat in the fridge.

"His name's Adam," Emma told me, "and he seems quite serious about the food so I wouldn't go eating any of it if I were you."

"I won't!" I replied, eager to present myself as easy to get along with. Emma turned around, then, and took me by the shoulders.

"You're so quiet, Paige. I thought I would be the quiet one, and you the extrovert. You know, that whole American versus British thing."

I looked down, unsure of how to respond. "Uhh, well. I guess I've always been a little –"

"It's OK!" Emma yelled, a decibel level I was soon going to get very used to. "It's totally fine! It's adorable, actually. I love quiet people!"

She wasn't kidding, either. Emma Wolf from the UK didn't even leave me the option of not being her friend, which ended up being A-OK with me because I liked her right off the bat. Sure she was loud enough to attract glances as we walked across the leaf-strewn campus on the way to class (and I'm ashamed to admit I chose many of my classes – a lot of English and History – simply because Emma herself had already chosen them), but she was irresistibly likeable, plain-spoken and warm. On the first day of classes, as I stood outside the main arts building wondering whether or not I was going to throw up with anxiety, she appeared in front of me with that big smile of hers and a cup of hot chocolate.

"Here you go," she grinned, pushing it into my hand. "You can't be down if you've got hot chocolate. Why are you standing here like a little lost lamb anyway, Renner?"

That was another one of Emma's habits – calling her friends by their last names. "I – uh, I couldn't find the classroom," I told her. "It says room 038 but I couldn't find anything lower than 100."

"It's in the basement," she replied, tucking her arm through mine and leading me back inside. "You didn't think they'd let us undergrads into the grander rooms, did you? The ones they put in the prospectus? Of course not! Now we're here and we've paid our fees, it's off to the dreary basement with us!"

"The pros- what?" I asked, still not entirely used to Emma's rapid-fire speech patterns.

"Prospectus. The catalog, you know, the book they send with all the photos of happy students and gourmet meals to convince us to apply. Now come on, you're almost late. Are you going to drink your hot chocolate or not? Because if you're not, I will."

***

It took me awhile to accept that I had suddenly, and almost as if by magic, become 'normal.' Emma happily bulldozed me into friendship and with her came all of the other people she had done the same with – and our roommates. Within weeks I found that I was hardly ever at the apartment, because there was always some social event to attend, always something to do. At first, I just floated along happily, like a leaf caught in a burbling steam of sociability. I hung back behind Emma, letting her take the lead, clutching at her arm as she ran on ahead of me.

Soon, though, and slowly, I started to gain confidence in myself. I started messaging people myself, rather than just letting Emma take care of everything. I began inviting people to the apartment instead of just joining in when Emma took the lead. She liked to have 'suppers' as she called them, usually on weekend afternoons and evenings. A whole chicken would be put in the oven to roast, bottles of wine would be opened and people would drift in to eat and drink and talk with us late into the evening.

It was after one of these suppers, when everyone had left and I was doing dishes in the kitchen while Emma sat at the table, finishing the last of the wine, that I found myself suddenly sniffling and tearing up.

"Oh God!" Emma cried, jumping up and wrapping her arms around me. "What is it, Renner? Were the potatoes that bad? I swear I should have left them in the oven a little longer!"

I giggled a little, comforted by my friend's joking, but I needed to tell her what was in my heart. "The potatoes were fine," I whispered, running hot water over a soapy plate.

"I know that, you silly sausage! Now come on, tell me what's gotten you all upset."

"I'm not upset!" I said, aware of how ridiculous I sounded making a pronouncement like that as a tear slid down my cheek. "I mean, obviously I look upset but I'm not. I'm – I'm happy."

Emma pulled away and gave me an exaggerated look of skepticism. "Are you? You don't look it."

I remember doing that thing, then – that thing you see little kids doing after they've been crying when they inhale and their breath is all shaky. I did that and Emma led me to the table, still strewn with wineglasses and plates. She sat me down and looked me right in the eyes.

"Now, Renner. Speak up. Tell me what's wrong. And don't go all silent and embarrassed like you always do."

I swallowed. "I meant it, Emma. I'm happy. I told you this before but I don't know if you believed me or if you understood. I really didn't have any friends in high school. None. Nobody liked me – a lot of them actively seemed to hate me."

"They're fucking idiots then," she replied.

"Yes, they kind of were. But I just wanted to say that I'm, uh, I'm grateful to have met you. I mean, not to be too awkward about this or anything but it means a lot to me that we're friends. That we do things like these dinners on the weekends. I never had anything like this before. I never," I broke off, sniffling again, and Emma gathered me into her arms.

"I know, Paige. I know. I believe you. Some people have a really hard time of it in school. I got bullied a little, when I was around 12 or 13 – I was taller than all the other girls, too loud, too enthusiastic, too everything. But I don't think it was anything like what you went through. But you're here now, aren't you? You're here with me and with the rest of us and things are looking up for you, my quiet little friend."

After my mother's death, I was never as close to another human being as I was to Emma. Not during those first years at college, anyway. I wanted to tell her everything about me, I wanted to bond even tighter. I wanted to tell her about Caistley. I didn't, but I wanted to. Sometimes I would think about it before falling asleep at night, in my little room that overlooked a tree-lined street. What would she say? What expression would she wear on her face? I was pretty sure she would suspect I was playing a joke on her.

There was a moment, one foggy September morning at the beginning of our sophomore year, that it was on the tip of my tongue to say something. Emma and I were up early, intent on getting a photo of the misty campus as the sun came up and before all the other students poured in. We were standing amongst the trees in the big field that the campus was built around and I commented, without thinking, that the air felt very much like England. By that time I thought of England as the place where Caistley was located, even though no one from Caistley would have recognized the word.

Emma turned and gave me a sharply curious look. "What?"

"Oh, I, uh," I stammered, "I meant it feels like how I imagine the air in England would feel."

But Emma wasn't quite buying what I was saying. "Huh," she said, still looking at me. "You've never been to England, right?"

I made a weird shrugging, head-shaking gesture with my body that I hoped managed to walk the fine line between not revealing the truth and not outright lying.

"Because it does feel like England this morning," Emma continued. "Exactly like it. That stillness in the air, the way everything is slightly muffled by the fog. I'm actually feeling a little homesick – and I never get homesick."

She was right, too, and I so badly wanted to join in, to tell her of the grey, foggy fall days in Caistley, the smell of the wood smoke and the sea all mingled together. I couldn't, though.

Emma sensed I had something to say. She waited quietly – something she hardly ever did – peering at me, waiting for me to come out with it. But I couldn't. We left it at that, she got her photo, and we both went off to our first classes.

It was around this time, too, that I developed my first real crush. I mean, I'd been attracted to certain boys before, but never to somebody I actually knew, somebody I might have a chance with. This particular boy was named Brandon and he was on the Grand Northeastern swim team. He wore sweats in navy and gold – the college's colors – with 'SWIM TEAM' written across the back, and I spent a lot of time staring at those letters from my spot directly behind him in one of my history classes. He was tall and gangly – the muscular kind of gangly – and he had a deep, foghorn-y type of voice. I'm not even sure what I saw in him. He wasn't ugly, but he wasn't particularly attractive either. What I don't want to admit to myself and what is therefore the most likely truth, is that I probably liked him because he paid attention to me.

Make no mistake, I was not one of the 'popular' girls at Grand Northeastern. I had friends then, sure. Some of those friends were male. A couple of them even liked me, if their sweaty palms and nervous stuttering around me were any indication. But most of the boys still wanted to date the same girls they'd wanted to date in high school. Cute little giggling blondes with white teeth and flawlessly tawny skin and a certain way of making those sophomore boys feel more like the men they had not quite become yet.

Emma had a boyfriend, but she wasn't one of those girls. She was, as she'd said before, too loud, too tall, too in-your-face for those handsome boys who needed their girlfriends to be an admiring audience of one, not competition. And it was Emma herself who noticed I was spending entirely too much time commenting on Brandon from history class.

"You've got a thing for this guy, huh?" She asked me casually one night while she picked at some pasta-based casserole I had made for dinner.

"What?" I asked, failing so badly at feigning innocence that even I had to laugh. "Fine. OK. Yes, he's cute, I guess."

"You guess, huh? Is that why I get a report on what Brandon was wearing and what Brandon said and oh Brandon is so smart after every class you have with him?"

I threw a piece of pasta at Emma's head. "Shut up."

She ducked and laughed. "Well invite him over then. How about Sunday? I'm making another roast, Adam and Jake will be there, Sarah, Bryan, Alison – a bunch of people. It'll be easier that way, too, because if you go all silent and shy there'll be other people there to pick up the slack."

Emma wasn't wrong. It would be more comfortable in a group. Friends or not, social life or not, I knew I wasn't in any way ready to handle myself like a normal human being in any kind of one-on-one situation with Brandon.

He said yes, though, when I asked him after our next class together, staring at my feet the whole time. Well, first he asked me who else would be at the dinner, but I assumed he was just making small talk. I texted him the street address to our apartment and then scuttled away, glowing and trying to keep the enormous grin off my face until I was out of sight.

Chapter 15
21st Century

When Sunday finally came I insisted on Emma answering the door when Brandon showed up. I was too shy to face him that early, I needed a few sips of wine first. When he walked into the living room I barely looked up as he set down two six packs of beer and Emma introduced him to everyone.

"And here," she said, in a voice that was thankfully free of any innuendo, "is Paige. You know Paige."

"Uh, yeah. Hey Paige."

"Hey," I responded, suddenly very interested in a speck of dirt on the surface of the coffee table. Later on in the kitchen, while Emma and I prepped potatoes and carrots, I looked at her expectantly. "Well?!"

She kept her eyes on the carrots. "Well what?"

How could she not know what I was talking about? "Well what about Brandon?" I asked excitedly, turning around to check that we were still alone. "What do you think of him?"

"He seems nice. Can you pass me the butter?"

I should have taken the hint, but I didn't even know Emma's lukewarm response was a hint until it was too late. We ate dinner at the table, some of us standing up leaning on the counters because there wasn't enough chairs, and afterwards Brandon hung around. I ran into him once, on the way to the bathroom, and smiled.

"Hey."

"Hey Paige."

And I was so besotted, so in that mode where I was interpreting everything he did as fascinating and charming, that even then I didn't hear the lack of interest in his tone.

The hallway was narrow, though, and we were standing close together. I remember being very conscious of how close we were, of how I could smell his cologne, of how easy it would have been for him to reach out and touch me. And I really wanted Brandon from the swim team to touch me.

He didn't, though. Instead he just raised his eyebrows at me and continued back through to the kitchen, where everyone was hanging out.

It was later that evening, after running into him again on our tiny little back balcony, where I had gone to get some air, that he shattered my hopes. I was happy to see him at first, my heart leaping with joy to see that he was alone, that he was coming to spend time with me, specifically.

"This is a nice apartment, " he said. "I'm still in one of the dorms – the swim team members get it free so I figured why not save a little money, right?"

"Yeah," I replied, probably grinning more than I should have been. He was right next to me, leaning over the railing and looking down the alley. He was so tall.

We chit-chatted about various things, mostly all school-related, our history professor etc. And then he asked me about Emma.

"Oh, Emma?" I asked, surprised.

"And that girl Sarah, you're friends with her, too?"

I nodded, confused. Why was he asking me about my friends?

"Is she single?"

The sensation, the feeling of a sudden shrinking in my soul, felt real – physical. I turned away from Brandon and looked out over the alley myself, because I didn't want him to see the expression on my face.

"Uh, yeah," I replied. "Yeah, I think so."

"And is she – well, does she like guys?"

I nodded stiffly. "Yes I think so."

"Cool. Do you think I could get her number from you? I mean, you don't have to or anything, but we know each other from class and I just thought –"

As Brandon babbled I went through my memories of him, illuminated as they now were by a new light. Sarah had a class that ended the same time our history class did. Sometimes she would wait for me outside and we'd have coffee together. And yes, looking back it suddenly seemed so obvious. Brandon was usually there, talking to me, when she was there. All of those efforts to talk to me in class, all of those total misinterpretations on my part.

"So wait a sec," I said, cutting off whatever it was he was saying. "Did you just act friendly with me so you could get to Sarah?"

"Huh?" Brandon replied, looking genuinely surprised. "I don't even know what you're –"

"Well all those times you talked to me during class – and after class – those were just to use me to get closer to Sarah?"

I didn't like the shrill tone in my voice but I couldn't make it go away. Brandon held his hands up.

"Wait. Paige, are you mad? I talk to everybody, I'm a friendly guy. I don't know what you thought –"

"I thought you liked me!" I squeaked, knowing I shouldn't be saying anything even as the words were spilling out. "Why do you think I invited you here? I thought – I thought –"

It was the look on Brandon's face that shut me up. Embarrassment. Not for himself, either – for me. He backed away a little, gingerly, and it hurt so much to feel that, to feel his total lack of interest, his fear that I might do something stupid like try to kiss him.

"I didn't mean to, uh – Paige, I didn't think that... Maybe I should just go?"

"Maybe you should!" I snapped, not looking as he went back into the house and left me there on the porch. At least I managed to wait until I was alone to cry, like some stupid high-school girl, because some stupid boy who never even had the slightest bit of interest in me wanted to date one of my friends.

Emma found me about fifteen minutes later, dry-eyed by then and filled with self-loathing. She didn't even have to ask what had happened, after she saw the look on my face.

"He asked me for Sarah's number," I said flatly. "I'm so fucking stupid, Emma."

"No you're not. Don't say that, Renner."

I turned to her, then, distraught. "I don't even know who I thought I was kidding, you know? I'm still me. I'm still that outcast girl who nobody liked. What, did I think I was suddenly hot property because I had friends? I'm not blind. I know I don't look like a cheerleader! The worst part of this is he's not even that great, is he?! I saw it when he was out here, blathering on about Sarah and oh he was just being friendly to me and he's friendly to everyone blah blah blah oh God, please don't let the ugly girl try to touch me."

"You're not ugly, Paige. Stop it. Stop saying this stuff."

"I'm sorry," I laughed bitterly. "You want to hear the worst part? The only reason I'm acting like such a psycho right now is because this is the first time a boy I liked ever even talked to me! So of course I fell in love, like some pathetic little puppy. Well, yay I guess. This just needs to happen a few more times and I'm sure I'll toughen up."

Emma was gentle, putting her arms around me and pulling me in for a hug. I apologized later, as we sat in the living room finishing off the very last of the wine after everyone else had gone home.

"I'm so embarrassed about acting like that," I started, but she shook her head angrily.

"Don't, Renner. Don't do that. You don't need to apologize for having emotions, OK? What do you think, that I never got worked up over a boy? And it's weird isn't it, the way it's always the kinda shitty ones who get you the most worked up? Anyway. Don't say sorry. I've spent entire days – weeks! – of my life ranting and raving about this or that guy whose name I can't even remember now. And they've done the same about us, believe me. This hurts. I know it hurts. I know how it feels. It's probably going to hurt tomorrow, too, and the next day. But you will get over it – and probably a lot quicker than you think."

* * *

It wasn't that anything Emma said to me the day of Brandon's rejection was wrong, it's that I was too caught up in it at the time to really see how right she was.

I think maybe I got a little cocky. I got to thinking that the person I was at Grand Northeastern was entirely different to the sad girl from River Forks, the unpopular girl with no friends and no life, the girl who watched her peers grow up, begin to get boyfriends and girlfriends, start going to parties, start getting jobs and cars as she hung back at the periphery, always watching, never participating. And the drama with Brandon just revealed my 'new' life to be the sham it was – or so it seemed to me at the time. There was no 'new' life. I was still me. Still insecure, still undesirable for anything more than friendship.

Looking back, I can see how silly my assumption that I was undesirable because swim team Brandon didn't want me. But I was 19, naive even for my age, inexperienced and, although I was improving, getting to know and like myself a little, still prone to fits of self-doubt.

My friends tried to help but most of them were normal, and for that reason most of them assumed I was normal, too. They didn't know about my dead mother, or that the only friends I had ever had before them existed in a different millennium. So even as they dragged me out with them to various parties or dinners or errand-runs and did their best to shore me up and support me, none of them really understood just how thrown off course I was.

I kept it together for the rest of the semester and most of the next one. I made it to most of my classes, and passed my exams. When summer started, though, and without the pressures of coursework and papers being due, I found myself drinking more. I liked drinking – I had liked it ever since Emma introduced me to red wine with our dinner parties. I liked the way it seemed to make everything look like it was in soft-focus, the way it made conversation seem more profound, somehow, more meaningful. I started looking forward to it, the warmth of the alcohol dissipating out to my fingers and toes, the exhalation of breath that came with tipsiness. Before long, I wasn't just drinking wine anymore. I was coming home from my summer job at one of the local grocery stores and mixing my own rum and Cokes and vodka and orange juices with the frost-fogged bottles of hard liquor we kept in the freezer for parties.

It didn't get too far. My roommates – Emma, Adam and Jake – noticed. Adam came home one Monday afternoon after a weekend away to find me sprawled across the sofa, drink in hand, music cranked up loud. He turned it down, sat on the chair next to me and asked me if I knew what time it was.

I sat up, struggling a little, and laughed at how drunk I was – sometimes it's difficult to tell just how much you've had until you try to do something like sit up or walk to the bathroom. "Uh, six?" I ventured.

Adam held up his phone so I could see the time. "It's not even three, Paige. You're drunk. I'm going to make some coffee."

"I'm not –" I began, but Adam was already headed to the kitchen.

College is a strange time. Like grade school, it involves throwing a bunch of people who have very little in common other than age together and waiting for them to cluster into groups based on – well, often on not much at all. A shared apartment, randomly sitting next to someone in class, dorm rooms next door to each other. Little things.

They stepped up, though, these people I had only known for not even two years. It went on for awhile, the afternoon drinking. There were a few embarrassing incidents, too. A shouting match at a party with a girl I thought had looked at me the wrong way, a ruined dress after a night at the bar and my own drunken inability to keep the spaghetti Emma was trying to force down me to sober me up on the fork and not in my lap.

"What are you doing?" She asked me the next day as we drank coffee in our living room and fanned ourselves with advertising flyers because our landlord, who paid the electric bills for the entire building, had forbidden air conditioners.

I was miserable, hung-over, shielding my eyes from the too-bright sun. "Drinking coffee," I replied, not having seen the look on her face.

"Paige."

I looked up, and saw it then. "Oh," I said. "Oh, what am I *doing?*"

"Yeah."

"I don't know," I smiled sadly. "It seems like I'm sliding down a short path to some kind of alcohol problem."

"And why are you doing that?" Emma asked. She wasn't lecturing. She wasn't being judgmental. She was being a friend. I couldn't take it though.

"Just a sec," I told her. "Just let me pee, I'll be right back. I promise we can talk about this."

But instead of going to the bathroom I went to the kitchen and turned the tap on so Emma wouldn't hear me opening the freezer door. And then I took a big, long swig of vodka right out of the bottle and stood there for a few seconds afterwards making faces and trying not to retch.

When I sat back down with Emma she was none the wiser. An hour – and a few more trips to the kitchen – later, I was nicely toasted. It made the conversation easier. The cloud of shame was lifted, temporarily.

"This isn't just about Brandon, is it?" Emma was saying. "I mean, it was months later that you started drinking – that thing with him at the party was so minor. He was just some boy you thought was cute, wasn't he? Is there something you haven't told me?"

I looked up at Emma as she perched on the chair opposite me, her golden-brown eyes full of concern and her long, auburn hair piled messily on top of her head. She wasn't cute, not the way the little blonde cheerleaders were, but there was something stately about my best friend.

"Yeah," I said, only just managing to keep the slur out of my voice, barely conscious of what I was saying because I was half thinking about Emma's stateliness. "Yeah there is something I haven't told you."

"Would you like to tell me?" She replied. "Paige, if anything happened with Brandon – if he tried anything, if he did anything to you that you didn't –"

"Oh it has nothing to do with him," I responded breezily, waving my arm in the air. "I just need to pee and then I'll tell you, OK?"

I stood up, then, and yelped in surprise when Emma grabbed my wrist hard and yanked me back onto the sofa. "Paige! Do you think I don't know what you're doing?! You're totally wasted! Seriously, just sit down and talk to me. Now."

She meant it. I could see it in her eyes. She'd threatened to call my father a few times over the summer already and that was something I really, really wanted to prevent from happening. My dad couldn't keep the pride and happiness out of his voice whenever we spoke on the phone, there was no way I wanted him to have even the slightest clue as to how bad things had deteriorated for me. So I sat back down, because I didn't want Emma to have to even consider calling him.

"Why are you doing this?" Emma whispered, her voice cracking. "If something happened to you, Paige, I swear to God I will kill the person who did it. Is that it? Do you – if you need someone to go to the police with you –"

"It's nothing like that," I sniffled.

"Are you sure? And Brandon –"

"It's nothing to do with him. He didn't do anything. I mean, I wanted him to – but he didn't."

"Is it your home life?" Emma continued, clearly desperate to find a reason for my spiraling situation. "You told me how it was for you in high school, Paige. About your father, too. Is it that? I know you think therapists are useless but maybe you could talk to someone about this? We don't just get over our pasts, you know."

"I did have friends," I blurted suddenly, urged on from someplace in the depths of my drunkenness.

"You – what? I know you have friends, Paige! I am your friend! Adam and –"

"No," I cut her off. "I know I have friends now. I'm talking about back home, in River Forks. I said I had no friends but that was a lie. I did. I had two friends."

"OK..."

Emma was skeptical, looking at me like she wasn't sure if it was me talking, or the alcohol. And because I was drunk, it just made me angry.

"I know it's hard to believe," I spit bitterly. "Someone being friends with me, of course. Gross Paige Renner, Paige Renner the witch, Paige Renner the weirdo."

"That's, uh, Paige – that's not what I'm saying at all. Or thinking. You just haven't ever mentioned any friends from River Forks. You've actually been pretty clear that you didn't have any, and that it was really tough for you. I understand if you didn't –"

"They weren't in River Forks. They were actually in your country – in England. Well, not that they call it England but..."

"You have friends in the UK?" Emma asked. "Where from? You mean, like, internet friends?"

I laughed, even as a little voice spoke up from the back of my mind: *Shut up, Paige. Shut up, shut up, shut up.*

"Ha, no, not internet friends. They don't know what the internet is. They don't even know what a car is, or an airplane."

Emma's expression was curious. She wasn't upset with me, she was just trying to figure out what the hell I was talking about. And I, in my drunken haze, was quite enjoying dangling the secret in front of her.

"I'm sorry," she told me, "I don't understand, Paige. I don't know if you even know what you're saying right now."

"Of course I know what I'm saying!" I shouted. "How drunk do you think I am?! Not so drunk I'm just blathering nonsense."

"OK." Emma reached out and put her hand on my knee, giving it a squeeze. "OK, Paige. You don't need to get angry with me, I'm honestly here to listen to you right now – to anything you have to say."

And just like that my dumb, momentary bravado was gone and I was suddenly hunched over my own knees, crying, as memories of Caistley and Willa and Eadgar flooded my consciousness. "I miss them" I choked out, wiping my tears away on the back of my wrist and sniffling hard. "I miss them so much. I never even said goodbye, I just left. They probably think I'm – " I broke off, properly sobbing by then. "They probably think I'm dead!"

Emma grabbed one of my hands and took it between hers. "Hey, Paige. Paige, look at me. If you haven't talked to these friends for awhile, or if you've lost touch, we can find them online. You have their names, right? We can find them on Facebook and you can send them a message. I'm sure they'll understand, if they were real friends. They'll know what it was like for you, what a difficult time it was."

I laughed again, through my tears, as I imagined typing 'Willa' or 'Eadgar' into Google. As far as I knew, nobody back then even had a last name and between that and the whole over-a-thousand-years-ago situation, I didn't think Emma's plan would be very effective. She was trying to help, though.

"They won't be on Facebook," I said quietly, taking a few shaky breaths. "They won't be online at all."

"Are – are you sure?" Emma asked. "Even if they don't have any social media it's still pretty easy to find people online, you know. If they're in the UK and you have their names I'm pretty sure we can –"

"We can't," I said sadly. "I'm telling you, we can't. I haven't seen either of them for years now – their names were Willa and Eadgar, they were brother and sister. I spent half my childhood with them."

We were quiet for a few minutes. Emma got up and went into the kitchen and came back a short time later with a steaming cup of coffee and a peanut butter and jelly sandwich.

"You should eat, Paige."

I picked up the sandwich and took a bite to prove I was making an effort, before putting it back down. it was pretty good, though, and I remembered I hadn't eaten for hours, so I took another few bites.

"So," Emma said gently, "what's the story with Eadgar and Willa? Were they Amish or something like that?"

Although I was still quite drunk at that point, common sense was beginning to assert itself. I couldn't tell Emma the real story, of course I couldn't. "Well they're more religious than you or I, that's for sure. But no, they're not Amish. I shouldn't have even brought them up, that was dumb. I didn't lie, though, Emma. I want you to know that. I really didn't have any friends in River Forks – that's the truth."

Emma put her arm around me. "It doesn't matter, dummy! Like, even if you did lie – and I know you didn't – I know this is hard for you, I know you're still sensitive about it. I understand."

We left the conversation there and, over the next few days, I made a real effort – and a mostly successful one – to stop making so many trips to the freezer when no one else was looking. My roommates noticed, too. They didn't make a big deal out of it, because they didn't want to embarrass me, but they were quietly supportive, free with their smiles and hugs. It was a few days into the start of the first semester of our junior year that Emma yelled from the living room one day as I washed the dishes in the kitchen.

"Paige!"

"Yeah? What?"

"Do you spell Eadgar like E-A-D or just E-D?"

I rinsed the soap suds off the mug in my hand and walked into the living room, drying my hands on a kitchen towel. Emma had her laptop open on the coffee table.

"It's E-A-D," I told her, watching as she typed the name into Google.

"Were their parents weird hippies or something?"

"No," I replied, a little worried about where the conversation was going, because I didn't want to have to lie to my friend. "Why?"

"Because Eadgar is an ancient name. Anglo-Saxon. Hold on." Emma typed some more. "Huh, it looks like Willa is, too. Anglo-Saxon, I mean. Were their parents big history buffs?"

I shook my head and Emma looked up, noticing the look on my face. "I'm sorry, Paige," she said. "I was – I just thought maybe it would help you to find these friends of yours, and even if they are from some crazy internet-free family, there should be something online, some –"

"They won't be online," I reply. "I promise you they won't be. It's a waste of time looking."

Emma narrowed her eyes. "But," she responded, confused. "How do you know that? Why wouldn't they be? Everyone is online, even if it's just on one of those white pages sites or something."

I flopped down on the sofa and sighed. "I actually wish I could tell you this story, Emma. I've never told anyone – well, when I was older, anyway. I blabbed about it to everyone as a kid."

"Well why can't you?"

I looked up, catching her eye directly. "Because it would make you think I'm insane."

Emma balked at that, and laughed. "What? No it wouldn't. Unless you're joking with me right now. Why would it make me think you're insane? Paige I don't know how many times I have to tell you that I understand that things were different for –"

"This isn't just about things being different for me," I cut in, because some part of me was actually finding itself persuaded by Emma and I didn't want that to happen. "It's about what you would think if Adam walked in here right now and told us he had a pink unicorn back home in Ohio. Not a horse that got painted pink, or an imaginary friend or a toy or anything like that but an actual pink unicorn. Something impossible, something that can't exist, that can't happen. If he walked in right now and seriously told us that, what would you think?"

Emma laughed. "I'd think he was nuts."

"There you go."

I was just about to go back to the kitchen to finish the dishes when Emma spoke again, slowly and carefully.

"So what are you saying, Paige? Are you saying that your story would be the same as the pink unicorn story?"

"Yeah," I admitted, because it was the truth. "I am. You would definitely think I was crazy. You'd call my father. You might even call an ambulance."

Emma stared at me intently, trying to figure out if I was playing a joke on her or not, trying to reconcile what I was telling her with what she knew of me.

I'm not a woo-woo person at all. A week before that conversation in our apartment I'd annoyed Emma by making fun of her going with one of our other friends to get her tea leaves read. She knew I was pretty hard-headed about that kind of thing, so I can see why she wasn't totally convinced it wasn't all a big joke when I told her how unbelievable my story actually was.

"How about if I promise not to do any of those things?" She asked finally, as her curiosity got the better of her – not that mine wouldn't have, in the same position. "What if I promise not to think you're crazy or call anyone or tell anyone else? And you know I wouldn't, Paige, you know I wouldn't say a thing."

I did know that. I wished in that moment that Emma actually was an untrustworthy blabbermouth because damn if telling someone about Willa and Eadgar and Caistley and everything they – and that place – were to me wasn't tempting. Not some therapist who didn't give really give a damn, but someone who cared about me.

"I want to tell you," I said, sitting back down. "You have no idea how much I want to tell you this, Em. But I'm not kidding or exaggerating – you would not believe it. And I don't want you to think less of me. Even if you don't call an ambulance, I still don't want you to think I'm nuts."

"But you're not nuts. I know that – I can see it. I live with you, Paige! I think I'd know if you were crazy!"

"You're right," I agree. "I'm not crazy. It's just – it's not believable. If someone came to me and told me the same story, and none of the things that have happened to me had happened, I wouldn't believe them. Not in a million years."

"Oh my God!" Emma sighed, punching a pillow in mock frustration. "You're killing me, Paige. Damn!"

A weird recklessness descended over me that evening. After the mistake of telling my therapist as a child, and after the bullying in school, after all of it, I was still desperate, the way human beings are when something extraordinary has happened to them, to spill. Not to tell so much as to be believed. To have someone hear me out and talk to me about Eadgar and Willa as if they were real people, as if Caistley was a real place. Which they were, and it was.

And who better than Emma? She wouldn't tell anyone. She was solid. She was my best friend and she had my back. I knew that. So what if she thought I was a little nutty, as long as she didn't do anything else?

"You have to promise not to do anything," I said, still disbelieving that what appeared to be about to happen was actually going to happen. "No calling anyone, no telling anyone. You have to *promise*, Emma."

She looked me right in the eyes. "I promise. I won't tell a soul."

"And you won't think less of me. Even if you think I'm a little crazy, because you're going to think that – you won't let this affect our friendship. Promise."

"Well," Emma said, and I found I was actually comforted by how seriously she was taking things. "As long as this doesn't involve you telling me you're a serial killer or something."

"No," I reassured her, "it's nothing like that."

"OK, well then I promise not to think less of you. I promise that it won't change our friendship. I don't think it will – if anything it'll make us closer, don't you think?"

"I hope so," I responded, my voice heavy with what was about to happen.

We sat there looking at each other for a few moments, waiting. And then I spoke.

"So you know I told you they live in England, right? Willa and Eadgar?"

"Yes."

Was I really doing it? I was. My skin prickled with the anticipation that it could still go very wrong. But Emma was my best friend. I knew her, I trusted her. If I couldn't tell her, who could I tell?

Looking back, I see that my thoughts on Emma's reaction were incredibly naive. I very badly wanted her to believe me, and so I just convinced myself that she would. Or, if she didn't actually believe me, that my story wouldn't change anything between us.

"They do live in England," I continued, swallowing hard as I came up on the big reveal. "They just don't live... now."

Emma tilted her head to the side. "They don't live now? What do you mean by that?"

"I mean they don't live in 2016."

I let the words hang there in the air as Emma gazed at me. After a little while she shrugged. "I'm sorry, Paige, but I have no idea what you're talking about. You knew them when you were younger, you mean? Before 2016?"

There was a little inkling, then, in my mind. A little hint, something in Emma's expression telling me I shouldn't go any further. But, stubborn and already committed, I ignored it.

"No," I replied. "That's not what I mean. What I mean is they live in the past. As far as I've been able to tell they live sometime in the 9th century, in what would be East Anglia on a modern map."

Emma was silent for a little while, and then she laughed. It was an uncomfortable laugh. "What?" She asked. "Paige, you're joking. This is a joke, right? Ugh, I thought you were really going to tell me –"

"It's not a joke."

Poor Emma. She had no idea how to respond. I couldn't blame her, because I knew I would have been just the same way in her situation, as would everyone else we knew. "But," she said, searching for words, "what are you – how did you spend time with them, then? Are we even talking about real people here, Paige? Did you read about them in a book as a child and then imagine they were your friends or something?"

"Oh they're real," I assured her. "They're as real as you sitting there on the sofa, or me telling you all this right now. I've collected oysters with them on the beach outside Caistley, I've played hide-and-seek in the woods close to the –"

"Caistley? Is that where they live? Or, uh, lived?"

"It's where they still live, as far as I know," I replied, feeling a little wobble in my heart at that phrasing – 'as far as I know.'

"And Caistley is," Emma paused, "in the past?"

I nodded.

"And you're saying you've been there? You've been to the past? You're some kind of time-traveler?"

By that point in the conversation, I could already see that I was being 'humored.' Emma was being polite, but even she couldn't completely hide the horrified reaction I thought I glanced on her face for a split-second, before she turned away. And why wouldn't she be horrified? I know I would, if someone I knew and loved came to me with something that sounded like the delusions of a crazy person. But I pushed on anyway, stupidly hoping that if I just kept explaining the details, she would see how sincere I was and that would lead her to believe me.

"I guess I am, yeah. It's, uh, it's been going on a long time. Since I was 5 years old, just after my mom died. So I guess it never really seemed like that big of a deal to me."

"Just after your mom died?" Emma asked.

"Yeah. Why?"

I watched my friend lean back on the couch and put her hands over her face for a second. When she looked back at me I could tell she still wasn't buying anything I was saying. "Just after your mom died, Paige? That's a bit of a coincidence, isn't it? Hasn't it ever occurred to you that maybe a 5 year old who just suffered an extremely traumatic event could come up with a fantasy world or an imaginary friend as a way to cope with it?"

I felt my spine stiffen with offense when Emma said that. "Well," I replied, "I suppose it probably would have occurred to me if Caistley was a place I only remembered from being a little kid. But I kept going there. That's what I'm saying. The last time I went was over two years ago. I know the difference between a dream and reality, Emma. Don't you think you would, too?"

"Are you getting upset with me?" She asked, noticing the change in my tone of voice. "Paige, you must have known I would be skeptical. It's like you said – you're telling me something unbelievable. You can't be mad at me, can you?"

She was right. Of course she was right. But I was still irritated – probably more at myself for ever thinking it would be a good idea to tell anybody else about Caistley.

We continued to talk for awhile – quite a long while, actually, over an hour. Emma asked questions about Caistley, and Willa and Eadgar, and I answered them. But I knew Emma by then, and so I knew she was just being polite. I'd seen her do that before, pepper someone she didn't like or wasn't interested in with questions, feigning an interest she didn't feel. I didn't know if it was a personal quirk or something to do with her Britishness but it didn't feel good to have it directed at me. I felt patronized, humiliated by her lack of belief – which she did not have to state out loud because it was all over her face, and evident in her body language.

And as much as she'd promised nothing would change, it was like I could already feel her pulling away, putting distance between us.

I cried when I went to bed that night, because I knew it had been a mistake to tell Emma, and I knew that my hopes that it would bring us closer together had been dashed – and the opposite affect achieved. I cried for Willa and Eadgar, too, because I missed them and because I still couldn't get the thought that they were out there somewhere, wondering if I was alive or dead, out of my mind.

What I didn't do was drink. I had that one thing going for me. Sleep came blissfully quickly and all night my dream-self ran through the sun-dappled woods outside Caistley, a child again.

In the morning I woke up and stayed in my room until I was sure Emma had already left so I could avoid an awkward situation at breakfast. I had decided, and seemingly during the night as I slept, that I was going to go back home for the weekend. And when I was at home, I was going to go to Caistley again. It was the autumn semester of my junior year and after the disaster that was trying to tell Emma about my childhood experiences in another place and another time, I simply realized that nothing was going to make me feel better or reassure me that Willa and Eadgar were safe and fine and not worrying about my whereabouts except seeing them, speaking to them again.

It was asking for another awkward situation, I knew that. My friends were very likely going to be furious with me for abandoning them without a word. But I couldn't just let them go. So I went home on a Friday evening after my last class got out and had dinner with my dad. After he went to bed I convinced myself to make a short trip to Caistley that night, just to see if everything was still in place, if the tree still took me to where it always had, and then to go again the next day when it was light and Willa and Eadgar would be up and about.

As I lay my hands on the trunk of the tree, I was even thinking about possibly staying the night in the woods outside Caistley, if it was warm enough. Eadgar and I had built a crude tree-house when we were around 11 and 12, far enough off the ground to be safe from any animals, and I thought it might be nice to re-experience it. Of course as soon as I got there and saw that strange orange glow in the sky – the one that was to lead to the events that would change my life forever, I forgot all about the tree-house.

Chapter 16

9th Century

I am in the Jarl's roundhouse, alone now after the servant girl who had come in with an armful of fresh logs with which to stoke the fire has left. Gudry and Anja bathed me again after the feast, and I am now dressed in another silk tunic. At the back, it dips so low I feel the breeze on the top of my buttocks when I move, and at the front the fabric has been wound around a thin necklace of hammered gold around my neck. If I so much as lean the wrong way, my breasts will fall out. It's garments like the one I am wearing right now for which the term 'side-boob' was invented. I smile, very briefly, thinking of the term – thinking of the world of cars and shopping malls and celebrity tabloids for sale at grocery store checkouts. And then I look around again, and see where I am, and think about who will be coming for me soon.

Eirik. The Jarl. A sharp-toothed frisson of anticipation runs the length of my body at the thought of him. He is on his way to see me. Where is he? An hour away? Twenty minutes? Twenty seconds? And when he gets here, what will happen?

I am standing, walking around the roundhouse, nervously picking up objects and putting them back down again. The bed has been piled even higher with furs tonight, some of them silver-grey and tipped with white, others as black as the night sky. I gaze down at them, trying to get a handle on how I feel.

How do I feel? I don't know, I can't tell. I'm wound up tightly, I feel that. I feel a thrum of energy running under my skin, a certain tremble that threatens to seize my fingers as I hold them out in front of me and watch the firelight flickering between them.

Am I afraid? Yes, I think I am afraid. But then, the natural follow-up question – do I *not* want to see the Jarl? I cannot answer yes to that one. So how is it that I am both afraid and filled with a jumpy kind of longing? How is it that the thought of one of his big, rough hands on my body both thrills *and* intimidates me?

As I'm wrestling with these questions, aware that I might not have the time to ponder for long, the leather flap door opens and there he suddenly is.

I look up at him, at first because the simple act of him entering the roundhouse has drawn my attention and then because I can't look away. I have never seen a man like the Jarl before, and by that I don't mean I have never seen a man dressed in leather and furs or a man who wears his hair long and braided, with the braids near the front pulled tightly away from his face – although it's true, I hadn't seen a man like that before I met the Jarl. But it isn't what Eirik wears that draws my attention the way a burning torch draws moths to its light, and it isn't his hair or even his great height and breadth. It's something else, some inherent quality, a kind of purely male mastery that I have realized, after spending time with the Vikings, is not often to be found in modern men.

"Paige," he says, not moving from where he is standing in front of the doorway. "Are you warm girl? I told Hildy to send someone to build up the fire – did she do it?"

"Y-yes," I respond, my voice a whisper.

The Jarl unties a leather strap at his waist, unwinding it once, twice, and then setting his sword aside with a clatter. He is big, the kind of big that would make most men his size unwieldy, but instead of lumbering or stomping, Eirik moves like a panther – swift and powerful even in the smallest movements.

I am still standing up. The Jarl slides one of those rough-skinned hands, that I was thinking of not five minutes ago, around my neck and tilts my head up to him, rubbing his thumb over my chin and studying my eyes. Then he lies down on the bed of furs and reaches for a slice of apple on the wooden plate that has been left for him, should he get hungry in the night. I stay where I am, as if frozen to the spot.

"You're afraid."

"Yes," I reply, awkwardly resting my arms stiffly against my sides as I develop a sudden consciousness of their existence.

"It's as it is," Eirik says calmly, swallowing the apple as I try to decipher what he means. "You seem more afraid than most, though. Most, you can see behind their eyes that they want the thing they fear. You I'm not so sure. Maybe you prefer other girls, like yourself?"

I do a double-take at that comment. Have I just been asked if I'm a lesbian? In the 9th century?

"I, uh –" I start. "I –"

Eirik laughs. "You Angles are such funny people. Some men are born wanting men, and some women are born wanting women. What use is there in pretending it doesn't occur? As it is, girl, am I describing you accurately? Does your center grow soft and wet only at the thought of another's center doing the same?"

I shake my head no, just a little, and mumble the word 'no.'

"What was that?" The Jarl asks, his eyes demanding a clearer, louder answer.

"No," I say again, louder.

He reaches out, then, and caresses my ankle, slipping his fingers up over my calf until my knees feel as if they might just give way. "I'm teasing you, girl. You think I couldn't smell the hunger on you the other night?"

My cheeks begin to burn. They burn even brighter when I look down to see that the leather wrapped around his thighs has fallen open. As soon as I see it I turn away, as if my eyeballs might be scorched by the sight. I can feel my heartbeat pounding in my throat.

Eirik chuckles, utterly at ease with himself and his own arousal. "What is it?" He asks, and we both know he knows perfectly well what it is. "I don't believe you've never seen a man in such a state before. Besides, it's you who caused it. I'd be willing to guess that if I was to slip my hand up under that tunic, you'd be as slippery as a sun-warmed oyster."

As he speaks, the Jarl pulls me down onto the furs and does the thing he's talking about – slipping his hand up under my tunic. I don't breath at all as he pushes the silk out of the way, watching my eyes closely for a reaction.

It happens automatically, the second I feel his fingers on my sex, sliding between my lips. I reach down and push his hand away, even as a strange little sigh escapes my mouth, and then I look up, suddenly fearful when I realize what I've just done.

But the Jarl isn't angry, or even slightly upset. He's looking at his finger, shiny with my wetness, and then at me. "You're not afraid of me, girl. You're afraid of yourself. You've no need to worry, Paige with the pink cheeks. It's as I said – I won't rape you. You can relax, let yourself lie easy on the furs."

What does he mean when he says I'm afraid of myself? I don't know. I also don't know that I can trust him not to force himself on me, even as I'm not at all sure that he isn't the only thing I want.

"No," he says, his voice a low rumble, "I won't take you against your will."

The Jarl's eyes slide down from my own. The thin fabric of my tunic has slipped, half-revealing one of my breasts. I exhale quietly as he runs his thumb over it and the nipple pebbles under his touch.

"Beautiful," he murmurs, leaning in unexpectedly and closing his mouth around it.

I gasp loudly, shocked, almost undone by the syrup-thick sweetness of the sensation.

"There," the Jarl whispers, drawing me into his mouth. "There you go, girl."

Things are moving fast inside me. Thoughts, desires, it's all suddenly sped up, like a roller coaster rushing down the slope after a long, slow climb. Maybe not thoughts – I'm not thinking. Eirik pulls my tunic the rest of the way off my breast and takes it in his hand and my hands sink into his hair as I pull him into me.

"Oh my God," I breathe, reaching, grabbing desperately at him.

And then he stops, his hands tight on my wrists. He's laughing. I'm not laughing – I'm lying on my back, breathless, not entirely sure of what just happened. I can't think. I don't feel like I can breathe. Eirik looks down at me, his eyes a deep, stormy blue.

"I told myself I'd be soft with you, girl. A man knows how to be soft with a maid, how to take his time. And I'll take my time with you. But you make it difficult when you reach for me like that, when you look at me as you are right now, with all the things you need from me written all over your pretty face."

He's not kidding, either, about it being difficult. Even his voice sounds different – slower, deeper. He's holding back. An ache between my legs, one that I'm only just now dimly aware of, makes itself known. How can that be? If I 'fear' anything it's specifically that – the pain. Although I only saw him for less than a second, Eirik's manhood is of similar proportion to the man himself. How can I want something at the same time that I fear it? I don't know. I don't know. But I do.

I open my mouth like I'm doing everything else tonight – out of instinct, not consciousness. The decision is never made, my lips fall open for him because there is nothing else that could happen. And when they do, he slips his tongue between them and tightens his grip on my breast, squeezing and caressing until my body sings. When he stops, I'm panting.

There are no more words left in me. Whatever the time was for words is over. I reach up to my throat as the Jarls' eyes bore into me, and pull the top of the tunic out of the gold necklace, revealing my breasts completely. I see something in his eyes, then. A naked, animal thing. And when I see it, at the same moment I know in my heart that it won't be denied, there is no part of me that wants anything other than to indulge it.

"It's too much now, girl," Eirik says, grasping the tunic in his hands and yanking it the rest of the way off. He moves on top of me, pushing my thighs apart with one hand and I realize it's going to happen. Right now.

"Wait," I gasp. "Eirik. Please. Wait."

Why am I asking him to wait? I don't know. He doesn't either. He growls and buries the fingers of one hand in the fur, before balling it into a tight fist.

"Don't ask me to wait. Don't reveal yourself that way and then ask me to wait, girl."

"But I don't know what to do!" I say. "I don't know – I don't want to do the wrong thing – I"

Everything is heightened at this moment. Even as I'm terrified of doing something wrong, or stupid, my body is opening itself up, blooming for him. I don't want him to wait. He's right – it isn't him I fear, it's myself. As it always is.

It's all erased, though, my mind cleared utterly of anything except the Jarl, when he wraps his hand around himself and guides his full length into me not one second later. My back arches up off the furs and I suck air in, in, in to my lungs, scrabbling at the furs, at him, my eyes tearing up with the pain even as I want it – all of it.

Eirik holds me, puts his hands on either side of my face, forces me to look at him. And that alone brings me back to myself, calms me. I open my mouth for his tongue as he begins to move in and out of me and he gives it to me.

"I haven't been with a woman since that night," he breathes, propping himself up on his forearms and sinking into me over and over. "I chose – I wanted it to be you, Paige. Does it hurt, girl? Does it hurt? I don't mean to hurt you but you're so wet, my sweet one, so wet and tight around me. Voss...voss!"

I don't know what 'voss' means but the way he says it it sounds like he's swearing. Pain radiates out from my center as the

Jarl takes me, but I make no move to stop him, I don't cringe away. Why? Because he's becoming incoherent. His breath is coming faster. His mouth hangs open and his eyes darken and nothing I have ever experienced in my life has been as good as this, as good as this man in this state. When he puts a hand on my belly and holds me down, fucking me harder, I curl my body up to him even as I'm still not entirely convinced any of this is physically possible.

"Paige. Oh, girl. I'm almost there. You've almost got me there. I'll put my baby inside you and you'll be mine. Is that what you want? Do you want –"

"Yes," I whimper, not thinking at all, just feeling, just reacting. It's not that I don't mean it, though. I do. An entire lifetime of messaging, years of sex ed, of lectures and warnings and it's gone in an instant. It's so gone I'm not even giving permission, I'm begging. "Yes. Eirik, please. Please..."

"Voss," he growls, moving faster. It's now that I start to feel it. A little tickle, a little something inside, a spot he's hitting. I angle my hips up.

"Look at me, girl. Look at –"

He takes my chin in one hand and turns my head towards him just in time for me to catch his face melting into a grimace of pleasure as he slams himself into me again and holds himself inside this time, his body rigid. I strain up to him, force my body open, starving for what he's giving me.

I watch the Jarl as I take all of him, I see the way the urgency melts away. He reaches down between our bodies and pulls himself out of me gently. I'm sore, out of breath, oddly restless.

As he collapses onto the furs beside me, catching his breath, I surmise that it must have happened – he must have come. Just the thought of it sends a shiver through my sex. And with the shiver comes another sensation – wetness, warmth. I slip my hand between my legs and draw my fingers across my thigh, looking for proof.

Eirik is watching me intently. When he sees what I'm doing he laughs. "Are you making a point?"

I catch his eye, confused. "What? No – I was just, uh, I was just checking to see if, um –"

He flattens one of his palms on my belly and leans in to kiss my mouth. "You really are an innocent, aren't you? Not anymore, I've taken care of that – but the look on your face, one would think you'd never pleased a man before. You seem to think of it as some difficult thing."

"I haven't pleased a man before," I reply, squirming on the bed of furs as what I think is bemusement – do I really have the power to please a man like the Jarl? – turns as if by some earthy alchemy into an even deeper desire. I wanted him before, even before he was inside me, but it was a chaotic wanting. Looking at my fingers, feeling the evidence of his pleasure, knowing I caused it – it's too much. I roll towards him and bury my face in his warm chest, hooking one of my legs over his hip. He grins.

"Come dawn, girl, you'll be weeping tears of my essence."

It takes me a few seconds to figure out what he's saying, but when I do, when I realize he's just told me he's going to spend the entire night filling me with his cum, a hot flush of lust seizes me and I wrap my arms around the Jarl, pulling him to me even as the painful throbbing between my legs has yet to die down.

I see that he's almost ready again, but instead of pushing me open again – something I'm dying to feel once more – he pulls away, easily holding me down on the furs with one hand.

"Eirik –" I sigh, impatient.

He pushes himself down, kissing my breasts, then my belly. "Mmm," he murmurs, going lower still. "I like the sound of my name on your lips, Paige. I think I will give up being Jarl and stay here with you for the rest of my days if you promise to never stop speaking my name in that way."

I've never been the girl who caused this kind of response. I've looked at other girls enviously, wondered how it felt to inspire such carnality in men, but never even seriously considered that I might have the same power. And now that I'm tasting it for the first time I am utterly intoxicated. A tiny sigh from me and Eirik growls, opening his lips against my bare thigh like he's just barely controlling the urge to devour me. And all I want is more of that – more of him, more of his need.

"Eirik," I whisper as he slides his arms under my ass and beings me up to his mouth. I'm about to say it again when he bends his head – his stubble prickly on my thighs – and suddenly I'm moaning like an animal, digging my fingers into the solid flesh of his shoulders. White hot bliss radiates out from the spot where his warm, wet tongue slips over my clit and everything that was diffuse is suddenly focused, concentrated.

"Oh my God," I whimper, my eyes rolling back into my head. It's way too much. Nothing I've ever done to myself has felt like this perfect, slippery pressure. I push my fingers into the Jarl's hair, unthinking, and pull him against me as my thighs quiver.

"Eirik," I cry out as he hesitates for a brief moment at exactly the right time, letting my orgasm build and build before pushing his tongue over me again and not stopping even as I beg and scream and claw at his shoulders.

And then my mind is blank. I don't hear the sounds I make, there is no consciousness of anything except the pleasure spooling out from my very center, coming and coming and coming until I'm a sweaty, half-giggling, half-panting mess on the Jarl's bed of furs.

When I regain the ability to speak – and who knows how long it's been – one minute? Ten? I shake my head, disbelieving. My body is limp, wrung out. And when I open my eyes, there he is, looking at me.

"How did you do that?" I whisper softly, because speaking any louder is going to take effort and I don't even feel I have the strength to move a single finger at this moment.

Eirik smiles and settles down next to me, sweetly unable to keep his hands off my body. "Sometimes it just happens that way, girl. Sometimes two souls are both at exactly the right place. I had an idea it would be like this, though."

"Did you?" I ask, looking down and then right back up again when I see he is completely hard. "Wait – um –"

"Do you want to do something about that?"

Yes. Yes I want to do something about it. It's new to me, this need to satisfy, and it warms my belly even as I haven't quite come down from what Eirik just did to me. Perhaps his comment about me weeping tears of his cum by the morning was a simple truth instead of a figure of speech?

"Are you afraid of it?" He asks, as I eye but don't touch his rigid cock.

I shake my head. "No. I – uh, no. It's just –"

"Here," he says, taking my hand in his and guiding it down, using his own fingers to wrap mine around his length. And when he feels me, his eyes close and he exhales heavily. It's like a drug, that reaction. All I want is more of it.

Tentatively, I slide my grip down, and then up again. The Jarl's hips jerk forward, pushing himself harder into my grip. "Like this?" I ask.

"You're killing me," he responds, moaning quietly. "The way you ask so sweetly, the look in your eyes – you really don't know, do you? You don't ask to make a show of your innocence, you ask because you really don't – ohh," he stops, looking down, watching my hand around him, "ohhh. Paige. You're going to finish me again, girl, and too soon once more."

"It's not too soon," I insist, leaning in and kissing Eirik's cheek, his temple, his neck, filled with a desperate urge to please, to take care of him in this one way. "It's not too soon. I – I want you to."

He grimaces. "Don't say such things, girl. You only guarantee it."

But he's stiffening in my hand, a brand new sensation for me, and clear liquid is leaking out, running down over the head of him, over my fingers. He's moving quicker, too, and so I move quicker.

The Jarl's eyes consume my body as he gets closer. They linger on my breasts as they bounce and move with the intensity of our rocking movements, and on my bare belly, my lips before he opens his mouth against them, pushing his tongue in deep, deep. There's aggression there now, and I find myself wanting nothing more than to fan its flames, to push it higher and higher.

"Voss," Eirik groans, pushing two fingers between my legs. "Paige, voss! Paige, Paige –"

The thought pops into my head as the Jarl gnashes his teeth with lust, slipping his fingers into me, palming my sex like it belongs to him, that nothing could be better than this. Nothing could be better than him like this. He grabs my wrist tightly, controlling my hand's movements when he begins to come and I look down, watching it, watching him spill himself all over my hand, my belly, the furs. He keeps holding on tight, too, until he's wrung every last drop out of himself, and then he looks down at my white hand and lets go quickly.

"I'm sorry, girl, I didn't realize –"

"Don't be sorry," I sigh, starry-eyed, totally drunk.

I roll over onto my back and look at the roof of the longhouse – the trunks of young trees arranged laid out around a small hole at the center, to let the smoke from the fire escape, and then the gaps filled in with mud and straw. What's happening to me? I almost ask the question out loud. I'm warm, relaxed, as content as I have ever been in my life. I can't look at Eirik either, even as I feel him there next to me, his jewel-like blue eyes still focused only on me. I'm afraid to look at him. He picks up on it immediately, and with such accuracy I wonder for a moment if he's some kind of mind-reader.

"Why do you look away, girl? Are you frightened?"

I nod, and am shocked to feel tears spring to my eyes. They're not sad tears, though – in fact they're unlike any tears I have ever experienced before. The Jarl runs his fingers tenderly over my cheek.

"What is it that frightens you?"

And even though I have a strong feeling he knows what's happening in my heart better than I do, I respond anyway. "It feels like I might drown," I tell him. "Right now, if I look at you, it feels like I might lose myself. I'm sorry, I'm babbling, I don't even know what I'm talking about."

"Oh but you do," Eirik says, pulling me back against him and holding me tight. "You said it yourself – you might drown. You don't know enough yet to know that there is nothing sweeter in life than drowning in another person."

I roll back over so I can look him in the eyes. "That just makes it scarier."

I'm telling the truth. Lying there naked in the Jarl's arms, with his wetness still slick on my thighs and the fire warming us both, it feels like it wouldn't take any effort at all to let go, to drift off into whatever it is that's happening between us and forget all about 2016, as if I had lived my whole life in the past and the whole of my life in the future had been nothing more than a dream.

I fall asleep with Eirik's body curled around me, a dull ache between my legs and the feeling in my heart that things are not anything like as simple as it feels to be in his arms.

Chapter 17
9th Century

Things change for me after that night with the Jarl. I sleep with him now, every night. I no longer work, there is no more grinding of grain or washing of pots or mucking out of the pig sties. I eat better, too, two full meals a day – one when I wake up and the second in the evening. In between there is dried fruit and apples and cheese to snack on, and no one to slap my hand away when I reach for them.

Eirik is busy during the days, ensconced in the longhouse with his higher ranking men discussing things he does not discuss with me or hunting for deer outside the camp walls and returning sometimes with a buck. On those evenings when the hunt is successful there is a communal feast, Viking women and children included. The Jarl always brings the loin to the table himself, rare and bloody, and cuts off the choicest piece for me before anyone else eats. I sit during these times, humming with the joy of being cared for, and accept his offering with great respect and affection. He is a good hunter, a good warrior – a good *man*.

And yet I am not free to go.

Two things happen, as my days in the Viking camp turn to weeks, and then to a month, two months, and so on. The first thing is my certainty that I must leave. I'll be missing now, at home. The police will be involved. My father and my friends will be sick with worry. These are not small things to me. They are the biggest things in my life. And there is nothing to be done but to get back to them. To do otherwise would be to condemn them to lives of loss and worry. I cannot do that.

The second thing is the nights. I spend them with the Jarl, in his arms, and I come to know him in a way I did not think it was possible to know another human being. Sometimes I think I know him better than I know myself. I begin to know what the smallest, most fleeting expression on his face means. I begin to divine his moods in the angle of his shoulders, the sound he makes as he sits down in the roundhouse with me after a long day.

"I feel sometimes as if I'm getting a degree in you," I say sleepily one night after he has satisfied me three separate times and I feel as if I will spend the rest of my life limp on Eirik's fur-laden bed.

"Mmm?" He asks. "A what? A dekree?"

A shiver runs through me – I'm usually more careful than this. It's become automatic now, the simple exclusion of certain parts of my life from all conversation. I would no more discuss a car engine with Eirik as I would my time-traveling with a casual acquaintance in the 21st century.

"Oh," I reply, "nothing, I'm tired, I don't know what I'm saying. I just meant that it feels as if I know you better than anyone else knows you. Almost as if I'm not a fully separate person from you, sometimes."

The Jarl pulls me to my hands and knees, then, and enters me, bending his body down over mine, clasping his hand around the back of my neck. That's how it is for us now. There is no real line between us, he takes my body as if he owns it and no part of me would have it any other way. In the mornings, I wake him up with my mouth or my hand, or simply by pressing my naked body back against him until his own arousal pulls him from slumber. And when he leaves the roundhouse, stopping at the door to pull me close and cover me with kisses before heading off to meet his men with the bouncing lope of a man who has just been completely satisfied, I am content in a way I have never been before.

As fall turns to winter, the nights become frosty. Sometimes a light snow falls, and the morning sun glistens and sparkles in the ice crystals that form on every surface. The Jarl returns late one night, hours after the sun has gone down, and finds me braiding pieces of straw into a rope, the way Anja and Gudry have taught me.

"They say when I have enough I can link them together for a hat," I say, keeping back the part where I think this hat might be useful on a long journey down the coast if it's during a hot or sunny time. I look up and see instantly from Eirik's face that he is not concerned about my hat.

"What is it, babe?" I ask, using a term of affection he has only ever heard from me, but one he has decided he likes. "What's wrong?"

The Jarl sits down at the wooden table and beckons for me, pulling me onto his lap, undoing the knot at the back of my neck that holds up my tunic and burying his face in my breasts. He looks up a minute later as I run my fingers through his hair and kiss his dirt-smudged cheeks.

"It's going to be a long winter, Paige."

"Is it?" I ask. "Are you worried there won't be enough food?"

"No, we have enough grain and pigs to last us three winters. But this is our first winter staying here. Usually, my people raid the land of the Angles when it's warm, and return to the our land when the frost comes. Soon there will be more of us here, more coming, but until then I worry we're vulnerable in exactly the same way the Angles have been vulnerable to us – sitting out here in the open, not moving, with a barely-dug ditch to keep out the King's men."

"There's more than a ditch – those palisades are pretty sturdy," I say, taking what I remember of my reading on the Viking invasions of Britain and trying to apply it specifically to our current situation. "Does the King even have enough men? We're in the Kingdom of the East Angles now, aren't we? They have enough to worry about with the Mercians on their doorstep to care about such a small group of Northmen, I think."

Eirik looks at me sharply. "How in Freja's name do you think you know so much about the military concerns of the King?"

"I don't," I reply. "I'm just guessing."

"No you're not. I know it because what you say is correct."

"Then why are you worried?"

"Because it's my lot to worry. There's no one above me, girl. If the people starve, if they're killed by the enemy, it's on my head isn't it? It's my duty to think of these things. The women don't weave precious stones into my leathers for nothing, you know. I don't eat the best meat for no reason. I am given those things because I earn them. Because keeping me strong means the people keep themselves strong. And you still haven't told me how it is you're advising me on the strength of King of the East Angles!"

"I'm not," I say hurriedly. "It was just a guess!"

Eirik harrumphs. "You're full of guesses, girl. And it's a mighty coincidence that so many of them turn out to be truths. You're right about the King. But he's never had an encampment of Northmen sitting on his coast, has he? It doesn't take a wise man to see we make a tempting target."

"Set the men to digging the ditch deeper," I say, thinking that if the ditch around the camp is deep enough, and the ramparts outside it tall and wide enough, those things alone, combined with the palisade, would keep out even a large force of men – even on horseback. "And set more of the women to making arrows – I don't know why Hildy needs so many to help her with the washing."

The Jarl laughs suddenly, a sound I love. "She doesn't – but the washing is her task, and so she pretends she needs a small army of girls to get it done."

"Well tell her to stop! Double the number of arrows in camp if you worry about invaders. Which will be more useful – cleaner cooking pots or arrows?"

I wrap my arms around Eirik's strong neck as he stands up and he whirls me around in a circle. "Tell Hildy to stop, you say?" He grins. "Are you trying to get me killed, girl? I should send Hildy out to meet the King of the East Angles, shouldn't I? One harsh word, one switch with her little willow branch and he'll be running off into the hills, never to be seen again. And now you, too! Perhaps you can accompany her, and advise the King on how to do his job?"

He's in good humor, I can see that, but when he sits back down and gets to running his hands over the curve of my waist and then around, sliding them down over my buttocks and pulling me in closer to him, I'm afraid I've gone too far.

"I don't mean to tell you what to do," I say, because now he's unwrapping his own leathers and that look is in his eye and I know there is not much time left for talking. "I don't intend to –"

"Of course there are more arrows being made," Eirik says, freeing himself from his leathers and cockily enjoying my reaction. "I don't need you to tell me that. You're a smart one, though, Paige. It's almost a shame you're a woman, I could use someone like you on my side when Veigar is trying to convince everyone that we should attack the King's men in the middle of winter."

He's gazing up at me as I stand between his legs, waiting for a reaction – waiting to pull me down onto that thing I can't take my eyes off. "It's a shame I'm a woman?" I whisper playfully, pushing Eirik's dark hair off his face because I want to see that expression he always makes when he first feels me around him. "Are you sure about – ohhhh..."

He maneuvers me onto him before I can finish speaking, pulling me all the way down, impaling me on his cock until the rest of my words disappear into a moan. I lean my head back, closing my eyes and letting Eirik take control.

It doesn't take long. I'm still gripping his shoulders hard, the sweet little tightenings still running through me, when the Jarl lifts his hips up off the chair and holds himself there, panting and staring into my eyes as he empties himself, all his tension, all his pleasure, into me.

Chapter 18
9th Century

It's sometime in what I think is late November when I finally accept that I will be with the Vikings for the duration of the winter, at least another three months – probably more, barring an exceptionally early spring. I tell myself that this is a good thing, that it will allow me more time to integrate, and to allow everyone else time enough to forget the idea that I might try to escape. When the moment comes, no one will be expecting it – that's good for me, it means I'll get a head start when Hildy and the Jarl and everyone else just assumes I'm off washing in the stream or collecting oysters at the beach.

But I know, because the process is already well underway, that the others in camp are not the only ones getting used to a new situation, to new people. I am getting used to it, too. I'm coming to know some of them – not just the Jarl – and coming to like them. I spend a lot of time with Gudry and Anja who, after realizing I'm not Hildy and am not going to beat them for smiling the wrong way, both prove themselves reliable friends and confidants. Even Hildy herself has grown on me, now that she is no longer allowed to physically chastise me. She has a husband and two daughters, and they live in an oddly modern arrangement whereby she spends all day running the domestic side of the Viking camp and her husband makes sure their girls are fed and healthy.

And then there is the Jarl. There was never a period when I seriously thought I was somehow 'playing' the Viking leader, never a time when I didn't feel something for him. But as time passes I find myself more and more unable to think of my life without him. He doesn't just make my head – and other parts of me – explode on a nightly basis, he takes care of me. And the more I get used to this luxury, the more I cannot imagine being without it. It's not one-sided, either. He's come to rely on me, too – a fact he does not make any effort to hide. He comes back sometimes, after one of his men has been injured in the taking of a village or Veigar has been too stupid to understand an instruction, and buries his face in my neck for a minute or two or five, silently breathing me in, recovering from the trials of the day. He'll look up at me then, searching my face with those limpid blue eyes of his, and tell me he doesn't know what he would do without me.

And when he tells me that, and I see that it's true, my heart seizes up slightly from knowing that he is going to have to do without me – and sooner than he thinks.

He comes back late one night, after what was supposed to be a minor raid on a small gathering of peasant huts just up the coast – not even a village – and his eyes are dark with trouble.

"What is it?" I ask, immediately aware that something is wrong. "What happened? Are you alright?"

I spring to my feet, lifting his leathers, turning him around so I can see his back, searching for blood or injuries, my heart in my throat.

"Look at you," he smiles sadly, tenderly down at me. "Such busy love, Paige. Such womanly worry. Where would men be without women to worry about us?"

He's thoughtful, the way he often is, but I'm still in a slight panic. "What happened?" I ask again. "Why do you look so –"

"Asgald has been wounded, girl. Here," he turns his forearm up to me and drags one finger across the center of it. "It's deep, he's going to lose the hand – maybe the arm. He will die before the next full moon, I think. And if he does not die, he won't be able to fight again."

I shake my head, disbelieving. "Asgald?" I ask, thinking of the young man – 18, younger than me – with so much promise, the man Eirik has taken under his wing. "But you said it was just some peasant huts! You said –"

"I know what I said. One of those peasants had himself a sword, didn't he? Who knows which of the King's men he stole it from, but he caught us out, we weren't expecting a fight. He didn't even know how to wield it, he just came out of his hut and started chopping away, as if he were cutting logs for the fire. Asgald wasn't even looking."

I've met Asgald before, feasted with his parents. He's blonde, hazel-eyed and almost as tall as Eirik – although not even close to as broad. He's funny, too, capering around for the little kids, telling me tall tales about the time he and Eirik bested a giant and then goofily insisting that it's all true. Now he's going to die? Tears spring to my eyes.

"Eirik," I whisper, pulling his head down and pressing his face against my neck. "I'm sorry. Are you sure he will die?"

"I don't know. Hildy has the healers tending to him but the wound is deep, almost through the bone, and the rot may already have set in."

"Did you kill him?" I ask, suddenly infuriated. "Tell me you fucking killed the bastard who did it, Eirik!"

The Jarl pulls back and gazes down at me. "You're becoming one of us, girl."

"What?" I ask, still desperately needing to hear that the peasant who attacked Asgald had been made to pay. "Did you kill him or –"

"I see you sometimes," the Jarl continues, ignoring my question. "You think I don't see you trying to hold yourself apart from us? You still have plans to escape, to go back to your home."

I look up at him then, my mouth open, because how does he know this? And if he does know it, how is he calling it out so casually, as if it doesn't matter? "I – no," I protest. "No, Eirik – I don't know why you would, um, I don't –"

He turns my face up to his. "It doesn't matter, Paige. Because even as I see you trying to keep yourself apart from us – from me, even – I also see the roots of your life taking hold in our earth – in *my* earth. You keep yourself apart because you feel it too, because you're scared of how inevitable it is. Look how angry you were just now when I told you of Asgald's wound – look how you crave the news of a peasant's death. Look at your panic when you thought it might be I who was injured! And even now, your eyes betray you, my love, they speak so much more than your mouth."

I pull away from Eirik, unsure if I'm angry, or embarrassed, or oddly relieved. "What do you mean?" I bark, settling on 'angry.' "You don't know what I'm thinking, Eirik. Sometimes, maybe, but not all the time. You don't know everything of me!"

"Oh but I do, girl. It's no particular talent on my part, I'll say that. It's you – you give yourself away like a child. You've no cunning in your heart, and no skill for it. Even now it's written all over your face that I'm right."

"Well," I respond immediately – and defensively – "if you think I want to escape why don't you watch me more closely? If you know all these things why am I free to wander the camp – to go to the beach, even! You're just saying these things to make yourself seem smarter than you are!"

The Jarl is watching me, and a smile is playing at one corner of his lips. When he doesn't respond I throw my hands in the air. "And now you have nothing to say! How convenient! Look at you – you can barely hide your smile – you won't be smiling if I do escape!"

As soon as the words have left my mouth I feel that I've gone too far. I look away, and then when the Jarl says nothing, I look back. His expression hasn't changed. The smile still threatens.

"What?!" I'm yelling now. "You won't be! You won't be smiling if –"

"Yes, girl," he replies, holding up one hand. "I heard you. And you're right, I won't be smiling if you escape. Is that some kind of victory to you? Have I showed a great weakness in admitting it? You're a strange one, Paige, even still after this time with us. I smile because I know already that you won't escape. You can try, if you must, but you won't succeed."

"How do you know that?" I demand, as a hollow feeling seizes my stomach – I won't succeed? How can he know that? He can't. And even as I tell myself he can't know it, I believe him anyway, because it's him saying it, and because without even noticing it I've found myself in a place where I simply accept the things Eirik says as the truth.

He reaches under my tunic and casually cups one of my breasts. "I can answer the question if you like."

"Yes," I tell him defiantly, even as something inside my begins to crumble under his touch.

Eirik sits down at the wooden table and pulls me onto his lap, taking one of my hands in his and placing my index finger on the far left side of the table. "Here. This is where we are right now." He drags my finger in an uneven line across the table. "And this is the direction you have to travel to get back to the village where my men took you. Do you understand?"

I nod and he continues. "It's not a short journey, especially without a horse, and the land is wet and spongy – impassable."

He's waiting for me to say something, to reveal myself – maybe to reveal my plan, if I have one. Which I don't, beyond 'get from point A to point B, somehow.' When I don't speak, he continues. "There are long stretches of this coastline where the wet land and the sea are indistinguishable, neither man nor horse can pass. You need a ship – and you don't have a ship, girl, nor the ability to sail one. I suppose you could go inland but it would be too far, you would go hungry or, more likely, you would be taken again – and by far worse than me."

I remain silent, but it occurs to me that the Jarl is very possibly exaggerating. He and his men travel on ships. They sail the coasts. The Kingdom of the East Angles is not his homeland any more than it is mine – how is it that he has come to have such an intimate knowledge of its geography? I don't think he has. Yes, there is marshland between the Viking camp and Caistley, but 'impassable?' That I doubt.

Eirik runs the fingers he's using to guide my hand lightly up my forearm, sending a shiver of desire through me.

"Why do you wish to leave?" He asks, and there is genuine bafflement in his voice. "You were a maid when we took you, so it's not a man or children that pull you away. You see that even the slaves here eat better than they did in their homes, don't you? You see that –"

"Yeah but they were always on the edge of starvation in their homes," I chide, because it's not like the Vikings are exactly feeding them generously.

"There you go again," Eirik whispers into my ear, kissing the lobe gently.

"What?" I ask, enjoying the feeling of being on his lap, so small against his bulk, so protected.

"You constantly speak as if you're not one of them, girl. And you're not, anyone can see it. But you won't tell me where you *are* from, and that's one thing I haven't figured out yet – why you won't tell me. It wouldn't matter if you were the Queen of the East Angles herself. You're ours now. You're *mine* now."

He's hard, I can feel it against my back. I feel it between my own legs, too, the answering wetness, my body having a conversation with his outside of the words coming out of our mouths.

"I could tell you," I whisper, turning to him as I slip my hand under his leathers and caress his entire stiff length with my fingertips. "But I'm not sure you'd be listening too well."

I watch his face, because I love to see the way his expression changes when he's aroused, and he watches me watching him.

"There's something else," he tells me, pulling my hands closer, tighter around him.

"What is it?" I ask, kissing his cheek, and then his chin. It feels so easy to do this for him, to please him, to give myself to him, after the day he's had. Knowing it's the one thing he needs more than any other makes me glow with a kind of pride at the fact that it's only me who can do this for him now, only my body that can satiate him.

"Come the thaw, girl, we'll be married. Hildy was cursing me just yesterday, for allowing the women to keep their hopes –"

Did he just say what I think he just said? And in the tone of voice one usually reserves for telling a person what restaurant you'll be meeting them at? I pull away. "Eirik. What did you just say?"

"Hildy says as long as it goes unannounced the women still hope, that it's making them turn away their own suitors until –"

"Before that," I reply. "About – about getting married?"

It is the Jarl's turn to gaze at me as if I am some alien creature. "Yes, come the thaw. Are you offended, Paige? Hildy asked some of the women from your village and they reported no feasting between the families, no real rituals before the wedding. I suppose if you wish me to bring my family to meet with yours –"

I laugh out loud, because what else can I do? Eirik asks me why I'm laughing.

"This just – this isn't how imagined it," I reply, half telling myself none of this matters anyway because I'll be gone come the thaw – no matter what Eirik says about impassable swampland – and half helplessly besotted, even as the proposal is nothing like what I had ever imagined. If I can even call it a proposal! "This isn't how it works in – I mean, where I'm from. We don't do it this way."

"Neither do we," Eirik chuckles. "In my country, I would come with my mother and father to the house of your mother and father, and many formalities would be observed, many discussions would take place, our parents would need to be assured that our marriage would be good, and prosperous. In the end it would be your father who gave permission, and if he gave it a date would be set then. The wedding itself would involve days of feasting between our families, an intertwining not just of ourselves but of our parents, our brothers and sisters, aunts and uncles. A wedding is a joining of families as much as it is of a man and a woman."

"And we can't have that," I say quietly, "because you took me from my family, and because you don't care what my father would say."

"So you don't wish it?" The Jarl asks, pulling away to look at me like I am even crazier than he thought.

I laugh again. "How can you not see this?" I ask, leaning against his chest and playing with the beads on the leather straps wrapped around one of his wrists. "How can you be so smart, Eirik, and not understand that just because I eat better now, and just because I have you to protect me, it doesn't erase what happened? It doesn't erase the fact that I haven't seen my father in months? That he most likely thinks I'm dead – and that this keeps me up at night, long after you have fallen asleep, thinking of how he must be suffering?"

The Jarl and I gaze at each other, each equally mystified by the other. Eventually, he speaks. "How can I not see it, girl? *How can I not see it?* You ask me this, when it is you who lacks vision? It's as if you're angry that you can't have everything just as you want it. Even a King doesn't get angry at such things, because even a King knows what you seem not to know – that this is life. You are here with me because I took you, yes. And I would be dead and rotting in the ground if your King had found a way to make it so. It's as if you're a child sometimes, with a child's ideas, crying because someone has taken her straw doll. But a child grows up and learns that life isn't having what you want all the time, that this is an impossible thing. How many times have I reminded you that you've never eaten better, you've never been as protected from harm – that you live a life with me that would be the envy of your own Queen?!"

Eirik's voice rises as he finishes, but he doesn't seem angry. He just seems vehement – and still genuinely confused. Just as I am.

"And how can you not see that I miss my father anyway?!" I reply with equal vigor. "How many times do *I* have to say it? Can you imagine how you would feel, if the King's men came and took you away from here, and fed you roasted pork every day, sent you the prettiest girls? You would miss your people, wouldn't you, even if the food was good and the girls beautiful? You would miss the North? You would think of your family worrying for you, and it would trouble you. You would miss *me*!"

"Of course I would," the Jarl replies at once. "But I wouldn't fight the way you've been fighting since the day I first laid eyes on you. I would understand that my life was changed, I would accept it. And believe me, your King would no more feed me roasted pork and send me pretty maids as he would welcome my warriors with a feast and hand over his lands to us with a smile."

"So that's it?" I ask. "I should just accept it? I should just accept that I have no say in any of this?"

"You have a say, girl," Eirik responds, and for the first time in our conversation I hear a hint of irritation. "If it's not your wish to be married then we won't be married. You would be very stupid to decide as much but I speak the truth – you won't be forced. It isn't our way to force women into marriages they don't want."

I've made it worse. He has come to me after Asgald's wounding to be comforted, to be held, and I have made it worse. I look up from my place near his chest and shush him gently when he goes to speak again. "I'm sorry," I whisper. "I believe the things I say to you, but it isn't the time. Your friend has been hurt, you worry for him, and I heap more worries onto your head."

Eirik looks down at me, his expression soft. "I can't be heated with you, Paige. If anyone else spoke to me the way you do..." he trails off and bends down to kiss my mouth. "But you – it seems nothing you can do will truly test me."

He's wrong about that, I think, but tonight will not be the night we find out. I turn to face him, still straddling his lap, and pull my tunic the rest of the way down. There is a level of complete comfort with the Jarl that I never even dreamed of reaching with another person. My self-consciousness about my body has gone, melted away like ice under a summer sun. When his eyes drink me in I tremble with nothing but anticipation. He bends down and takes one of my nipples into his mouth, running his tongue around the very tip of it until it stands up small and firm and shiny-wet in the firelight.

"You need me, girl."

He's not asking. He's not even telling, he's just stating the truth. I know it, and I know he knows it.

"Yes," I whisper, exhaling audibly as he repeats himself on my other nipple, pinching it gently between his fingers before he moves away. "Yes, Eirik."

"And you'll be mine. Come the thaw, you'll be my wife."

He wraps his muscular arms around me and flattens his hands against my back, pulling me in close as he draws my nipple into his mouth again, harder this time, and deeper. An arrow of lust flies down, directly to my sex, and I arch back, gasping with pleasure.

"Yes," I moan. "Yes, Eirik. Yes."

He stands, then, lifting me with him and placing me on the edge of the table, where he has just drawn the escape route he claims I will not be capable of following, and spreads my thighs with his hands. I tighten with anticipation, pushing my hands into his hair and crying out his name as he runs his tongue up under my clit and over it, over and over until my body is slick with sweat and my voice shaky with need.

"You're mine," he says, pausing just before he brings me to orgasm, as I squirm and beg and try desperately to pull his mouth back to me. He waits for another second and says it again, a confirmation: "You're mine."

And then he slips two fingers into my slippery, aching sex, drags his tongue over my clit again, and then one more time, and makes his words true, whether I want them to be or not.

I reach for him with weak, shaky arms a minute later, almost crying with the intensity of the orgasm he's just given me. He lets me catch my breath for a moment, but I know we're not finished, I know the Jarl needs me still.

I reach down and wrap one hand around him, smiling at the sound he makes as he thrusts himself up and further into my grip. His eyes find mine and he kisses my mouth, letting me taste his hunger.

"I wait all day for this," he says, his voice so deep it's barely more than a rumble. "When we sail, when we discuss plans in the longhouse. Even when we fight – I think about this. About you."

Eirik's hands are on my breasts, my body – everywhere – as he speaks. His breath is coming short now, I can feel the power inside him building. I look up into his eyes.

"So do I. I think about the way you are right now, that look on your face, the way your breath sounds. I thought you finished me just then but now, seeing you this way, I need you again."

The Jarl tilts my head back so he can kiss my neck, open-mouthed. "You need me again, girl? There's no gentleness in me tonight, you understand? I don't know if you can take –"

It's too much. He's trying to warn me, I know, but it's not having the intended effect. I get off his lap and we look at each other for a few seconds, saying nothing. I keep my eyes on his even as I turn away, until the very last second possible, and then I bend down over his table, offering myself up like a choice cut of venison on a platter.

"Voss," he whispers, and I feel his fingers between my lips, opening me up, readying me. I know I should be scared – the Jarl is so much bigger than me, and strong enough to snap a grown man's bones – but there is no resistance, no hesitation inside me.

"Eir —"

The word dissolves into a little high-pitched scream as he fills me, suddenly and completely, and makes no effort to slow himself, even from the first moment. I can't turn my head, either, because one of his hands is flat against the back of my neck, holding me down against the table, and the other is clasped to my hip, keeping me exactly where he needs me.

This isn't a conversation between bodies any longer, this is an invasion, the sweetest and most longed-for conquering. I submit, relaxing underneath him, breathing in time with his thrusts, because there is no other way to do it.

His movements are soon frenzied, his body tight as he covers me. It's too much, *he's* too much, and yet it's all I want in the world, to give what I can to please him. I know I'm going to come again, but I'm somehow not involved with it. He's going to decide how it happens, when it happens. I cry out a little when he sinks his fingers into the flesh of my hip so hard I know there will be bruises in the morning, but he's almost lost now, moaning my name, pinning me to the edge of the table.

And when those exquisite few seconds come, just before he finishes, and I hear his breath catch in his chest as I wait, my own body gives itself up at just the right moment. A wave of fiery bliss crashes over my head as the Jarl leans his head back and bellows his own pleasure into the smoky air, filling me, yanking me back against him until everything he needs to give has been given.

We stay where we are for a few moments, and the only sound is our breathing. Eventually, Eirik slips his hand around my waist and pulls me up to a standing position.

"Have I hurt you, girl? Let me see you, come here..."

He turns me around to face him and looks me up and down. I see his eyes widen and then look down myself. A belt of redness runs across my hips, deeper at the crest of the hipbones themselves.

"What —?" I ask, confused. "What's that?"

"It's from this," Eirik replies, running his hands along the edge of the table. "You'll be bruised come sun-up, my love. I'm sorry, girl – it was not my intention to leave marks –"

His expression is genuinely remorseful and something about him right now, in the difference between the aggressive hunger of a few minutes past and the current gentleness with which he runs his fingers over my reddened flesh, fills my heart.

"It doesn't matter," I say, stretching out on the furs and pulling Eirik down with me. "I wanted it the way it was. I wanted you that way." I look away, afraid to finish my thought.

"And?" He asks, reading me like a book. "What is it you keep back?"

I take my tunic, lying within arm's reach, and begin to play with the thin leather belt that hangs from a loop at the waist. I do not look at Eirik. "I liked that I – that I could make you feel those things," I say, very quietly. "That you were, you know, that you were like that because of me."

"Your cheeks are as rosy as the dawn, Paige. You wear the marks of passion on your body and yet you flush at words. What a strange little creature you are."

"I am not a 'strange little creature!' I protest, smiling.

"Oh yes you are. Beautiful, yes, and sometimes I fear smarter than myself – but undeniably strange. No matter, tomorrow I will tell my people that I intend to marry the strange little Angle – if that's even what you are."

I stretch out luxuriously and a phrase from the psychology class I took during my first year at college pops into my mind: cognitive dissonance. The stress or upset at holding two opposing ideas or thoughts in one's head. Eirik speaks of a wedding, and part of me melts away under his blue-eyed gaze, happy – eager – to be carried down the current of his river. Another part of me knows there will be no wedding. When I take his goodnight kiss and tell him yes,

yes, we will marry, it isn't a lie. Even as I know it cannot happen, it isn't a lie.

Chapter 19
9th Century

Five days later, I stand next to the Jarl as his wife-to-be in front of a great structure built of sticks and logs all carefully intertwined so as to hold themselves up. Around this structure stand the higher Vikings – Eirik's men, their wives if they have them, Hildy, the healers – all women – and, at its foot, Asgald's parents. Their faces are stern but I see them clutching at each other under the furs that blow up in the gusting wind. The sun has just set and darkness creeps across the sky from the east. The stars emerge over our heads and Asgald, the young warrior, lies dead atop the pyre.

There are many long pauses in the ceremony, many times we find ourselves facing silently into the biting winter winds. No one turns away. I do not understand the words being sung, or all the meanings of the gestures being given, but it could not be more obvious that respect is being paid.

Finally, Eirik himself steps forward, approaching the young man's parents and kissing them gravely on their foreheads. They kneel before him, each kissing the back of his hand and then standing again. Still, the only sound is the howling wind.

"He was green!" Eirik suddenly bellows, turning to face his people. "He was green but he was not weak! His was the strength of the young birch, flexible still, yes, but speaking of the real hardness of the full-grown man to come. Perhaps I should be glad of his death, for he surely would have challenged me, in time..."

The Jarl's voice rises over the weather as he speaks of Asgald's life, of his childhood in their homeland and his skill as a warrior. I do not know how long his speech is, because most of my body is numb with the cold, just as most of my mind is too caught up in the spectacle unfolding in front of me to be thinking of anything else.

"We light the fire now," Eirik shouts, holding a wooden torch wrapped with linen and soaked in oil over his head, "to bid the valkyries come and take his soul to the Great Hall! We do this even as all of us here know they are here already, howling with the wind, demanding the young warrior for their procession!"

I watch, awed, as the Jarl, clad in his finest furs and bare-chested even in this chill, steps to the side and dips the torch into a small fire to light it. He hands it to Asgald's mother, who steps stiffly forward and pauses for just a moment before holding it to the base of the pyre. The kindling catches almost at once and the fire begins to spread. Next, the young man's father does the same, holding the fire to the opposite end of the pyre. When he steps away he grabs for his wife desperately and I see that they will fall if either one of them loses their grip on the other.

Everybody stares, transfixed, at the funeral pyre. Tears fall and freeze immediately on windblown cheeks. The Jarl takes the torch and steps towards the center of the structure, holding it again to the base. The fire is everywhere now, licking and crawling its way upwards, reaching for the stars.

"A son!" Eirik shouts, holding the torch aloft again. "A brother! A warrior! Asgald! He flies away from us now, to Valhalla!"

The last two words – 'to Valhalla' are screamed, and I swear I hear Eirik's voice crack on the final syllable. I can't be sure, though, because the words are echoed now, by the assembled crowds.

"To Valhalla!"

And just as their voices mingle with their Jarl's, a shower of sparks explodes from the fire, bright orange against the black of the night, and my breath is stolen from my chest.

I am not religious. I was not raised religious. I do not believe in God, or Gods, or any of it. But something happens there, as I stand beside the pyre – a sense of leaving, a loss, as real as the quick turn of one's head when somebody leaves the room in a hurry. *You're imagining things, Paige. You've been with these people too long, you're starting to adopt their superstitions.*

Maybe so. Maybe I am starting to adopt their superstitions. But my heart is pounding and I am looking around, wide-eyed, at the solemn Vikings, barely able to hold back my astonishment. *Did you hear that?!* I want to ask, even though I'm not sure it made a sound. *Did you see that?!* Even though I am not sure I saw anything beyond sparks.

A short time later, after the fire has reached its peak and begun the work of turning the young warrior's earthly remains into ashes, the Jarl leads us back to the longhouse, where a feast awaits. The parents stay behind, and I grab at Eirik's hand, trying to tell him they're not with us. He knows what it is I'm going to say.

"They will stay until the end, girl. Alone. It's as it is."

'It's as it is.' The Vikings say it all the time. I reach for Eirik, wanting the comfort of his arm around me, but he holds me away and speaks sternly.

"It's not the time, Paige."

I fall back, a little hurt, mostly overwhelmed by what I've just witnessed. The people are silent as we make our way back. In the longhouse, they begin to talk somberly, a low murmur that never picks up. I am not seated with the Jarl for this feast, but at the opposite end of the table, with the women and the old men and boys. Casks of ale are brought in, along with huge platters of cold ham, bowls of fresh butter and dark, heavy loaves of bread. A simpler feast than usual, but just as generous. My stomach rumbles at the smell of the food, but there is another speech to be made – this time, by Veigar.

By the time he finishes I'm almost salivating. I look to the women seated around me, waiting for the signal. Hildy soon grabs one of the loaves, tearing off what looks to be a good half of it and I reach for my cup of ale, prepared to fill my belly.

Something odd happens, though, when the scent of the ale reaches my nose just before I take a sip. There's something sweet in it – sickly sweet, almost like rot. I slam the cup back down on the table and a couple of the women seated by my side look at me questioningly. So does Hildy. She laughs when she sees me try again, only to place the cup back on the table with even more force.

"It's the light ale tonight, girl. The dark is only for the higher people, not for communal feasts. Have you gotten so used to fine things already?"

"I, uh –" I start, meaning to deny Hildy's claim – I hadn't even noticed the ale was any different to what I drink with the Jarl in the roundhouse – but my words stick in my throat. My stomach suddenly feels very full. I look up, confused, and Hildy stares right back. I think she realizes what's about to happen before I do, because she's up on her feet before I've even managed to clap my hand over my mouth, hauling me towards the door.

We make it outside, thankfully, before I vomit over the frozen ground. I look up afterwards, sweaty and bemused, and then do it again.

"What the fuck," I mutter, angry at making a spectacle of myself like this, especially in front of Hildy, and also because I'm genuinely surprised. The feeling of sickness had been so fast, so out of the blue.

"What's that you say, girl?"

"Nothing," I reply, running my hands down over my thick woolen tunic, checking for splash-back. Hildy is standing there with her arms crossed over her bosom, smirking at me. Emboldened now, because my engagement to the Jarl is known throughout the camp, I make a face at her.

"Why are you looking at me like that?" I demand. "It's not like I could help it. You didn't even have to come out here with me, Hildy, I don't know why this has to be about you. You always –"

"Shut up, girl," she replies easily, before reaching out and grabbing one of my breasts. I leap away, slapping at her hand.

"What are you doing?!" I shriek. "Get your hands off me! I'll let the Jarl know you –"

Hildy grabs me by the shoulders – I am once again reminded of how surprisingly strong she is – and gets in my face before I can finish threatening her. "How the Jarl saw fit to take you as a wife I will never know," she says, rolling her eyes. "Perhaps he enjoys the fact that with you never shutting your mouth, he isn't called on to say much when he retreats to his roundhouse?"

I struggle and think about kicking at her shins, but Hildy holds me steady and fear of what she could do to me before Eirik hears my screams holds me back.

"Gudry and Anja say you missed your last moonblood, girl – is it true?"

"What?" I ask, indignant, as she finally lets go of me. "Moonblood?"

Oh, *moonblood*. My period. Wait a minute.

"My what?" I cry. "My moonblood? Why are Gudry and Anja – why the hell are you creepers talking about my moonblood, Hildy?!"

Hildy doesn't know what a creeper is, so she doesn't get angry at being called one. Instead I am treated to another eye roll, this one dripping with condescension. "You're to marry the Jarl, girl, are you not? Has he come to his senses and changed his mind? No, I think not. He announced it this week but the women have known for awhile now, the way it is with these things. It's Gudry and Anja's job to care for you, you understand that – right?"

I nod, prickling with annoyance at Hildy's tone of voice, the way she speaks to people like they are small children. "Yes," I reply shortly. "I understand that."

"Good. So you understand why we discuss your moonblood then. Do you? I see from that cow-like expression on your face that you do not. They watch your moon cycles for signs, girl. And your breasts – look at the way the tunic pulls tight over them, even now. Your belly won't be flat for long!"

'Cow-like?' Jesus. I stumble backwards a little and catch myself on the edge of the grain-house we stand beside. I don't know why I'm so affected by an insult, it's not like Hildy ever sees fit to hold back. Cow-like. Damn. But she said something else, too. I look at her in the darkness, and the whites of her eyes glow under the moon as it peeps out from behind a cloud. "What?" I say, breathless. "What did you call me? What did you, uh, say?"

She smiles then, and shrugs. "You're a trial, girl, but sweet in your way. Perhaps I can see some of what he sees in you. But you stumble against the grain-house like this comes as a big surprise! Have you not been in his bed for many a night now? Maybe I soften to you because I love our Jarl, and because I know what happiness this news will bring him – especially now, after we have sent Asgald to the Great Hall and the men hang their heads low."

Happiness? What is Hildy talking about? Why is my heart pounding out of my chest? A surprise? My belly. My belly won't be flat for long. *My belly won't be flat for long?*

My hands find their way to my midsection and my jaw falls open in disbelief. The sound of Hildy's laughter rings through the night. "It's your first, girl. I understand. Even as we know how a baby finds its way into our bellies, the first is always a shock. Gudry and Anja must be told of this – I'll fetch them now."

"No," I whisper, taking Hildy by the sleeve of her tunic. "No. Wait. Wait!"

She turns back to me, just for a second, and caresses the flat expanse of my belly. "Smile, girl. Motherhood will be good for you."

And then she's marching officiously off, already calling for Gudry and Anja, and I'm half-collapsed against the side of the grain-house as the fog of my short, panicked breaths dissipates into the night.

Motherhood.

Motherhood?!

But Hildy's right, even as it all seems too far-fetched to consider. What did I think was going to happen? I knew it was a possibility. I look up at the moon as the clouds race across its face, and I have to admit to myself that I more than knew it was a possibility – I actively hoped for it, in that bone-deep part of my soul that has nothing to do with reason or rational thought. Did I? Yes, I did. And now my shock might have more to do with not daring to believe it rather than any real confusion about how it happened.

I don't know how long I stay there. Long enough to start shivering. Gudry and Anja find me there, my teeth chattering against each other, and erupt with tender concern, tearing their own thin leather wraps from around their shoulders and throwing them over me.

"Why are you out here?" Anja demands as they lead me to the roundhouse where I am routinely tended to. "You're frozen! Paige! It's time for you to be careful with yourself now, do you understand?"

I'm so cold, when they get me undressed, that just dipping a toe into the hot bathwater causes a pins-and-needles-like explosion in my foot and I jump back, yelling.

"OW!"

"Forgive me," Anja whispers softly. "You need to warm up first."

They dip their fingers into a bowl of oil and begin to rub me down, pressing their lips together when I catch their eyes, to hide their shy smiles.

"It's alright to say something," I tell them. "You can talk about it. I just – I hope Hildy hasn't made a mistake. How does she know? How *can* she know?" I look down. "Look, my belly is flat."

I watch as Anja and Gudry give each other a look. "Your breasts, lady," Anja says, running one finger over a nipple. I am used to being touched by these girls now, so much so that I don't even flinch away when they do it. It's the same as going for a leg waxing – a grooming ritual. "Look here, do you see? The flesh is darker."

My nipples do look darker. Or do they? Are my eyes playing tricks on me in the dim light from the fire?

"You'll be a mother by the next harvest," Gudry says, looking to Anja for agreement. Anja nods.

"Yes, around harvest time. And a wife, too."

My two friends are happy for me, even as they respectfully avert their eyes more than they used to, now that it's known throughout the camp that I am to marry the Jarl.

"Hildy will be telling the Jarl now," Gudry says, taking my hand and helping me into the bath now that I have warmed up enough to stand the hot water. I freeze.

"What?!" I cry, dismayed. "But I should be the one to tell him! Help me get dressed, I'll go and find the Jarl myself."

But Anja puts a hand on my wrist. "Lady, he'll know already. It's as it is, this is how we do it. Come, let us bathe you before you go to see the Jarl."

"Everyone?" I ask. "Even the servants? Does Hildy tell every man when his woman is pregnant before she can?"

Gudry giggles, the way she always does when she thinks something I've said is especially absurd. "No, lady! Only the highers, and the Jarl. Any baby is welcome, of course, but the Jarl's baby – the Jarl's first baby – that's special. There are customs to attend to. After you feel your womb quicken the women will take you into the woods for a moon ceremony and you will ask Freja for a good and quick birth, and a healthy child."

Before I leave the bathing roundhouse, Anja hands me a small cloth sack of what looks like dried herbs. "Put a pinch in your cup, and then fill it with boiling water if the sickness comes back."

And then the two of them, and Hildy, escort me to the Jarl's roundhouse. There's a feeling of formality, of gravity in the air. I'm not sure if it's the funeral for the lost warrior Asgald or the news of my pregnancy or some combination of the two. Perhaps it's all in my own head. Even as I am not as sure as the others seem to be that I really am pregnant, the possibility that I am isn't exactly lighthearted news. I know the statistics on birth before modern medicine. I know pregnancy in this place is a risk to my very life – and to my child's, if there is indeed a child in my belly.

When I see the expression on Eirik's face, a great sadness wells up in my heart. He's happy. As soon as the women leave us alone he's on his feet, cradling my head against his chest and then pulling me far enough away so that he can look in my eyes.

"Is it true?" He asks.

"How do I know?" I reply. "I have no idea! I can't take a pregnancy tes– I mean, I know as much as you do."

"But you have the mother's sickness. Hildy said –"

"The mother's sickness?" I ask, and it dawns on me it's just the Viking term for morning sickness. I know what that is. "Oh – yes, well, I did get sick. But I've been sick before, and it was never a baby."

"But do you feel any different?" The Jarl asks, looking me up and down, searching for the difference he asks about.

His eyes are full of hope – he desperately wants the news to be true – and it makes my heart ache. "I don't know," I tell him softly, caressing his cheek. "I can't tell yet."

He's gentler when he makes love to me before we go to sleep. As we lie in the weak orange light from the embers in the fire-pit, both on the verge of sleep, he runs his fingers over the string of bruises running between my hipbones.

"I didn't mean to hurt you, my love," he murmurs. "I shouldn't have been so passionate. I should have been more careful with you."

I roll over to face him and nestle into his chest, shushing him with a kiss. Minutes later, and just as I'm about to drift off, he places his hand on my stomach and sighs deeply before closing his eyes.

Chapter 20
9th Century

The winter months pass slowly. I spend my days observing – who goes where, who speaks to who, who outranks who – because there's not much else to do. Due to my pregnancy, I'm being allowed to do even less than I was before the news got out. Gudry and Anja accompany me almost everywhere, constantly trying to get me to eat and admonishing me if I so much as dare to pick up a piece of firewood. Hildy keeps a beady eye on me, too, and if I'm seen to be doing anything she considers out of the ordinary, I know I can count on Eirik bringing it up later that night, after she's tattled to him. Thankfully, he's usually got a smile on his face when he does.

The taking of villages continues, but Eirik doesn't lose any more men – the death of Asgald weighs heavy on him and he's more careful, less confident that the peasants are entirely without the will or the means to defend themselves. My pregnancy is obvious now, undeniable even to myself as my belly swells with Eirik's child.

It's sometime in what might be April, perhaps May, just as the teasing warmth that's come and gone for the past few weeks feels as if it's beginning to settle more permanently over the camp and the gentle, rolling hills and woods surrounding it. It's daytime and I'm bored, having just spent the last two hours in the bathing roundhouse, letting Gudry and Anja dangle various charms and objects over my midsection, trying to divine the sex of the baby. The results of their experiments have been inconclusive and I'm itching to get out for a walk, maybe even outside the camp. But when I get to the eastern point where the palisades stop, intending to slip out and gather wildflowers to put in Eirik's roundhouse, I hear the commotion of men coming from the direction of the beach.

"The warriors!" Gudry shrieks, her eyes lighting up. "They're back early! Let's go and meet them, shall we?"

I grin. Gudry is unmarried, but has recently begun a dalliance with one of the Jarl's men, and she's as effusive and over-excitable as a schoolgirl. Anja reaches out and grabs her wrist, though, before she can tear off down to the beach and throw her arms around her returning warrior.

"Get a hold of yourself, girl," she snaps at her companion and Gudry's head drops, even as she sneaks a look up at me and smiles, still. "Stop flinging yourself at him in this way – don't you know a man needs to feel a challenge? No, we'll wait right here for them, and you will be containing that ridiculous, pig-like squealing."

So we wait, just outside the camp, with a few other people who have happened, like us, to be there at the right time. Anja's words have had no effect, though, because the minute Gudry spots her boyfriend she's rushing towards him, throwing her arms around his neck and covering him with enthusiastic kisses. He lifts his head, grinning sheepishly under Gudry's loving assault.

Anja rolls her eyes. "She'll have a baby in her belly soon, and then she'll be even more useless than she is now!"

"Oh she's fine," I say, intending to defend Gudry to her constantly aggrieved companion, to say something about how she manages to do her work in the end, even if she pauses a lot to giggle and gossip. But before anything else can come out of my mouth my eyes lock onto the line of captives being led up the path from the beach by Veigar. I take a step forward, my heart suddenly in my throat at the site of that flaxen head, bent low.

"Is that –?" I start, before remembering that I am the Jarl's wife-to-be now, as well as the future mother of his child, and I no longer have to ask permission to do almost anything. I step forward into the chain of prisoners, grabbing the wrist of the woman who has caught my eye. Briefly I spot a bedraggled clump of children behind her but then she looks up and I'm pressing my hands to my face, sobbing.

"Willa," I weep, as her eyes widen in recognition and she clings to me. "Oh my God, Willa. I thought you were – I thought you –"

But we can't talk, because our voices are breaking. People around us are staring but we hold on to each other tightly. When Veigar approaches I lean in and whisper in Willa's ear.

"I'll come see you. Soon. Tonight! I can help. Where is –"

But Veigar jerks her away and smirks at me. "Get back, woman, these are the Jarl's prisoners, not yours."

"Stop!" I shout, before he can drag my friend off. "I want to talk to her!"

Veigar leans in, although I notice he doesn't lean as close as he could. "Have you gone deaf, idiot? These are not your prisoners, it's not for you to –"

"LET HER GO!" I bellow as he digs his fingers hard enough into Willa's flesh to make her yell.

Veigar responds by shoving Willa roughly aside and coming at me. I stand my ground, meeting his eyes, daring him to do something that's going to piss Eirik off. And fortunately I'm not made to pay for my recklessness because Eirik is suddenly between us, staring at Veigar like he thinks he's lost his mind. Instantly, the big lummox's body language changes and he goes from tough guy to naughty toddler.

"I'm trying to get the captives to their quarters, Jarl," he says, angrily gesturing at me. "And this mad-woman of yours is getting in the way, as usual. Tell her to let me do my job and I'll cause no more trouble to you."

Eirik, who has an expression on his face that tells me – and, I think, Veigar himself – that Veigar has just come very close to doing something he would have been made to pay for, turns to me, expertly defusing the situation. "Is it so, girl? Are you getting in Veigar's way? Why are you even out here? Anja – why is she –"

"She wanted to pick flowers, Jarl. For your table. We had no idea you would be returning early. Here, lady, take my arm, we'll go back to the bathing house and –"

"No," I reply, staying where I am.

Eirik turns to me sharply. "What craziness have you got inside you now, girl? What is this about?"

By now, I know there are two Eiriks. There's off-duty Eirik and on-duty Eirik. Neither one is a jerk, but when he's busy being a leader – rather than a husband- and father-to-be – he's focused entirely on that. I know he's got things to do now, after what looks to have been another successful raid, and I know he doesn't have time to listen to any lengthy explanations from me. So I keep it short.

"This is my friend," I say, gesturing at Willa and glaring angrily at Veigar. "Please ask this pig to keep his hands off her. I also wonder, my Jarl, if I might be allowed to take her with me, now, to the bathing roundhouse. She's dirty and –"

"They're all dirty, girl," Eirik shoots back, and I can hear the impatience in his voice. Veigar chuckles, just quietly enough so that Eirik doesn't hear it.

"Please," I whisper, lowering my head respectfully so no one witnessing the scene will have cause to think their Jarl is being henpecked by his crazy Angle.

Eirik looks at me, then at Veigar, and then at his man Gunnar, who has replaced Asgald in the inner circle. Then he looks back at me again and finally shrugs. "Fine. Take her. Anja – you and Gudry help this one to get cleaned up. I'll see *you* tonight, my love."

He looks right at me and emphasizes the 'you' and I can't quite tell if he's being good-humored or if I've genuinely annoyed him. Not that it matters right now. Right now, I need to get Willa away from the smirking – although happily somewhat humbled – thug standing over her.

"Come," I say, taking her hand and helping her up.

"Wait!" She cries. "My children!"

We all turn to the filthy little waifs standing silently behind their mother – how many of them are there? Three? Good Lord. Eirik speaks before I even have time to entreat him to let the kids come with us.

"No, girl. They'll be taken with the other children and fed, there's nothing to fret about. Take her, clean her up, Hildy will take care of all the little ones."

Eirik does not understand that telling me Hildy will be 'taking care' of the children engenders absolutely no confidence in me, but there's nothing else to do about it. I look at Willa. "Come. You heard him – they'll be fed."

She doesn't want to come with me, and she makes a weak attempt at stopping it as one of the other men usher the children along with the rest of the captives, into the camp.

"I'm to be his wife," I whisper, leaning in close to my exhausted-looking childhood friend. "He is trustworthy, don't worry, they'll be fed."

"And they'll be kept here?"

"Yes," I nod. "We'll take care of you and then we can see to them. Alright?"

I get the strong feeling that Willa wouldn't even be close to agreeing to such a separation if she didn't perfectly understand the situation – i.e. if she didn't understand that she has no say in any of it, anyway. She takes the arm I offer her. Veigar lunges at her one last time as we walk away, like the overgrown child he is, and Anja laughs out loud at him, which makes me laugh, too.

I can't be as free with my conversation as I would like, as we make our way to the bathing roundhouse, although from the look of Willa, whose eyes are falling closed even as she remains on her feet, I'm not sure it would be any use to ask questions.

When we arrive I instruct the two women to warm a bath for my friend and they do, although both of them wear irritated little grimaces on their faces throughout.

"You can leave, if you like," I tell them, annoyed. "I can do this myself."

"We can't leave," Anja replies coolly. "The Jarl asked us to stay with you."

"Fine then," I snap. "I don't know why you two have bugs up your butts about this – you have to bathe me every damn day!"

Anja narrows her eyes at me, aware I'm being short with her, but not aware, specifically, of what it means to have a 'bug' up her 'butt.'

It's amazing how much of a pain in the ass a person can be, even as they technically do their work. Both of them move slowly and resentfully, wrinkling their noses at Willa's stench and making faces like helping to clean her up is the worst task they have ever been asked to participate in.

"Oh my God!" I shout, about twenty minutes into something that should have taken five, at most. "Give me the cloth, I'll do it myself!"

Instead of waiting to be handed the cloth I just snatch it out of Anja's hand. Willa is in the tub of warm water, half-asleep, her head lolling back on the edge. She jerks awake again at the sound of my angry voice. Anja moves to snatch the washcloth back from me and I hold it away, eyeballing her.

"Go get Hildy if you like, but I'm going to do this myself. If you don't like it, take it up with her – or the Jarl!"

At that, Anja abruptly stands up, announces that she's going to do just that, and flounces out.

"Lady!" Gudry moans, as Anja's stomping footsteps fade. "Now Hildy is going to be angry! Now we're going to catch a whipping!"

"You're not going to catch anything," I tell her. "Just stop being such a pain and help me with this, will you? Don't worry, girl, I won't let Hildy touch you."

Gudry edges forward and we set to work on Willa's scraggly hair, so unkempt it's twisted itself into knots.

"This is going to take forever," Gudry sighs.

But it doesn't take forever. It only takes a couple of hours. I help Willa out of the bath, the water of which is now as dark as the earthen floor, and help her to lift a tunic over her head. She's even thinner than I remember, each rib painfully visible when she raises her arms, even from the back.

"What's happened to you?" I whisper, aching with guilt. My friends used to count on me for food, they used to be chubbier than the other kids in Caistley, and it was down to me. Now Willa is thin again, almost shrunken, and she looks far older than her 25 years.

She shrugs. "Nothing. Babies. I've had a little one on my breast now for longer than I can remember – they suck the life out of you. I see you're about to have the same."

I look down at my belly with Willa and she reaches out, running one bony hand over my almost shameful roundness.

"I'm sorry," I whisper. "I'm so sorry, Willa. I didn't mean to leave like–"

"WHAT'S ALL THIS?!"

Hildy barges in, hands on hips, and stares me down. I stand up, putting myself between her and Willa.

"The Jarl said I could take her to get cleaned up," I say calmly. "That's 'all this.' She's very tired now and we need to find a grass bed so she can sleep."

The Jarl and I sleep on furs, but almost everybody else in the camp sleeps on what to me look more like body pillows than beds – long sacks stuffed with dried grasses and only changed once a year, in the springtime. I wasn't sure if Willa even had a grass bed, back in Caistley.

Hildy raises one eyebrow at me. "Your Jarl said you could clean her up, girl, but make no mistake – she's a captive, and I'll be taking her with me, now."

She moves to step around me and I move in the same direction, blocking her from getting close to Willa.

"Girl!" She barks. "Get out of the way!"

I know she isn't going to hit me – she can't, not with my pregnant belly and my place at the Jarl's side – and that makes me braver than normal. Willa makes me braver, too. I've already let her and Eadgar down once, I'm not about to do it again.

Instead of hitting me, Hildy snatches a handful of my hair in one of her fat hands and I scream, enraged, and kick out at her. She dodges out of the way and I kick out again, lashing out with my fists now. We scrap like that for a good minute or more, until Hildy suddenly sees something I don't and immediately drops her arms to her sides. I take my chance and shove her, hard enough to almost send her flying, and then feel a firm, familiar grip on my upper arm.

"Voss! What is happening here?!"

It's Eirik and his eyes are flashing with real anger. I step away from Hildy quickly, and nobody looks him in the eye.

"What is this?" He demands again, jerking my arm a little. It's not painful, not enough to even leave a temporary mark, but suddenly – and for the first time with my Jarl – I see red. I yank my arm out of his grip and because he's not expecting it, it works. Then I jump away as he tries to grab me again.

"Stop it!" I shout at him as everyone – including Hildy – shrinks away, shocked. I don't shrink away, though. Nor do I avert my eyes. Those I turn up to him, meeting his gaze directly. "Why are you shouting at me?" I demand, not waiting for an answer. "I told you this woman is my friend – it's not a lie, Jarl! She is my friend, a true friend. Why do you stand there looking like you want to kill me? Would you not do the same, for a friend? If someone came to hurt Gunnar, or Veigar – or me? Wouldn't you try to stop them?"

I stop, panting with emotion, but seeing the looks on everyone's faces – Willa, Gudry, Hildy – just underlines that I'm breaking a very serious rule right now and that just makes me even angrier. "You want me to do this?!" I demand, gesturing at Hildy. "Is that what you want of a wife? You want me to cower away from you? What would you think of a man who did the same, Eirik? What would you think if somebody came to take Veigar and you were too scared to try to stop him? If you understand why that would be impossible for you, then you understand why it is impossible for me!"

My voice rises on the last sentence – I'm really yelling at him, my chest tight with rage.

We stare at each other, the Jarl and I, me poised defensively, more than ready to come to Willa's aid should anyone wish to try me. I know I won't win – not even against Hildy – but if he thinks that means I'm just going to let her be dragged off into –

"Fine, girl."

I frown. "What?"

Eirik shrugs and lets out a very long sigh. "Take her to the roundhouse, I'll have Hildy bring her some bread and ham."

Hildy lets out an indignant snort but one glance from the Jarl and she's quiet again.

"Do you mean it?" I ask, worried some kind of trick is being played on me, or some sort of test being run. "You're not –"

"Girl, I have forty new captives, more pigs and grain and ale and my men are tired and – if you can believe this – even grumpier than you. I don't have time for this." He nods at Hildy. "Take them to my roundhouse. Bring them bread and ham. And bring some of the tincture for this one, here."

"Shall I stay with them, Jarl, when —"

"No, there's no need, one of my men will be on guard."

I resist the urge to smirk directly at Hildy, who is visibly pissed off now that her plan to thwart me has itself been thwarted — and by the one person she can't just smack around. The mention of the tincture, a foul brew of various plants and herbs that is meant to calm a person who is nervous or hysterical, is horrifically patronizing — but just as the Jarl is going to deal with me later, I, too, am going to deal with him.

Chapter 21
9th Century

Watching Willa eat gives me a feeling of immense satisfaction, even as I'm nervous about what she might have to say about Eadgar when she finishes.

"Aren't you hungry?" She asks between mouthfuls of heavily buttered bread and gulps of ale.

I shake my head and she looks like she wants to question me further. Instead, she goes back to eating. And she keeps eating for quite awhile, until I'm worried I'm going to have to call for a very irritated Hildy and ask her to bring more food.

Thankfully, it doesn't get to that point. Willa looks up, swallowing the last bite of ham, and asks me when she can see her children.

"Soon," I say. "You have to understand, it isn't my decision. We're lucky I was even allowed to take you away from the rest of the captives. Just – when the Jarl returns, be quiet, try not to anger him."

Willa throws her head back, laughing. "You ask *me* not to anger him, Paige? Forgive me but I don't think I'm the one who needs to be told not to anger my highers!"

I'm about to agree, but instead I just put my arms around my friend and hold her tight. "I'm so glad to see you," I whisper into her ear. "You don't know how glad. Your children will be fine, you just let me speak to the Jarl about it."

Willa kisses my cheek. "Aye, Paige, we missed you too. Eadgar said you must have got married to a higher, maybe even one of the King's men. We always knew you weren't one of us, that one day there would be no more games in the woods."

"So," I begin, tense at the mention of his name, "Eadgar is – is he here? Did the Northmen take him, too?"

Willa shakes her head as we sit side-by-side on our chairs, our arms thrown around each other's shoulders in the same manner as when we were children. "No, he was away tending to the pigs with my husband. They'll have seen what happened, though. They'll know I – and the children – were taken."

Everyone in the past still seems to hold faith with a kind of fatalism that I don't see in modern people. But if there's one person who might be prone to the same kind of stubborn refusal to accept her circumstances, it might just be Willa. And before I even have time to ask her if she's thought about it she's speaking of escape.

"I'll slip away with the children, after darkness falls," she says, leaning in close to me so there's no chance the guard outside will overhear. "You'll help us, Paige."

She's not asking – she's telling. And I don't quite know how to respond.

"Wait," I say. "*Tonight?* I – I don't know if that's the best idea. The guards will be alert tonight, as they always are when we have fresh captives."

Willa looks at me sharply.

"What?" I ask.

"'We,'" she replies.

"We – what?"

"Are you one of them now then, Paige? You use that word 'we' like these are your people. What happened? Did they take you, too? How long ago? Do you intend to tell your Jarl of my plan?"

I feel my eyes widening with surprise, followed quickly by offense. "Yes they took me!" I reply shortly. "And no, of course I'm not one of them! I've been planning for months to make my own esc –"

I stop talking when I see Willa staring pointedly down at my belly.

"But you haven't escaped," she says plainly. "Here you are – and not without some power, I see. Power – and a Jarl's baby in your belly."

"But that doesn't mean –" I begin, but Willa shuts me up with a wave of her hand. The feeling from childhood, the respect for her as the older and more experienced sister I never had, remains.

"You don't have to explain yourself to me, Paige! Look at your fat cheeks – and the Jarl himself, as fierce and striking as a wolf. He loves you, I saw it in his eyes when he looked at you – and when he didn't beat you for speaking to him so sharply! You've no reason to leave, you don't need to explain it to me."

I shake my head, frustrated. "But I do! They took me, Willa. They took me just like they took you! Then the winter cold came and I've been waiting for the spring to come."

"When did they take you?"

"About 8 moons ago, around harvest-time. They took me from Caistley! I came back to see you and Eadgar, to see how you were, and the Northmen were there but you weren't. Did you see them and hide in the woods?"

Willa shakes her head and runs her finger through a smidgen of butter left on the plate before bringing it to her lips and licking it off. "No. The ealdorman moved a couple of families to another place for a fortnight, to gather the apples and berries for winter. Eadgar and I – and my husband and children – were in that group. When we came back to see the village burned we cleared the debris and built just enough dwellings for the small group we were then, close to the original site. A second Caistley.

"And your mother?" I ask.

"She died two summers ago, after a fever came through the village – nearly took my second child, too – he was just a babe at the time."

As ever, people in the past speak of death with a plainness of manner I cannot share. I reach out and put my hand on Willa's arm and tell her I'm sorry.

"We were sorry too, Paige, but she lived longer than expected for a woman of her place, and we're grateful for it."

Willa is flagging. I'm not surprised, but I'm also not finished talking to her. "Wait," I say, when she moves to curl up on the furs I have laid out for her next to the fire. "Wait. Before you sleep you need to know that tonight cannot be the night you escape. We need to make a plan, first."

"You and your plans," she smiles. "I forgot how much you like making plans. Fine, I'll wait, but you'd best not be pulling my leg – or telling the Jarl of my intentions – because I'm going. One way or the other, I'm taking my children and going home."

"I'm not pulling any legs," I reassure her, laying a woolen blanket over her as her eyes close. "Sleep now. We can talk when you wake."

I return to the table as Willa sleeps, preoccupied. She's not kidding about escaping – I know that. And the warm weather has come, the season I told myself I was waiting for before making my own attempt. I look down at my belly and think of the walk back to Caistley – one day, maybe, probably two or three. I can take food, and the nights are warmer now. Warmer, but still cool. I wonder if I can persuade my friend to wait for a few weeks, maybe another moon, until summer? Then even if we get wet we won't freeze to death come nightfall.

"Planning your escape?"

I jerk my head up and then immediately away so the Jarl doesn't see the guilt on my face.

"No," I reply, accepting a kiss on my forehead. "No. I was thinking of – I was thinking of you. I was wondering how angry you would be with me when you returned this evening."

Eirik sits down in a chair opposite me and gives me a wry smile.

"What's that look for?" I ask.

"It's the look I give girls who think they're smarter than me," he replies quietly as Willa stirs in her sleep but doesn't wake. "You and your questions, Paige. As if I don't understand that the lower people care for their friends and their families just as much as the higher people do. I don't think it is I who lacks understanding."

Eirik's massive shoulders are slumped forward slightly, he rests his forearms on the table. He's tired. I don't want to cause any more trouble for him, but he seems to be looking for a response. "So you understand," I say, "but you still get angry with me? You still seem to expect some people not to fight when you yourself would do so?"

The Jarl reaches out, takes my hand, and pulls me onto his lap. "It's not about what I expect, girl, it's about what's smart and what's not smart. If you hadn't been there this afternoon what do you think your sleepy friend here would have done? Do you think she would have screamed and yelled and carried on the way you did? Do you think she would have challenged Veigar like you did?"

I shake my head no.

"And why is that?"

"Because it probably would have gotten her killed," I reply. "And she knows if she dies her children will die, too."

"Yes," Eirik nods. "She knows, the way everyone except you seems to know – how to behave. She understands the hierarchy. You do not."

"No," I protest softly. "I do. I know it as well as anyone. It doesn't mean I accept it. It doesn't mean I think it's right."

Eirik nudges his chin down against my shoulder and puts one hand on my bump. "Is this why you plot to escape?" He asks, continuing before I can figure out how serious he is. "You have a man who loves you, girl. Not just a man – a Jarl. And you have a baby in your belly. You say to me that you understand how things are, but how can I believe that? Where will our baby be safer than here?"

I open my mouth but nothing comes out. Nothing can come out. What can I say? Nothing, the same as all the other times I've discussed this with Eirik. I can't tell him the truth, so I can't tell him anything. I can't say no, actually, our baby would be much safer being delivered in a hospital, because Eirik doesn't know what a hospital is, just like he doesn't know about grocery stores or college or just about everything else from my other life.

"And you never say it back," he continues, pulling my hair aside so he can kiss my shoulder. "You think I don't notice, that I don't see that furtive look in your eye."

He doesn't have to tell me what he's talking about. I know it, and he's right. I haven't told him I love him yet – I haven't said the words, anyway. I can't say them, and it's probably more because they're true than anything else. It's as if uttering them out loud will prove to be a kind of incantation, a spell keeping me physically in one place – the past. And I am not ready to cast such a spell over myself.

"Eirik –"

"Don't. You don't need to say anything. I already know, Paige. You keep thinking I don't know, but I do. I know you love me. I see it in you, I see the way you look at me when I come back to you in the evenings, I see the relief when you catch sight of me after I've been leading the men on raids. I don't need you to speak the words aloud. It's your own fear that keeps you from speaking. There's something else, I know that too. You won't tell me what it is, but I know it's the reason you look so guilty when I come home and tell you to stop plotting your escape. I –"

"I can't tell you," I whisper, the way I have so many times before.

"You say that, the way you always do, but it makes no sense. I put up with it because I love you, Paige. There is no other reason. But you must know it hurts me to think you keep things from me. It —"

"You wouldn't believe me," I cut him off again. "You would think me mad. You would make Hildy pour the tincture down my throat every day."

"Yes, and you say that, too. You might be surprised, girl."

We're talking in soft voices, because Willa is asleep. I'm beginning to tire, too, and the fire-warmed air in the roundhouse is only making it worse. A sudden recklessness, like that which overcame me earlier in the day, rushes through me again. I turn slightly, nestling into Eirik's comforting hugeness. "There's always enough to eat where I come from, you know. You keep telling me there's more here, but you're wrong. Where I come from, there is always enough food."

Eirik chuckles, and I assume he thinks I'm joking. "We found you in a field outside a peasant village, girl."

"You did," I reply, "but that's not where I'm from. If you thought it was, you'd stop asking me all the time."

"So you are a daughter of a King's man? Or the daughter of the King himself. I've thought as much for many moons now, girl. It's not just all those gleaming white teeth in your mouth – there's no explanation for those, other than luck – but it's when you act the way you did today. As if you are owed a deference no peasant or slave would ever dream of expecting. You act as a higher."

I shake my head. "I'm not the King's daughter, though. I'm not a higher. And my teeth are white because I go to the dentist every year."

"Dentist?" Eirik asks, and I almost laugh at the sound of a modern word coming out of his mouth. "A healer?"

"No, a dentist. Dentists are like healers, but they only care for people's teeth. And they're much better at it than a healer."

Our voices are light as we speak, affectionate. We're both dancing along the line between a playful, unserious conversation and a different, much more serious one. But what harm can it do? I am with the Jarl, and he isn't going to hurt me. I can give him some details, it's not as if he'll be able to guess.

"And where is this place, then?" He asks, and although his tone is exactly the same as mine, we both know this is precisely where this conversation has broken down every other time we've had it. "South of here, by the village where we found you? Is it outside the Kingdom of the East Angles? Maybe it's south, across the sea?"

"Yes," I say, very quietly. "It is across the sea. But not south. Southeast. Past the land, past the Kingdom of the East Angles, and Mercia."

"Eire?" Eirik asks. "The Green Isle? My people are there, too, you know. We raid all up and down the coast of that land as well as this one. Is that where you come from, girl? And if it is, how did you get here?"

I shake my head. "No, I don't come from Eire. You don't know the place where I come from. No one here does. You don't even know it exists."

"Ah, that's interesting," the Jarl whispers in my ear and I can tell from his voice that he thinks we've passed out of our real talk and into our joking-talk. "And how is it a maid of ten and ten years came from this land that nobody knows exists to the Kingdom of the East Angles? Did you build a ship yourself?"

"I don't know how to build a ship."

"I know it."

"I didn't come on a ship. I didn't walk. I came here in a different way to all of those ways. It would be very hard to explain, because the truth is I don't understand it myself. I know I came here because here I am, sitting here with you, but I couldn't tell you how, Jarl."

We sit silently in the warmth for a few minutes until Eirik pats my thigh, indicating for me to stand up. "I'll call Hildy to take your friend here back to her children. She –"

"Did they –"

"Yes, they ate. They're being cared for. Give her a blanket to take with her when she leaves."

***

Willa makes no attempt to escape that night, or that week. Eirik is smart, though, and he's made sure to have Gudry, Anja and Hildy be extra watchful with me. He's posted more guards close to the roundhouse – his own, and the one where Willa and her children sleep. He makes no attempt to stop me from bringing them food, though, or new clothes to replace the oldest boy's garments, which are so full of holes they can barely be described as clothing. By the end of the first week the kids are noticeably more energetic than they were when they arrived, and it makes me smile to see them running around their mother's legs, playing games with each other as she works.

And Willa does work, because Eirik has drawn the line there, telling me he wouldn't be able to explain it to his men or his people if he suddenly let a captive live as one of them. Willa and I talk when we can, snatching little two minute or five minute conversations before one of my attendants drags me away. She still plans to escape, and she says it'll be when the Vikings relax their current levels of security a little, which she knows they will.

"Eadgar knows," she whispers to me one day when I've managed to slip away from Gudry. "So does Aldred . We discussed the Northmen many times, because we knew they would come for us, sooner or later. They know I'll be trying to get back to them, they'll be waiting. When I get back we'll try to ask the ealdormen to move us further inland, away from these raids – they're moving people already, on the King's orders. It'll be soon, Paige. I'll have to take the children and leave here soon."

"Don't leave without me," I implore, although even as I'm begging her not to go without me I don't know if it's about me not wanting to miss my opportunity to escape or me not wanting to lose Willa again, and possibly forever this time. Neither of us needs to say it out loud, we both know if the Vikings catch her there will be little I can do to convince them to spare her life. "Please."

That night, as I lie in Eirik's arms, I wonder if it will be one of the last times I do so. He's right when he tells me I love him, and he's right that I'm too afraid to say it, but after all this time I still don't have a choice. It's not just my father now, or my friends at home – it's not just their suffering pulling me away, making it impossible for me to stay in the past. I'm going to have a baby soon, and my main concern is for whoever the little fluttering in my belly will turn out to be. Even if there was no one waiting for me back in 2017, which it must now be at home, I still couldn't find it within myself to risk my own life – and therefore my child's life – to stay in a past where death is so common and expected that people treat it the way they treat having breakfast, or stubbing their toes. Could I?

And as it turns out, the decision is confirmed for me four days later when Eirik returns from another raid with an already foul-smelling wound across his right shoulder and a fever even I can feel. I find him in the healer's roundhouse, taken there by his men, after Hildy comes to tell me, in grave tones, where he is.

He smiles when he sees me, trying to play it down. He's sitting up, strong as ever, his eyes are clear – but there's no mistaking the smell.

"That needs to be cleaned," I bark at the healer as soon as it hits me. "You need to boil water from the stream and clean the wound, you need to –"

"Girl," Eirik takes my wrist. "Let the healers do their work. They're preparing a poultice right now, to speed the closing of the injury."

I look up and sure enough, the healer and her two female assistants are busy preparing herbs of some sort, mashing them into a bowl of pig's fat and approaching the Jarl with a big gob of it a minute later. When one of them reaches out to apply it I slap her hand away.

"No!" I yell. "Don't put that on a dirty wound! Damnit, you have to clean it first, didn't you hear me? Someone needs to go get a bucket of water right now and –"

I stop talking when I see that no one is listening. They're just staring at me like I'm crazy. I shouldn't be surprised, the concept of hygiene – at least in terms of injuries and keeping them clean – doesn't exist with either the Vikings or the Angles.

"Fine," I tell them, grabbing a wooden bucket. "I'll go fetch the water myself. *Don't* put that on the wound – not yet."

I rush to the stream, fill the bucket, and return as fast as I can. It's to no avail, the pig-fat-and-herb substance has been applied and the healer's assistants are wrapping a definitely-not-sterile linen bandage around the Jarl's shoulder and upper arm area.

"You shouldn't have done that," I say to the healer. She looks up at me and then quickly at Eirik, probably waiting to see if he's going to shut me up. Eirik says nothing, but he doesn't look especially happy.

"If we don't treat the wound, lady," one of the assistants says to me, "the rot will spread, it will get into his blood. If that happens, it could be very bad. We don't want –"

"You're right!" I respond, just barely keeping my voice below shouting volume. "We don't want it to spread to his blood! Yes! Correct! That's why we have to clean it first – that's why we shouldn't be applying whatever the hell that concoction is to it, or wrapping it in dirty –"

"Girl."

It's Eirik. His grabs my upper arm, his grip firm. I stop talking and he politely asks the healers to leave, which they immediately do. Then he turns to me.

"I'll be glad when this child is born, Paige. I fear pregnancy is softening your mind."

I press my lips together, hard, to keep words I'll regret from coming out, but I can't withhold an eye-roll. The Jarl pulls my body towards him – not so hard as to hurt, or to cause me to stumble, but hard enough to let me know he's not joking around.

"Let the healers do their work," he continues, clearly exasperated. "Why do you insist on acting like you know how to do everyone's work better than they do? It's not right, Paige. It makes people think ill of you, and I don't want my people thinking ill of you. Why can't you just keep your mouth shut when it's called for? Don't you want my wound to heal quickly?"

"Of course I do!" I reply, my voice rising with helplessness. "That's why I told them to boil the water, and clean the wound before they dressed it! if they don't do that –"

"Enough!" Eirik yells, getting to his feet. "I'll send for Hildy and some tincture for you. You don't listen to me, girl, even when I really need you to. What am I to make of that?"

"But Eirik," I say, reaching out for his hand as he goes to leave. He dodges my touch and sets his jaw. "No, girl. Go back to the roundhouse. Have a nap. Have some tincture. Have something! Stay here until Hildy arrives – if I hear anything about you wandering off, I'm going to be very angry."

He leaves and I sit heavily down on the bare earthen floor of the healer's dwelling, my eyes prickling with tears of frustration. He's angry with me, because he thinks I'm thinking about myself, that I'm being a know-it-all, making his wound about me and not him. Even though the truth is the exact opposite.

I submit when Hildy arrives, hanging my head and silently allowing her to drag me back to Jarl's roundhouse. When he returns that night he doesn't say much, and I can see he's favoring the shoulder already, wincing when he uses the arm.

"Eirik," I say, very softly, "you should let me wash –"

"QUIET!" He bellows, turning to me with such speed I think he might strike me. He doesn't, though. He doesn't make love to me, either, before we go to sleep. I lie awake, worried about his shoulder as he tosses and turns all night.

Chapter 22
9th Century

Less than a day later and the Jarl's shoulder is visibly worse. The foul smell has grown and Eirik is sweaty with fever now, still speaking but not always making sense. The sense of panic around us is palpable. Veigar and Hildy, usually enemies, speak in low voices outside the roundhouse as I tend to him inside. When they come in, both of them look to be expecting a fight from me, but I give them none. I have other plans.

Before they leave, I grab Hildy by the arm – Veigar is an idiot, I know he won't listen. Hildy, for all her bluster and cruelty, is not an idiot.

"Wash the wound with boiled water," I hiss in her ear as she tries to pull away. "Dress it with nothing, wash it and expose it to the fresh air. He's going to die if you don't!"

"No one's going to die, girl," Hildy replies, freeing herself from my grip. But I can hear the fear in her voice – she's trying to convince herself more than she's trying to convince me.

As soon as they're gone, I take advantage of the fact that the whole camp is bound up in the Jarl's worsening injury – no one has been left behind to guard the roundhouse – or me. It's a warm night but I pull a woolen tunic over my head anyway, and slip my feet into the crude leather sandals Eirik had made for me. I grab a cloth sack, into which I shove the loaf of bread and the apples that have sat uneaten on the table for the entire day. Then I slip out into the night, to find Willa.

Thankfully there is no one at her roundhouse, either, and it's easy for me to whistle in the distinctive tone we developed as children, so she knows it's me. She emerges a couple of minutes later.

"What is it, Paige? Are we to leave now?"

"Yes," I reply, glancing from side to side, ready to duck into the roundhouse myself if any of the Vikings come near. "Get the children. The Jarl is unwell, everyone tends to him, this is our only chance."

There is no hesitation from Willa. She steps back into the roundhouse and comes back with two small children in her arms and another just behind her. I take the largest of the two little ones – all three are as silent as mice – and we make our way swiftly, carefully to the place where the palisade stops on the eastern edge of the camp, facing the sea. No one is there. We slip out, still not saying a thing, and follow the path to the beach, where we head south.

It's twenty or thirty minutes later before we feel safe enough to talk.

"I brought some bread," I tell Willa. "And apples. The children can eat."

"You must eat, too," Willa tells me, nodding down at my belly.

"This isn't how I planned it," I say as our pace naturally slows the further away we get. "I did not plan to escape with a big belly holding me back, or with three little ones to carry. Do you think we have even a chance?"

Willa turns back, eying me. "If you didn't think you had a chance, Paige, why did you leave? Even if the Jarl dies, they'll find you another husband. You're beautiful and strong, they know your babies will be as beautiful and strong as you."

"The Jarl isn't going to die!" I cry and Willa, never one to hold back, looks baffled.

"Then why are you leaving?"

"Because I need to get him something to save his life. Some med–" I cut myself off, because Willa doesn't know what medicine is. "Some, uh, plant. A plant. It grows in the woods outside Caistley. Yes, a healing plant. I need to find it and bring it back, to heal the Jarl."

"Wait," Willa says, stopping. "Let's take a short break, alright? Just until we catch our breath. And you will tell me what craziness this is you speak of. You plan to return? Is that it?"

We sit down in the tall grass that runs along the top of the coastline, each of us with a sleeping child in our aching arms. I don't like the fact that my arms are aching already – it's been less than an hour, how do we propose to keep going for many more hours without becoming too tired to continue? I push the question out of my mind. Willa is staring at me waiting for a response.

"Yes," I nod, looking out over the sea at the moonlight dancing over the waves. "He's going to die if I don't."

Willa watches me for a few seconds and then joins me in gazing out over the water before responding. "You love him. I thought as much. Is it a wise thing, Paige? To love one of the Northmen? Do you think, if your healing plant works, that he will live a long life? I suppose it doesn't matter, none of us are wise when it comes to love."

My mind is trying to get ahead of itself, I'm already picturing the pharmacy in River Forks, wondering how difficult it will be to break the glass with a rock in the dead of night, thinking maybe I should bring one of my father's tools to help. I'll need to get online, too, so I can find out what particular variety of antibiotic I need to steal. What if my bike has a flat tire? Can I walk to the pharmacy? What if there's an alarm? I won't have the energy to run from –

"Paige?"

"Huh?"

"We should keep going – it'll be too hot in the middle of the day, the children can sleep then. We should take advantage of the dark."

So that's what we do, and the walk isn't too arduous at this stage. It gets easier when the gray dawn begins to swallow the darkness and we can see where we're putting our feet. Willa is right, though – by the time the sun is high in the sky it's too hot to keep going, and our bellies are grumbling with hunger. We retreat into the woods and sit in the shade. Willa and I tear pieces off the loaf of bread for the children, and hand them apples. We drink from a stream, as we have been doing since we left the Viking camp, and then we all fall into a deep sleep.

Willa shakes me awake sometime later and I immediately see from the light that it's late afternoon. Beside us, the children sleep restlessly and I notice the oldest, a boy named Rowyn, has a bright pink sunburn across the tops of his shoulders. Willa wakes them as I take the rest of the bread and apples, and the various tunics we've shed in the heat, and stuff them into the linen sack I took from the Jarl's roundhouse. Thinking of the Jarl urges me on, even as I fear I am too late, that he was too sick when I left, that there isn't enough time for me to travel all the way back to Caistley and then all the way back to the camp – not to mention the trip to 2017 in between.

"He's strong," Willa says, scooping her youngest baby into her arms and seeing the expression on my face as we set out again. "He's the strongest man I ever saw in my life, Paige. I wouldn't have believed such men existed until I saw your Jarl. If anyone can fight off a fever, it's him."

Please be right. Please be right.

Soon, we come to a place where the land is marshy all the way out into the sea. I take a few steps into it, sinking up to my knees, and realize there's no way it's passable, even if we were without the little ones.

"The marshes go inland a far ways." Willa says. "Miles. Perhaps someone has built a bridge over it, out of wood? There is such a thing in the marshes north of Caistley – or so the people say."

I look to the west, inland, and then east, out to sea, shielding my eyes against the setting sun with one hand. "Is this the marsh north of Caistley?" I ask. It's *a* marsh north of Caistley, I know that, but I don't know if it's the same one Willa speaks of.

"I don't know," Willa replies. "I've never been so far north – until your Jarl and his men took me."

"We're going to have to swim," I announce. And even as I announce it I am fully aware of Willa's feelings about swimming. Not only does she not swim, she actively fears the water – be it the sea or the deep stream that ran through the woods near Caistley. Both she and her brother seemed to associate the water with disease, bad fortune, death. I could never persuade them to do so much as stand in it up to their knees, and neither of them ever made an attempt to hide the fact that they considered me completely insane for swimming in it – even in the harmless, slow-moving sections of it that passed through the woods.

Willa shakes her head immediately, chuckling with humorless disbelief. "No. No, Paige. I'll not have the children anywhere near the water."

"Where will you have them, then?" I ask. "Back at the Viking camp, without their father? Without their uncle? Because that's where they'll be if we don't get around this marsh. The Vikings won't just let me go, you know. I'm carrying their Jarl's baby – and you're an escaped captive. They'll be coming after us, and some of them are likely to be on horseback.

"We're not going into the sea!" Willa shouts, distraught at what I've just said, because she knows it's true. "We'll go inland, we'll walk along the borders of the marsh. We'll find a wooden walkway or we'll just go all the way around."

"But so will the Vikings, if they choose to come after us!" I exclaim, grabbing her by the shoulders and giving her a little shake. "They'll be expecting us to do that – they know the Angles fear the water, and they don't know I don't. You don't even have to swim – we can use pieces of wood, we can use these dry logs from the woods to float, we can find some big enough for you to hold yourself and the children with, to keep your heads above the water!"

Twenty minutes later, I am swimming out into a calm evening sea, gasping at the cold of the water and dragging a large, floating log behind me, onto which cling Willa and her three children, all nestled between her arms and bawling with fear. Willa is silent, but I see from the pallor of her skin that she, too, is terrified, and that she is only holding it together enough to contain her own screams so her kids don't have to hear them.

Their shrieks get louder, too, as I drag them further out, but I have to do that because the sand underneath my feet remains marshy and eager to suck my legs down into it for quite a distance. Once we are at about chest depth, I can swim freely.

It takes a long time. I knew it was going to. I knew there was no choice. But there are a couple of times during the swim that I wonder if I am going to have the strength to complete it. I can't go back to the land, because the land isn't solid, we'll drown there as sure as we'll drown out in the sea. I ask Willa to help, showing her with a little demonstration how to lift her legs up behind her, near the surface, and kick. She learns quickly, and that makes my job easier.

Soon, though, I am experiencing a kind of fatigue I have never felt before. It's the kind of tiredness you just know cannot be overcome by willpower or believing in yourself or any of that motivational talk. I am simply running out of gas, like a car – and when I do I'll be as much use as a car with an empty tank on the side of the road. I turn back towards the land as the sun slips below the horizon, and pray to the universe that when we reach it, it will be solid.

"Are we past the marsh?" Willa asks, her voice a whisper.

"Yes," I reply, because I have to believe that's the truth.

The children are silent as we close in on the dark shore, their teeth chattering now as their mother whimpers and frets and as I tentatively move to set my feet down beneath me and discover if my friend and I and her babies are going to drown in this cold sea, or if we might still have a chance.

I cry out, a raw sob of relief that rings through the night, when I feel pebbles under my feet. Willa lifts her drooping head. "Are we past it, Paige? Have we found the solid ground again?"

But I am too tired to respond. I just keep pulling the log, and the people attached to it, until the water is thigh-deep and Willa feels the ground for herself. She stands up and gathers the kids in her arms and we make our way through the final feet of water to the beach, saying nothing until we step onto it. And then we collapse, all five of us, into a heap of cold, wet, exhausted humanity. No one has the strength to weep or speak so we just lie there, unmoving, panting, for a half an hour – maybe longer. We're soaked, and all of our clothing is soaked.

"We need to get higher," I say finally. "We need to get to the grass or the dry sand at least – we need to dry off."

So Willa and I drag ourselves – and the children – up to the grass at the top of the pebble beach, and then we fall asleep.

I wake first, and it is still dark. The youngest of Willa's babies, a girl, sleeps with her body curled neatly around my bump. So as not to wake her, I don't move. We ate the rest of the bread before the swim, knowing it would be ruined by the water, and we only have three apples left. We need to find Caistley soon. As much as I want to let them sleep, we have to keep moving. I shake Willa gently.

By what feels like mid-morning, we are seriously flagging. My whole body aches with fatigue, muscle-strain and hunger. We're stopping every five or ten minutes now to rest, barely able to carry the smaller children. During one of these frequent rests, Willa looks up at me as she feeds a chunk of apple to Eadgar, her second-born son.

"I won't make it too much farther, Paige. Even you look weak, and I've never seen you look weak before. Promise me if I die that you'll keep going with the children. Eadgar and Aldred will be waiting, they'll be looking for me – for us."

"No one's going to die," I say, but both of us know, as we look grimly into each other's eyes, that it's just as likely to be a lie as it is the truth. "If you get too tired I'll go on, I'll find Eadgar and come back for you. But no one's going to die."

We keep going, trudging along, too tired to do anything but put one shaky foot in front of another. It's late afternoon, the sun just beginning to drop towards the horizon, when Rowyn stumbles to his knees and doesn't get up.

"Up!" Willa commands, and even as she tries to hide her fear from her babies I hear it there, the shaking in her voice. "Up, boy! We'll see your father soon – don't you want to see your father?"

But Rowyn does not get up. He doesn't raise his head. Something is wrong, and Willa and I both know it. My heart begins to pound as she kneels beside her son and lays him on his back. I see that he's barely conscious, his eyelids fluttering.

"Is he tired?" I ask, my breath coming short and quick. "Is that it? Does he need to sleep? He can sleep now, Willa. We can take a break now. Does he want some more apple?"

Rowyn is 6 now, the oldest of Willa's children, and he has been walking as much as his mother and I have on this journey, because neither of us has the strength to carry him.

I watch as Willa lifts him to his feet and lets go, her face contorted with fear. The boy's knees buckle and he lurches to the side like a drunk before falling over again and curling up into a fetal position. Willa screams.

"Is he dying, Paige? Is that it? What can I do? He's my first baby. My first! I can't – I can't –"

I lean over the child, terrified, but am soon close enough to hear his breath. I look up at Willa, who has her hands pressed tightly to her mouth as she tries to contain herself. "He's breathing," I whisper. "He's alive. We have to let him rest. Stay here with them, I'll go and find a stream."

I stumble off into the woods that lie just to our right, and wait until I'm far enough away so I won't be heard to crumple to the ground, sobbing. I look up at the sunlight as it peeks through the leaves, an image I have seen so many times before, and think of how happy I was in woods like this as a child. Now I'm no longer a child, and there is no happiness at all. Willa's son is not dead, but he will be soon and I don't need a medical degree to see it. We have less than a single apple left.

An image of Eirik's face enters my mind and, at the same time, I feel the fluttering sensation that is the growing child in my belly – *his* child. I have to keep going. There's no other choice. I force myself to my feet and stumble on, pausing every now and again to listen for the sound of water. And then, suddenly, I hear something. Not water. Voices. I'm on the ground before there's even time to think, trying to figure out which direction they're coming from. They're close. Too close. I move to scramble deeper into the undergrowth but then I hear them right there, feet away.

"Who is this trying to snuffle for acorns like a pig?" A male voice asks and I give up, knowing I don't have the strength to run or fight. I take a deep breath, put a submissive smile on my face, and turn around.

A man, clearly a peasant, carrying no weapons. He doesn't look threatening. Behind him, another man whose face I can't quite make out until he steps forward, into the sunlight, and I gasp.

"Eadgar!"

My childhood friend wears a dark, scraggly beard now, and something about his face his different, rougher. But it's him. He steps forward, narrowing his eyes.

"Paige?" He asks, stunned. "It can't be – am I seeing things? Is it you?"

He reaches out and pulls me to my feet and we fall into each other's arms.

"I thought I was never going to see you again," he says when we pull away to look at each other, still disbelieving. "We thought you married one of the King's men, but," he looks me up and down, taking in the state of me, "you don't look like you – Paige, what are you doing out here in the woods? And with a baby in your belly – where is your hus –"

"Come," I say, grabbing Eadgar's hand and gesturing to the other man, who I assume is Willa's husband. "I am with Willa and the children – they're resting right now but the oldest isn't well. I'll take you to them."

At the mention of their sister and wife, both men race on ahead of me as I go back to her, and then Eadgar and I stand back, watching, as the family is reunited. The children use the last of their strength to reach for their father and he scoops them up, all 3 of them, and holds them tightly.

"They need food," I say. "And water – that's what I was looking for when you found me. We've been walking for close to three days with only bread and apples. Rowyn is the weakest."

Willa and I, exhausted, sit back and watch as the children's father and uncle tend to them, pressing pieces of the bread to their mouths, giving them sips of water from their waterskins. I wait for a few minutes, until Rowyn manages to sit up on his own, and then I turn to Eadgar and speak quietly.

"Are we close to Caistley? I need to get back there very –"

"It's gone, Paige. Burned down by the Northmen – we've set up a smaller settlement close to it, though. it's just a little further –"

"I know," I whisper. "I just – I need to get back to Caistley anyway – the old Caistley. Is it close?"

Eadgar looks at me, confused by the urgency in my tone. "It's just down the coast," he says, pointing south, past a stretch of rocky shoreline to a beach that, now I see it properly, does look familiar. I get to my feet and Eadgar grabs my wrist.

"Wait! Paige we've only just found each other again – do you need to leave so soon? We need to hear what's happened in your life since we –"

Willa cuts in. "Let her go, Eadgar. She's got business with her own family, a husband with the fever and a healing plant in the woods outside the village. But before you go, Paige, we should arrange a meeting spot. I know you need to get back to your husband but just – just in case. In case something happens."

As Willa speaks it dawns on me, as it should have already, that this might be the last time I ever see my friends. Because I'm not going to Caistley for a plant, I'm going to get back to 2017, and when I return – *if* I return – I'll need to go straight north again, there'll be no time for anything else.

"The clearing in the woods," I say, my voice shaking. "Where we used to make crowns and bracelets of the yellow flowers. That will be the place."

Eadgar helps Willa to her feet and we wrap our arms around each other.

"The clearing," Eadgar says. "It's close to our new settlement, I'll check it every day Paige. Every day between the work in the fields and the evening meal. I promise."

And then it's goodbye. We all know it. Willa gives me her husband's name very quickly, and tells me he already knows mine, as she and Eadgar always talk about their old friend from the estate.

I've never been as close to being torn in two as I am at the moment of leaving, of actually turning my back to them and walking away. And even as I know every step brings me closer to the moment when I will no longer hear their voices, and probably never hear them again, Eirik pulls me forward, on towards Caistley in spite of my aching body and my empty stomach.

I cry almost the whole way there, walking along the coast alone with the warm breeze playing through my hair. When I get to the path that leads to Caistley – still in use but more overgrown than I remember it, I turn around and look back. All I see is coastline, trees, darks rocks, sea, sky. I do not see my friends anymore. I jog, then, down the path, out into the clearing where the remains of the village stand, and then into the woods.

The sun has just set when I get to the place I'm aiming for – the tree. I have only the loosest of plans – go home, get online, break into the pharmacy in River Forks, steal antibiotics, return to past, go north. I know, even as I kneel beside the great gnarled roots, that I should give it more thought. But there's no time. I take a deep breath and hold it, and then I lay my palms flat against the base of the tree's trunk.

Chapter 23
21st Century

The light hits me first, and my response is to cower for a second, maybe two, before I realize it's nothing. It's just the light of the town reflected against the cloudy sky, the light from the streetlights that run the length of the road just a short distance away. It looks so strange though, after so many months away – so other-worldly. There's noise, too. A single car speeding, roaring down the road. Only it's not speeding – or roaring. It's just driving. I blink as my eyes barely manage to follow it. My brain has forgotten how fast things move in 2017.

The house. You have to get into the house. You have to go online.

I make my way out of the trees and up across the backyard, eying the house. Once again that sensation of deep familiarity melds with another – equally strong – of deep strangeness. The house looks enormous, monumental even, despite it being a very ordinary dwelling, of the type almost everyone I know in River Forks grew up in.

There are no lights on. That's good. My father must be sleeping. I try the back door and it opens into the kitchen. The smell of home floods my nostrils – laundry detergent, dinner, and all of those unidentifiable things that make one house smell unlike any other – and I almost feel dizzy from the wave of memories that washes over me.

I step inside, bare feet on old linoleum, and close the door gently behind me. Then I make my way through the kitchen with ease, because just the light from outside is enough for me to be able to see exactly where I'm going, on my way to check that the door leading upstairs is closed. Halfway there my hip bumps against something and I cringe at the sound of a large stack of papers hitting the floor. I don't move for a full minute, waiting for the sound of my father stirring upstairs. None comes. I make it to the door – it's closed.

It's now or never. I go to the desk where my father keeps the ancient desktop computer and nudge the mouse. A second later the screen blinks to life and I lift my hand to my eyes, shielding them from the brightness. One-handed (because the screen is still too bright for me to look at directly), I type various search terms into Google and then write down the answers on one of the many pieces of paper stacked on the desk. Ten minutes later I have a list of medicines, only one of which I've ever heard of, and two of which I have underlined: Cephalexin and Amoxicillin.

Before leaving the house I do four main things. First, I raid the fridge, and wolf down the rest of a pasta casserole sitting on the top shelf. Next, I put as much food in the linen sack as I can fit, and as I think I can reasonably carry. Then I go into the laundry room and find a clean pair of my dad's sweatpants and a t-shirt, both of which I put on, and a pair of my own sneakers, sitting untouched for months beside the back door. If anyone sees me, I want to look at least semi-normal.

Lastly, just before leaving again, I grab another piece of paper off the pile sitting on the computer desk, intending to write my father a note. But the light from the computer screen is just about enough for me to see something I recognize on the paper, just before I flip it over to write the message. I hold it a little closer to the screen and then gasp audibly when I recognize what I'm looking at.

I'm looking at myself – a picture of me. Emma took it in the kitchen of our rented apartment towards the end of our freshman year. I'm smiling widely, saying something to Emma – I can't remember what. Someone has cropped out the background and the rest of my body and just used my face. Across the top of the piece of paper are 7 stark capital letters: 'MISSING.' Underneath are my details, my name, height, weight, date of birth, where I was last seen.

I brace myself against the edge of the desk. *Don't sit down. You can't sit down, Paige. You have to go. You have to go right now.*

The rest of the papers are all the same. My father is upstairs. I could go and wake him right now, I could end the torment he must be in.

No. You can't. He won't let you go. He'll want to call the
police.

I grab a pen and write a note. My handwriting is messy because my hand is shaking – and because all the muscles I use to write with are out of practice.

"Dad –

I love you. I am safe. I am not hurt. I can't stay because someone I love needs me but I just want you to know that I love you so much and I'm OK. Say hello to the goblins in the woods for me, even the one with big ears! I love you. I miss you so much. Paige."

The part about the goblins is a secret message of sorts – silly stories my dad used to talk about when I was very little. The goblins in the woods were friendly, if grumpy, and the one with big ears was the grumpiest. Nobody else except me and my dad will understand what that's about, and I want him to know that it's me, and that I'm not being forced to write something against my will, or lie about not being in danger if I am.

I fold the paper in half, and then again and put it beneath the empty casserole dish in the fridge, because I don't want to risk him waking up early and seeing it before I've had time to get back to Caistley. And then I leave, taking my bike out of the garage and stopping along the side of the road on the ride into town to pick up a large rock.

Main street is deserted, but brightly lit. I see Johnson's Pharmacy, sandwiched between the dollar store and the fast food restaurant and I have my second serious moment of doubt since leaving the Viking camp. Am I supposed to just walk up to that door, throw the rock through it, go inside, find the medicine and leave? And cross my fingers no one sees anything, no one hears anything? And even then, how long has it been since I left Eirik? Three days? He was sick when I left, already saying things that didn't make sense. What are the odds he's even still alive? So many things have to go right and it doesn't seem possible that they all will. I sit down on a bench for a few minutes, thinking, but it doesn't help because there's no plan B – there can't be. I either get the medications or I don't, and every second I delay the worse the odds of anything working out become. I take the rock out of the sack and approach the front door, looking around me all the way. Nobody appears. I look into the fluorescent-lit pharmacy – I guess I'll be able to read the packaging easily enough – and close my eyes briefly. Am I really doing this? I am really doing this. Because there's no other way.

The rock bounces off the glass door and lands at my feet the first time I throw it. Damnit.

I pick it up again, throw it harder. It bounces off again. My heart hammers in my chest. Have I come all this way to be thwarted by a glass door? The next time, I don't throw the rock. I keep my fingers wrapped around it and bring it down hard against the glass, shrieking with the effort. A web of cracks appears at the place of impact and I smash the rock in that same spot again and again and again until there's a hole that I can kick at with my sneaker-clad foot. By the time there's a hole big enough for me to squeeze through without being cut to ribbons it's been about ten minutes and I'm sweating with effort. The doubts are still there, not even in the back of my mind anymore, and growing more and more insistent.

You could barely kick in a broken glass door, Paige. How are you going to make it back to the Viking camp? You're too weak. You can't do it. Go home. Give up. It's over.

I refuse to listen to them as I duck through the hole in the door and climb awkwardly over the counter at the back of the store. I hold the list I've written up next to my face as I start making my way up and down rows of shelves, each crammed with various containers and blister-packs of pills and bottles of liquids. None of the names on my list are coming up. Ten minutes later, still nothing. Another five minutes and I'm about to start crying with frustration. What if they're not here? That's not possible! This is a pharmacy – they must have antibiotics!

And then I see it, a box with 'Amoxicillin' written on it. There are eight boxes in total, and I put all of them in the bag. I'm obviously at the antibiotics now, I should keep going, just to see if they have the Cephalexin – better to go back with two possible treatments than one. By this point I'm moving so quickly I'm knocking things off the shelves, almost in a full panic, every instinct screaming at me to get the hell out of there.

A bright light – much brighter than the overhead lights – suddenly illuminates me and my surroundings. I look up and my eyes close, blinded.

"THIS IS THE POLICE. PUT YOUR HANDS ABOVE YOU HEAD."

Chapter 24
21st Century

My legs give way and I sink onto the cold, polished floor of the pharmacy, screaming with – with what? Rage. Grief. Frustration. I'm not imagining it, it's really happening. I can see the red and blue lights of the patrol car reflected on the ceiling above me. I don't move, though, even as they scream at me to do so. My mind actually goes strangely blank as the realization that it's all over, that my plan is screwed, that I'm not going to make it back to the Viking camp in time, hits me.

"SHOW US YOUR HANDS!"

No, I think. *No, I'm done. Do what you have to do, but I'm staying right here on this nice cool floor. You're going to have to come and get me.*

I stay where I am, and the shouts of the police officer – maybe there are two of them, I can't tell – seem very far away. I'm very tired, too. So tired it almost feels as if I'm about to drift off right now, right here on the nice cold tiles in the–

Before I can finish contemplating whether or not to fall asleep on the floor of the pharmacy I've just broken into, I'm flying through the air somehow. Wait, no – I'm not flying. Someone is lifting me. A cop. My body is limp, I don't fight. I do, however, catch the look of surprise on his face when he finally gets a glimpse of me.

"It's a girl," he says, and he sounds so shocked I actually giggle. "Dave! It's a chick!"

He's handling me roughly, probably because he's angry I ignored their demands to surrender, to show them my hands, all those things I thought only happened on TV. But he's managed to get me over the counter and now I'm standing in front of it as he holds me very tightly by the arms. Hildy's done that before, held me that way. I don't like it. For the first time with the police I fight back, trying to wriggle out of the officer's grip. But I'm weak and it's useless.

The other officer – Dave – is rifling through the linen sack.

"It's – uh, it's food," he's saying to his partner. "And antibiotics. Yeah, just antibiotics. Granola bars, peanut butter, amoxicillin –" Dave looks up at me, confused. "What the hell are you doing stealing antibiotics?" He asks. "What, did you think these were Oxys? Is that what you – oh shit."

The cop holding my arms looks at his partner's suddenly serious expression. "What? Got something? I know this little chicky didn't just come in here to steal anti –"

"She's pregnant."

Both cops look down at my belly, which is partially obscured by my father's baggy sweatshirt.

"Are you?" The one holding me asks, and I feel his grip softening even before I can answer. "Are you pregnant, I mean?"

"Yes, I am."

He shakes his head disapprovingly. "What the hell are you doing? You don't look like an addict – and pregnant! Are you crazy?"

I shake my head. "No, not crazy."

"Not that it matters, you're under arrest for –"

Just as he's about to launch into my rights, which I admit I am looking forward to in a very strange way, the other officer – Dave – has another 'oh shit' moment. Only this time, instead of saying anything his eyes suddenly get very big and he points at me and does a little on-the-spot dance.

"What's your problem?" My officer asks him and Dave puts his hand over his mouth.

"Dude. It's – I think it's her – that college girl, Paige something. The one who went missing last –"

I find myself suddenly spun around to face the cop who had been holding me this entire time. They both study my face for a moment.

"No *fucking shit*," he says slowly, a few seconds later. "It sure looks like her – is that you? Are you Paige, uh, Paige –"

"Renner," I reply. "And yeah, that's me."

They're going to find out anyway, soon enough. Why not spare myself whatever trouble it would take if I didn't just admit it?

It's been almost a year since I used my last name. I sniffle a little after I do it this time, and the officers both soften noticeably.

"Get a chair!" The first one barks at Dave, and Dave brings me a chair. I sit down. "I'm Jim," he says, looking into my eyes. "Officer Jim Granton – and this is Officer Dave Stiles. You're – you're OK. Are you OK? Are you hurt? You don't look hurt."

"Should we call an ambulance?" Officer Dave Stiles asks, and his partner concurs. An ambulance is summoned, as are more police.

"How did you get here?" Officer Granton asks me, looking shocked. "Did you escape from somewhere – from someone? Have you been held? You know the whole country has been looking for you since last September, right?"

"The whole country?" I ask, still not quite convinced any of this is really happening. The whole country? The state, maybe – that I could believe. But the country?

I watch, when more police and paramedics arrive, as Officer Jim Granton takes my bag of food and antibiotics out to his car, knowing I won't see it – or any of its contents – again. My mind is whirring, trying to come up with a plausible scenario for getting back to the woods behind my father's house, alone. They don't seem to be arresting me – am I free to go?

Five minutes later, wrapped in a blanket I don't need in the back of an ambulance, I look right at the woman shining a light into my eyes and asking me what my name is and tell her I'd like to go. When she makes a non-committal noise I move to get up and she puts a hand on one of my shoulders.

"Wait a second, Paige. We're not even close to finished here. We need to –"

I shove her aside, not roughly, and try to exit the back of the ambulance. A man in street clothes, who looks to be a detective from the way all the uniformed cops are deferring to him, takes hold of my wrist.

"And where do you think you're going?"

"Home," I say, not looking him – or anyone – in the eye. "My dad's house. I need to see my dad."

"Your father has been called, Paige, he'll be waiting for you at the hospital. Is there something we can get for you? Are you hungry? Thirst –"

I try to yank my arm out of the man's grip and fail. "Let me go!" I yell. "Are you arresting me?! I haven't done anything! Let me go home – I just want to go home!"

"We aren't arresting you," he tells me, "not right now. But if you try to leave we will – we just caught you stealing, remember?"

I go limp as my exhausted brain remembers oh, yeah, they actually do have a right to prevent me from leaving.

**

I wake up in a hospital room. Sunshine streams in through the window. To my left, my father sleeps in a chair, one hand barely clinging onto a disposable coffee cup. The moment I see him, I begin to cry and the sound of my crying wakes him. He looks up at me.

"Paige."

I have never heard the kind of relief I hear now in my dad's voice. Never. He stands up slowly and I see he is even more unsteady on his feet than I remember – this is a man who isn't even 50 years old – and we reach for each other desperately.

"I thought you were dead," he whispers, after we have clung to each other for many minutes. "Paige, I thought you were dead. I still don't even know if I believe what I'm seeing right now, I don't trust myself not to be dreaming. Is it really you? What happened? Who – who took you?"

"It's me," I smile through my tear-blurred eyes. "It's really me."

"The police said they found you in the pharmacy in River Forks, trying to steal medications. They say you haven't mentioned anyone yet – anyone you might have been stealing on behalf of, I mean. How did you – Paige, you have to tell me what happened. They say you're having a baby! Who did this to you? We have to find them. We have to –"

"Nobody," I answer. "What I mean is, nobody 'did' this to me – any of this. I –"

"Well what happened then?!" My father asks. "You disappeared into thin air, Paige. We found your phone, all your things, your bank account was untouched, none of your friends knew anything. Well there was that one girl, what's her name? Your roommate?"

"Emma?" I suggest, marveling at how soft the hospital blanket feels under my fingers, at how clean all the shining, modern surfaces are.

"Emma, yes, that's the one. She told some completely crazy story about time travel and, I don't know, it was absurd. And other than her, no one knew anything. We know you made it back to River Forks because there was CCTV footage of you at the bus station, and the police think you made it home because they found fingerprints in the house, but beyond that there was literally nothing. Honestly it was like aliens had kidnapped you! And now you're back and – it feels the same as your disappearance, just out of nowhere, no explanation, nothing. Not that I'm complaining, Paige. The only thing that really matters is that your home and that you seem to be fine, physically. I just – if someone hurt you, I want them to pay. You should want them to pay, too. Even if they convinced you they were you friend, you should –"

"Dad," I say, because I can feel my father getting away from himself. "I told you no one hurt me. No one convinced me they were my friend."

I'm aware that what I'm saying is not strictly true. Someone did hurt me – Veigar with his rough handling when I was captured, Hildy various times after that – but telling my dad or anyone else about it isn't going to do anything except make them think I'm crazy. Because as soon as I admit I've been hurt, they're going to ask me who did it and then I'm either going to have to lie or admit that it was some 9th century Vikings that hurt me. From there, I doubt it's a very long distance to the psychiatric ward.

After a few more attempts to get information out of me, my dad finally gives in to my pleas to be allowed to go home and disappears to talk to the doctors, or the police, or whoever it is who gets to make the final decision on the matter. He returns not 10 minutes later, and I can tell from his expression that the news isn't good.

"No!" I protest. "Dad! Ask them again – please! Why am I even in here? Nothing is wrong with me, I'm fine – and I just want to go home."

I've got a vague plan formed in my head right now. I can't just go home and leave my poor father again. No, I have to tell him the truth. I will tell him the truth. But not here in this hospital, where I can see he's not completely convinced my mind hasn't been affected by whatever it is he thinks I've gone through. I have to tell him at home. I have to convince him to come with me.

My brain pauses, throws itself into reverse. What? I have to convince him to come with me? Yes, I do. I also need to know if Eirik is alive or dead. If he's alive, then I need to be with him. Our child needs to be with him. And my father needs to be with me, the only person keeping him tethered to his own life. He already looks like he's about 75 years old, I know he won't survive losing me a second time. If Eirik is dead – my mind skips over the possibility even as I am fully aware that it's likely – then the decision is made for me, I will return to the present and live the rest of my life with my dad and my baby and my friends in this world, with its bright lights and hospitals and student loans.

But I have to know. I have to know if the man whose very being, mind and body, is now as familiar to me as I am to myself, has lived. I know he probably hasn't, but I can't go on to live in 2017 without knowing for sure.

So I have to get out of this hospital. I have to get home.

"Dad," I say, pushing myself up into a sitting position. "Dad. I have to go home. I – I can't relax here, I can't think. Please, you have to –"

A woman I don't recognize walks into the room – a doctor. She smiles at me, and then at my dad, and asks me how I'm feeling.

"Fine," I reply, instantly regretting the shortness in my tone. If I'm going to get out of here I need to start being nice to people. I need to start acting like I just want some time to heal, to process, to do whatever it is people are supposed to do in a situation as messy as this.

"I'm Dr. Lawson," she says, offering her hand to me and then to my dad. "I'm just here to talk to you, Paige. Do you think we could be alone for a little while?"

My father balks at leaving, I can see he's about to protest when one of the detectives walks in and reassures him it's fine, that there are two cops posted outside my room and a further two at the entrance to the ward.

"Wow," I say to Dr. Lawson. "Four guards?"

The doctor pulls a chair up next to my bed. She's a psychiatrist, I can tell already. Something about the cast of her eyes, the mask of gentle concern. "Eight guards," she replies. "We have four posted at the entrances, to keep the media out."

"The media?" I ask. "For – me?"

Dr. Lawson doesn't answer. Instead, she asks me a question. *Definitely* a psychiatrist. "Are you surprised? You've been missing for months, Paige. Normal college girl, no history of criminal activity or running away, doing well socially and in her studies, just disappears into thin air? And then shows up just as suddenly months later, pregnant? This story is huge."

Why is she telling me all this? Isn't it her job to help me get myself together? Not that I intend to ask her any of this out loud, of course.

"So," she continues, leaning in the way some mental health professionals do, almost as if you're just two friends sharing a juicy secret. I don't like that tactic – never have. It's fake and I don't buy it for one second. "Can you give me your full name?"

I answer, and Dr. Lawson follows up with questions about where I think I am, the name of the university I attend, the year, the president. I answer all of them correctly. Some of them she repeats, as if trying to catch me out. I decide about halfway through that I don't like this woman at all. Eventually, though, she moves on.

"And can you tell me where you've been since last September, Paige?"

I know exactly what I have to say. I also know I need to make her believe me, and I'm not so sure I can make that happen. As ever, though, I don't have a choice. Can't tell the truth, can't tell an obvious lie – because it'll get found out right away. Got to go with the 'I forgot' defense. I look down at the white blanket covering my legs and then up, into the doctor's eyes.

"I don't remember."

She gives me a tight little smile and writes something down. "You don't remember anything? Do you remember last night, at the pharmacy?"

"I, uh – yes. I think so. I remember one of the officers lifting me over the counter."

"And do you remember why you were at the pharmacy?"

Yes. I was there to steal antibiotics so I could take them back to the 9th century and give them to the Viking who fathered the child I am pregnant with. "Uh, no. I don't. I'm sorry."

"You had antibiotics in your bag when the police caught you. Some food, too. Is someone you know injured? Were you trying to help somebody? Has someone threatened to hurt you?"

When the doctor fails to get anything out of me with regard to the pharmacy visit, she asks me what the last thing I remember is, from the time before I went missing. I tell her I remember coming back to River Forks, that I think I recall being in the house, but that's it.

"So just to be clear," Dr. Lawson asks, just before leaving. "You remember events leading up to the day you went missing, and you remember events after the police found you at the pharmacy last night, but you remember nothing in between?"

I hesitate before answering because I sense she's trying to catch me in something. But what can I do? I don't know a single thing about real amnesia or how it manifests, I don't know if what I'm claiming is true is possible or not. I do know she can't force me to talk about specific things, and if I don't talk about them then they cannot be used against me.

"Yes," I reply softly. The doctor makes another note and then looks at me. "Thank you, Paige. I'll let you get some rest now but we'll be seeing each other again."

But there's no time to rest because after Dr. Lawson leaves a female detective comes to question me. She's kinder than the doctor, but just as full of questions. She wants to know if I understand that I'm pregnant, if I remember how I got pregnant, who got me pregnant, when they got me pregnant, where it happened, if I wanted it to happen and on and on and on and all I say in response is that I don't remember.

It goes on like this for a long time. I don't mean hours, I mean days. Everybody keeps telling me it's time to rest and to recover, but I keep getting bombarded with the same questions from the same people, until my own frustration seems to match theirs and I get the distinct sense that nobody has a single clue about what should be done with me. The police aren't going to charge me with anything for breaking into the pharmacy, because they're worried about how it's going to look to the media, who are hanging on every detail – or so I'm told, I haven't been allowed to access the internet or talk to anyone who isn't my dad or somehow involved in the case since they brought me to the hospital.

Finally, after almost three weeks, I start refusing my food. There's no intention to take it far enough to hurt myself or my baby, but I don't tell anyone that. In fact, I try to give off the specific vibe that I'll keep it up for as long as I have to. A few days later, I'm free. I mean, I'm 'free.' Free to go home. Not free to do as I please. Not free to leave the house. Who's keeping me inside? Not the police, not my dad, no. My new jailers? The media. When I am discharged from the hospital there is a hoard of them waiting outside the doors – more than I have ever seen, even for a movie star or a disgraced politician. My dad and two of the guards – both of whom are coming home with us to 'keep an eye on me' (whatever that means) use their bodies to shield me, hustling me quickly to the car as camera flashes and shouted questions fill the air.

"Who's the father of your baby, Paige?" "Do you know who the father is?" "When are you due?" "Do you remember anything?" "Are you a member of a cult?" "Have you experienced alien contact?"

I'm too shocked to notice how outlandish some of the questions are. They don't enter my mind. All I want is to be far away from the bright lights. Once I'm in the backseat of the car I cover my head with my arms and think of Eirik. Eirik wouldn't have let any of that happen to me. None of those reporters would even have dared to show up if they'd so much as gotten a glimpse of the Viking Jarl in all his fur-and-leather finery, staring them down.

But Eirik isn't here. Eirik probably isn't anywhere. He's probably dead, Paige. Because you screwed up. You got caught.

The media follow us home. They follow us home and then they set up camp at the bottom of the driveway and in the empty lot next door. And once they've set up camp, they don't leave. There's so many of them they don't even seem to sleep – even at three, four o'clock in the morning, all that has to happen is for me to open the front – or even the back – door, and the shouted questions and flashes resume.

I go online almost immediately, and am horrified to discover that the mainstream media camped outside the house are the least of it. There are whole websites dedicated to the theory that I'm an alien being, that my disappearance – and now my return – is the first step in a process that ends with the rest of the aliens coming to earth and enslaving the human race. There are countdown clocks to this 'invasion.' Grand Northeastern has had to ban reporters from campus, after they started harassing my fellow students for stories. There are whole message-boards convinced I'm lying, that my father and I have made the whole thing up in order to secure a lucrative book deal – that my baby is a pillow, or, disgustingly, the product of incest.

There are months and months of these stories, pages and pages on these message-boards. The volume alone of the incorrect information just makes it seem that I could never say enough to counter it.

I go to sleep that night with a creeping sense of horror. I'm stuck here. Stuck as the seeming star of an almost infinite number of stories, powerless to correct the role I've been shoved into by strangers all over the world. This can't be my life now, can it?

And just before I drift off, the certainty, again – if Eirik were here, he would do something about this. He would not allow any of it to happen. But Eirik isn't here, and I fall asleep with an aching emptiness in my heart.

Chapter 25
21st Century

Almost a week after I return from the hospital, I'm starting to feel stir-crazy. I can't leave, because leaving means dealing with the media and I just... can't. Not yet. So all my time is consumed by two main activities – obsessively reading the stories about myself online and half-mourning a man that I can't even talk about, because talking about him would mean explaining who he is, and how he came to be the father of my baby.

There are some things I enjoy about being back in my own time. I enjoy the feeling of silky, well-conditioned hair after a shower. I enjoy hot water straight out of the tap, on demand. I enjoy sleeping on a mattress, and having a washing machine to wash my clothes. But it's amazing how small these things actually are, how seemingly inconsequential.

It's also amazing how many things I don't enjoy, that I thought I would. There's more food than I've had for months – tons and tons of food, the refrigerator, freezer and every cupboard in the kitchen stuffed to bursting with it – but it doesn't taste very good. It's bland and sweet and no matter how much of it I eat, it's nothing like the earthiness of roasted venison loin or even like the little cakes the cooks in the Viking camp would make out of boiled peas and the wild, onion-like vegetables that grew beside the streams. There was less food with the Vikings, but it tasted better. My father watches me with astonishment as I cook rare steak after rare steak, even resorting to serving it with barely-cooked onions in a fruitless quest to re-create what I miss from the Viking feasts.

"Are you anemic?" He asks me one night, eying me as I use my spoon to capture the last juices of another bloody steak. "We should take you back to the hospital to check if –"

"No."

"Paige, how long do you plan to –"

"I'm not going out there!" I declare, slamming my spoon down on the table. "I don't want to speak to any of those awful people – I don't even want to see them! I'll go see the doctor when they leave."

My father goes back to eating his dinner – a frozen burger of the type that I can no longer bring myself to force down my throat – but I can tell he's got more to say.

"What?" I ask, when he doesn't say it. "What is it, Dad?"

He hesitates and I prompt him again. "Dad? What?"

"Well, I just think I should tell you, Paige, that I have arranged for a lawyer to come over tomorrow – to meet with us."

A lawyer. Good. "Really?" I ask, brightening slightly. "Do you think they can get those reporters to leave us alone? I mean, how long are they –"

"No," my dad says, "it's not for the press. They have a right to be there – believe me, I checked."

"Well what's it about then?" I ask.

My dad's expression is suddenly serious. Worryingly serious. He looks at me and I see that he's holding back tears. My stomach drops.

"Back at the hospital, Paige – there was some talk. Some talk of –"

"Of what?!" I cry when he trails off. "Dad! Talk of what?"

"Of your baby."

Terror surges into my veins. "My baby?" I ask, my voice trembling. "What about my baby, Dad? What about my baby? Is something wrong with –"

"No! No, Paige – the baby is fine." My father cuts in when I jump to my feet, on the edge of losing it completely.

"Well then what is it?!"

"Sit down and I'll tell you. I – just sit down."

I sit down, light-headed with dread – I really don't like the look on my father's face right now. Not at all.

"OK," I say slowly, trying to show that I'm calm enough to discuss the matter with. "Please tell me what they said about the baby."

My dad looks away suddenly, but not before I see that he's emotional. "They said they're not sure if, uh, if –" he breaks off and presses a hand to his mouth. "They're not sure you're in the right place to care for a newborn. Psychologically, I mean."

The blood in my veins feels as if it's turning to ice. The sound of my own heartbeat thuds in my ears. "What?" I ask, because surely I've misheard.

"They're not talking about taking the baby away from you for good, it's nothing like that. But Dr. Lawson and the rest of her team seem to feel that he – or she – might be in danger if you were allowed to take full custody right after birth. She says there can be, uh, hormonal issues after a woman gives birth, that can exacerbate any psychosis already present, or bring on a crisis of some –"

I stand up, shaking my head. "I'm not hearing this," I say out loud. "I – Dad – what are you saying? *Psychosis?* Since when am I psychotic?! Do I seem psychotic to you? This can't be legal! How can this be legal? You said the lawyer is coming tomorrow?"

He nods, but he still won't look at me. "Yes, tomorrow. But she already said she wasn't sure if –"

"This can't be happening," I say quietly and then again, a few seconds later and not so quietly. "THIS CAN'T BE HAPPENING! Are you kidding me right now, Dad?! They think I'm psychotic? Do you think I'm psychotic? Is that why you won't look at me? DAD!" I'm screaming now, slamming my fists down on the table.

"No!" My dad responds, angrily swiping a tear off one of his cheeks. "No, Paige, you don't seem anything like what I thought psychotic people were like. But the doctors, they say it's not always obvious, that sometimes it seems as if people are perfectly sane."

"Well isn't that fucking convenient?!" I shout, beyond caring about cursing in front of him. "So even if I don't show any of the signs of being crazy, they can just –"

"Paige, they said you don't have amnesia. You don't have any of the signs of amnesia – there are two different kinds, the doctor said, and you don't fit the criteria for either one. And then there was that stuff that came out a few months ago, that interview your friend did, about the, uh, the time travel."

I clench and unclench my fists, concentrating on breathing in, and then out. In, then out. I'm on the edge of something, I can feel it. Finally, a couple of minutes later, I sit down again and look my father in the eye.

"What friend?" I ask calmly, even though there's only one 'friend' it could be. "I'm not sure what you're talking about."

"Your roommate, the one you were living with when you went missing. She did an interview with one of the big news shows, and she mentioned that you'd written some weird story about time-traveling, or told her something about it. I can't remember, it all sounded so ridiculous I just put it out of my mind. But then I re-watched it one night and I remembered you used to talk about similar things when you were a little girl – do you remember that? You used to talk about those imaginary friends of yours? William and, uh – do you remember?"

There is a hollow feeling in the middle of my chest, like someone has just drained all the blood out of my heart. Betrayal. Emma talked about what I told her – *what she swore she would never talk about to anyone* – on national TV? My mind can't decide whether to weep or rage. In the end, both happen at once.

"I'm – Paige, I can see that you're upset but I think what you need to understand here is that when you were missing, everyone who loves you was willing to do anything, to follow any trail of breadcrumbs – to find you. And now that we've found you and there's still no real answers..." my dad trails off as I sit in front of him, desperately trying to gulp back the sobs that are erupting out of me.

"I just want you to be OK, Paige," he continues, "I want you to be able to deal with –"

"So just to be clear," I ask, my voice shaking. "You told Dr. Lawson about that childhood stuff – about my friends in the woods? You –"

"I didn't have to tell her," he replies, looking at his hands. "One of your old therapists came forward – Dr. Hansen, I think it was? From when you were a little girl, just after your mother passed? So when Dr. Lawson asked me about it, did I remember anything etc., I didn't want to lie. You did used to talk about those things, Paige. And I want you to be OK! Your friend who went on TV just wants you to be OK, too."

A fact presents itself to my mind: the media are not allowed on the property. They have to stay at the bottom of the driveway, and in the lot next door, outside the property line. I could make it down to the woods. They might see me, but what would it matter if I disappeared before they got to me? And if, this time, I never returned?

I get up and slip my shoes on. It feels like being on some kind of auto-pilot, like my brain is in some kind of very practical, basic mode. Shoes. What else? Food. I open the cupboard under the kitchen sink and grab a couple of the plastic grocery bags my dad has always insisted on keeping, for some reason. There are bananas in the fridge. Cheese, peanut butter, bread, butter, a bag of oranges. They all go into the bags.

"Paige," my dad says, after watching me quietly for a few minutes. "What are you –"

"I'm going for a walk," I reply. "I'll stay on the property, don't worry."

"A walk?" He asks, confused. "Why do you need to take all those groceries on a walk? Where are you – Paige, what are you doing?"

I can hear my father's voice getting more concerned. I don't have much time, he's either going to try to stop me or he's going to call someone – the police, the paramedics, who knows.

"I'm going for a walk," I say again, adding two bottles of water to my load.

"But," he protests, clearly thinking about blocking me and then stepping aside at the last minute as I open the back door. "Paige! Wait! This doesn't make any sense! What the hell are you –"

I turn around and kiss my dad on the cheek. "I love you, Dad."

And then I turn and step out into the backyard. My father shouts after me, telling me he's calling the hospital, begging me to stop. But I don't stop. They're going to take my baby and that's something that I simply cannot allow to happen. Eirik may be alive, he may be dead, but I'm going back to the past, back to my friends and, hopefully, to him.

When I'm almost at the bottom of the yard, and about to enter the woods, my dad starts to chase me. I pick up my pace a little, but not much – he's in no condition to catch me, even as pregnant as I am. But a few seconds later I see a bright light to my right, also in the woods. It's bouncing, like someone is carrying it.

"Help!" A voice shouts – my father. "Catch her! She's trying to leave again!"

The light is getting closer. Soon, there is a voice.

"Paige? Paige Renner? I'm Brian Watlin from KPYU News – can we have a minute of your –"

FUCK. I whirl around and shove the reporter to the ground before he can get another word out of his smarmy mouth. And the bastard is actually narrating what's happening as it's happening.

"She's just pushed me to the ground. Paige Renner has just pushed me to the ground. We're in the woods, out back of the Renner property, she's running. Mike! She's running!"

I am running. The reporter's tone indicates that this is a game to him, excitement, something that's definitely going to play well on the six o'clock news. But I'm running for my life. For my child's life – for our right to be together.

Suddenly my mouth is full of dirt, the smell and taste of dry leaves. Someone is sitting on my back. Someone else is pinning my arms to my sides. People are breathing heavily, after the chase.

"We've got her," the reporter says. "Tell the paramedics we're in the woods behind the house – I've got my light on."

I've either tripped or been knocked off my feet. Either way, it's over. I won't be getting away. Not now. Maybe not ever. An image of Eirik's face fills my mind's eye. Those piercing blue eyes, as changeable as the sky. If he was here, none of this would be happening. I never should have left him. I never should have been so arrogant as to think I could save him all by myself.

I turn my face back into the dirt, because the cameraman with the reporter has recovered and is now filming me, and begin to scream. Not incoherent screams. It's just one word, over and over: Eirik.

Chapter 26
21st Century

I'm back at the hospital again. There's a guard at my door, and this time I know he's there to keep me in as much as he is to keep any imaginary bad guys out. I'm restrained, my wrists held by soft cuffs to the side of the bed. It's ridiculous, and I know who's behind it, too – Dr. Lawson. What is it about people like that? Some of them – like her – are even highly qualified, but there's something there, some narcissism of their own, some need to be seen as the expert, the one who is never wrong, the one who sees what other people don't.

Because I've had people think I'm weird before. Oh, that I'm used to. Therapists, fellow students, from the time I was very small. I'm used to being 'weird.' And I even learned not to talk about Caistley, or Willa and Eadgar, at a pretty young age. But Dr. Lawson is looking for reasons to condemn me and that's the part I can't quite understand. Who am I to her? It begins to become clearer, however, over the days (and then the weeks) that I spend having 'sessions' with her in my hospital room.

Dr. Lawson is smart. OK, that's become debatable. Dr. Lawson is somebody who *needs to be seen as smart*. She spends hours a day with me, asking me the same questions over and over – 'Do you ever feel like you might hurt yourself?', 'Do you ever feel like you might hurt somebody else?', 'Do you ever feel as if you have difficulty distinguishing between what's real and what's just in your mind?' – and always receiving the same answers – no, no and no. How long will it go on, I wonder, until she accepts I'm not lying, and that she never had any real reason to think I was nuts – or possibly even violent – in the first place?

But as the questions continue and the answers remain the same, I begin to sense something that feels almost like hostility in the good doctor's tone. It only takes a few comments – about how I must think I'm so smart for fooling so many highly qualified people, or how only a deeply disturbed person would invent stories of time travel and alien abduction (Dr. Lawson turns out not to be so great at doing her research, because I have never, not once in my life, ever brought up alien abduction – that's entirely on the tabloids) while their friends and family have spent the past months, almost a year, losing their minds with worry. She even seems to suggest, in her vague and passive-aggressive way, that I have somehow manufactured my own kidnapping. But she's a doctor, and she knows how to say these things without really saying them, in ways that I can't really call out without looking like the crazy one myself.

She gets up one day, as we're talking in my room, and walks over to the window, looking thoughtful. "Interesting," she says, to no one in particular – definitely not to me. "I've never had a patient try so hard to pull the wool over my eyes"

And there it is, I realize. That's her problem. She thinks I'm making her look bad. She hasn't been able to get to the bottom of my disappearance, and her ego can't deal with that. After all, I'm just some attention-seeking college student to the doctor. And now it's all starting to look bad, because as hard as some people in the press – and even one or two police officers, if reports are to be believed – try to establish that I have, in fact, faked everything, they don't seem to be able to find any evidence of it.

It gets more explicit as time passes. Dr. Lawson begins to openly hint that if I just tell her what really happened, I'll be allowed to give birth and take my baby home right away. It's a lie, I can tell. I respond to it the way I respond to everything else she says to me now – with silence.

I haven't given up – not even close. It's just that there's nothing else to do on a locked psych ward, if one is sane, except work at proving one's sanity. My father comes to visit me as often as he's allowed – which is about twice a week after Dr. Lawson decides his presence is hindering my 'self-reconciliation' (whatever that means), but I'm angry at him for calling the paramedics that night I tried to leave, and he knows it.

They can't keep me here forever, I tell myself. Even as my belly grows to the point where I can barely find a comfortable position to sleep in, and the nurses tell me I'll go into labor at any time, I remain cooped up, subject to the never-ending questions of a woman who thinks she has me all figured out and can't allow herself to be wrong.

I'm not a particularly strong person. I'm only strong through this ordeal because I have something – some*one* – to be strong for. My baby. Eirik's baby. Whoever this person is in my belly, I owe it to them to do everything possible to keep them safe, to get myself out of the predicament I'm in and build a life around them. Eirik is with me in this, keeping me strong, steeling my resolve every day. It's his face I see before I go to sleep at night, and his blue-eyed gaze I feel in my heart when Dr. Lawson is hounding me with questions. I talk to him sometimes. Not prayers, and not the act of a crazy woman – I know he's not physically with me. And not out loud, either. Just in my head.

I'm trying, Eirik. I'm trying to come back to you. I'm trying to do the best for our baby. And I'm going to keep trying for as long as I can.

***

One day, I turn away from the window where I constantly sit, watching the world outside and thinking of my time in the Viking camp, to see Emma standing in the doorway. I blink, not sure if I'm finally actually crazy, or if it's really her. She looks different – her hair is longer, she's thinner than I remember.

"Oh my God," she says – her first words to me in almost a year. "You really are pregnant!"

I stand up awkwardly, pushing my big, disproportionate body up out of the chair using my arms, and just look at her for a few seconds. "Yeah," I say eventually. "I am. Due any day now, apparently."

My instinct is to wrap my arms around my friend and squeeze her until neither of us can breathe. I don't do that, though. I don't move from my spot. I remember the interview my father told me she did, spilling secrets she'd sworn to keep. She made me look like a nut, she helped get the ball rolling on this whole 'Paige Renner is a crazy person' thing. She knows why I'm not hugging her, too, I can see it in her eyes.

"You don't know how hard it was to get in here to see you," Emma says, after a long and awkward silence. "I've been talking to your dad for weeks, trying to negotiate a visit the whole time. They've really got you on lockdown."

"No shit."

More awkward silence. Finally, she just blurts it out.

"Look, Paige. I'm sorry. I think you know that's what I'm here to say. I'm really sorry. You don't understand what they said to me, though, before the interview. They made it sound like I would be helping you if –"

"Helping me!?" I ask, spitting out the words bitterly. "Helping me? Well shit, Emma, you've got a funny way of helping. I suppose I'm misremembering the part where you *promised* never to say a damn word about any of that to anyone, aren't I? I seem to be misremembering so many things these days!"

Emma's staring at me, and it just makes me angrier. "What?" I ask. "Do you think anything they're saying about me is actually true? Do you think I'm really nuts? Oooh, better run away fast before I beat you to death with my fucking pillow!"

"Paige –"

"What?!" I yell. "You PROMISED, Emma! You fucking promised me!"

"I know," she whispers. "And I would have kept that promise if you hadn't gone missing, Paige. If I didn't think you were dead, or in some psycho's basement! You don't know how it was, the police were questioning everyone, the media was going crazy, everyone was just telling the people who knew you to give any information they had, that any little thing could give them a lead. The producer on that show told me I was helping you! He told me if I didn't tell them everything I knew then I could be making it more difficult to find you. And, Paige, all I wanted to do was find you. I had to withdraw from school for two semesters over this. Every single night I went to sleep with all these horrible images in my mind, all these terrible things I thought someone might have done to you and I'm just – I see now I did the wrong thing and I am so sorry. Please believe me, I am so, so sorry. I never wanted to hurt you. I just wanted to find you. You're my best friend."

I try to blink away my tears but that just sends them rolling down my cheeks. Emma is crying, too, but I'm still too angry to give her the hug I know we both want.

"Why do you think I'm in here?!" I reply, my voice choked with emotion. "Why do you think everyone thinks I'm nuts, Emma? That interview just gave everyone an excuse to think I'm just some delusional attention seeker. And now I'm about to have a baby in a fucking psych ward!"

I collapse into my chair. A few seconds later, I feel Emma's hands on my shoulders, trying to comfort me, and shrug them off.

"I'm sorry," she repeats miserably. "I didn't know, Paige. If I had known –"

We stay there like that for ten minutes, fifteen, sitting across from each other, miserable. When the height of the emotion passes, I look out the window at a passing school-bus full of kids.

"Did you really withdraw from both semesters?" I ask finally. "Are you back in classes again now?"

Emma inhales, and her breath shakes the way it does sometimes after you've cried a lot. She nods. "Yeah, both semesters. And yes, I'm back now. Technically, anyway."

"What do you mean 'technically?'"

She shrugs. "I mean I'm enrolled. I only go to about thirty percent of my classes, I'd guess, but all my professors know who I am, they're mostly going super easy on me. I'd definitely fail every single one if they weren't."

"You shouldn't be missing so many classes," I tell her, allowing a smidgen of sympathy to soften my heart.

Emma nods. "I know, Paige. Believe me, I know. It's seriously so dumb for me to even be talking about this right now, as if somehow I'm the one who has suffered the most here. I came to apologize. I understand that you can't forgive me. I just wanted you to know that I've never felt worse about anything in my life – it kills me that I hurt you, that I made things more difficult for you after everything else that's gone on."

"Everything that's gone on," I repeat, rolling my eyes a little when Emma's not looking. "The worst part of it is this, right now! I'm not allowed to leave, the doctor is convinced I'm some kind of psycho – you know they're talking about taking away the baby, right? Because I can't even look after myself so how can I look after a baby or some shit like that?"

"What?" Emma asks, confused. "They're thinking about – Paige, why would they take away your baby? You're the victim here!"

I shrug, trying to act tough, but even in the midst of the shrug I can feel the emotion rolling back over me like a wave. "I don't know!" I reply, my voice thin and high-pitched. "I don't know, Em! The doctor here – Dr. Lawson – she hates me. She hates me because she thinks this is all just some big con I'm pulling and –"

"And what's happening about that?" Emma cuts in. "Like, do you have a lawyer? Does anyone even know about this? Does your dad know?"

I nod. "He knows. We called a lawyer but he said we should just do whatever the doctors recommend, that if it went to court it'll look good, like I'm making a good faith effort to get better."

Emma shakes her head like she can't believe what she's hearing. "What?! Paige, I – I don't understand. 'A good faith effort to get better?!' What exactly is wrong with you? How are you the person who is in the wrong here? Are you seriously telling me they're threatening to take your baby? Because if you are, someone needs to intervene. Your dad needs to get a better lawyer or someone needs to tell the media or, I don't know – something! That's completely insane!"

The media. There's an idea. I haven't been allowed access to the internet for weeks and the only channels I can access on the ancient TV in my room only show nature documentaries and infomercials. "Does anyone even care about me anymore?" I ask. "Like, is this even still a story?"

"Are you kidding?" Emma asks. "This is still a huge story – people are super curious, there's some kind of huge bidding war between the networks over who gets to interview you first when you get out – it's crazy. They still call me at least once a day begging for another interview – which I promise you I am not going to do."

"And why do people think I'm in here?" I ask, as the first inkling that maybe the view from outside is very different from the truth comes over me.

Emma fiddles with the zipper on her purse. "Because you're pregnant, I think. That you're vulnerable, you're recovering from what happened to you." She pauses, because she, like everyone else, still has no idea what did happen to me. "I'm not going to lie, there are a few people who think you made it all up but I want you to know I don't believe that for –"

"Do they realize I can't leave?" I cut in. "Has that been reported?"

"No," Emma replies. "I don't think so. I haven't seen anything about that."

A flicker of hope lights up the darkness in my heart and I'm about to ask Emma if she thinks letting people know would change anything when the door to my room opens and a nurse walks in.

"Visiting hours are over," she says, setting a tray of tomato soup and plastic-wrapped saltine crackers down. "You're lucky Dr. Lawson even let you –"

"Tell them," I say to Emma as she gathers her things. I grab her and pull her into a sudden hug, whispering desperately in her ear: "I forgive you. I know you were trying to help! Tell them about the baby. Tell them –"

"Come on now," the nurse intervenes, pulling me away. "Time to leave – and time for you to get some rest, Paige."

Emma is looking at me questioningly. "Really?" She asks, as she's hustled gently out of the room.

"Yes!" I call after her. "Tell them!"

The door shuts and the nurse looks at me disapprovingly. "Dr. Lawson isn't going to let you have new visitors for long if you –"

"Fuck Dr. Lawson," I respond flatly, rolling over on my bed so my back is to the nurse. She leaves less than a minute later and I fall into a short, unsatisfying sleep.

It's dark when I wake up. I look around the room, because I've got a vague feeling like something specific has woken me, someone calling my name or a loud noise of some kind. But everything seems to be in place. I look out the window at the moon, filling my room with pale light.

"ARRRGH."

I sit up at straight, not even aware, for the first second or two, that the strange noise is coming out of me. My stomach hurts. My tired brain runs through the possibilities. Sick? Am I going to puke? Do I need the bathroom? No. The bed underneath me is wet. And my stomach really is quite painful...

Oh my God.

Without thinking I reach out and slam my hand down on the red button that summons the nursing staff. Then I do it again and again and again until I hear footsteps in the hallway outside. The door opens and someone turns the light on. I shield my eyes from the brightness and, just as I'm about to be asked what's wrong, I get up off the bed and myself and the two nurses look down at the huge wet spot.

"I think –" I start.

"The baby is coming!" One of the nurses finishes for me.

And then I remember the conversation with Emma, the advice to get a new lawyer. That was only a few hours ago. It's not enough time. I need a few more days, at least. Time for the story – that I'm not allowed to leave the hospital, that my doctor is planning to have my baby taken into custody – to get out. Time for my dad to find a lawyer who gives better advice than 'do what they say.'

"No," I say, in a strange half-asleep, half-panicked state. "No, I – I can't. I can't."

The nurse thinks I'm talking about giving birth – which in a way I am but not in the way she thinks – and pats my knee affectionately. "Don't worry, Paige, they'll get you set up with an epidural."

I look at her face. Hazel eyes, dark-blonde hair, about 30. *Help me*, I want to say. *Please help me. Get me out of here. They're going to take my baby.*

But I don't say any of that, because I know if I do that she might tell Dr. Lawson. I bite my lip, hard enough to taste blood in my mouth, as another sharp pain seizes my belly.

Chapter 27
21st Century

At some point in what is to become a mostly-blurry memory of pain, brightly-lit rooms and the antiseptic scent of the hospital, I am moved to a different room. I refuse the epidural because the anesthesiologist explains that it will numb my entire body from the waist down and some primitive instinct buried deep inside my lizard brain thinks I might be able to make a run for it when the baby is born.

I don't even notice when my father arrives, because I'm in another world by then, a world made of pain, pain and more pain. I'm only vaguely aware that I'm groaning and shrieking like a wounded cow, because every ounce of my consciousness is taken up with the task at hand.

"I feel like an animal," I gasp at one point, to a nurse who is kindly allowing me to crush her left hand. She half-smiles, half-winces down at me.

"Your baby will be here soon, Paige."

My eyes search the room as I give birth, finding my father's face at the last second. I push one more time when the doctor instructs me to do so, and then it feels like my heart is simultaneously exploding and being crushed as a slippery, tiny, naked creature is placed on my chest. I look down, somehow not quite seeing, and then up again at the medical staff, at my dad.

"Is it –?" I ask, because it doesn't seem possible. A minute ago there were five people in the room. Now there are six. Now there are six?!

Again, I look down. This time, I see a face. A very small face, the eyes dark blue and fathomless.

"Oh my God," I breathe. "Oh my God. He looks just like –" I catch myself. Even at that moment, when I should be free to say and feel everything, I have to catch myself. "He's beautiful," I continue. "He's so beautiful."

It's not a lie. He – because the child is a boy – *is* beautiful. And he also, and I have to keep this part to myself, looks so much like his father it takes my breath away. I clutch the baby to my breast and sob for Eirik's absence. He should be here. I sob for happiness, too, because I feel happy. How could I not, holding my baby for the first time?

***

Half an hour later, my son and I are alone in a recovery room, his downy head nestled into my neck. Everything is quiet now, soft, dim. Nurses speak in whispers, the lights are turned down low. I'm besotted. I'm also not thinking.

A knock at the door.

"Paige?"

"Come in," I whisper, beckoning my dad into the room. "Look. Isn't he gorgeous? Look at his little hands!"

My dad struggles to maintain his composure when I pass the baby to him. "You're right," he agrees. "He's wonderful. Beautiful. They're not going to take him away from you, Paige."

A sliver of ice cuts through the blissful warmth of a new mom and her baby.

"How do you know?" I ask, my voice so soft my dad has to lean in close to catch it.

"I spoke to your friend Emma yesterday," he says. "She came to the house after visiting you. I didn't think she was making sense, but she was so persistent. I – I called a new lawyer, someone famous – she offered her services a month ago but I turned them down. And then I –"

"Dad?" I prompt, as my son snuffles in his grandfather's arms. "What?"

"I called the news," he replies after a long hesitation, eying me like he's afraid this is going to make me angry. Which it would have, weeks ago. Not now. Now I see that my father and I are both on exactly the same page – every single possible thing must be done to keep this baby with me – with us.

"Not the local news," he continues. "The national news. CNN. They wanted me to do an interview and I, uh – I agreed to it."

I look up and say one word: "Good."

"They're not taking him away from you," my father repeats and there is something steely in his voice that I don't remember ever hearing before. "It's not right, I won't let it happen."

We sit, staring down at our new family member and making plans to keep him with us, for I don't know how long – hours. The new lawyer has been in touch, she thinks my dad should do the CNN interview. I don't want to be dealing with any of it. All I want to do right now is drown in the softness of my baby's skin, the way his expression, when he turns his head a certain way, is exactly the same as one I used to see on his father's face all the time.

But that isn't how things turn out. When Dr. Lawson barges into the room that evening, after a small commotion and some angry voices I can't quite make out in the hallway outside, I'm expecting it. All the same, my entire body tightens with anxiety and my arms itch to shove her away from the baby as he sleeps in my arms.

The doctor runs a hand over her hair and gives me the fakest smile I've ever seen. You'd think a psychiatrist would learn how to fake goodwill a little better.

"Paige!" She says brightly. "How are you doing? I hear the birth went well."

"You're not taking him," I reply calmly as my dad, who has fallen asleep in one of the uncomfortable hospital chairs, stirs awake.

Dr. Lawson ignores me and leans over, trying to get a look at the baby. I turn my body away.

"What are you doing here?" My father asks when he sees who it is. "Get out of here. My lawyer should have called the –"

"Mr. Renner," Dr. Lawson cuts him off. "Yes, your lawyer has been in touch with us. Don't worry, I'm not here to do anything nefarious."

She pronounces the word 'nefarious' like one would pronounce the word 'scary' to a small child – as if it's a joke. But it's not a joke, and her tone just infuriates me.

"Not here to do anything nefarious?!" I hiss. "You've been telling me for weeks that I'm not fit to care for a baby, that you're going to take him away from me!"

Dr. Lawson gives me the gently confused look you would give a crazy person who is ranting about nonsense. "Oh dear," she says, pretending to be concerned. "Paige, if you thought I meant *I* was going to take away your baby, I can assure you that was never the case. I'm just the psychiatrist, I can't just arbitrarily decide to take away a baby. Besides –"

"You know what I mean –"

"I'm as concerned for your son as you are, Paige," she continues, totally ignoring me. "I understand this is a very emotional time for you – all women are emotional during pregnancy and after giving birth. But I think if you take a step back and really think about this – about the situation you find yourself in at this point in your life, you might come to see that maybe I have a point."

Dr. Lawson's tone is totally different to anything I've ever heard from her before. She's trying to persuade me now, rather than straight-up accusing me of things. Instantly I know that the lawyer has contacted the hospital – and it sounds like she has had an effect, too.

I laugh bitterly. "I know you think I'm crazy," I say coldly. "But do you think I'm stupid, too? Do you think that any part of me buys anything you're selling, after all these weeks of you telling me I'm insane, a danger to myself and a danger to my baby?"

"Paige," the doctor responds, still using that same tone. I look at my dad, anger tightening into a red hot ball in my chest and he pulls his phone out of his pocket. "Mr. Renner," Dr. Lawson says, changing her focus. "There's no need to –"

My dad holds his hand up. No one says anything for a few seconds until my dad speaks to whoever has taken the call.

"She's here," he says, and I can tell, at once, that he is as close to violent rage as I am. "The fucking doctor! She's in the room *right now!* I need you to –" he pauses, listening. "Uh-huh. OK. OK. Two hours?! OK. Alright. Thank you. Bye."

He hangs up and looks right into Dr. Lawson's eyes. "You need to get out. Right now."

I watch as the faux-sincerity on the doctor's face curdles into anger. "Your daughter is not fit to care for a child," she sneers, not even looking at me. "She's a pathological liar, Mr. Renner, a borderline personality. Don't you ever wonder –"

"GET OUT!" My dad shouts. "NOW! Lady, I swear to God, if –"

A man in a suit and two worried looking nurses burst into the room.

"Sheila," the man says, stepping between Dr. Lawson – Sheila – and my dad. "I asked you not to come in here. Come with me, we can talk –"

"Don't touch me!" Dr. Lawson screeches, even though no one has touched her. "John, you're making a mistake. You're really going to cave in to some celebrity lawyer over this? This baby is in danger! You're going to have blood on your hands if –"

At that point, my dad loses it completely. He lunges at Dr. Lawson but the man in the suit and the two nurses hold him back.

"Call security!" The man yells at one nurse, and she disappears out of the room. Then he turns to my dad. "Mr. Renner!

Sir! Calm down, please. I am John Allan, the head administrator of this hospital – no one is going to take your daughter's child away from her. Please. Sir, please calm down!"

And my father does calm down, as soon as he hears that no one is going to take the baby away. He looks John Allan in the eye. "You better not be lying. You better not just be saying that so –"

John Allan looks harried and pissed off, but it doesn't seem aimed at my dad. He shakes his head. "I'm not just saying it, sir. Your lawyer has been in touch with our legal team and we realize some mistakes might have been made in the course of your daughter's care –"

"Bullshit!"

Everybody in the room looks at the person who has just shouted 'bullshit' – Dr. Sheila Lawson.

"She's psychotic!" She yells, pointing at me as John Allan moves to escort her out of the room. "She's been here for weeks, John! Weeks and she still hasn't said a thing about what happened to her when she was 'kidnapped!' Everybody knows she made the whole thing up and now you want –"

"Out," the administrator replies, coldly. "Right fucking now, Sheila. OUT."

And then they're gone. The argument continues in the hallway, but the loud, angry voices fade as Dr. Lawson is led away, hopefully to the end of her career. I look at my father. He looks at me.

"Damn," he says. "I guess that lawyer meant it when she said she was going to put the fear of God into this hospital's legal team."

"So what does this mean?" I ask, still not truly willing to believe I'll be allowed to just walk out, not after everything. "I – we – can just go?"

Less than 24 hours later, I'm free to go for good. I leave with my son and my father through a back entrance to the hospital, so as to avoid media attention. Before we leave, John Allan informs us that Dr. Sheila Lawson has been placed on paid leave, pending the outcome of an investigation into my care at River Forks Hospital.

The press appear to be breeding like rats, because the crowd outside the house is a lot bigger than I remember it. The presence of a newborn does nothing to dampen their enthusiasm, either, and they film, photograph and scream questions at us as we run into the house. The commotion wakes the baby and he begins to cry. As my father runs around, closing all the curtains and then fussing over the mess in the kitchen, I tentatively raise Eirik's son to my breast and almost melt into a puddle of hormonal emotion as he latches on and gazes up into my eyes, like I might be the most wonderful thing he has ever seen. Which, given he is only 1 day old, might just be true.

Later, when night has fallen, the baby is asleep and the house is in a much cleaner state than it had been when we got home, my dad and I look at each other.

"We can do this," he says to me. "We can do this, Paige. The interview is tomorrow – they're coming here to do it but they don't have to know you're here. You don't have to appear."

"You're still doing that?" I ask, barely looking up from my sleeping child's sweet face.

"Yes," my dad replies. "I have to – I agreed to do it, even if they've let you out of the hospital already. Besides, the interviewer says we can use this as an opportunity to – what did he say? 'Frame the narrative.' We can explain that you're a new mom, that we need peace and quiet, that you might talk about what happened when you're ready. Or not. Hopefully we can get those reporters to leave and we can get back to some kind of normal life here."

Bless my dad. He's not even that old, but he seems to live in an older world than the one I'm used to. A world where the presence of a newborn baby in a house is enough to get a crowd of desperate, ruthless media types off the lawn. We don't live in that world anymore. I know it and my dad doesn't.

"I'll stay upstairs," I tell him. "During the interview, I mean. I don't want to be on TV."

***

Time itself seems to have taken on paradoxical new qualities with the presence of my baby. The minutes themselves pass as if slowed, each second looming past as I do next to nothing beyond staring at him, running my fingers over the contours of his tiny, sleeping face, marveling at a soft hand as it wraps itself tightly around my thumb. And even as the lovesick haze of new motherhood seems to have delayed the ticking of the clock itself, time races by. I sit down at just past five o'clock, with the baby on my lap, and when I next check my phone – expecting it to read 5:30 or perhaps 5:45 – it reads 9:10 and I'm baffled – where have the hours gone?

My dad hovers sweetly, as enchanted as any grandfather would be. I feel him holding back, though. He comments at one point how he thinks he can see a bit of my mother in the baby's mouth and chin and then I notice him biting another comment back – a comment I'm almost certain would have been about the man my dad doesn't know – my son's father.

I desperately want to tell my dad about Eirik. I want to tell him so badly I'm near bursting with it. Not yet, though. I haven't figured out what I'm going to do, and I can't very well go telling half the story, can I? I can't say oh, yes, my baby's father is named Eirik and I love him, because that will inevitably be followed with questions about where Eirik is and why isn't he here with his child and how did I meet Eirik etc. etc.

I'm going to give myself a few days. To think. To be with my son. To settle in. I won't make any rushed decisions. I won't allow these precious first days to be tainted with stress – not anymore than they already are, anyway.

The media crew arrive earlier than expected and I disappear upstairs before they come in. Then I sit on my bed, with the bedroom door open, straining to hear what's being said. It sounds like a whole bunch of people, there are a lot of voices and sounds – furniture being moved, equipment being placed, preparations being made. The baby, his belly full, mercifully does not stir.

A couple of hours and two feeds later, my son sleeps again and my boredom and curiosity grows. I walk to the doorway and stand there cocking my head towards the stairs, but I still can't make out anything that's being said.

I look back at the baby. Still fast asleep. It's just a few steps down the stairs.

When I get to the bottom I lean my ear gently against the door. That's better. Now I can hear everything. A woman is speaking, her voice serious and authoritative. I recognize that voice – Joyce Williams, the 'prestige' interviewer. Wow. She's asking my father about the baby.

"He's beautiful," my dad us saying, and I can hear the pride in his voice. "Almost 9 pounds, beautiful and strong. I love him very much."

"And your daughter," Joyce Williams asks, "how is she?"

"She's great. She's like any new mom, just completely engrossed in her baby."

There's defensiveness in my dad's tone when he says that and I realize that's partly why he's agreed to do the interview – to try to introduce a different narrative to what has become a sensationalistic and negative story.

Joyce Williams pauses briefly before asking the next question. "And do you, Mr. Renner – or your daughter – have any comment on the statement given by Dr. Sheila Lawson just over an hour ago?"

My father has been caught off guard – so have I. Dr. Lawson is giving statements now? Is that legal? I lean harder against the door.

"Uh, Dr. Lawson?" My dad asks. "I – er – I didn't know that she, uh –"

"Of course Dr. Lawson is barred from discussing your daughter's case, Mr. Renner, but it was reported a few hours ago that she has been fired from her job at River Forks Hospital. When we caught her outside her home she – actually, Jim, do we have the tape?"

My stomach sinks. What has that awful woman said? She's smart, it's almost certain she's found a way to say something without actually, legally 'saying something.' There's a small commotion going on in the living room and I can't help but crack the door, just an inch. I have to hear what Dr. Lawson said.

My father is on one of our sofas, which suddenly looks very worn and old under the intense lights which have been set up behind the cameras, most of which are pointed right at him. Joyce Williams is seated facing him, slightly off to the side. A man wearing headphones is handing my dad a phone.

A few seconds later, Dr. Lawson's voice fills the room.

"As you know, I'm not legally allowed to talk about Paige Renner or anything to do with her care," she says, in a voice dripping with faux concern. "And I'll need to speak to my legal team before I can give you a more official statement. But what I will say right now is that I have spent my entire career protecting vulnerable children and young people from those who would do them harm. Sometimes it's their parents, sometimes their teachers, school bullies, anyone. And sometimes, it's themselves."

Dr. Lawson pauses dramatically after that statement and I feel the first bubbles starting to boil up in my blood.

"Some young people are a danger to themselves, through no fault of their own. Mental illness, personality disorders, the consequences of past trauma – it can be anything, and we should be compassionate in our approach to them. But if you were to ask me what I think about allowing an infant to be cared for by one of these damaged –"

"That's enough!"

My father, holding the phone, has stopped the video playing and is glaring angrily at Joyce Williams. I can see how hard he's trying to hold it together. I myself am lightheaded with rage. How was that comment from the doctor not about me? How is anyone listening to that ever going to think she's not talking about me? Of course she is!

"You're upset, sir."

Joyce Williams is addressing my father, whose face is bright red now. He looks to his side, at the man who handed him the phone. "You said this wasn't going to be a 'gotcha!' You said this wasn't going to be hostile!"

The man, off-camera, signals something to Joyce Williams and she turns to one of the cameras and announces a commercial break. Seconds later, my dad jumps to his feet and rips the microphone off his lapel.

"What is this?!" He shouts, at no one in particular. "You can't just ambush me with something like that, like I'm some goddamned rube! Get – get the fuck out of my house. Right now. All of you. Out. OUT!"

Immediately, Joyce Williams and about three other people surround him, speaking softly and kindly, assuring him they didn't intend to cause any upset, that this is his chance to defend me, that unless he continues the interview, he's wasting his chance to 'change America's mind.'

My father, bless him, knows bullshit when he smells it. He brushes off the entreaties of the perfectly coiffed, perfectly unctuous

Joyce and her flunkies and shakes his head. "No. I'm sorry, don't touch me. That was an ambush – you should have warned me that you were going to play that tape – live – of Dr. Lawson. We're done here. You do have to leave right now."

And as I watch the media team continue their efforts to convince my dad to finish the interview, something happens. Something like the camera suddenly being pulled way, way back in a movie. A new, wider perspective is suddenly laid out in front of me.

Even if these people leave, right now, they're not going anywhere. Not really. This is 2017, where scandals never die. They live on, zombie-like and constantly mutating online, in all those discussion forums and comment sections and Youtube videos. No, the media isn't going anywhere. Nor is the interest. I've barely glanced at my phone since coming home, and even I've seen enough to realize that this is the biggest story in the country – and that the interest in me and my story is not the kind, concerned interest of a loving friend or relative. It's viciously intense and, terrifyingly, not really interested in getting at the truth, so far as I can tell. No, it's become something else, some kind of cultural monster that has nothing to do with me and everything to do with reflecting people's own narratives about their own lives, about themselves, back to them. To one group I'm an innocent victim – ruined, of course, utterly ruined, destroyed by the unspeakable things they're certain have happened to me – but innocent. To another I'm the worst kind of manipulator, a brainless, heartless young woman desperate for attention and fame, toying with the media and using my own child as a way to keep the spotlight focused right on me. Those are the two main stories. Believe me, there are others. Countless others, from the mildly wacky to the truly insane.

I look back up the stairs, listening for any sound of fussing. It's not just me who's going to have to deal with this scrutiny, either. It's my father, my friends – my son. And he won't have his father around to guide him through it.

I peer back out through the door as the CNN crew continues to cajole my father, and I can almost feel it – the cold certainty of steel infusing my spine.

You can stop this.

Maybe it's Eirik, maybe he's the trigger for this sudden surge of strength – the thought of him, of what he would do in this situation. Maybe it's coming purely from inside me, a natural reaction of boiling anger to the whirlwind of lies and bullshit swirling around not just me, now, but my family – my baby and my father. I can't know, in the moment, what the cause is. All I can know is that I've had enough. Of everything. Something has to be done, a decision has to be made. I take a deep breath and step out into the living room.

It takes a few seconds for people to notice me. One of the crewmembers is the first to look up and see me standing there and I watch as her eyes widen and she paws at the man beside her and points at me.

"Jim, Jim – JIM!"

Jim, irritated already, almost brushes her off but she grabs his shirtsleeve and he looks up. And then his eyes widen, too. More people look up. A little ripple of whispered excitement runs through the crew.

"Is that her?"

"Get the lights back on."

"Where's the baby?"

Eventually, it's Joyce Williams herself who speaks directly to me. "Paige!" She smiles, extending her hand out to me. I take it and smile back, not buying it for a second. "Would you like to take a seat beside your –"

"No."

Everyone in the room stops what they're doing and looks at me when they hear the tone in my voice. If I'm not mistaken there is a slight edge of 'is-she-going-to-lose-it-right-now' in their interest, too. I don't bother telling them they're going to be disappointed.

"I won't take a seat next to my dad," I say, my voice firm. "He said the interview with him was over, and it is. I have something to say, and you can film me when I say it, but I'm not answering any questions. And if you want to do this we have to do it right now because my son will be awake soon and he'll be hungry."

Joyce Williams looks at her crew members. The crew members look at Joyce Williams. Jim, who seems to be in charge in some capacity, nods to a couple of people. "Do it, set it up. Now."

Less than ten minutes and one very short, very one-sided negotiation later I'm seated in front of the bright lights – bright enough that I can actually feel the heat coming off them. The camera is pointed at Joyce, though, and she's talking directly into it, explaining that my father has ended the interview early but that they now have me, Paige Renner, and that I've agreed to answer a few brief questions. It's one question, but I don't bother correcting my interviewer – if I have to walk off on live TV because she steps outside the bounds I've just laid out, that's her problem, not mine.

"And now," Joyce says, "we have an exclusive interview with the young woman America has been waiting months to hear from – Paige Renner. Paige," she turns to me, along with one of the cameras. "Is it true you've given birth to a boy?"

I control my breathing and keep my expression neutral. "Yes."

"And what can you tell us about the time after you went missing?" Joyce starts.

I shake my head, just a little. "I'm sorry, I don't want to talk about that. What I do want to say is that I am not mentally ill or delusional. I do not have amnesia or borderline personality disorder. I was not kidnapped by aliens, or any of the other insane theories I've seen floating around online."

"But what about –"

I keep going, ignoring Joyce's interruption. "What I want to say is that I love my son and I love his father. I won't be making any other statements to the media, and none of my friends at Grand Northeastern, nor any of the staff at River Forks Hospital, knows any more than any of you, so you can leave them alone. If I have anything else to say, I'll say it myself. Thank you."

Joyce waits, the way interviewers do, to see if I'll leap to fill the awkward silence after I finish talking with more information. I do not. Finally, she speaks again. "And does your baby have a name yet?"

I look right into the camera, realizing only at the moment the words come out of my mouth that yes, my son has a name. "Eirik. His name is Eirik."

"Eric?" my interlocutor asks, raising one eyebrow conspiratorially, as if we're just two girlfriends having a chat – and that the conversation is not, in fact, being broadcast live to the whole country.

"Eirik," I repeat myself, slowing down and pronouncing it carefully. "Ei-rik. Like 'eye' and then 'rick.' He's named after his father."

Joyce Williams can't believe the scoop she's getting. People have been speculating about the identity of my baby's father ever since I turned up in that pharmacy in River Forks. "His father?" She repeats, not quite managing to contain the excitement in her voice.

But I'm standing up already, removing the microphone that's been attached to my shirt even as Joyce pleads with me to sit back down. My dad steps in, getting between us.

"No, you heard her, that's enough. You have to leave now."

***

An hour later, my dad and I are sitting across from each other at the dinner table. The furniture still hasn't been moved back into its proper places but the CNN crew is gone.

"You know they're not going to leave you alone?" My dad says dejectedly, picking at a pile of instant mashed potatoes on his plate.

I meet his eyes, nodding. "Yeah, I know. I was just thinking the same thing."

"I hate this," he continues. "I hate that you – and my grandson – have to put up with this. With being stalked like animals. I wish I had enough money to just take all of us – I don't know, somewhere else, somewhere far away. I'm so sorry Paige. I'm so sorry I can't protect you. It's my job and I can't –"

I reach out and put my hand over my fathers. "Dad, stop. This isn't your fault – none of this is your fault. And you couldn't stop it anymore than anyone could – including me."

We sit quietly for a little while, picking at our unappetizing dinner. I'm thinking of how delicious a venison stew would be right now, straight from the gigantic clay pots that simmer for hours over the cooking fires in the Viking camp, when my dad speaks up again.

"So his name is Eirik, huh? How do you spell that?"

"E-I-R-I-K," I reply and my dad looks emotional. "Dad," I say, patting his forearm. "Dad. Dad! What is it? What's –"

"I understand why you don't want to talk to the media," he say, breathing deeply, trying not to cry. "And I know I haven't been a good parent to you, Paige. But –"

Suddenly, it becomes clear to me. My dad thinks I haven't told him anything about my life during the months I was gone because I resent him in some way, or I think he's been a bad father.

"No," I say. "No, Dad. No, that is not – that is not what any of this is about. I don't think you've been a bad father, that isn't why I haven't said anything. Oh my God, is that what you think? We talked about this a long time ago –"

"Why then?" He replies plaintively. "Paige, why? Why won't you tell me?

"I can't," I reply. "I can't tell you. But I can show you."

My dad looks at me, confused. "You can – what? You can show me? What do you mean by that?"

"I mean I can show you, Dad. I can explain it to you by showing you. Not right now, not today. Soon. Tomorrow, maybe. I need to talk to someone first."

"To Eric? Eirik, I mean?"

"Dad," I say, taking both his hands in mine and looking into his eyes. "Will you trust me? If I tell you that soon you'll find out everything, you'll understand everything about where I went and who I was with, will you just trust me?"

He sits back, still looking mystified, but he nods his head. "OK. I mean, I don't understand anything that's going on here right now, Paige, but OK. I trust you."

I force myself to eat a few mouthfuls of mashed potato, mindful of the need to keep my calorie intake high because I'm breastfeeding – and because I'm about to go back to a place where calories aren't always in such easy supply. A couple of minutes later, I ask my dad another question.

"Did you mean what you just said?"

"About what?"

"When you said you'd take us away if you could, somewhere far away, somewhere where no one knew who we were?"

My dad's face falls. He feels that he's let me down, and that hurts my heart. "Yes," he says quietly. "Yes, Paige. I'm not sure you understand that the only thing keeping me here – in this particular house, and this particular town – is you. Well, now it's you and little Eirik. I don't care where I am, as long as the two of you are with me.

Even when you went away to college, the only reason I stayed here is so you would have somewhere to come back to – a home."

My heart fills with love. "Oh Dad," I whisper. "Is that true?"

"Of course it's true, Paige. You and your mother are all that ever mattered to me. When she died, it was down to just you. I know I let you down –"

"No!" I say, standing up and going to him, wrapping my arms around his stooped shoulders. "No, Dad. Don't say that. No one let anyone down, OK? I told you this before, remember? Before I went to college? It's not what I feel, it's not what happened. We both lost mom, and losing her broke both of us. I've never resented you. Never."

My father's voice is very, very soft now. "You mean it?"

"Yes!" I cry. "Yes of course I mean it. I love you, Dad. I've always loved you. And I'm not going anywhere, OK? We're going to stick together from now on, all three of us."

As if on cue, Eirik begins to fuss and I reach down into the bassinet near my feet to pick him up.

Chapter 29
21st Century

"Paige?" Emma sounds suspicious.

"Yes," I reply. "It's me."

As soon as she hears my voice I hear a big sigh of relief on the other end of the phone. "Ugh, thank God. The media is going totally nuts right now – they're following me home! I thought maybe someone had hacked your phone or – actually, fuck it, it doesn't matter. How are you? I saw you on TV last night – that was so crazy! You totally handled Joyce Williams – ha ha! And – oh my God, Paige – when can I meet the baby? It's a boy? When can –"

"Emma!" I laugh, because this feels just like old times – begging my friend to calm down as she talks a mile a minute and loses me about halfway through. "Slow down!"

She laughs, too. "Yeah, sorry about that. I just – damn, I have so many questions that I don't even know where to begin. When can I see you? I mean, I'm not sure you can leave your house right now, I keep seeing shots of all the media trucks outside. It looks like a total nightmare."

"It is," I agree. "And I don't know if I can get out – not without getting bombarded anyway, and not anytime soon. They even followed my dad to the grocery store this morning, and then some stupid website posted that I must be breastfeeding because there was no baby formula in his shopping cart. They're seriously spying on groceries!"

"But we can talk on the phone, right?" Emma asks.

"Oh yeah. Eirik's sleeping right now and I'll have to feed him if he wakes up but I can talk at the same time. And as for visiting, I was actually kind of calling about that."

There's a brief pause before Emma replies. "So you named him Eirik? After his, um, his dad?"

She's afraid of saying – or asking – the wrong thing and upsetting me. But it doesn't matter anymore, because I'm not going to be around much longer. That means I can talk about it more freely, even if I do still have to be careful with the specifics.

"Yeah," I reply. "I did. We can talk about that if you want but I'm just also wondering if you can come over tomorrow afternoon? It's important."

"Tomorrow?" Emma replies, skeptical. "To your house?"

She's worried about the media. It's understandable. "Yeah, to the house. If you park in the driveway all you have to do is run to the front door. It's really important that I see you, Em. And it has to be tomorrow."

"Well I really want to meet the baby," she tells me. "And I guess I don't see any other way of doing it – not without you having to leave, anyway, and I'd rather it was me dealing with those reporters than you. Sure, yeah, I'll come tomorrow. Afternoon? How does one o'clock sound?"

"It sounds great! And Emma?" I ask.

"Yeah?"

"Can you do me a favor?"

"Sure – you need me to pick something up? I can do that, just –"

"No, it's not that – it's actually kind of a strange request."

Emma chuckles. "Just tell me, Paige. Everything is so strange lately it'll probably be fine."

"OK. It's – uh – can you wear something plain and boring? Like a plain t-shirt and skirt, in normal colors? Like not bright pink or anything like that?"

"Uhh..."

"Just humor me!" I tell her, trying to keep my voice cheerful. "Please, I'll explain it when you get here. You'll understand."

"OK," Emma replies, sounding amused. "Fine. You're such an oddball, Paige."

I end the call as quickly as possible after Emma agrees to come over the next day, because I don't want her to start asking questions again and I know she's going to if we keep talking.

She's coming at one in the afternoon. That means I have just under a full day to get ready. I look at Eirik, asleep in his bassinet, and my heart melts. Was I ever that innocent? That blissfully relaxed?

I suppose I was at some point. No longer. Now it's my job to protect him. I search my mind for doubts, because I am a naturally doubtful person and almost every decision I make is beset by worries and anxieties. There are very few this time, and it surprises me. Surely taking your baby and your dad – your only family in the world – to live in the 9th century, would produce some questions? And yes, it has. Will we have enough to eat? What if one of us gets sick? What if the Jarl is dead?

If Eirik is dead, we come back to 2017, we make a life here in the future, we make the best of it. If Eirik is alive, we won't have to worry about having enough to eat. We won't have to worry about our son growing up weak and sickly, like the villagers in Caistley, because he'll get the best of everything. And should tragedy befall us, should any of us ever fall sick in a way the healers can't deal with, there's always the tree – a way back.

Sure, we could stay. We could stay where there are hospitals and schools and paved roads and Google. It would be easier to stay, in so many ways. But I know if I stay, it will be a decision made based on fear.

Something inside me has changed since giving birth and escaping Dr. Lawson and the hospital room I spent so many weeks of my pregnancy in. Something is different, and it's not just my body. I feel it, bone-deep, when I look down at my son. The days of

Paige Renner making decisions based on her fears are over. I don't hope they're over, I'm not willing them to be over – they simply *are* over, already in the past.

I must be brave. For my baby, for my dad, and for the man who, whether or not he is still alive, has taught me the value of bravery. I grab a piece of paper and write down a list of items. Later, when I hand the list to my father, he gives me a look.

"What's all this, Paige? Are you planning for the zombie apocalypse?"

I laugh. "No, Dad. It's just some things I need."

"Antiseptic cleanser? Antibiotic cream? Sterile bandages? Meal replacement drinks? Multivitamins? What's all this for? It's going to cost a fortune."

I could tell my dad that his money is only going to be useful for around the next twenty hours, and then he's literally never going to use it again, but that would just get him thinking that maybe Dr. Lawson was right, that maybe I really am crazy. So I just smile and reassure him that I definitely need the things on the list.

"Merino wool socks?" He continues. "Can I even get those at Costco? I might have to go to the outdoors store for those. And five pairs? Paige, what the –"

"Dad!"

My dad looks up. "What?"

"Please. I need everything on that list. it just took me over an hour to write, and I've been thinking about it for days. I'm so tired, and I need to give Eirik a bath. Can you please get those things for me? I promise you I need every single one of them."

My dad stares at me for a few more seconds and then shrugs. "Ok. Sure, fine. But you've got baby formula on this list, Paige. I thought you were going to keep breastfeeding –" he stops when he sees the look on my face and holds his hands up. "OK, OK! I'll head out right now, then, because this might be a long trip."

I stand up and kiss my dad on the cheek. "Thank you."

And then I stand behind the heavy, closed drapes in the living room, peeking out as the reporters surround the car, shouting questions as my dad tries to pull out onto the road. Thinking about how they're going to react when it slowly becomes clear that my dad, myself and baby Eirik have apparently disappeared into thin air causes a grim smile to spread across my face.

I can't enjoy it for long, though, because I'm fretting now over whether I put everything on the list. I think I did. I mean, I must have, because Eadgar, Willa and Willa's kids have survived this long without any modern help – I just want to make things a little easier for them. And if they're confused by the pull-tabs on top of the meal replacement cans, so be it, because I don't mean to return to 2017 and I want to make sure those kids and my two friends go into winter with full bellies and all the vitamins and warm blankets they need. I'll worry about explaining what 'vitamins' even are when I get there. The medical supplies are for me to bring north, to where I will hopefully find the Vikings and the man whose unknown status as alive or dead I cannot quite force myself to face at this time, because doing so would make it impossible for me to take care of all the things I need to take care of. No one in the past – neither Viking nor villager – will know what to do with sterile bandages or antibiotic ointment. I'll keep them with me, just in case.

Eirik wakes as I stand at the window, hidden from the media, and then takes to my breast with such enthusiasm it actually has him panting. I stroke his cheek as he stares up at me, drunk on love and mother's milk.

"We're going to meet your daddy's people soon, my love. Your people. And you're going to grow up in the meadows and the woods, fat and happy and surrounded by people who love you."

I leave the second part of that statement unsaid, the part where I admit I don't have a crystal ball, that I can't actually know the future, and that sometimes bad things happen. My heart is still filled with courage, even as my mind is fully aware of all the possibilities. My son needs things he cannot get in 2017. I cannot be his father. I cannot be a full, functional community of people who care about him. I cannot be the deep, clean streams and the fields of white and yellow wildflowers he will play in, if everything goes well.

And if everything doesn't go well? I'll cross that bridge if I come to it. In the meantime, I claim ownership of my own destiny.

Chapter 30
21st Century

"Why can't we just use backpacks?"

It's just past noon on my last day in the 21st century. My dad and I are packing the items he bought yesterday into a series of plain burlap sacks he had to go to an agricultural feed store to buy, and he's full of questions. I ignore the one about the backpacks – not be rude, but just because I know answering it won't satisfy him and the interrogation will continue.

The burden of responsibility is on my shoulders, and it isn't just for myself and my son – it's for my dad, too. Although he isn't chronologically old, he has never recovered, not the way I have, from the loss of my mother. He barely coped without her for years, and I know he won't cope on his own at all. He's said as much to me over and over since I came back from my time away, repeating that I am all he has, that he doesn't care where we are as long as we're together. The Antarctic, he says sometimes when we talk, Siberia, Timbuktu, the middle of the Australian outback – it doesn't matter, as long as we're together.

Well, I think, as I carefully place a flat-pack of meal replacement drinks at the bottom of a sack, *we're definitely going to find out if that's true or not.*

Emma shows up just before one o'clock, dressed in a white t-shirt and a plain ankle-length skirt. Good. Both she and my father can feel the strange anticipation in the air – I can tell from the way they're watching me, waiting for me to tell them what's up. Before we go, I insist that we all sit down and eat the rest of the pizza we had delivered last night – and that I deliberately ordered way too much of. I want our bellies as full as possible.

We eat quietly, surrounded only by the sounds of chewing – and Eirik snuffling as he sleeps in his bassinet.

"Oh my God," Emma says, after finishing a single slice of cold pizza. "I shouldn't have eaten that – I already got a chicken wrap on the way here, ugh, I can't even move."

But I take another slice of pizza out of the box and put it on her plate anyway.

Briefly, I catch her and my father making very fleeting eye-contact. They're wondering what the hell is going on. I put down my pizza and look up at the two of them.

"So," I say. "I need to ask you guys a question."

"Sure." Emma replies.

"Do you trust me? I see you looking at each other, wondering if oh, maybe the doctor was right, maybe Paige really has lost her mind. I –"

"No," my father says. "No, it's not that. We're just full, Paige, and you keep making us eat more pizza. Why are you suddenly so insistent on stuffing us with pizza?"

"And what are all these bags of –" Emma starts, but I hold up one hand, stopping them both.

"Wait. Just answer the question. Do you trust me? I'm going to ask you two to come with me right now, on a short walk. And before we go – in fact right now – I want you both to promise you're not going to ask me any more questions. We're not going anywhere in the car, it's all fine and safe. But I need you to trust me. Just – trust me, and come with me."

Emma narrows her eyes and looks at me, checking for signs that I'm joking and seeing none.

It takes a few minutes, and they both attempt to pepper me with more questions, but eventually they do both give in, and agree to come with me on a walk in the woods behind the house. There's a brief silence when I inform them that we need to bring the bags of goods, but the stern look on my face keeps them both quiet. I'm sure it all looks totally nuts to them, but they're going along with it because a) they do trust me and b) as I said, what harm could it do – a walk in the woods?

I glance down at my phone just before we leave. Almost 2 p.m. Eirik is snuggled up against my chest in a linen baby wrap, the bags are packed, Emma and my dad are waiting. This is it. I usher them out the door ahead of me, but Emma notices me leaving my phone on the counter.

"Don't you –" she begins, but I eyeball her pointedly and she shuts up. "OK, fine. This better be worth it, Paige. You are acting like a right nutjob."

I laugh. "A 'right nutjob.' English people are so adorable!"

Emma grins and we're off. I'm so close I can almost smell the East Anglian air, and I'm terrified something is going to go wrong, that I'm going to be thwarted somehow.

But nothing stops us. We walk down through the yard and into the woods and Emma comments on the fact that it's a beautiful day. It is. Sunny and warm and with just the faintest whisper of autumnal crispness on the breeze. When we reach the tree, I come to a stop and, a couple of seconds later, so do Emma and my dad.

Emma puts down her sack, sighing exaggeratedly. "Ugh, this is so heavy."

Suddenly, I'm emotional. I thought I was going to avoid this. I thought I was beyond that now. Apparently not. All it takes is a single glance back through the trees, a little glimpse of the house. I'm never coming back here. I'm never going to feel the cool, dusty linoleum under my bare feet again on a hot summer's day. I'm never going to drive into River Forks with my dad in our battered old Ford again. I'm never going to sleep in the room where my mother used to kiss me on the forehead every night.

I can't remember what her face looked like, but I remember her voice clearly, and the mantra she would repeat after that bedtime kiss, just before she closed my bedroom door: "Goodnight, Paige. Goodnight, sleep tight, don't-let-the-bedbugs-bite."

"Paige?" My father says, stepping forward when he sees that I'm teary. "What is it?"

"It's nothing, Dad. Well, it's not nothing. But I can't explain it now. Maybe in a few minutes."

Emma is staring at me, concerned. "What are we doing here?" She asks gently, putting an arm around my shoulder. "Why are we all down here in the woods?"

I turn to her and take a breath. "You said you trusted me," I remind her. "You said you'd do this for me."

"And I will," she replies, looking at my dad. "*We* will. But – what do you want us to do? Right now, I mean? Why are we –"

"I want you to listen," I tell them, wiping my eyes. "It won't take long. But I want you to listen. And I want you to keep your promise that you won't ask any questions. I need five minutes. Just listen and do as I ask for five minutes. And then you can do whatever you want. Call the hospital, call Dr. Lawson, call the media, drag me off to the loony-bin. Anything. But I want five minutes. OK?"

They're both thoroughly confused – not that I blame them – but they both nod, agreeing to the five minutes.

I look down at Eirik, asleep on my chest, and run a finger through the downy hair on the top of his head. I breathe in, slowly, and then out again.

"Do you remember," I ask my dad, "those two imaginary friends I had, as a kid? Willa and Eadgar? From Caistley?"

My father can't quite hide the worry on his face, but he keeps his promise and just nods. "Uh, yeah. I remember that, Paige."

And do you," I say, turning to face Emma, "remember what I told you last year, before I went missing? The big secret?"

Emma is not as good as my dad at hiding her reaction. She looks at him, quickly, and then at me. "Uh, yeah," she says carefully, "yes, I remember."

I give them both a moment for it to sink in that yes, I am talking about the incredibly awkward thing that makes me look crazy and that they both desperately wish I would stop talking about. When I'm sure that neither one is going to make a run for it or call 9-1-1, I continue.

"Yeah, so about that. And before I say this I want to remind you that you promised me five minutes – you promised."

They both nod again, and I can almost hear the gears turning in their heads, trying to figure out a way to deal with me, to get me back to the house, without pissing me off. And I haven't even gotten to the best part yet.

"So," I continue, refusing to look shyly at the ground or otherwise act coy. "Eadgar and Willa were never imaginary. They're real. And everything I told you last year, Emma, that was all true."

A thick fog of pure awkwardness settles over us. Emma speaks first.

"So, OK," she says, choosing her words carefully. "You say it's all true – about the, uh, the time-travel? OK. I understand. So what are we – um, what does this have to do with right now – with us being in the woods right now?"

"Paige," my dad cuts in and reaches for my arm. "We can talk about this back at the house. We can –"

"No," I pull away. "You said five minutes. Both of you. You said you would do as I said."

"OK," Emma says quietly, in the gentle tone you use with a person you're not sure is sane or not. "OK. So what do you want us to do then?"

"I want you to do this," I respond, even though neither of them looks like they're expecting a coherent response. And then I kneel down in the fallen leaves at the base of the tree and move to press my bare hands and forearms against the root. I don't actually do it, of course, not yet, but I show them how to do it.

Emma kneels down next to me, and she isn't happy. She knows she promised, but I can tell she isn't pleased at all. She's worried, and not because she thinks she's about to time travel.

"Paige," my dad says, still standing. "What is this? This is ridiculous – what are we doing? We need to go back to the house – these bags are heavy and Eirik is going to get cold."

"Sure," I nod. "We can go back. But first you need to do this. Come on, humor me – if I'm crazy, nothing's going to happen, right?"

My dad shakes his head – both of them seem annoyed as well as worried, and crouches down next to the tree. My stomach does a nervous flip.

"Now," I tell them. Put your hands – and your arms – on the tree. Close your eyes first, and take a deep breath, and then just touch the –"

First Emma disappears, and then my dad. A thin scream, as if from a great distance, fills my ears. I grab the bags they have left behind and lean forward, getting as much skin in contact with the tree as possible without waking Eirik. Darkness expands around me, my baby jerks awake on my chest, and then we're there. I look up.

Emma is on the ground, coughing. My dad is next to her, staring at his new surroundings. Neither of them are speaking, both look to be on the verge of freaking out completely. I expected this. I knew this was going to happen.

"It's real," I say softly, standing up so I can rock Eirik back to sleep. "It's not a dream or a trick, I haven't drugged you. It's real. It's as real as where we just were – the house and the yard and the woods. It's just – different woods."

Emma is whimpering and looking around. "Paige – what did you do?" She asks, her voice shaking. "What did you – what is this? Where are we?"

"You already know what this place is," I tell both of them calmly. "It's Caistley. Well, it's very close to Caistley. This is the place I told the therapists about when I was a little kid – it's the place I told you about, Emma. This is it, all around you. As real as anything."

I wait quietly as my father and my friend get slowly to their feet, looking around like bears that have just emerged from hibernation.

"I must have had a seizure," my dad says, more to himself than me. "I passed out. I'll wake up in the woods behind the house any minute now. I hope you don't call an ambulance, Paige, I don't need one."

I smile at my dad's attempt to save money, even as he thinks he's passed out and having some kind of dream.

"I don't hear any cars."

I turn to Emma. She's got her head cocked to the side, listening. She looks up. "No planes, either. I don't hear anything. Just birds."

"Yeah," I say, unsure if she's accepted where she is or if she's just making observations on my skill at creating whole environments to play complex pranks on my friends and relatives. "It's always so quiet here. It was always one of my favorite things about it."

Emma faces me, her hands on her hips. "This can't be what you say it is, Paige. You know that, right? Time travel doesn't exist. Time travel *can't* exist. It's impossible."

I nod. "I know. I know it can't. But it – well, it does. Here, anyway. Right now. And all the other times I've come here."

"So where is this village, then?" She asks. She's not being combative, it's just her way of dealing with something that she believes to be impossible. "Where are these friends of yours? Willa? Edgar?"

"Eadgar."

"Eadgar, alright. Willa and Eadgar. Where are they? Off dancing with fairies and unicorns?"

I laugh. "Unfortunately not. There don't seem to be any unicorns here – or fairies. This is where Eirik's dad lives, though. Or, lived. Uh –"

I stop talking, unsure about what tense I should be using to speak of Eirik the Jarl and Emma and my father both stare up at me.

"Really?" Emma says. "*Really*? You were – Paige, you were here? That whole time?"

I nod. "Yes. Now do you see why I couldn't tell anyone? Everybody already thought I was nuts – how would they have reacted to me telling them I was a time-traveler? Even you two didn't believe me!"

"I'm still not sure I do," Emma replies. "So we're in a different place now. Not in the woods at the bottom of your garden anymore. But how do we know this is time travel? It just looks like trees and earth and sky to me."

As if on cue, a sudden rushing in the undergrowth fills our ears. I know what it is, but both my dad and my friend whip around, trying to figure out where it's coming from.

"What is that?!" Emma shrieks, grabbing my arm. "Paige! What is –"

One of the ruddy, hairy pigs that the villagers let loose in the woods to forage shoots out of the bushes and, seeing us, disappears right back into them.

"A pig," I say, remembering a long time ago, when I didn't recognize the creatures for what they were, either. "They have different pigs here – not the big, pink ones."

"Jesus Christ," my dad suddenly whispers, leaning heavily against a tree. "Paige – you were telling the truth? This whole time? Eirik's dad is here?"

"Yeah," I reply. "I was telling the truth. I was never crazy – I've been coming here since I was a little kid and it just took me awhile before I realized I wasn't supposed to talk about it, that other people didn't travel in similar ways."

We all stand quietly for a few moments, and I can feel my dad and Emma are taking everything in, attuned to every little sound, every scent, every tiny breeze around them. Eventually, Emma looks up at me. "I still don't believe it," she says. "I'm not saying I know what this place is, but time travel, Paige? *Time travel?* There's got to be – it has to be something else. Something I can explain. Prove it to me. Show me something. Show me this isn't just a trick."

"Show you what?" I ask. "It's more about what I can't show you than what I can. You already said you didn't hear any cars or planes. And you just saw the pig –"

"Yeah, I saw a pig," Emma agrees. "A weird-looking pig. That doesn't mean this is the past."

The plan had been to bring both Emma and my dad to the past, to show them that it was real, to give Emma a way to get to me if she needed to, and then for her to return to the modern world. But if she's going to refuse to believe we've actually traveled through time, what am I supposed to do?

As I try to come up with some way to 'prove' to Emma – and my dad – that we're not just in a different place but a different *time*, both of them slowly start to explore. They don't go very far, and they keep stopping to listen for the sounds of cars or lawnmowers or something that will out this whole situation as an elaborate prank. I follow Emma as she wanders out of the woods and towards the remains of the original village of Caistley. Burned debris remains on the ground, pieces of straw-thatched roof and scorched sections of wattle and daub walls that the villagers used for their own dwellings and for the animal pens.

"This looks like thatching." Emma says, pointing to a particularly well-preserved piece. "Like from a roof, I mean. I don't think you have thatched roofs in America, do you?"

"No," I reply, hanging back as the two of them keep going.

We head to the beach a short while later, and I watch as my dad and my friend search the horizon for ships I know they're not going to find. *Will it take?* I wonder. *Will they buy it? I was 5 when I first came here, they're both grown adults. Maybe something about the adult brain just isn't flexible enough to accept a thing like this?*

But there's no time to keep wondering because I suddenly hear the sound of footsteps behind me.

"What the —" Emma says, her forehead creasing with worry as she hears the same thing.

"Paige?"

It's Eadgar. He's with Willa's husband, and they're both standing there in front of me, plain as day.

"Paige!"

Eadgar and I throw our arms around each other as Willa's husband and two other very confused people look on. Eadgar finally steps away and looks down at the baby in my arms.

"Ah," he says. "The Northman's baby – is it a son? A daughter?"

"A son," I reply, smiling as Eadgar takes the baby's little hand in his own.

"And is he healthy? Strong like his father? Willa's told me all about your Northman, Paige. Is that why you're here? Are you going back to him? We spotted you in the ruins of the village, but Aldred wasn't sure it was actually you, so we've been watching the three of you from the woods for little while. I'm so glad to see you, Paige."

I can feel Emma and my dad hanging on every word, staring at Eadgar and Aldred, at their tunics and their dirty bare feet. I know they're waiting for answers, too.

"Yes," I reply. "Yes I'm going back to him – if he's still alive. He was sick when I left, from a battle-wound. I've brought my father, too. And my, uh, my – friend."

I step aside a little, and the two parties of two stare at each other in open wonderment. Eadgar and Aldred seem most fascinated by the shoes I forgot to ask Emma and my father to remove, and Emma and my father seem just generally shocked. I can't blame them.

"This is my father," I say to Eadgar and Willa's husband. "And this is my friend, Emma."

More than a thousand years have passed between these two pairs of humans, but some things remain the same. The people in the past don't shake hands, not exactly, but they do a single clasp sometimes, when meeting new people (which rarely happens). There is a process of introduction, too – I go through it now, naming names, informing Emma and my dad that it's more of a hand-grab than a hand-shake.

"I brought you food," I tell Eadgar, when everyone knows everyone else's name. "And some other things for Willa and the children. Are they near?"

He nods. "Yes, we're still in the same place we were when you left. A short walk from the old village."

"I'll have to come with you," I tell him. "I want to see Willa. And I – I need to explain some of the things I brought to her."

There has never been a tradition of inviting people for dinner in Caistley, not as long as I've known the place. The people are poor, always on the verge of starvation, and it's just not a ritual that would make any sense in those conditions. So it's not strange or odd that Eadgar doesn't ask us to eat a meal with his people. He understands I'll want to see Willa, though.

"Yes, it's very close," he replies, looking at my dad and then at Emma, clearly wondering if they'll be coming too. Eadgar, although he and I – and Willa too – all have an understanding that there is probably something more than me being from 'the estate' – still thinks of me, rightly, as an outsider. His hesitation is understandable.

"Where is it?" I ask. "My friend will be going back to the estate, but I will bring my father with me if it's OK?"

Eadgar explains that we should follow the coast south for about five minutes, and then back inland along a path that starts beside a large rock formation that looks 'like a man's head with a big nose.' He hugs me again before leaving with Aldred, and then I turn to Emma and my father.

"OK," Emma says, her face white. "OK, Paige. I think I believe you. I think – oh my God. I think I'm going to faint."

My dad and I help Emma to the ground. "I didn't bring you hear to scare you," I tell her, brushing a stray lock of hair off her damp forehead. "I brought you here because I'm staying. I think my dad is staying, too. And I don't want you to worry about me anymore, or think something terrible has happened to me."

She looks down at the ground, and I don't realize she's crying until I hear her breath catching in her throat. "You're staying!?" She wails, dismayed. "Paige – what are you talking about? What about college? What about – your *life?*"

I sit down beside my friend, being careful not to jostle Eirik and wake him again, and put my arm around her shoulders. "What kind of life am I going to have in 2017, Em? You saw those reporters outside the house, you've read all the stories online. And now you've seen this place you must know that I'll never be able to answer all the questions adequately, no one will ever be satisfied. Eirik would have to grow up with those questions hanging over his head, with all his classmates knowing the story." I pause. Emma seems to be listening. "He'd have to grow up without a father," I continue. "He'd have to –"

"So he's here, then?" She asks, sniffling. "Eirik's father is here? That's why you couldn't tell anyone?"

"I think he's here," I reply softly. "I hope he's here. You know they found me in that pharmacy, right? Remember that? I was there trying to steal antibiotics for Eirik's father – he was wounded in a battle and –"

"Oh God," Emma says again, putting her head in her hands. "A battle, Paige? Eirik's father was wounded in a battle? I *must* be dreaming this. I must be."

My dad, meanwhile, is sitting on the other side of Emma, offering what little comfort he can in the midst of his own shock and listening to everything I'm saying. "That's why you needed medicine?" He asks. "Because someone, uh, someone here was sick? You were going to bring it back?"

I nod. "Yes, Eirik's dad was sick – very sick. I don't know if he's alive or dead now."

"And will he be with these people we're going to give the food to? Willa and Ed – uh, Eadgar?"

I shake my head. "No. We'll have to go a little farther to find him, if we can. But I just – I want you two to listen to me. Emma, I needed you to see this place because I need you to know I'm safe. I choose to be here. I don't want you going through life thinking something terrible has happened to me, OK?"

Emma is crying openly now. "So this is it?" She asks, taking a shaky breath. "This is it, Paige? I'm never going to see you again?!"

I hold her for a few minutes before speaking again. "What would you do?" I whisper. "Emma, what would you do? If you had a baby and a maybe even a man you loved – in one place? And in the other, people you loved, yes – friends, yes, but also the things I have in 2017 – the media, the story, the attention. I brought you here so you won't worry but also, well, it wasn't just that..."

"What was it then?" Emma cries, clinging to me.

"I don't even think I realized this until right now," I tell her. "But I think I wanted you to know how to get here. Just in case you ever needed to. In case you needed to see me for some reason and it was –"

"What?" Emma laughs, but she doesn't sound happy. "So this is going to be like you're just in the next town over? Like I'll come and visit you for tea and, I don't know, guts-pie, every weekend?"

"Guts-pie?" I ask. "What's that?"

"I thought that's what people in the past ate," Emma says. "You know, guts."

The moment is serious, I know that. Maybe it's because it's so serious that I throw my head back and laugh out loud. "Guts-pie?!" I giggle. "Oh my God, Emma. They don't eat guts! Well, I guess they do eat more parts of the animal than we would, but –"

She looks up at me, smiling sadly. "See? Guts-pie. I don't want to eat guts-pie, Paige."

"I know you don't," I tell her. "And no, I don't mean you'll come and visit me every weekend. For one thing, I don't think I'll be too close to this place – to this tree – and this is the only way to get back and forth between 2017 and... here. But also because I spent years going back and forth as a child and I know it doesn't really work to live in two places during one life. It just means living half a life in two places, rather than a full life in one. I don't want that for you. I don't want it for myself, or my son, or my dad."

"But you've picked this place, haven't you?" Emma says, and I can tell from her voice that she already knows the answer to her question. "You've picked this place, and now we'll be so far away from each other."

"We will," I agree, my heart aching because I know this is goodbye. "But you'll have a good life, Emma. A full life. Everyone loves you. You're smart and funny and beautiful and you charm the pants off everyone you meet. You have a family that loves you, so many friends. And one day you'll probably have children of your own, with someone you love. And then you'll understand why I'm doing what I'm doing."

"I already understand," Emma smiles sadly. "I do, I get it. I'm just. I'm – I'm going to miss you, Paige."

We hold onto each other, crying, and neither of us wants to let go.

***

Just before Emma leaves, after I've explained in detail how to use the tree to get between one world and the next – the fact that there needs to be skin contact, that anything brought along needs to be touching your body – we're standing together like two condemned women, knowing this is the moment of parting, not wanting to acknowledge it. I hug my friend one more time, both of us sobbing, and then stand back, leaning against my dad, as she kneels down to touch one of the tree's roots.

"Wait!" I shout, at the very last second. "Wait! Emma! Wait! We should – um, we should have some kind of a signal. Something we can leave at the tree – in this world or in 2017 – so if one of us happens to be in the woods in our world, and we see the signal, we know the other needs to get in contact."

"Yes," Emma says. "Yes, yes, that's a good idea. What should we use – should we mark the trees somehow or –"

"I don't want to mark the trees," I reply immediately. "I obviously don't know how any of this actually works but I think we should leave the trees alone."

"OK. How about an object then? Something that could only be from our – uh, our respective places."

I reach into one of the bags and pull out a can of strawberry flavored meal replacement drink and hand it to her. "Here. Leave this. Right, uh – right here –" I point to a place off the path, under the bushes. "No, wait. The pigs will get it. How about a branch? Tie it to one of the branches. How about this one? It's out of the way so no one walking by will see it, but I'll know to check it. And I'll know if it's there that you left it, because no one else here has canned strawberry drink."

"And what about you?" Emma asks. "What can you leave?"

I wrack my brain for a minute. "A pot! Like, a clay pot or a bowl. That's what they use here, and they're everywhere, even the villagers have them. I'll leave it near the tree, against one of the roots. So you'll know, if you see it, that –"

"That you left it. That you need to see me."

"Yes."

Emma looks up at my dad. The moment of parting is upon us, I feel it. "Goodbye, Mr. Renner," she says. Then she looks at me. "Goodbye, Paige. Take care of yourself. Take care of each other. I won't ever mention this place to anyone. And I won't ever forget you. Even if –" her voice breaks.

"You don't know the future," I tell her gently. "Neither do I. We're saying goodbye for now, aren't we? That's all we can say, because we don't know what will happen."

She nods. "Yes. You're right. So it's goodbye for now. Goodbye for now, Paige."

"Good –"

Like a phone call ended before one person has managed to get the entirety of their final goodbye out, my father and I are suddenly, brutally alone in the woods. The place where Emma was is now just the leaf-covered ground, the tree root she laid her hand on. I turn to my father and he holds me.

Chapter 31
9th Century

We – my dad and I – bring the sacks of food and supplies to Willa, who we find ensconced in a little hut just like the ones that used to stand in the first version of Caistley, before it burned down. I ignore her questions about where the items have come from – the cans of meal replacement drink and the plastic containers of vitamins are clearly not of the world we are in. And because there has always been that unspoken understanding between us that 'the estate' is something much more than an actual estate, she doesn't keep asking them. She knows I mean it and she believes me, she trusts me when I say I brought these things for her and her brother, her husband and her children. I show her how to pull the vitamin capsules apart, explain that the powder should be mixed into food, not too much, that after another summer has passed they won't be of any use anymore.

There's so much to explain. At some point during the explaining I begin to wonder if I haven't brought half of these things in order to spare myself the awkward conversation I fear is coming – the one where Willa and Eadgar ask me why it is I'm leaving them again, to go and live with the people who destroyed their village.

But Willa doesn't need to ask why I'm doing what I'm doing. She knows. So does Eadgar. I'm doing what I'm doing because I have a child, and because I'm in love with his father.

Before we leave, Willa kisses my cheek and ignores the toddler tugging at the bottom of her tunic. "And if he's not there," she says, "the Northman – you'll come back here, won't you Paige?"

I nod, looking at her and Eadgar. "Yes, I will."

* * *

When my dad and I have made it back to the beach, and I've managed to get my emotions under control, we approach the point where the path leads back into the woods – and back to the tree that could take us back to 2017. I stop when we get to it. To our right, the sea crashes against the rocks as a high wind begins to pick up.

"There it is," I say to my dad, pointing to the path. "That's the way back to the tree. I told Emma you were probably going to stay with me but –"

I stop talking, because if I try to speak even one more word I'm going to break. My dad puts his arm around me and leans down to kiss the top of Eirik's head. My son is asleep again after having his dinner while I explained how to use the pull-tabs on the meal replacement cans to Willa.

I wait for my father to speak, to say something. But he doesn't, not right away. Instead he just keeps walking, his arm slung around my shoulders, right on past the entrance to the path.

"Is this the right direction?" He asks a few minutes later. "North, right? You said we had to head north?"

"So you're – you're – dad, you're –" I say, but I'm barely coherent.

"Yes, Paige," he replies. "I'm staying."

I have questions, I need reassurances, but nothing I'm trying to say is coming out properly because today has been filled with too many goodbyes and I'm terrified my dad, even if he says otherwise right now, is going to come to his senses soon enough. And if he does that, then I'll have another goodbye to add to the list – my own father, my baby son's grandfather. I don't know, if it comes down to that, if I can do it.

My dad looks north, following the coastline with his gaze, and then out over the waves. "If this is a dream," he says, "it's the most realistic dream I've ever had. I can smell the saltwater, I can feel the warmth of the sun on my face."

"It's not a dream," I say, wiping my red, tired eyes one more time.

"As I said," he replies. "I don't think it is. But if it's not a dream – what is it? We could be anywhere right now – the United States, Europe – anywhere. And as for the time, well, how do I know what time it is here? Your friends wore strange clothing, they spoke oddly, but none of this really proves we're not in 2017 anymore, does it?"

I know he's not saying any of this to doubt me or to 'prove' me wrong – he's saying it because, as Emma said, what I claim is happening is technically impossible. And I certainly don't have a technical response to the question of how it *is* possible.

"I can't tell you why," I tell my dad. "I can't tell you how, either. I can't explain what is, I can just tell you what is. This isn't 2017. It's not the United States. It's the Kingdom of the East Angles, and it's sometime between the years 860 and 880 A.D. – as far as I've been able to work out, anyway. I read up on this place when I was a kid, when it started sinking in that Caistley wasn't the kind of place I was going to be able to find on Google maps."

"The Kingdom of the East Angles? So – England?"

"Well, yes. But 'England' doesn't exist yet – not in the way we think of it, not as one country."

A gentle gust of wind comes in off the sea and it is as I remember it since childhood at this time of year – warm, salt-laced and seemingly infused with the sunshine that only deigns to fall over this part of the world for any extended length of time during the summer. It's September now, and the days are as ripe and sweet with the summer as the fat, dark berries – the ones that look a little like blackberries – on the bushes.

"I was 5 when I came here for the first time," I say, picking a few of those berries, popping half of them in my mouth and then handing the rest to my dad. "When you're 5, you still believe in Santa Claus. I did, anyway. I'd also just lost my mother. What I mean is that 'impossible' things seemed very possible at that age – probable, even. And I didn't even understand the whole story, then. How could I? I didn't know I was going back in time. For a few years I just thought that there were some place near River Forks where they had very different hygiene standards, and a lack of grocery stores."

My dad chews the berries and looks surprised. "These are delicious. These are – these are the tastiest berries I've ever eaten."

I chuckle. "Yeah, that's one thing about this place. There's not as much food as there is at home – not even close – but what there is tastes a lot better."

Eirik stirs and squawks. He's going to need to be fed again very soon. My dad and I are still standing on the beach, talking. Not heading north. I look at him as he looks down at my son.

"So you'll stay?"

"Of course I'll stay," he replies, as if it's the most obvious answer in the world. "It might have been good for you to warn me that –"

"You would never have come, then!" I interrupt. "You wouldn't have come down to the tree, you would have thought I really was crazy. It's OK, I don't blame you – but it had to be this way."

My father catches my eye, smiling. "I suppose you're right about that. And listen, Paige, it's like I said. I still don't know I'm not dreaming. Part of me still expects to wake up in bed in a few seconds. But it also doesn't matter. If it's a dream, I'm staying with you and Eirik. If it's not a dream, I'm staying with you and Eirik. We need to stick together – it really is the only thing that matters."

We begin to walk north again, after I breastfeed the baby, and I'm trying to calculate in my head how long it's going to take. It took between two and three days to get south to Caistley from the Viking camp. So – three days? Probably two? We can move faster without Willa's small children in tow.

At one point I reach into the small amount of supplies I've kept for my dad and I and take out two tuna sandwiches, handing one to him.

"Mmm," he says approvingly. "This is great. I'm actually really hungry."

I smile. "Yeah, that's another thing about this place. You actually have time to get properly hungry. I don't know why a tuna sandwich tastes nicer after walking, after genuinely being hungry, but it really does."

"What are you going to do," my dad asks as we continue, "if there's not enough? Food, I mean? You said earlier that although it tastes better here, there's not as much. And you're eating for two right now, Paige. What if –"

I swallow a mouthful of tuna sandwich. "It's not like that, Dad. Not for – uh, not for me, anyway. Eirik's father is the Jarl, the leader of the Vikings. He and his family will always have enough to –" I stop talking abruptly when I see the look of pure bewilderment on my dad's face.

"Vikings?" He says, shaking his head as if he's certain he hasn't heard me right. "Paige, did you just – did you say *Vikings?!*"

I smile, mostly at myself – because I really should have anticipated this reaction – and nod. "Um, yeah. Vikings. That's another reason I've been able to pin down what time period this actually –"

"VIKINGS?!"

I nod again as my dad gives me a look of straight skepticism. "And you better get used to the idea, Dad, because they're going to think you're strange if you react this way when you meet them."

We walk on in silence, tracing the edge of a small bay with our steps as the sun sinks low in the sky and illuminates everything with a golden light.

"We're going to have to find somewhere to sleep soon," I say. But my dad is not thinking about where we're going to sleep.

"So this – this Viking – the King, is he? He's Eirik's –"

"Not King," I reply. "Jarl. It's their word for leader. Eirik is the Jarl."

"The baby's father is the Viking leader, then?"

I nod. "Of this group of Vikings, anyway. Other groups have other Jarls, there isn't one centralized leader for everyone."

"And how did you come to meet this 'Jarl?'"

To our left, at the top of the beach, sand dunes dotted with clumps of grass stretch inland. The sand itself is fine, soft. We could sleep here, out in the open where hopefully the animals that lurk in the woods at night might be less willing to approach?

"Paige?"

"Oh," I respond. "Yeah, sorry. It's just that I think we should stop here for the night. If we keep going the beach might get rocky and I don't want anyone to fall over a rock in the dark and sprain their ankle. That's something we don't –"

"Are you avoiding my question?"

"No," I reply, pulling the one blanket I kept for us out of the bag, thinking to myself that that is actually exactly what I'm doing. How do you tell your own father that the man you love began the relationship by kidnapping you? The Vikings kidnapped a lot of other people that day, too, but somehow I don't think it's going to matter. "We should get some sleep. We can talk about it in the morning if you want."

My dad grunts a grumpy agreement and I know he isn't going to let the topic slide. The temperature drops as the stars come out, but we keep the blanket mostly over Eirik, who is nestled between us.

I wake throughout the night to feed the baby and gaze up at the bright, countless stars over our heads. I haven't discussed with my father what we will do if Eirik is dead. I haven't even really discussed it with myself. Even thinking of it now, even thinking the word 'dead' in the context of the Viking leader, is almost impossibly difficult. I'm operating on faith, I realize that. And faith is dangerous, especially in such a harsh world. I turn away, both physically and psychologically, curling my body around my son – and delaying, once again, the facing of my own doubts.

***

We wake up bleary-eyed, damp with the dew that has fallen in the night, and in need of the kind of good, hot showers we will likely never have again. I feed Eirik as my dad cuts oranges with his pocketknife and puts together a rudimentary breakfast. When he hands me all four orange segments, and half of his own tuna sandwich, I balk.

"Dad, I –"

"Eat it," he insists, nodding down to the baby. "You need to keep strong so you can keep him strong. I've still got this – " he pats his own not-entirely-flat belly – "to keep me going."

So I take my own sandwich and half of my father's and marvel at how quickly and easily I have forgotten just how it feels to be truly hungry. We need to find the Viking camp soon.

And what if it's gone? What if they've sailed home? What if Eirik is dead?

I push the questions out of my mind. Eirik told me the camp was only the first outpost, that they intended to stay in lands of the East Angles, to move further inland and up and down the coasts. It wasn't just an invasion, he told me – it was a settlement. So it has to be there, still. *He* has to be there.

My father and I walk all day and into the evening. At one point we come to what might be the same place I had to swim, with Willa and her children in tow, around the marshland. At this time of year, though, it's just dry enough to be passable, and we manage to cross it on foot. The next day, as we get going again at dawn, we say little. Our bellies aren't empty exactly, but they're not full either. The worry is beginning to set in – are we ever going to get there? What if we're going the wrong way? Even though I know we're not going the wrong way, what if we can't find the Viking camp? And my dad, who doesn't even have the reassurance of knowing the place is real, is having his own doubts, I can feel it.

"It think it took three days," I tell him as the morning sun rises in the sky and begins to offer the first real warmth of the day. "About three days, anyway, to get back to Caistley from the Viking camp."

I'm trying to offer reassurance – and not just to him.

He nods. We're talking less now, due to fatigue and hunger. Our sentences are shorter, more efficient. A few minutes later he speaks again. "You were going to tell me how you met him. The Viking Jarl."

"Yeah," I reply. "I was. Next time we rest, I'll tell you, OK? I'm warning you though, it's kind of a long story." I can feel my dad staring at me. Eventually I look up to meet his worried eyes. "What? Dad, I promise I will tell –"

"It's not that, Paige," he replies, waving away my protest. "It's – well, look at you. You're out of breath. You've just had a baby! For God's sake, what are we doing here?! We hardly have any food left and –"

I drop to my knees suddenly, dragging my dad down with me. He's still talking. "What? Paige, are you listening to –"

"Dad!" I whisper. "Be quiet!"

There are two men further up the beach, I've just spotted them. They're only about forty feet away, and they're walking in our direction.

After the split second it takes my brain to register this basic information I notice something else – the men aren't dressed in the plain tunics I associate with the East Anglian peasants. No, they're in leathers. One has a sword strapped to his waist and the other carries an axe in one hand. Vikings.

I look at my father. He looks back at me. Are these Vikings with Eirik? Are they from that camp? Are there even any other camps? Their footsteps and chatter get closer and I can see my dad is thinking exactly what I'm thinking – the thing that almost every human being thinks when danger approaches: *run*.

And just as my rational mind is attempting to remind me that neither of us is in any condition to run – we're hungry, we're tired, and one of us has a baby strapped to her chest – my son chooses that moment to let out a sudden loud cry. Instantly, the men stop.

For a few seconds there is nothing, and then one of them asks the other if it's an animal they've just heard.

"That's no animal," comes the response. "That's a baby."

"Didn't the Jarl say she might have a baby with –"

The Vikings don't finish their conversation, because they've seen us. They're on us almost right away, looking down as my dad and I cower beneath them and I clutch my son tightly to my chest.

"Who's this then?" The larger one asks, and I realize to my dismay that I don't recognize either one of them. "What village are you from?"

The smaller one, the one with the axe, is studying me. "Look at her," he says, as his eyes take in my features. "The Jarl said she had long dark hair like this – and her teeth – girl, open your mouth."

I open my mouth. And then, making some effort to keep the fear out of my voice, I speak.

"I'm Paige," I say, getting to my feet and helping my dad up after me. "And if the Jarl you speak of is Eirik, then I believe I am the one you're looking for."

The moment they understand who I am, when they hear their Jarl's name trip off my tongue, their body language changes completely. They both become respectful, almost bashful, and they step a few paces back so as not to seem so menacing.

"Lady," the one with the sword says, "the Jarl has been searching for you for four moons – every three days he sends fresh men south, to walk the coastline. That's what we're doing now. Tell me, is this the child he speaks of? Is this my Jarl's child?"

Even in the few minutes it takes for the Vikings to begin treating me the respect I had come to get used to during my earlier stay in the encampment, I feel my own esteem returning to me. I am not Paige Renner, undergraduate student, single mom and probable crazy person here. Here, I am Paige, wife-to-be of the Jarl, mother of his son. And the fact that the two Vikings speak of the Jarl in the present tense has not missed me.

Still, I must be sure. "It is," I confirm. "And before you continue with your questions you must tell me of the Jarl himself – when I left he was very sick, I was going to find some healing plants to –"

"The sickness faded," the axe-wielding Viking replies. "Everyone thought it was the end, even the healers said that all they could do was ease his pain. But that night, after you left, the fever lifted."

"Valhalla will wait many years now, for the Jarl to sit at the feast," says his companion.

"So he's alive?" I ask, hardly daring to believe it. "He's – he's fine? What about –"

"His arm is still healing," the Viking. "There is stiffness in it still, but it fades with the herbs the healers apply to it every night.

The Jarl is the strongest man in the world – even with one arm tied behind his back he could beat a whole pack of the King's men."

Somehow I doubt that, but I don't say it out loud. And not to spare the Jarl's dignity, either. No – the reason I don't speak is because I can't. He's alive. I stumble in the soft sand, sobbing. Baby Eirik wakes at the sound of his mother's cries and I hand him to my father.

Why am I sobbing? Relief. And underneath the relief, underneath the emotion, something else. Confirmation. I knew he was alive. Did I know he was alive? Or does it just feel like it in this moment, as I am told he is? I can't tell. And I suppose it doesn't matter. All that matters is that Eirik is still here, still flesh and blood and bone. I look up at my father.

Nothing can hurt us now, I want to say. I don't say it, because I still haven't told him the story of Eirik and I want to do that first, but I know it in my heart. Eirik is alive. And as long as he's alive, we – myself, my son and my father – are safe.

The Vikings tell us their names – the larger of the two if Ivor, and the smaller is Fridleif. They are new to Eirik's personal guard, both of them 19. They offer us food – fermented milk from the water-skin, chunks of cheese, the heavy dark bread whose taste on my tongue makes it so my nose believes itself to be smelling the scent of wood-smoke in the roundhouse.

My dad and I eat. And then we eat some more. And after we eat, we sleep under the dappled light at the edge of the woods, guarded by Ivor and Fridleif, who say we are a few hours walk from the Viking encampment.

Chapter 32
9th Century

My legs feel lighter and quicker as we travel north after that, knowing what awaits me. As the sun begins to sink towards the horizon, Fridleif leaves Ivor to stay with me, my baby and my dad and runs on ahead. A tingle of excited anticipation runs up my spine – we must be getting close.

"So I guess you could say he kidnapped me," I say to my dad a few seconds later, out of the blue. He's going to meet Eirik soon, he deserves to know the truth. "Not just me – everyone his men could get their hands on in Caistley."

My dad has slowed his pace to match mine and he's looking at my face, searching for signs of pain or trauma. In fact I know exactly what he wants to know – what any parent would, in the same situation. His daughter has just told him the father of her child kidnapped her. And so the question arises naturally.

"He didn't rape me," I say plainly. "You need to know that. In fact he saved me from being raped – or worse."

My dad stops walking and puts his arms around me. "Oh thank God, Paige. Thank God. I thought that maybe –"

"I'm not saying the Vikings don't do things that people from 2017 would consider wrong," I say quickly, not wanting to give my father the expectation that he is walking into some kind of cuddles-and-rainbows community. "They do. You'll see it for yourself. But I don't know them to be unnecessarily cruel. They're just – I don't know how to explain and it's as I said – you'll find out for yourself. They're very wedded to their way of doing things, that might be a good way to put it. And it will be good for both of us to remember that."

More questions follow. I do my best to answer them all. How old is Eirik? How did he treat me when I was first captured? Will he be angry that I left, even if it was because I feared for his life and wanted to help? What does he know about where I come from?

On that last question, I am halfway through the answer – underlining to my father that under no circumstances can the Vikings know anything of where we're *actually* from, and that their being of the opinion that we're from one of the higher social orders of East Anglian society is good enough for now, when Ivor lets out a yell.

My dad and I both look up at him and see immediately that he's waving at someone. My gaze follows Ivor's north and suddenly, there he is. His men follow on either side of him, and trailing behind. But there is no mistaking who I'm seeing, even at a distance. The Jarl. Eirik. *My Jarl.*

I close my eyes as my nervous subconscious pokes at me: *make sure it's him first. Make sure it's not a mistake. Make sure you're not dreaming.*

But it's not a mistake and I'm not dreaming and that is Eirik walking towards me, resplendent in his fur mantle, shirtless underneath, sword slapping against his muscular thigh with each step he takes. I don't know whether to laugh for joy, or cry, or scream. I lift my hands to my face, disbelieving, as my heart beats fast in my chest.

"Here," my father says, helping me to extricate myself from the baby wrap. "Let me take him."

I pass my son to my father and run forward, still barely trusting what my eyes are seeing because it seems too good to be true. Even as I race across the sand towards him part of my mind is still in denial – it can't be! It's a trick! You don't get a happy ending, Paige – happy endings were never meant for people like you.

Only when Eirik takes my face in his two strong hands, lifting it up to his, do the voices quiet down.

"Eirik," I whisper. "Eirik."

He says nothing right away. He stands strong and steady, his sapphire-blue eyes locked on mine. In those eyes, I see the uselessness of words. Eirik doesn't need to tell me he missed me, or that he thought we would never see each other again. He doesn't need to tell me that he needs me, either, or that I need him, or that the place where I am meant to be is at his side. He doesn't even need to say that he forgives me.

"Look at you," he finally whispers, a phrase I remember. "Look at you, Paige. You came back to me."

"I did," I reply, burying my face in his chest as he pulls me close, breathing in the familiar scent of him. "You were so sick," I tell him. "And I knew of some healing plants growing in the place where your men first found me – I, I wanted to gather them and bring them back to you but then –"

The Jarl silences me with a shake of his head. "There's no need to explain, girl. I knew you were either dead, or that you would come back to me. You weren't dead, so here you are."

I smile, remembering his habit of making statements like this, of stating simple truths in ways that my over-excited, worry-prone mind would never come up with. "And you," I say, touching the scar on his shoulder. "The healers were so worried, I thought you were going to die. I had to leave, I had to try to find the plants!"

"How could I die?" Eirik smiles down at me, his happiness as bright as sunshine. "Without knowing you were safe? Without –"

My father and Ivor are approaching, and baby Eirik is fussing. The second the sound hits his father's ears I see something inside him – some stoic, male thing – slip.

"Is that – a baby?" He asks hesitantly, and I see that it is no longer me who is doubting my own eyes – or ears.

My father hands me my grumpy son and I turn back to Eirik. "Yes, it's a baby. Your baby. Your son."

"But I thought –" Eirik replies, staring down at the little, noisy bundle in my arms. "I thought – your belly is gone – that the child was lost somehow. I –"

He stops talking, then, because it doesn't take a genius to see the parentage of the baby I'm holding. Everyone is watching the Jarl, their eyes following his finger as he reaches down and runs it over his son's cheek.

"Gods," he whispers. "Gods, Paige. I thought there was no way. Is the babe a boy or a —"

"A son," I say again, handing the baby to his father.

"A son?" Eirik repeats, his voice breaking on the word 'son.' He stares down at his child, examining him, running his fingers down each chubby arm and each chubby leg, counting the fingers and toes, tracing the outline of a tiny nose, a tiny chin.

"His name is Eirik," I say, not just to the Jarl but to the other Viking men who are present, a kind of informal introduction.

When the Jarl is finally able to tear his eyes away he looks up – first at me, and then at my father and his men.

"There will be a feast," he announces, his voice loud and strong again. "The longest feast our people have known in their time. Eight days! Eight days for my son, and for the return of the woman who gave him to me! It is to begin at sundown tomorrow!"

The Vikings – all except Eirik – scatter at the pronouncement, running back to the encampment to announce the news and to begin the preparations for the feast. Soon it is just myself, the Jarl, my father and the baby, and the latter's cries are becoming increasingly demanding.

"He's hungry," I say, taking him back from his father and offering him a breast. The cries cease immediately.

The crisis of a fussy baby dealt with, Eirik turns to my dad, and then back to me.

"Your father," he says, his tone questioning.

"Yes," I confirm. "His name is Daniel Renner – Dan. Eirik, this is Dan, my father. He's going to be living with us now."

Eirik takes the hand my dad is offering, unsure of what to do with it, and then pulls him into one of the chest-out, single-clap-on-the-back hugs the Vikings reserve only for other high-ranking men.

"You are welcome, Dan. Paige and I will be married soon, but we're already a family. Which makes you family, too. I'll have a roundhouse built for you by the middle of the feast, at the high point of the camp."

The highest point of the encampment is reserved only for the highest-ranking Vikings. When Eirik leads us back, I hang back and explain to my dad what it means to be offered a roundhouse in that spot. I think he understands, but the look on his face is one of pure astonishment.

"A few days ago, I was writing a Costco shopping list on my phone," my dad says to me, smiling bemusedly as the camp ramparts come into view. "And now I'm being told – by the Viking who is going to marry my daughter – that a roundhouse is being built for me in the Viking village."

I put my arm around his shoulders. "I know, Dad. I had years to get used to this, to being in the past – and even after years, the Vikings were still a shock. But Eirik is showing you respect, and that means everyone else here will show you respect, too. I'll be with you as well, to show you how things work, to help you with whatever you need."

My father's expression is doubtful, but not unhappy. "I don't know, Paige. I'm almost 50, which must be – what? The equivalent of 90 here?"

"No, not 90. There are older people here, some even in their seventies and eighties – it seems to be that if a Viking makes it to 35, they get as old as we do. Almost. They won't think you ancient."

"It doesn't really matter, Paige. You're here. And he," he looks down at my son, "is here. So I'm here. And if it means living in a – what was it? a roundhouse? – then so be it."

He's expecting the living conditions to be unpleasant. I can't blame my father for this, anyone taken from 2017 and transported suddenly into the 9th century would feel the same way. All the same, I think he's going to be pleasantly surprised when he sees what life is like for someone of higher rank. There definitely aren't going to be any more trips to Costco in an old beater car – here, his meals will be brought to him, and they're going to taste a lot better than the processed crap he's been living on since we lost my mother.

***

I don't spend my first night back with the Jarl. Gudry and Anja, neither of whom are able to contain their shrieks of happiness when they see me again, explain in the bathing hut that when a Viking woman gives birth, she is kept from her husband's bed for a moon – two if the healers deem it necessary. Instead of keeping her man warm she spends her nights in a separate roundhouse, resting on a bed of furs and drinking specially-prepared teas, eating a specific diet to help her heal and keep her milk supply abundant. Most of the woman will share the 'Mother's House' with others, but I am to have my own.

The two of them question me as they bathe me, saying that the answers will determine what I am fed and given to drink during my time in the Mother's House. Am I still bleeding? A little. Is my milk abundant? It seems to be. Does the baby fuss after he eats? Does he draw his knees to his stomach? Does he fall asleep at the breast? Do I dream of wild animals? Of forests, or rivers? On the night the child came into the world, was the moon waxing or waning?

Eventually, I drift off to sleep in the hot bath water, with baby Eirik sleeping on a pile of furs beside me and Anja and Gudry attending to the important matters – like how clean my fingernails are and which floral essence to scent my hair with.

Later that night, as I sip a bitter tea that Anja insists I must finish before I'm allowed anything to eat, and as my son suckles noisily at my breast, Hildy comes barging in.

She takes one look at me and nods knowingly. "Ah, so it's true. You've given the Jarl a son, girl. And you've brought him back to us, I see! How kind of you!"

Hildy's being mildly sarcastic, a sort of 'thanks for blessing us with your presence' thing, but I let it slide because Hildy is going to Hildy, and I'm not going to be able to change that. She softens, though, when I show no signs of talking back, and edges onto the furs where I'm lying, so she can get a look at baby Eirik.

"Beautiful," she says. "A beautiful child, he looks just like the Jarl! And strong – they can probably hear him eating all the way from the beach!"

Soon enough, Hildy reveals the reason for her evening visit – and it isn't what I expected. She's not here to harangue me, or try to involve me in one of her power games. No, she's here to ask me about my father. What was it he did all day, before he came to the Viking camp with me? Does he enjoy hunting? Where is his wife?

I try to answer the questions as best I can, but the truth is my father dropped most of his interests when my mom died, and spent the next decade and a half surfing the internet and living off the money my mother left him.

"Hildy," I say at one point, when she refuses to stop badgering me for information. "I'm not trying to be difficult right now. My mother died five summers after my birth, and since then my father – well, he doesn't do very much. He doesn't have a lot of interests. I think mainly what he's interested in is me being happy – and now, my baby being happy, too."

Gudry, who has been listening quietly, pipes up. "My mother's sister is the same. Her husband died of a fever eight summers ago. Eight? Maybe nine? But she's taken to her bed ever since, and she grows as thin as a skeleton even as my mother brings her buttered bread every day. All of what used to make her happy – growing flowers for the healers, playing with the children – only seems to make her tired now. We have to drag her to the garden, and then she complains that it's cold and her back aches and she wants to go back to bed."

Hildy, who I expect is about to smack Gudry upside the head for talking out of turn, instead looks at me. "Is this the way with your father, girl?"

"Yes," I reply, mildly irritated. "That's what I've been trying to tell you."

Hildy is thinking. "It's not always possible that people who get lost like that, halfway between life and death, can be brought out of it. But sometimes they can. Usually it's love that does it – family, friends. He has a new grandson now, that's something. We'll have to find him some companions, too. I'll see to it, girl. Now – Gudry, Anja – is she ready for the feast tomorrow night? The Jarl wants her there, and the baby, too. Jarl Magnar and his people will be in attendance. Everything must be perfect."

Anja bows her head respectfully. "We'll have her ready, Hildy. The baby, too."

I wonder, briefly, if they're going to clean the baby's fingernails as well as mine, and scent him with rosewater.

* * *

Eirik does not come to see me before I fall asleep for the night. I'm not really expecting him, because there is a level of activity in the camp that I don't remember seeing before – he's busy, and we're not allowed to share a bed, anyway. Still, I long for him. To see him on the beach, to see the look in his eyes and feel his hands on my body, and then to be kept from him, is something like a sweet kind of torture.

He doesn't come the next day. Neither does my dad. When I ask Hildy, as she rushes in to deliver a bundle of dried herbs to Anja, where he is, she shakes her head at me impatiently. "The feast is tonight, girl! And it is not just any feast! Your father is fine, he's been assigned four men – four! – so there's no need for you to worry. You'll see him tonight – him and the Jarl."

'Assigned' four men? I want to ask Hildy what that means but she's already gone.

As the afternoon progresses, the tempo in the camp – and in the Mother's House – rises by the minute. Gudry and Anja are almost frantic as the light starts to fade, anointing me and the baby with various oils, braiding and pinning my hair, deciding it isn't quite right, unpinning it, pulling the braids apart and then starting again. When my hair is done Gudry slides a silver cuff up my right arm, until it rests around the upper portion.

"Only a mother can wear a silver cuff like this," she tells me, "around her upper arm. Maids aren't permitted to wear any silver bangles, and wives only on their wrists until they've borne at least one child. When you marry the Jarl, you'll have a silver circlet on your head, the sign of a wife."

When the two women are satisfied with my hair and adornment, and baby Eirik has been pressed to my breast one more time (they want his belly as full as possible for the feast, so he doesn't fuss), they dress me. Another silk gown, this one open at the back. When I protest, they remind me that I'm still bleeding slightly from the birth, and show me the cloth pillow, stuffed with soft grasses and herbs, that I'm to sit on. Over the dress goes a light wool overcoat, sleeveless and split up the back, again to allow me to sit on the pillow with no clothing in between. Gudry shows me how to use the ties to tie it closed if I need to get up, and how to open them and pull the garments out of the way when I sit down at the feast.

"It's almost time!" She whispers excitedly, after poking her head outside the roundhouse to check how close we are to sunset. "An eight day feast, Paige! The Jarl must love you more than any man has ever loved a woman before – I never heard of an eight day feast before!"

Chapter 33
9th Century

The feasting longhouse has doubled in size since I last saw it. Instead of a single row of tables running down the center, there are now two rows, and a series of narrower tables in the middle, all laden with the familiar massive pots of stewed pork, loaves of bread, plates of the little rosewater-flavored cakes that the Viking women seem to be partial to, fruits, roasted vegetables and more casks of ale than I can count. At one end of the room the Jarl's table sits on the higher platform.

Gudry and Anja seat me at this table and stand to the side, signaling to Hildy, who waits by the main entrance. Next, my father is led inside by two younger Viking men, and seated at the same table as me. I am pleased to see that he looks better than I've seen him in years – more alert, somehow, more present. His eyes seem brighter, his cheeks less pale.

"Dad," I say, reaching for his hand. "How are you?"

"How am I?" He whispers in reply. "They're treating me like a damned king, Paige! There are four of them – four! – whose only job, it seems, is to make sure I have everything I need at every second. Do you know that they cleaned my ears this afternoon? My ears, Paige – what a disgusting task! It's like they think I'm a total idiot – but in a good way."

I laugh. "Yes, they're very serious about cleanliness here – for some people, anyway. They don't think you're an idiot – they know you can clean your own ears. It's just part of being the Jarl's father-in-law. Father-in-law-to-be, anyway."

My dad is about to keep going, and I myself am also dying to talk to him, to hear how everything has gone for him, what he thinks of his first day with the Vikings, but more guests are being brought in. I don't recognize many of them but I can tell from their dress, and the deference the servants are showing to them, that they're important people.

It takes over an hour for the longhouse to fill with people. Eventually, there is only a single empty seat left – the one next to me. And I know Eirik has entered the longhouse before I hear or see him, because a hush falls over the people and it can only be a reaction to his presence.

"Friends!" He begins, walking up to the table where I am sitting and laying one of his enormous hands on my shoulder. "Welcome!"

An introduction follows – Jarl Magnar, his men, Eirik's men, the women in attendance. And after each and every person's name has been spoken aloud by the Jarl, a ritual that confers Eirik's respect – and therefore his people's respect – on the visitors and on his own clan, he lifts his sleeping son from my arms. I look up, knowing it would be inappropriate to swoon at the spectacle of a hardened Viking warrior cuddling a tiny baby against his muscular chest, and only just managing to stop myself.

"We welcome Jarl Magnar and his kin," Eirik intones, not taking his eyes off the baby. "But this is the first feast of eight days – I think even our old people don't remember the last eight day feast – and I have a more personal welcome to announce. My son, named for his father – Eirik."

He holds the baby aloft and the room breaks into loud cheers, shouts of 'Eirik!' and the sound of cups being slammed back onto the table after long swigs of ale. Of course, the din wakes the sleeping child, and Eirik smiles at the sound of his cries. "Listen to that," he says proudly. "You can already hear the strength in his cries – Veigar, Fridleif, you two better be careful or my son will be claiming more East Angle's grain than the two of you combined!"

Eirik hands the baby back to me, and I soothe him into contentment, whispering that there's nothing to worry about, nothing to be afraid of, because his father is the most powerful warrior in the land. Baby Eirik stares up at me, almost seeming to understand my words.

"It's not just my son," the Jarl continues, his tone becoming more serious. The longhouse grows quiet. "The woman you see beside me, captured twelve moons ago in one of the southern villages of the Kingdom, has returned. Most of you know her – she's not easy to miss!" Chuckles ring out, and although I'm not certain what Eirik means, I'm pretty sure it has something to do with what the Vikings see as my inability to know my place. "The moon is full on the final feast day, and we'll marry at dawn. If she'll have me."

I'm watching the baby as I listen to Eirik. It takes a few seconds to register that an even deeper silence has fallen over the hall. I look up. A question. He asked a question. Did he? Am I meant to answer? The Jarl leans down and whispers in my ear:

"You must speak your answer aloud, girl, so the people can hear it."

"Uh –" I start, and Gudry suddenly appears at my side, helping me to my feet. "Yes."

I look at Eirik. Have I said the right thing? He grins. "Louder, woman. So everyone can hear it."

"Yes!"

"Louder!"

"YES!"

Another eruption of cheering, drinking, shouted congratulations. Eirik and I gaze at each other, smiling. At each end of the longhouse, a small crowd of servants waits to serve the food. But Eirik isn't finished yet. When the merriment finally dies down slightly, he holds up one hand.

"There is one more thing," he says, his loud voice booming easily down to the people sitting at the far end of the hall. "My wife to be, and the mother of my son, brings another with her. Dan, her father. Rise, Dan."

My father stands, and I can see from the look on his face that he's worried there's something he's supposed to do, or say, and that he doesn't know what it is. But Eirik flattens his hand over his own chest, and then reaches out, repeating the move on my father's much smaller chest. "Dan is one of us now," he tells the crowd. "As much one of us as any of you. A member of my family. He's to be treated with no less than the respect you afford to myself – and that includes you, Hildy."

Everyone laughs at the line about Hildy. My father sits back down, after a short bout of listening to his own name being shouted out loud by a large group of half-drunk Vikings, and Eirik signals the servants. "Right," he shouts. "Eight days. Any man I catch sober or hungry on the eighth day, I'll remove his head myself. Eat!"

The servants pour into the space between the rows of tables, but this is a Viking feast not a formal affair, and they're only there to facilitate the doling out of food that cannot be reached from where people sit. What can be reached – bowls of yellow butter and pyramids of dried, candied fruit – are attacked immediately. Eirik stands for a few minutes, overseeing his people, making sure all are eating, and then he finally takes his place next to me.

"You seem a vision," he says to me, unembarrassed, not bothering to keep his voice low so no one else at the table can hear. "It's as if Freja herself dines with me tonight."

He reaches out and traces one finger down one of my cheeks, dropping his eyes to the baby at my breast. "You've never been so beautiful, Paige."

My cheeks tingle with happiness as much as self-consciousness – I am not used to be spoken to that way in front of other people – especially my dad.

The Jarl sees to it that my dad, myself and all the people at the high table are taken care of, that our bowls are never empty of stewed pork and our cups never empty of ale - or of bitter herbal tea in my case. It's too loud in the hall to really have a conversation with anyone, and I want to talk to my Jarl and my father, but in the end

I'm happy to float along on the current of celebratory joy that fills the longhouse and stretches on into the evening.

Speeches break out throughout the evening – the visiting Jarl speaks for a good twenty-five minutes on the joys of marriage and the beauty of Eirik's new son and wife-to-be. Some of his men make speeches, too. There are children at this feast, and none of them stay in one place for long – at one point I catch one of them under the table, scrabbling about for a nut one of his companions has rolled between the feet of the seated adults.

By the time my eyelids are heavy, things don't seem to be dying down at all. Eirik sees that I – and my father – are tired, though, and signals Gudry and Anja.

"Take her back to the Mother's House – and take her father to the temporary roundhouse. They're tired still, from their journey. Bring them warm milk and let them sleep."

Chapter 34

9th Century

The feast days continue, but after that first night, I am gently encouraged to retreat to the Mother's House by Gudry, Anja and Hildy. At first this rankles me, because I still have my 21st century mindset and I see it as an exclusion rather than what it actually is – a luxury that many new mothers in the modern world would kill for.

The Mother's House is an oasis of purely female space, of gentle touches, soft voices and the gauzy, milky haze that is mothering a newborn. Baby Eirik fusses less when his mother has nothing to do but attend to him. And I worry less when I have my every need attended to by the two women I have come to trust completely. The rhythms of adult life blur into each other, the baby is brought to me when he's hungry and then held and rocked by my attendants when I need to sleep.

Men aren't allowed into the Mother's House, so don't see my husband-to-be or my father for seven days after the feast night, although Hildy assures me they are both fine and enjoying the festivities. Not that she doesn't manage to get a little dig in about how my father has no idea how to handle a bow – which I allow, because my father does, indeed, have no idea how to handle a bow.

"What did he do before?" Hildy muses on the eighth day, after Gudry has been to summon me to the bathing house after my days of rest. "What kind of man doesn't know how to use a bow, Paige? Did he have hundreds of slaves – and warriors to defend his land?"

I laugh at that, half wishing I could just straight up tell Hildy how far off she is, and she asks me what's so funny.

I shrug. "If only I could tell you, Hildy. Slaves? Warriors? It was nothing like that."

Hildy stares at me pointedly, then, and for long enough to catch my notice. "What?" I ask, impatient for Gudry to come back and take me to begin the preparations for the wedding ceremony that is to take place at the break of dawn the next day.

"I believe you," Hildy replies, and her tone is one of a person disclosing a fairly weighty secret. "Maybe the Jarl believes you, too."

"What does that mean?" I ask. It isn't like Hildy to be cryptic.

"That night," she says, "the night you left with your friend – we thought the Jarl would be in the halls of Valhalla before the sun came up. He was taken with fever, seeing things that weren't really there, speaking of things no one knew. We told him, even though we doubted he would understand, that you were gone. And in his sickness he said his men wouldn't catch you, even if they set out on horseback, or with dogs. He said you weren't from a place where we could go. When we tried to make sense of it, of what he meant, when we asked where you were from if not from the this world," Hildy gestures with one arm, to our surroundings, "he said that he didn't know where it was. Only that he knew it wasn't here."

I'm listening to Hildy intently. Too intently. I don't want her to think that I'm taking anything she's saying seriously. But it's too late and she's too smart. "And seeing your face right now," she says, as she gathers loose linens that will need to be washed in the stream, "I think maybe our Jarl was right. When I was alone with him that morning he asked me if you were a dream, he wanted to know if we saw you as he did, as real as any one of us."

Gudry walks in at that very moment, just as I'm searching for some way to say the Jarl was out of his mind, irrational with fever, that nothing he said during his sickness should be taken seriously, and relieves me of my duty to do so. Hildy's expression curdles into a scowl and she throws the linens on the ground and gets in Gudry's face.

"Girl, this is not my work! It's yours! Now take these to the washerwomen at once, before I have to tell the Jarl you let his mother's son languish in a filthy room!"

I smile and lie back, reassured that the strange moment with Hildy has passed. She rushes out of the roundhouse and Gudry looks at me, worried.

"Lady, I –"

"It's fine, Gudry. If this place got any cleaner, you all could use it as an operating theater."

"What?"

"Nothing," I smile, as Anja enters with my baby in her arms. "It's – nothing. Is he hungry, Anja?"

***

That night, I am roused from sleep in the darkness, as I have been warned to expect, and hustled into the bathing roundhouse, which is lit with more candles than I have ever seen. Gudry and Anja bathe me and dot my forehead and the nape of my neck with an oil I've never smelled before.

"What is that?" I ask, when the heady, floral scent fills my nose.

"It's from the south, across the sea," Anja says, brushing my hair out so she can braid it. "Rarer and more precious than gold – even the highest women can only wear it on their wedding day."

Whatever it is, it smells like heaven. I am beginning to wake up. When the gown is brought in, draped over Anja's arm, I gasp. I've never seen anything like it before – not in the past, anyway. It's cream, like most of the garments worn by the Vikings, but it's trimmed with colors I didn't think existed here – red and blue. In places, it's sewn with golden thread.

"Oh my God," I murmur, when Anja unfurls it in front of me. It even *sounds* beautiful, the heavy silk falling against itself with a whisper and the click-clack of the precious stones and beads that have been sewn into the neckline.

"He loves you," she says, when she sees the look on my face. "I've never seen a man love someone so much. When you were gone, he tried to keep everything as it was, but everyone knew if you didn't come back —"

She stops herself.

"What?" I ask. "What if I didn't come back?"

Anja shrugs. "I don't know, Paige. You came back, so how can I say what would have happened if you didn't? All I know is that the Jarl's sadness was a heavy weight over this place. And nobody knew how to help him. It's good you came back — see to it that you don't leave again."

I feed the baby one last time before I am dressed in the gown. It's the first time I regret the lack of mirrors or cameras in the past. I would like to have a photograph of this moment — of myself — to show to my baby when he grows up, or just to look at for myself, when I am no longer a young woman.

When I am dressed, and my braids have been extravagantly arranged on my head, I am led out of the camp in complete darkness, and complete silence. I try to ask where we're going at one point, and am shushed by Anja immediately.

We're going to the beach. I can feel the grasses brushing against my ankles as we walk, but the darkness is thick. Soon, the ground underneath my feet turns to sand and there is just enough light to see that we are on the rocky headland that juts out on the south side of the bay where the Vikings anchor their ships. In front of me stands Eirik, who I haven't seen for days. I can't see him, all I can see is the absence of stars where he blocks their faint light.

"Ei —"

"Shh," he responds, caressing my cheek with so much tenderness that it makes me ache.

I wait for a little while, to be told what is about to happen. Is this where the ceremony will be? Are we waiting for someone?

Where is my father? What if the baby gets hungry? No answers come. At some point I sense that Eirik and I are alone, that Gudry and Anja have left.

I'm confused, at first. What's happening? Why is no one saying – or doing – anything? But after one more attempt to speak to Eirik, and being lovingly shushed again, a kind of peace comes over me. The wind that blows off the sea is tangy with salt, the sand beneath my toes dry and cool. I'm suddenly so conscious of everything around me, so present in each moment as it comes upon me and then slips easily by.

And in all of this, there he is. Even as I cannot see him, the strangeness of standing together, alone with each other in the night, brings Eirik himself into an intense kind of focus. Slowly, my eyes become barely aware of a faint light in the east. Dawn. How long have we been standing out here? Forever?

And as the dawn begins to fill the sky, I find myself teary as the light picks the man I love out of the darkness. I look up into his eyes, unafraid of showing myself to him as the emotions rush through me, and it's all so perfectly clear. He is the center of my life. He is the sun around which I happily orbit. He's everything. I bring a hand to my mouth, overcome with the sudden nakedness, the complete acknowledgement of who Eirik has become to me, and stifle a sob. And then I don't bother to stifle the next one, or the next. And he stays where he is, not moving, as solid as an oak tree. He doesn't have to say anything, I am comforted by his presence alone.

The tears pass soon enough, but the feeling only intensifies. And soon there is enough light for me to see that people are approaching us. Not a crowd, not at first. At first I see my father, accompanied by e Viking woman I don't think I recognize. He seems to be walking a little differently. Is he holding his head higher than usual? Is that pride I see shining in his eyes as he gets closer? He seems to be about to say something to me when he gets within a few feet of me but the Viking woman whispers something in his ear and he stays quiet.

Others follow my dad. Eirik's men, Hildy, Hildy's family, Gudry, Anja, one of the healers. And slowly, as the sun itself mounts the horizon, the trickle of people gets heavier. I look back at Eirik, who hasn't looked away from me once, and breathe deeply. Soon we are surrounded. Everyone is quiet. The only sound is the wind, and the incoming tide.

I don't know what's going on, because I'm not a Viking. I don't know what to do, or what to say. What I do know is that I have never felt as full of love and connection and peace as I do right now. Eirik seems to see what I'm feeling because he smiles at me, and I see in his eyes that he is feeling what I'm feeling. I see how much he loves me.

We stand like that in the wind until the sun has lit each and every one of us with its pink light, and then someone hands something to Eirik. I look down. In his hands he holds a silver circlet, which he lifts, slowly and without breaking eye-contact, and places on my head. When the circlet is secure he steps back, gazing at me for a moment, and then draws me suddenly, rightly into his arms and kisses my mouth.

And in that moment all the theory in the world, all the things I have ever read about love or thought about love or wondered about love become real. I am loved. Completely. It's all there in that kiss, the lifetime stretched out ahead of us, our two paths coming together into one. The tears are running down my cheeks again when Eirik steps away. He smiles, and uses his thumb to wipe them away.

"Look at you," he whispers.

A few second later, there is a random – or, so I assume – whoop of joy from one of the crowd. And following that one whoop, many more, until it seems the whole camp is shouting their joy into the bright morning sky.

I don't need to ask, not really. I already know the truth. I feel it. But old habits die hard.

"Are we –"

"Yes, my love. Yes. The dawn ceremony binds us, and the silver circlet seals us. We are husband and wife now."

Somebody pushes a bouquet of wildflowers into my hands, and the Viking women surround me, pushing more flowers into my braids, laughing, kissing my cheeks and hands. Anja emerges from the crowd with the baby in her arms and Eirik takes him from her. I look up at him as he watches the women decorate me with flowers.

"I've never been so happy in my life," I say. Nothing I've ever said has been truer than those words.

And after me, it's Eirik's turn. The Viking men push new rings onto his fingers, lift new necklaces of precious metals over his head. They pick him up on their shoulders, cheering and dancing and singing songs, and carry him back into the encampment.

"You won't see him again until night falls," Gudry whispers in my ear. "But every bride says the wait is worth it!"

"Leave me here," I say, as the women move to lead me back to the bathing roundhouse, where I know I have hours of pampering ahead of me. "I'll be there soon. Just – just give me a little while."

And so they take their leave of me in little giggling groups, until only my father and I remain on the headland. I turn to him when we're alone and see that he looks happy, too. Happy like I have only the vaguest memory of him ever being, somewhere deep in the past, before my mother left us.

"Dad," I say, meaning to ask him how he is, but he pulls me into a hug and holds me tight.

"My sweet girl," he says, kissing my cheek. "Your mother would be so proud of you."

We sit down and I take his hand. "Good," I say. "I want to live a life that would have made her proud. But I want to make you proud, too. And, Dad, I want you to be happy. How has it been for you – being here, I mean? I know it's still too soon to –"

My dad laughs. "Did I ever tell you that your mother was a huge Star Trek fan?"

I giggle at the seemingly random piece of information about my mom. "No, I don't think so."

"Well she was. She used to have a whole bunch of episodes on VHS, and we would watch them sometimes, on dates at her apartment. Anyway, there is actually a point to this revelation. I think I remember one episode about one of the characters being in a coma, or sick or something. Not for long, but while he was unconscious he lived this whole life – years, got married, had kids etc., in the space of what was a very short time in the real world. That episode stuck with me for some reason, how strange it was to think you could be dreaming your whole life."

The wind plays with a lock of my hair that's come loose from my elaborate bridal hairstyle. I tuck it behind one ear and look at my dad. He does look healthier – younger, even. His face has some color to it, his back a straightness I don't remember seeing before.

"Is that what you think this is?" I ask. "A dream?"

"I don't know," he replies, shrugging helplessly. "I honestly don't know, Paige. I mean, you're here. You seem real. All of this seems so real. If it is a dream, it's not like any dream I ever had before."

"And even if it is a dream," I continue. "Is it a pleasant one? Are you enjoying it?"

My father looks down at the grass, rolls a few of the blades between his thumb and forefinger. "Yes," he says, a few moments later. "Yes I am, Paige. There's no computers here, are there? Nothing to do in the roundhouse except sleep – not even any books! They're treating me well, even if I can see it in their eyes that they can't believe how incompetent I am. One of the young men had to teach me how to hold a bow the other day. Not shoot an arrow, we're not there yet – he had to teach me how to hold the bow. And Kelda is helping me plant a little garden, just west of the encamp –"

"Kelda?" I ask, remembering the woman from the marriage ceremony. "Is that the woman I saw you with?"

My dad chuckles at my tone. "Yeah, that's her. She lost her husband a few years ago, in battle. We've just been talking about that, about what it's like. She has a daughter, too, just a few years younger than you."

My heart is near bursting with happiness. So much so that part of me wonders if my dad's theory about it all being a dream might be true. It certainly seems too good to be reality.

But it is reality.

"And we know how to get back to the tree," I say. If you ever change your —"

My dad looks at me. "I only want one thing, Paige. I want to be with you and Eirik — and I suppose now I should add your new husband to that shortlist too, huh? Wherever you are is where I want to be. I want to watch my grandson grow up. And if this is where I get to do it, in this beautiful place, then so much the better."

He puts his arm around me and we sit quietly like that for a long time, looking out to sea.

Chapter 35
9th Century

Sometime in the late afternoon, after Gudry and Anja have finished fussing over me and the baby has been fed, they lead me out of the bathing roundhouse in a second silk gown, this one less adorned, and offering decidedly less coverage than the one I donned for the wedding ceremony.

I assume we're heading to Eirik's roundhouse and a low, steady hum of excitement sets up deep in my belly at the thought of being with him after all this time. But we don't go to the roundhouse. Instead, we leave the Viking camp and walk into the hills to the west. I'm just about to ask where exactly it is we're going and whether or not I can have a wool tunic to keep the early evening chill away when I see it.

A spring – a hot-spring, I realize, when we get closer and I spot the steam rising off it.

"Wait here, lady," Gudry says, smoothing my tunic down over one shoulder as Anja inspects my already completely-inspected braids.

I turn as they go to leave, both of them smiling like Cheshire-cats, and ask what I'm to do.

"Am I to bathe? In the spring?"

Anja demurs. "No, lady. You must wait."

"But –" I start, noting that the sun is sinking in the sky and I'm outside the camp's boundaries.

Gudry, never good at biting her tongue, bounds back to me and leans in close to my ear. "I promise if you wait, something good will come."

So that's what I do. I wait. The tunic is silk, so thin I might as well be naked for all it hides of my body, and a breeze blows over my bare, pampered skin. I'm in the midst of shivering with the sensual delight of it all when a noise from behind alerts me to someone's presence.

Eirik. He stands naked and at ease beside the hot-spring, a colossus in the sun's golden rays. A physical sensation of heat rushes through my blood at the sight of him, a softening I can no more control than I can control the tides or the changing of the seasons.

"Paige," he says, beckoning me towards him. "Look at you, my love - as ripe as a late summer flower. And I as eager as a bee."

I giggle at the comparison Eirik makes between himself and a bee and he pulls me into his arms. We're both tense with anticipation, aware that we need to take things very, very slowly if we're to enjoy the full measure of each other after all this time.

"Why do you laugh?" He asks, burying his face in my neck and taking a long, noisy breath of me.

"Because you compared yourself to a bee," I tell him. "It's funny, bees are so cute and fuzzy. I don't think of you as very bee-like."

Eirik open his mouth against the warmth of my neck, kissing the place where my heart beats rapidly beneath the thin, pale skin. "Mmm," he says, "maybe not – but I'll have stung you more than once before the night is out."

I turn towards him as he speaks, helpless to stop myself, reaching for him like a drowning person reaching for shore.

"Wait," he chides, stepping away from my greedy hands. "Paige, I'm going to have you how I want you tonight. How *I* want you. You're my wife now, and you'll do as I say."

He's grinning, half-teasing, looking to get a reaction out of me. But I don't know if he's going to get one, because the last of the sun's light is catching his blue eyes and if he told me in all seriousness that it was now my life's work to please him whenever and however he wanted, I'm certain I would simply acquiesce. He must see it in my expression, too – that I'm not up to pretending I feel anything other than pure need right now. Without a word, he takes the hem of my tunic in one hand and lifts it up, pushing his strong, rough-skinned hand up my inner thigh and slipping one finger between my lips.

"Voss," he whispers, suddenly breathless as he feels what the months away from him have done to me. "*Voss*, Paige, your thighs are slippery with your need."

I look up into his eyes. "That's your fault. You did that. I can't even –"

I'm about to tell the Jarl that I can't even think of him when he's not with me without the same thing happening, but his hands are on me hard now, and suddenly. He tries to untie the intricate knots Gudry and Anja have tied down the back of the tunic and, when that doesn't work, he simply grasps the fabric in both hands and tears it off me.

"I'll have you now, girl," he pants, sitting down with his back against one of the boulders that circle the hot-spring and pulling me down with him. I don't know what I'm expecting – a few more seconds, maybe, or a finger inside me – but there's none of it. Eirik takes his manhood in his hand and guides it into me before I've even settled, yanking me down, impaling me on it in one swift motion.

I cry out, digging my fingers into the corded muscles of his shoulders at the unexpectedness of it – the sheer *size* of him.

"Paige," he breathes, one hand clamped onto my hip and the other cupping one of my breasts, lifting me up and down, not giving me one second to ease into it. "Paige, I need – I –"

He's trying to apologize, I realize, even as he completely fails to slow himself down. But I don't want the Jarl to apologize. I don't want anything except to give him what he needs. And if he needs to take me like this – deep and hard and fast – then that's what I want.

"No," I whimper, pulling his head against my breasts. "Don't say – don't –"

Jesus I can barely speak he's fucking me so hard. I try again, but now he's jerking his hips up sharply each time he pulls me down and that little spot inside my sex is starting to ache for more, even as it's already too much. "Eirik," I sigh, my breath quick and ragged. "You don't have to be sorry. You, oh my God, Eirik. You don't – Eirik!"

My voice rises to a near scream and he's done, we're both done. He jerks me down again, all the way down the length of him, and then he holds me there as I gasp and squirm and fills me with every drop of his savagery. I come, too, when he's nearly finished, as I feel him throbbing inside me. My sex twitches around him and a warm, wet rivulet of his cum runs down my inner thigh, pushing me right over the edge. I scream his name as an explosion of bliss spreads out through my body, a sensitivity so heightened it's almost but not quite pain and Eirik pushes his tongue into my mouth, breathing me in, holding me, waiting for me to float back to earth.

I don't climb off his lap right away because my legs feel like jelly, all my strength is gone. Eirik is panting, as unable to speak as I am, but he manages to lift me off a few moments later, with a gentleness that was not recently in evidence.

"I love that," I whisper as he wraps my body, my arms and legs, around him. "Eirik, I love –"

But I can't finish, not yet. I still need to catch my breath.

"What?" He asks. "I know what you love, Paige. I know what –"

"No," I say. "I mean yes, *that*, of course. But I mean that thing you do, how rough you can be with me and then how sweet. The difference in you, the before and after – I love it. I love causing it. I love doing that to you."

He locks one arm around me and slips into the hot-spring, taking me with him. Then he kisses my cheek. "Sometimes I fear I'm *too* rough with you, Paige. Even as I planned to show you this place tonight I told myself I would control it, I wouldn't let my desires get the better of me. But girl, it's been so many moons since I was inside you and as little as you are in comparison to me you have some kind of hold over me, some ability to bring an animal out of my chest."

"An animal out of your chest," I repeat, smiling. "I even love the way you say things. I love everything about you."

I move to settle in against that broad chest, but he holds me back, looking into my eyes.

"What?" I ask innocently.

"It's what you just said," he replies. "Say it again. Repeat it."

"I just said I liked what you said about –"

"Paige!"

I bite my lip and grin, knowing I'm testing him, but also knowing he's in a mood right now where I can probably get away with almost anything. "I said I love everything about you, Eirik."

"I know it, girl. I've known it for a long time. But it's the first time you've said the words – did you know that?"

I nod, suddenly a little shy, but the Jarl doesn't allow me to turn my face away. "What is it?" He demands. "What is that look on your face, Paige-from-across-the-sea?"

When I speak again, my voice is no longer filled with the cocky pride of pleasing my husband. It's quieter, quiet enough so he has to lean in and stop splashing the warm water up over my back so he can hear.

"So you're not angry with me?" I ask. "You're not – because I left, I mean? I wasn't sure if –"

"Stop." He says. "Why do you always ask questions you already know the answers to, my love?"

"Because I don't know the –"

"Oh yes you do. You know I'm not angry. I said it many moons ago, girl, I cannot be angry with you. And I said this, too – that you would come back. You love me, and I knew you would be back. I don't know what it is you had to do – my men said you sought a healing plant for my arm, but I think it's not the whole story. No matter, I knew you would return. And here you are, where you should be."

"You're right," I say softly. "It's not the whole story – it's not a lie, though, I did leave to find a healing plant. Something to save you. I thought you were dying."

"I was dying. But I didn't. They told me in my fever that you were gone and the gods knew I had to stay alive, to be here when you returned to me. How could I leave this world, knowing you would come back for me, and find me gone? Perhaps one day you will tell me the rest of the story? Perhaps not. What matters is you're here. Our son is here, and he's healthy and strong and as bright as the dawn – like his mother."

The Jarl runs one hand down the length of my back, casually cupping one of my buttocks, and I know he'll need me again soon.

"I have a marriage gift for you, Paige," he says a moment later and I look up, thinking he's making a dirty joke. His expression is serious, though.

"Oh?" I ask, scooping up the warm spring water with one hand and letting it run down his neck and chest.

"I've sent Veigar south, to bring your friend – the one you left with. What was her name? Willa?"

I sit up straight, filled with a sudden, desperate hope and terrified it's a game of some kind, a trick. "Please don't say things like that," I say, "if they're not true. Eirik, please –"

"Why wouldn't it be true?" He asks, bemused. "You said she was your best friend, and I saw how you worried about her and her little children. I thought it would be a way to show my love on the occasion of our marriage, to bring your friend and her people here to live with us, as part of our family. Is it unbelievable?"

"No," I whisper, even as I'm afraid to believe it. "No. But – Jarl, she has a brother, Eadgar. He is my –"

"Girl, they've all been sent for. All her people. They know you're here waiting for them. Don't worry."

"Do you mean it?" I ask again.

"It pleases you, then?" He replies, tilting my head to the side and kissing my neck. "It gives your heart peace?"

"Yes," I breathe, wrapping my arms very tightly around his neck. "Yes, Eirik. You have no idea. I have been so worried about them for so long. You don't know. All I've ever wanted – although I didn't realize it until quite recently, and you played a part in that – is for the people I love to be safe and healthy and well-fed."

"You only realized that recently?"

I rest my head on one of his massive shoulders, basking in the simple joy of not being worried about a single thing. "I told you it's different where I come from, Eirik. It's not just our clothing or our accent. It's what we value, what we do with our lives. In some ways it's the opposite of this place, where people often go hungry and a small injury can lead to lifelong struggles – or even death. Here you have to deal with all of those threats, every day. Where I come from the people don't worry so much about those things. But we're not as close to our families or our friends as your people, we don't spend so much time with those we love."

"What do you do?" Eirik asks and then sees that I haven't understood the question. "What do you do when you're alone, is what I meant. When you're not spending time with your families and the ones you love, what are you doing?"

I laugh quietly, thinking of how long – how many days and weeks – it would take me to explain to a 9th century Viking what it is we in the 21st century spend so much time doing. And yet somehow I know that even if I could do an adequate job of explaining what the internet is, or TV or commutes or mortgages or any of those hallmarks of modern life, I still wouldn't be able to make my husband understand why it is 'my' people spend so much time attending to them. I don't think I know anymore myself.

"I don't know," I say. "I don't know what we're doing. I thought I was going to miss so many things from my old life. But the truth is the only things I miss are people, and only a few. I don't miss my –" I pause, because I won't even be able to explain something as alien as missing 'things' to Eirik. "I guess it just took me longer than some people to figure it out," I smile. "To figure out what matters, and what doesn't."

"Sometimes," the Jarl says, pulling me in even closer, "I worry the people will learn that you're the sharper of the two of us. I worry they'll all wake up one day and realize that their Jarl's wife is the one who should be planning all our raids. But other times you tell me things like this and I know my position is safe."

Laughing, he ducks my playful slap, and catches my wrist midair. "Are you happy, Paige?" He asks, suddenly serious again.

A wisp of smoky lust spirals up through my body from the way Eirik is looking at me. "Yes," I say. "Yes, I'm happy."

"Good," he tells me. "Because I want all of my people to be happy, Paige. But I don't want anyone to be happy as much as you."

We hold each other in the hot-spring, naked in each other's arms, and the only sounds are the gentle lapping of the water as we shift our bodies and the sounds of our own breathing. It doesn't take long for the Jarl to grow hard again and I sigh, my heart full of love, when I feel it against my belly.

"We need a daughter now," he whispers in my ear as holds me tight, pressing my bare breasts to his chest. "Perhaps if we try very hard, we can have one before summer?"

"I don't think it works like that," I chuckle. "I'm breastfeeding your son, Eirik, I think we may need to wait a little while."

The Jarl takes my face in his hands and pulls me in for a deep, slow kiss. I can taste it in him – the hunger returning.

"You're probably right, girl. But don't get heated with me if you've got a baby – two babies, perhaps – in your belly come the winter."

"Two?!" I exclaim, and the feeling of Eirik suddenly sliding himself between my legs – not inside me, but almost – transforms my words into a whimper. "Two?" I ask again, my voice much softer now. "Where I come from – oh – women sometimes have three babies. Or four. I think one even had eight! I don't know if – ohhh. Oh my God –"

He's teasing me, running himself up and down between my lips and then pulling away every time I move my body into a position for him to slide into me.

"Eight," he teases, biting my earlobe gently. "I think if we start right now we could get there, Paige. I could put eight babies in your belly, my love. I'll have the servants carry you around the camp when you grow as big as the moon."

It's too much. The ache that seems to emanate from my very center is too acute, I can't listen to him talking about being inside me anymore without him actually being there. I reach down between our bodies and guide him into me.

It feels different this time – slower, gentler, but no less intense. My back arches as my new husband fills me with himself once more. I lean back as he takes me, floating in the water and gazing up at the stars.

Author Information

Amazon Author Page:

https://www.amazon.com/Joanna-Bell/e/B0768K811G

Sign-up to become a member of Joanna's Readers Group (notification of new releases, awesome monthly giveaways and freebies/deals on romance novels):

http://eepurl.com/c2jWP1

Contact Joanna: authorjoannabell@gmail.com

How To Catch A Cowboy: A Small Town Montana Romance

https://www.amazon.com/dp/B075FF65S3/ (available in paperback)

Reviews for How To Catch A Cowboy:

"Holy smokes, this book was beautiful...Ms. Bell was really able to develop her characters and give a meaningful story behind Jack and Blaze. I'm not even going to lie, I cried, but mostly happy tears."

" Great characters that were well developed...really sweet and heartwarming!"

"This read was amazing, the characters, the story, the writing everything was done perfectly and as I was reading it time passed not realizing that hours and hours had gone by as I couldn't put it down. It was a long book but it was thorough and flowed beautifully with great character development and no page seemed unnecessary to me. "

"I love this book. Of all my many Kindle books, this is my hands down favorite."

"Absolutely a love story that goes from rags to riches. Jack and Blaze meet under not so friendly circumstances and love blossoms from there. This union leads to lost treasure and lost families being brought together. Eternal love reunited families, a must read book."